CHANGING GROOMS

CHANGING GROOMS

Sasha Wagstaff

headline
review

First published in 2009 by REVIEW

An imprint of HEADLINE PUBLISHING GROUP

Cataloguing in Publication Data is available from the British Library

ISBN 978 0 7553 4888 6 (Hardback)
ISBN 978 0 7553 5252 4 (Trade paperback)

Typeset in Garamond by Avon DataSet Ltd,
Bidford on Avon, Warwickshire

Printed and bound in Great Britain by
Clays Ltd, St Ives plc

Headline's policy is to use papers that are natural, renewable and recyclable
products and made from wood grown in sustainable forests. The logging
and manufacturing processes are expected to conform to the environmental
regulations of the country of origin.

HEADLINE PUBLISHING GROUP
An Hachette Livre UK Company
338 Euston Road
London NW1 3BH

www.headline.co.uk
www.hachettelivre.co.uk

To Anthony . . . for Mauritius and everything else

Chapter One

Breathing in a healthy gulp of Cotswold air, Tessa Meadmore sped towards the village of Appleton. Beautiful countryside flashed past, neatly fenced fields bleached by the late June sun and chocolate-box cottages barely registering as Tessa roared by in her garnet-red Audi A4.

She screeched to a halt by a quaint pub with fragrant hanging baskets trailing down over the doorway. She checked her map and was about to take the turning for the B&B when she caught sight of an attractive older man jauntily waving his Bloody Mary at her. He had faded golden hair, not dissimilar to the honey-hued stone wall behind him, and sexy, bloodshot eyes. He was chatting up a pretty young barmaid who was crossly, but not very convincingly, slapping his hand away from her derrière. Tessa responded by giving him a cheery wave before speeding off in the opposite direction.

God, Adam would love this place, she thought before she could stop herself. After sharing exactly one year of their lives together and one messy break-up, it no longer mattered what Adam would love. It was over and she was ignoring his pathetic pleas for their reconciliation with as much dignity as she could muster in the circumstances.

Tessa cringed as she remembered how she had discovered his deception.

'Ta da!' Adam had cried, appearing in the doorway with 'I love you' scrawled across his chest in lipstick. He placed a tray laden with hot buttered muffins, Laurent-Perrier champagne and her two best Marc Jacobs for Waterford champagne glasses on the bed and made a show of waving his bottom at her. She had giggled as he clenched the velvety red rose between his bare buttocks and demonstrated a couple of swaggering dance moves. Taking one look at Tessa's mussed-up chestnut locks and naked breasts covered in massage oil, he was soon sporting an impressive hard-on, like a horse straining at the start tape of the Grand National.

As Adam prepared to launch himself between her thighs, a phone started beeping and Tessa grabbed the nearest one. It was one of those moments when picking up the right phone would have meant the difference between blissful ignorance and painful reality. As it was, it wasn't her phone and the text message that popped up had jokingly demanded to know when Adam might make 'an honest woman' of the sender after 'three years of living together . . .'

All hell had broken loose. Adam had desperately denied everything, the red rose falling to the floor, no doubt let down by his panicked sphincter. His hard-on had followed suit, deflating like a let-down party balloon.

Tessa knew exactly how it felt. Calling him every name under the sun, she had hurled one of her prized champagne glasses at him. Adam had made a mad dash for the door, shrieking girlishly and cupping his genitals. After shoving him naked and gibbering on to the street, Tessa had decided against being grown-up and brave. Instead, she had given in to her instincts, curled up in the foetal position and howled like a baby.

Three weeks later, she pulled herself together. Jilly, her boss at the TV station, had phoned about a celebrity wedding project in the Cotswolds and, without hesitation, Tessa had packed her life into her car and offered her Putney flat to a friend who was in the throes of a messy divorce.

Tessa grimaced. Even the sight of charming antique shops and old-fashioned tea houses nestling in the countryside could do little to lessen her sense of humiliation. She had been foolish, but there had been no reason to suspect Adam's absences and pleas of pressing work commitments weren't the act of a hard-working lawyer.

Cheating bastard, Tessa thought, shooting into the car park of the B&B and narrowly missing a decrepit-looking ginger cat that was lazily enjoying the afternoon sunshine. The B&B was small but cosy-looking with a white wooden gateway and a thatched roof. Tantalising wafts of old-fashioned pub food reached Tessa's nostrils as she searched for a place to park her car.

Look on the bright side, she told herself firmly. Sure, her heart was slightly battered . . . OK, make that very battered. And her ego was bruised beyond recognition. But the pretty little village of Appleton could provide the perfect hideaway. She could lick her wounds, get over Adam and, more import-antly, give her career a much-needed boost at the same time. She parked alongside a showy black Porsche 911 in the corner and wrinkled her nose in distaste. It must belong to the docu-mentary director she had heard so much about   Jean-Baptiste. According to Jilly, he bedded pretty much everyone he worked with and practically came with a government health warning.

Tessa pursed her lips as she hauled her battered Louis Vuitton luggage out of the car. Men were off the agenda as far as she was concerned, so Jean-Baptiste had better not try anything or he'd be wearing his privates as a neck scarf.

Squaring her shoulders, Tessa headed inside the B&B with grim determination. Nothing – and certainly not a man – was going to distract her from making this documentary a phenomenal success.

'Thanks again . . . I can't tell you how pleased I am that you've managed to finish in record time.'

Will Forbes-Henry shook the project manager's hand gratefully and waved to the team of dust-encrusted builders as they left in their vans. Renovating the family home and turning it into a boutique hotel had been an ambitious plan to say the least. And slick plumbing work, a new heating system and extensive replastering were only the start of it; every inch of the house was about to be revamped by must-have designer Gil Anderson.

Capitalising on the trendiness of the Cotswolds with Kates Moss and Winslet frequently in attendance was a risk, Will knew, especially with the spectacularly beautiful manor house in Upper Slaughter only a few miles down the road. But when he turned and glanced up at his family home, he was sure he'd made the right decision. Appleton Manor was a gorgeous, rambling house made of traditional Cotswold stone the colour of golden syrup and set in some of the most stunning landscaped gardens in the area. The manor begged to reach its full potential and be appreciated, but not everyone in his family agreed.

Striding indoors and scooping up the post on his way, Will headed for the sun-drenched sitting room at the side of the house. From fifty yards away he could hear his parents bickering like children.

'You really think turning our house into a hotel is a good idea?' Caro regarded Jack in horror, smoking frenetically. 'We could have all manner of riff-raff wandering in and out of here!' She was taut with tension, her yoga-toned body as rigid as the wicker chair she was sitting in.

Seriously hung-over from his liquid lunch at the pub, Jack shrugged and shakily stirred the vast Bloody Mary he was wielding with a rather wilted stick of celery. Like him, it had seen better days. 'Could be fun,' he commented mildly. 'We could be like Basil and Sybil in *Fawlty Towers.*'

Caro looked affronted. 'Speak for yourself! I couldn't look downtrodden if I tried.'

Jack laughed heartily at this and headed over to the drinks table in search of some more vodka.

'Mother, do try not to be such a snob,' Will said with a sigh as he walked in, fiercely tearing open an envelope. He adored her despite her flaws, but she really could test the patience of a saint.

'*Dar*ling, there you are!' Eyeing her eldest son with deep affection, Caro leapt out of her chair. Deeply tanned and as broad as a professional rugby player, Will looked divine, but as his navy-blue eyes met hers with a flinty stare, she knew he wasn't going to stand for any nonsense. She kissed his cheek effusively, enveloping him in exotic fragrance and almost taking his eye out with a flick of her flame-red hair.

Drawing him close, she lowered her voice. 'I can't thank you enough for not telling Jack about that little . . . ahem, financial problem, darling. It was an inspired idea to say it was down to that other company going into liquidation rather than my silliness.' She lifted her baby-blue eyes to him in a way that had charmed many. 'So embarrassing. So . . . unfortunate.'

Will winced at her choice of words as he glanced down at the bill he'd just opened. *Unfortunate?* His mother's decision to invest the family savings in the ill-fated business venture of one of her toy boys had been 'unfortunate' to say the least. The Forbes-Henry family now found themselves without any savings to speak of, with disgruntled bailiffs gagging to get their hands on the period furniture and nothing but a stunning house to save their bacon. A house that seemingly guzzled enough gas and electricity to power Russia, Will thought, stuffing yet another red bill into the back pocket of his jeans.

'So wonderful of you to rush back from France like this to save us,' Caro said grandly, as if it were she who had made the magnanimous gesture, not Will. 'Leaving your beautiful fiancée behind as well. We *do* appreciate it, darling.'

Will raised his eyebrows. He wasn't sure his mother appreciated his intervention at all; she certainly didn't seem to have the first idea of how serious things were.

'Thank God you're so rich, darling,' Caro said comfortably. 'You've done so well with your property business. You could probably buy Appleton Manor fifteen times over.'

Will was saved from having to admit he'd just spent the best part of his capital having the manor's plumbing and heating brought into the twenty-first century by Tristan bounding into the room.

'Doesn't the house look fantastic?' Tristan clapped Will on the back. 'Great job, bro.' His T-shirt was splattered with Alizarin crimson paint as usual and his hands were caked with it.

'Darling, I do wish you wouldn't use that bloody awful colour,' Caro pouted as she sashayed past him. 'It looks like you've bled all over yourself.'

Tristan absently raked his paint-stained hand through his mop of blond curls. Far from being a 'bloody awful colour', his favourite bluish-red left an intensely rich finish on canvas or skin. It was a luscious ruby red that he used because it represented high energy, passion and love, but what would his parents know about that? He watched them ignoring each other with the belligerence of teenagers. Poor Will, he thought, catching his brother's eye in sympathy. Caught in the firing line as usual.

'Don't suppose you'll be investing in the hotel, Tris?' Jack drawled, turning a rather steely gaze towards his youngest son as he swigged from his Bloody Mary. 'I doubt you've made much money from selling your little sketches.'

Tristan jumped up from his chair and poured the dregs of a bottle of whisky into a glass to steady his nerves. He was thirty, for heaven's sake, far too old to be defending himself against his bully of a father. What was his problem, anyway? Thank God Will was back to bring some sanity to the family.

'Tristan *is* investing,' Will pointed out with a frown. 'He's far too modest to admit it, but his "little sketches" actually sell for six figures. You wouldn't even have a roof over your head if he hadn't flogged several of them over the past few years.'

Jack grunted.

'Good for you, Tris,' Caro commented distractedly. 'I do wish they'd put stuff like that in *Tatler* and then we'd all know about it.'

Tristan and Will burst out laughing and Caro gazed at them, puzzled.

'I can't believe Rufus is getting married here,' Jack said suddenly. 'Not exactly the marrying kind, I wouldn't have thought.'

Caro perked up immediately. Rufus Pemberton was one of Will's old rugby mates, a pretty boy with delusions of grandeur who'd packed himself off to Hollywood some years ago. He had little acting talent but oodles of ambition, and a recent engagement to Hollywood royalty in Oscar-winning actress Clemmie Winters had put Rufus at the top of everyone's party list. Caro couldn't help being terribly excited about the idea of a celebrity wedding in her very own back garden, *and* of starring in a TV documentary about it.

'Not so upset about Appleton Manor being turned into a hotel now, are you?' Jack said slyly.

Caro gave him a withering stare, as Will and Tristan regarded their parents with a mixture of frustration and affection. Jack and Caro Forbes-Henry – the Taylor-Burtons of their time. Jack, once a strikingly handsome man with sparkling green eyes and golden hair, had gone to seed from too much drinking and sex; the eyes now a bloodshot sage-green and the hair the lacklustre colour of sun-bleached straw. Caro, wiry-thin with pale, freckled skin like a dappled fawn and flirty flicks of vibrant red hair was the perfect, glamorous foil for Jack's faded charm.

She turned to Jack sweetly. 'You could be the bellboy when we open the hotel,' she taunted. 'I can just see you in one of those little hats with the elastic under the chin.'

Jack glowered at her. 'And what role will you play, I wonder,

7

my darling? A maid? At least all that time spent on your knees wouldn't be wasted.'

'You can talk! You're hardly a paragon of virtue yourself with those wandering hands.'

'Better than wandering knickers. You keep La Perla in business single-handedly by losing yours so often.'

'Shut up!' yelled Tristan, standing between them. 'We're all tired of you two fighting all the time!'

Jack and Caro went silent, resorting to mutinous stares that, as usual, swiftly turned into something more suggestive. Seconds later, they had leapt from their chairs and were charging up the stairs two at a time. Within moments, sounds of their noisy, passionate love-making could be heard downstairs.

God, his parents were monstrous, Will thought. If they weren't both so lovably screwed up, he might be able to dislike them. As it was, he felt a fierce loyalty towards them and was determined to see them looked after in their old age.

'Aren't they dreadful?' Tristan commented as he strolled out into the garden, whisky in hand. 'Talk about growing old disgracefully. I don't think there's a barmaid or gardener in the village they haven't deflowered. God knows what the score is on either side. I've lost count, frankly.'

Will rubbed his chin ruefully, then did a double take when he caught sight of their sixteen-year-old cousin Milly at the bottom of the garden with another girl. 'Bloody hell! That girl with Milly – India, or whatever her name is. You can practically see her bum cheeks in that skirt . . . belt . . . thing. Aren't they supposed to be revising or something?'

Tristan peered at the girls in the distance.

'They're taking their exams this month. Yes, India is Milly's new best friend. She's an absolute menace. Poor Aunt Henny has been tearing her hair out, petrified Milly will end up pregnant or run off with a biker. And you should see David. He's all gangly limbs and macho posing these days.'

'Is he still hanging around with Freddie Penry-Jones?'

'Unfortunately, yes. Supplier of the best dope in the area, if rumours are to be believed.' Tristan grinned. 'We've got an interesting summer ahead of us, Will. Just a matter of keeping teenage pregnancy and drug overdoses to a bare minimum and turning this place into a fabulous hotel in time for the wedding. Oh, and it might be advisable to hire some ugly staff our parents won't have sex with.' He flung his arm round Will's big shoulders gleefully. 'Welcome back to the madhouse, brother! You couldn't get this kind of fun in France, even if you were shacked up with the lovely Claudette.'

Will pulled a face. 'I've got enough to think about with this TV crew turning up any minute. Some celebrity correspondent called Tessa Meadmore is going to be nosing round here.'

Tristan looked enthralled. 'Tessa Meadmore? Wow, she brightens my day on TV every morning. She's an absolute fox!'

Will looked dubious. He had met several journalists whilst promoting his property business and had also watched Rufus being mauled by a few of them since his career took off. From what he'd seen, they were all shallow and ruthless and eager to sniff out sordid gossip. He couldn't see why this Tessa Meadmore would be any different.

Tristan gave him a playful shove. 'Come on, Will, stop being the grown-up for once. This could be fun!'

Will smiled weakly. He knew his family thought he was too serious but this reality TV thing had disaster written all over it and Will wasn't sure he should have allowed himself to be talked into it. Still, Rufus was an old friend and, with things the way they were, the money would be a godsend. Poor Rufus and Clemmie were probably going to find every aspect of their lives under scrutiny, with even the most private of details finding their way on air.

And what about Appleton Manor? A film crew trampling across the floorboards just when the expensive designer he had hired was due any minute – the timing couldn't have been worse. And more worrying than that, the Forbes-Henry family would most likely be captured in the background in all their dysfunctional glory. On *national television*.

As for this Tessa Meadmore woman, Will thought as he grabbed Tristan's whisky, what if she discovered the family were on the brink of ruin? It would be the end of the hotel. Ignoring Tristan's cries of protest, Will necked the last of the whisky and hoped to God he hadn't made everything a hell of a lot worse.

Milly took the spliff from India and inhaled deeply. They were sitting on a stone wall soaking up the sun, their bare feet surrounded by GCSE revision notes, avidly watching the goings-on outside a rather majestic house up in the hills.

'I wish I knew what I wanted to do with my life,' Milly murmured as she blew on the end of the spliff speculatively. 'I can't even decide what A levels to take, let alone what to do at uni. David's off to read French and Law at Bristol, as long as he gets his grades – which he will – and I haven't got a clue. I'm a hopeless case, India.'

India shrugged laconically. She wasn't in the least bit academic and she knew her limitations when it came to exams. Besides, she had always thought there were other ways to make a good living.

As afternoon slid into evening and the red-gold sun glowed like a dying fire, Milly and India watched several removal vans pull up outside the house on the hill. Their contents were swiftly unloaded and carried inside. Tons of wooden tea chests with mysterious ornaments poking out of them, stylish furniture swaddled in bubble wrap and a plethora of expensive-looking suitcases flashed enticingly in and out of view.

Milly couldn't help feeling a flicker of anticipation. 'How exciting that Rufus Pemberton's back after all this time.'

'I know. He's such a stud.' India stretched back languidly

until her knickers were almost on show. 'He's getting really famous now; I read about it in *heat* magazine. He's marrying Clemmie Winters, though – *bummer*. She's old enough to be my mother.'

Milly rolled her eyes. 'I'd prefer her to mine.'

India shrugged. She didn't really understand why Milly had it in for her mother; Henny always seemed so kind and motherly. And it was hardly her fault Milly's father had died and left them homeless.

From a distance David, Milly's brother, cupped his hands round his mouth and shouted, 'I can almost see what you had for dinner, India. Put it away!'

David was eighteen, lanky and something of a sex pest. Munching on a doorstop chicken and mayonnaise sandwich, his A level French book tucked under his arm, he strolled up to them with his right-hand man Freddie Penry-Jones in tow. Freddie looked casually elegant, sporting a long, lightweight coat over jeans and boots, in spite of the warm weather.

Milly hurriedly raked her fingers through her blond hair and wished she'd put more lipgloss on. India stayed put, aware that the tantalising glimpses of her pristine white cotton G-string were probably driving David crazy.

David made a point of sitting on the other side of the wall and tossed his French book on to the grass. He'd always thought India was rather stuck up but it wasn't her fault. He reasoned that he wouldn't find her half as intimidating if she were called Joanne. She was pretty, though; there was no denying that and he hated himself for sneaking a pervy look at her honeyed thighs and skimpy underwear.

'Want some?' He held out his sandwich to Milly.

'No thanks,' she said primly. 'There are probably thousands of calories in that.'

'Let me know if you need any more dope,' Freddie said in his terribly well-spoken voice. 'Plenty more where that came from.'

He flicked his almost-black hair out of his eyes as he deftly rolled a spliff.

Milly stole a glance. The son of one of the richest men in England, Freddie was glamorous and untouchable and the subject of many a secret, dirty dream. She felt a rush of pleasurable shame flood through her body at the unspeakable things she had imagined him doing to her last night, feeling as painfully inarticulate and embarrassed around him as she always did. Freddie was tall, with eyes like crushed blueberries and long fingers that looked as if they could do incredible things to a girl.

Gallingly, he treated her like his kid sister. As if to prove a point, he pretended to cuff her under the chin.

'How are you, Milly Vanilli?'

His pet name for her left her wobbly at the knees but, deep down, she knew he meant it to be affectionate, not pornographic.

'Not bad. We're watching Rufus and Clemmie move in.'

'I can't believe Tessa Meadmore's going to be doing the documentary!' Freddie's eyes went dark with lust. 'She's *so* fit.'

David tore his gaze from India. 'Is she that bird off breakfast telly? Wide mouth, sort of long nose?'

'Face of an angel, body made for sin,' Freddie confirmed. 'She's got legs up to her armpits and moss-green eyes you could just dive right into.'

Milly's heart sank. That was all she needed, Freddie fancying the TV presenter. She let her blond hair fall over her face so he couldn't see how devastated she was. It was probably his father's fault; Hugo Penry-Jones was on his third wife already and they got younger each time he remarried. Freddie probably thought age gaps were all the rage.

'If I were a lesbian,' India drawled huskily, lifting her head slightly, 'I'd have sex with Tessa Meadmore.'

'Now, there's a mental image.' Freddie whistled.

David felt as if he might explode. God, she was provocative!

He wished he could say India left him cold but he'd be lying. He had a weakness for pale-skinned redheads and India, smothered in fake tan and possessing ginger locks rather than Titian, wasn't exactly his idea of perfect, but she was female and she was up for it, so as fantasies went, she was going to have to do for now.

'I wonder if I could pull Tessa.' Freddie narrowed his eyes as the smoke trailing from his spliff spiralled upwards.

India idly flipped her strawberry-blond hair out of her eyes. 'Shouldn't you both be concentrating on your A levels?'

Freddie looked unruffled. He was about as academic as India but his father had good connections so he was equally unaffected by the stresses of exam-taking. He hadn't even touched a revision book so far.

'More to the point, Tessa's twice your age!' Milly snorted.

'Yes, but I'm very handsome,' he deadpanned. 'And she's only human.' He and David fell about laughing.

Milly felt sick. Didn't women in their thirties adore young, attractive boys like Freddie? He looked much older than his eighteen years and he was sex on a stick.

Scuffing her bare feet against the wall, Milly decided she needed a plan. She could set Tessa up with someone – that would do it. There was Will, he was incredibly handsome and manly . . . oh, no good, he was besotted with his fiancée Claudette. Tristan, then. Milly smiled to herself. Perfect. Tristan was between girlfriends at the moment and an absolute sucker for a pretty face. Admittedly, he didn't always have the best taste when it came to women, what with one disappearing into thin air and another threatening to make dog-à-l'orange out of their faithful golden retriever Austin when Tristan broke up with her, but surely even *he* couldn't cock up a relationship with a stunningly attractive TV celebrity?

Feeling better, Milly boldly took the spliff from Freddie's long fingers and sucked at the end his lips had been clamped round seconds before. She sighed happily. It was better than nothing . . .

Back at the B&B, Tessa was warmly greeted by Joe the cameraman and Susie the make-up artist, both of whom she had worked with before. Laughter and chatter engulfed her as the rest of the TV crew shouted out in welcome. She edged her way through the packed bar, air-kissing and shaking hands as she went, and was just about to order herself a stiff drink when a swarthy man smoothly handed her a large glass of red.

Holding his other hand out he drawled, 'Jean-Baptiste – JB to my friends.' His sexy black eyes glittered as he gave her the benefit of his piratical smile. His accent was unashamedly French and he grasped her hand briefly, standing aside politely to let her sit down before taking his seat.

'So, 'ave you made many documentaries before, Tessa?' He smelt of cigarette smoke and cologne, and displayed the blasé confidence only a truly successful womaniser possessed. This was a man with a voracious sexual appetite – it was evident in the heavy-lidded eyes, the sensual mouth and the thrusting groin.

'A few,' she lied airily.

'I 'ave made many,' he told her with some arrogance. 'I will . . . show you ropes, I theenk you say?'

'That's *very* kind of you.' Meeting JB's gaze head on, she refused to fall into the limpid eyes and let her eyes travel down his body unabashed. She took in the well-cut red shirt and dark, low-slung jeans. He was lean like a whippet, not perhaps the tallest of men but what he lacked in stature he made up for in charisma.

'I don't usually do this kind of thing,' he volunteered suddenly. 'You probably know I am famous in my country for, 'ow you say, art-house French cinema?'

Tessa shrugged, amused that he thought he was so well-known. JB was known more for his brooding moodiness and bossy attitude than anything else.

'There was a death in my family, you see – my grandfather. Sometimes it is good to do something different, to get away, *n'est-ce pas?*'

Tessa couldn't agree more. And JB didn't know the half of it. Her boss Jilly had offered her the job in the Cotswolds on the clear understanding that it was a make or break situation. The whole Adam debacle had made her take her eye off the ball, professionally speaking. She had been so wrapped up in him towards the end, she had barely known her own work schedule and when the relationship had finally fallen apart, she had been forced to take her remaining holiday allowance in one hit just to get herself together.

Tessa glanced round at the excitable film crew, wishing she shared their enthusiasm. Aside from pointing out her recent lacklustre performance on her daily slot on *Good Morning UK*, Jilly also took a dim view of Tessa's long-harboured idea of writing her own novel. Before Tessa had left for the Cotswolds, Jilly had laid the law down unequivocally: either Tessa came up with the goods on this documentary or she was out on her ear, at which point she was at liberty to write any damned novel she pleased.

Tessa sighed, wondering how she had ended up in this situation. Her glittering TV career, so hard-earned, so carefully nurtured over the past ten years, was dangling by a very thin thread. Jilly was expecting great things, that much was clear. She had an idea Rufus Pemberton was hiding something and she wanted dirt; more than that, she wanted it yesterday. And if it meant Tessa getting down on her hands and knees to dig for it, so be it.

Oblivious of her inner soul-searching, JB interrupted Tessa's thoughts.

'Tomorrow, you are due to meet the family, the Forbes-Henrys,' he pronounced the 'h' with bad grace, 'so you can get to know them. We need to work out where to do interviews and find out about the wedding itself, where it will be 'eld, what it involves. And we need to make the family feel comfortable with the whole theeng, you know?'

'Definitely. I'll make sure I keep them sweet.'

Jilly was always encouraging her to ingratiate herself with the owners of the properties they filmed at but, in her experience, they tended to want the TV crew to shoot their footage and get the hell out of their lives. In this case, it was probably worth getting to know the family; after all, this was a long-term project – it would last for months and the cooperation of the Forbes-Henrys was critical to the success of the documentary. Tessa hadn't had time to do much research but she knew there were a couple of brothers and some cousins running around – a bunch of stuck-up aristocrats with trust funds, no doubt. She wasn't sure how old the cousins were but she hoped they were out of nappies; in her experience, screaming children made filming excruciating.

JB's dark eyebrows knitted together. 'The family are very rich, I theenk . . . crazy eccentric types, you know? There's the parents who 'ave some sort of open marriage, it seems, Tristan the bad-boy painter and the older brother Will who is very serious, so I 'ave been told, but worth getting to know because he's an old friend of Rufus's.' He caught the eye of a petite blonde with an impressive cleavage at the other end of the room, his dark eyes flashing at her suggestively. He brought his attention back to Tessa with difficulty. 'Jilly, she tells me she wants to know everything about Rufus and Clemmie – what they eat, *if* they eat, 'ow often they 'ave sex, if they like it kinky – you know the kind of theeng.'

Tessa nodded briskly. She knew exactly what was required. So why was her heart sinking slightly?

'You 'ave a big challenge on your 'ands,' JB stated silkily, getting to his feet. 'And something to prove, *n'est-ce pas?*' He bent down, his mouth close to her ear. 'Jilly tells me you 'ave – 'ow you say – lost your edge?'

She felt her cheeks turn red. How could Jilly tell JB such a thing? Mortified, she tightened her fingers around the stem of her wine glass.

'No matter, I told 'er I would keep an eye on you and make sure you still 'ave what it takes.' JB winked at her then gestured to the busty blonde who had caught his eye earlier. They disappeared outside, the giggling girl almost bursting out of her blouse.

Furious at being shown up by Jilly, Tessa barely knew what to do with herself. Feeling absurdly grateful when Joe the cameraman called her over to join them for drinking games and not even caring that she was due to meet the Forbes-Henrys bright and early the next morning, Tessa started downing neat tequilas like a pro.

Chapter Two

'So I'm thinking cosy yet decadent,' finished Gil Anderson, the designer Will had hired to revamp the manor. 'Something luxurious along the lines of rich colours, sumptuous fabrics and flattering lights. How does that sound?'

Will nodded cautiously. He and Tristan had bonded over a bottle of Scotch the night before and his head was beginning to ache. 'As long as we have the budget, that all sounds great. But there are eighteen rooms to decorate so we need to be . . .'

Already in love with the manor house and full of visions of how magnificent it could look, Gil ignored Will's protests about budget, his eyes lighting up as yet another brilliant idea came to him. 'And we're going to need some personal touches, something wildly romantic like organic candles and fresh rose petals, gorgeous silk eye masks – or mini bottles of Veuve Clicquot, perhaps?'

'Won't that cost a fortune?' Filled with trepidation, Will could see his budget spiralling out of control before they'd even started.

'At the Forbury in Reading, guests receive goodie bags with rubber ducks and slippers,' Gil informed him dismissively. 'If you want to play with the big boys, I'm afraid you have to speculate to accumulate, or whatever the phrase is.'

Will could see his point but he was beginning to wonder if he had made a huge mistake hiring Gil. He seemed to have a complete disregard for money and his taste wasn't so much expensive as outrageously lavish. But Will happened to know that Gil came with superb credentials – design school, followed by a long stint with Colefax and Fowler before creating his own company, 'Gilmore Designs'. His impressive portfolio included commissions for private homes of the rich and famous, as well as a recent Designer of the Year award for an exclusive boutique hotel in Knightsbridge. Having splashed out on an expensive overnight stay there in the name of research, Will could vouch for the fact that it showcased some of the most stunning interiors he had ever seen.

Doing his best to squash down the sense of unease Gil's ideas were giving him, Will headed downstairs, gesturing for Gil to follow him. 'I understand your fiancée will be joining us shortly?' He had been surprised at the number of times Gil had mentioned his fiancée Sophie since he arrived; he was as camp as Christmas and Will had assumed he was gay.

'She arrived this morning. I rented a darling little house in the village and surprised her with it.' Gil ran a hand through his spiky, highlighted hair. Being rather slight of frame and favouring brightly coloured shirts, he bore a passing resemblance to Noel Edmonds. 'It's been a bit tricky – childcare arrangements, that sort of thing, but it's all sorted out now.'

About to ask about deadlines, Will jumped when Gil let out a shriek. He was brandishing a dusty antique mirror he had unearthed at the bottom of the stairs.

'This is very rare, Italian gilt, highly decorative,' he gasped in awe. 'Look at the roses and the exquisite acanthus leaf design, Mr Forbes-Henry!'

'Er, very nice. And it's Will.'

'Sorry, *Will*. Nice, you say? I'm no expert but this is probably worth two thousand pounds, maybe more!'

'Really?' Will eyed it doubtfully. 'Christ, don't tell my parents; they'll hock it.'

Gil looked traumatised for a moment but he recovered himself. 'That reminds me, your brother, Tristan Forbes-Henry.

Would he consider showcasing some of his artwork in the manor? Guests love that kind of thing and there's nothing wrong with a bit of self-promotion, in my opinion.'

Tristan loathed 'self-promotion' but Will could see that Gil had a point. Tristan's rich canvases could look fantastic against the colour schemes Gil had in mind and some of the period fireplaces were crying out for a showpiece. He made a mental note to discuss it with Tristan *and* to supervise his selection; knowing Tristan, the walls would end up decked out with explicit nudes with very recognisable faces.

'I have two commissions lined up in Upper Slaughter after this job finishes,' Gil was saying chattily as they crossed the vast hallway. He admired the crystal chandelier hanging from the ceiling, certain it was an antique Flemish design worth thousands. 'But don't worry, I've warned my clients I simply won't be available until this job is finished – more celebrities, you know.'

Will frowned. He might be doing Gil an injustice but he had the air of a star-fucker about him.

Catching sight of his Aunt Henny struggling through the front door with a basket laden with bulbs, Will went to help her. She had a warm, friendly face and a comfortingly rounded body beneath her saggy cardigan and grubby overall. Pushing the sandy hair that was so like Jack's out of her eyes, Henny greeted Gil with a rosy-cheeked smile and dirt-streaked hands.

Eyeing her hands distastefully, Gil was distracted by a mounted photograph. 'Oh my God, is that who I think it is?'

Will glanced at the photo. Probably taken when he was around fifteen, the picture showed him in rugby shorts, his arm round a dark-haired youth sporting smudged eyeliner and a crooked grin. Realising he hadn't done Gil any injustice at all on the star-fucker front, he nodded. 'Yes, that's Rufus Pemberton. He's an old friend from school.'

'How thrilling!' Gil's eyes lit up. 'I take it the rumour about him getting hitched at Appleton Manor can be believed after all?'

Will said nothing but the deepening flush on Henny's cheeks gave the game away.

Gil could barely contain himself. '*Marvellous!* And is there really a film crew on its way to capture the whole thing?' He tapped the side of his nose knowingly. 'Oh, absolutely, mum's the word. And just so you know, I'm more than happy to be filmed at work.'

I bet you are, Will thought tetchily. Gil looked as if he was ready for his close-up already. What did he think this was, *Changing Rooms*? He hoped Gil didn't have secret ambitions to host his own TV show. And Lord only knew what he would be like when A-list celebrities like Clemmie and Rufus were in the vicinity.

'I'm not sure you'll have time for filming, not when half of the rooms need to be completed in time for the summer party. And the penthouses need to be started too.'

Going rather pale, Gil looked vexed. 'Summer party? Penthouses?'

Will exchanged glances with Henny. 'It was all in the pack I sent you. The summer party is at the end of August and I'd like to use it to showcase the rooms to the public. The penthouses are on the top floor of the manor. My parents usually occupy them but I've put them in cottages for now, like the rest of us.'

'I'll get on to that right away,' Gil called as he charged out of the front door as if he'd been shot.

Henny turned to Will. 'I'm so sorry I gave the game away about Rufus. I can't believe I put my foot in it like that. And thank you so much for letting me act as temporary wedding coordinator; I won't let you down, I promise.'

Will shook his head reassuringly. 'I know you won't. And not to worry, news about the wedding will spread quickly enough.

I'm more concerned about Gil pitching for his own series when he's meant to be working. By the way, his fiancée Sophie has just arrived.'

Their eyes met for a second.

Henny faltered. 'It must be a different one. What are the odds?'

'Exactly. Hey, I'll catch you later. I need to call Claudette.' He pulled his BlackBerry out of his pocket and dialled his fiancée. He was missing Claudette like crazy. They'd only been together for seven months but it had been an intense relationship, a lifetime seemingly crammed into a very short time. They had met at a party, quite by accident, and had been inseparable ever since. It had been passionate, exciting – overwhelming, in fact, and no one had been more surprised than Will when he had proposed to Claudette two months ago. But they had so much in common it seemed foolish not to make things more formal. Claudette loved the things he loved and seemed to want the same things out of life. Hadn't she always said she longed for a simple life in the countryside surrounded by family?

Hearing her husky voice in his ear as if she was standing next to him rather than being hundreds of miles away in Paris, Will felt his stress begin to melt away.

Nosing her car down the long, gravel driveway towards Appleton Manor, Tessa groaned and clutched her head. What on earth had possessed her to get so drunk last night? She knew she was stressed out over Adam, and JB's jibes had really got to her, but she'd picked a hell of a time to let her hair down. The drinking game had gone on into the early hours and she didn't even know what time she had tumbled into bed.

God, she could kill for an espresso! But, glancing at the rolling green fields surrounding the manor, Tessa was willing to stake her life on the fact that the nearest Costa Coffee was probably several miles away. And she was already hideously late for her meeting. She knew she didn't look her best – her long dark hair was pulled back into a low ponytail and the rose-pink blusher she had applied didn't seem to have made her look any less zombie-like. Not that she cared, she thought grumpily; she was hardly looking forward to meeting this eccentric family who'd probably never done a day's work in their lives, the lucky sods.

Turning the corner, Tessa almost crashed her Audi into a hedge as she caught sight of Appleton Manor. She pulled over and gaped in astonishment. Nestling in the golden glow of the glorious Cotswold Hills, it was a charming old house with mellow, honey-coloured stone walls and a quintessentially English air. It was covered in Virginia creeper which was a deep, glossy green, glistening in the late June sunshine, but it would no doubt turn russet and gold in autumn and cover the manor in a riot of rich colour. The manor house was surrounded by breathtaking, landscaped gardens and a river which ran around one side of the house and widened out into a lake.

Whoever had thought of turning this property into a hotel was a genius. Appleton Manor stood regally, like a prized jewel in the Cotswold countryside, but it was far too splendid to be kept hidden away. A house like this deserved to be shared and enjoyed by as many people as possible. Tessa couldn't wait to get inside and explore and she screeched to a halt by the front door. Taking a moment to drink in the view of the tranquil lake with its pretty stone bridge, she felt her tensions begin to slide away. She hadn't expected anything this beautiful and, secretly, she had assumed Rufus Pemberton and his American bride-to-be might have plumped for something ostentatious and tacky. But they had great taste; the manor house was romantic in the way only period English properties could be. It was classy, traditional and breathtakingly gorgeous.

Taking a peak into a gleaming Air Force blue 1938 Rolls-Royce Phantom parked outside, Tessa smiled with pleasure. It was clear that someone had treated this car like a lover; the interior was spotless, the dash buffed to within an inch of its life and the dove-grey leather seats looked as soft as butter.

She knocked on the door of the manor and was surprised when it swung open. Warily she stepped inside. This was obviously one of those lovely, safe areas in the country where locking your front door was considered gauche. Worried she had dented the divine hallway floor with the spike heels of her boots and gawking at a splendid chandelier she knew she would never be able to afford, Tessa swiftly headed into the first carpeted room she came to.

It was a library, brimming with charm. Heavy, blood-red drapes framed a vast picture window and at the foot of it fat piles of over-stuffed cushions begged to be sat on so the view of the lake could be admired. Battered sofas in shades of crimson and old gold looked as if hundreds of bodies had squashed them down but they looked invitingly comfy. Tessa couldn't resist and, without thinking, she sank into one of them, allowing the squashy cushions to mould themselves around her body.

Glancing up at the bookshelves that lined two walls, she saw stacks of poetry books nestling incongruously amongst autobiographies, bonkbusters and *Playboy* manuals. There were also dozens of cracked spines boasting the names of classic novels and some erotic fiction by Anaïs Nin. The Forbes-Henrys were clearly a well-read family. Pulling a book out from between the sofa cushions, Tessa saw that it was a collection of poems by Byron, the pencilled notes in the margin and torn pages suggesting it had been read over and over. Someone in the Forbes-Henry household shared her passion for the romantic poet, she thought with a smile. She heard a loud squeal and guiltily stuffed the book back between the sofa cushions.

'Oh my God, I absolutely *love* your boots!' An exceptionally pretty girl in a navy school uniform held her hand out. 'I'm Emilia . . . Milly. I'm Will and Tristan's cousin. Seriously, my friend India would kill for those boots. Are they Charles Jourdan?' She was a tall girl, leggy and slim with the last vestiges of teenage puppy fat. Her blossoming chest threatened to become matronly if she wasn't careful but she was ravishing all the same.

'Tessa Meadmore. And yes, they are. But I hope the heels haven't put a hole in that gorgeous walnut floor out there.' Tessa felt rather out of place next to this impossibly glamorous girl with her platinum-blonde hair. She realised the cousins were indeed out of nappies and, glancing down at her skinny black jeans and vintage grey Rolling Stones T-shirt, she instantly regretted her choice of outfit. She had thrown the clothes on earlier, thinking it was the right image for a successful TV presenter from London but against this backdrop of upper-class homeliness, it looked rather contrived. Tessa longed for some wellies and a big, comfy jumper.

'I didn't notice but we can always blame Austin, our dog.' Milly sat on the edge of the sofa and stretched her long legs out. 'And you're so pretty – that makes things a lot easier.' She was determined to put 'Plan Freddie' into action and push Tessa in Tristan's direction at the earliest opportunity. She was relieved to find that Tessa looked a bit pale and tired in the flesh but she was still lovely and befriending her was going to be fun.

'Makes what easier?' Tessa looked confused.

'Isn't it exciting about the documentary?' Milly said quickly, cursing herself. 'Rufus is de*lish*.' She nodded at the book tucked next to Tessa's denim-clad thighs. 'That's my cousin's favourite book. Better be careful with it – first edition and all that.'

Tessa searched her memory. 'Cousin Tristan?'

'Cousin *Will*!' Milly screamed with laughter. 'Tristan's more likely to be found with his head buried in a *Playboy* manual – or maybe *heat* magazine.' Realising she'd made her cousin sound superficial, she hurriedly added, 'He's not what you'd call the bookish type but he's utterly gorgeous, of course.'

25

Tessa wasn't remotely interested in hearing about Tristan. However gorgeous he was, she was here to work. 'So, how long have you lived here?'

'Me? About six months.' Milly reached out to touch the colourful Pucci scarf that held Tessa's long dark hair at the nape of her neck. 'Daddy died of cancer a year ago and left loads of debts, and bloody Mummy said we should sell our house in Oxford and move here. Great timing – I had to leave all my friends behind and I'm taking my GCSEs this month. I've got History tomorrow.' Her blue eyes narrowed crossly. 'Frankly, it'll be Mummy's fault if I flunk all of them.'

Tessa unwound the scarf and handed it to a scowling Milly. 'Have it, please. It was a gift from someone I'd rather forget about. Perhaps your mother didn't have any choice.'

'That's what she says but I'm still pissed off. Wow, are you sure I can have this?'

'It's yours. Is this one of Tristan's paintings?' Tessa stood up to get a better look at it, extricating herself from the sofa rather inelegantly. The painting depicted a naked young woman reclining on a ruby-red sofa, her luscious white curves contrasting starkly with her background. Tristan's exquisite brushwork had brought his subject to life, making her seem three-dimensional and disturbingly real rather than just a flat portrait.

'He's brilliant, isn't he? He painted one of Mummy once – not nude, of course, that would be icky, but he made her look quite attractive. Daddy loved it.' Milly's voice cracked and she wound the scarf round her long plait absently.

'You miss him?' Tessa tore her eyes away from the painting. Close up, Milly looked much younger, pale freckles breaking free from an unnecessary layer of foundation.

'Not really. He was a high court judge so I barely saw him, he was always too fucking busy to spend time with me.' Her eyes flashed with anger.

Not sure whether she was more taken aback by Milly's language or her sangfroid, Tessa felt a rush of compassion for her. She was either seriously well-adjusted or hiding some very hurt feelings. Tessa guessed it was the latter. Milly reminded her of herself at that age; she obviously wasn't the only one who missed having a father figure. She quickly pushed the thought to one side.

'Introduce me at once!'

Tessa looked up as a tall, blond man strolled in confidently, his bright blue eyes dancing with interest. 'Wow, you're *lovely*. Are you one of Milly's friends from school?'

'Don't be silly, Tristan!' Delighted, Milly gave him a shove. He was playing right into her hands. 'This is Tessa Meadmore, the TV presenter. She looks young but she can't pass for sixteen, you idiot.'

Taken aback by Tristan's height and the cap of golden curls, Tessa was rendered speechless. He was wearing an old blue Ralph Lauren polo shirt streaked with a rainbow of watercolour paint, and a pair of combats tucked into battered old Timberland boots splattered with drops of colour. He was probably one of the handsomest men she'd ever seen.

Tristan gave her a cheeky smile. 'OK, so the comment about your being a teenager was lame. But I meant the one about you being lovely. You have the most interesting bone structure – gosh, I'd love to paint you.'

Tessa felt absurdly flattered, and somehow she managed to shake his paint-stained hand, feeling rather hot under the collar. She stammered a greeting but was more focused on getting her body to stop tingling all over. I hate men, she reminded herself sternly.

'As for you,' Tristan nudged Milly with his elbow, 'you're too precocious for your own good.'

Milly gave him a sly smile. 'Whatever you say. Tessa's a big fan of yours, by the way. Of your work, I mean.'

Tessa wished the ground would swallow her up. Milly had made her sound like some kind of groupie.

'Is that so?' Tristan moved closer until he almost had his arm round her. 'That's very kind of you,' he told her, wafting minty breath in her direction. 'I think the admiration could be mutual. Where are you staying?'

She named the B&B.

'Sweet place but you could easily stay here. The cottage next to mine is free. You could be available twenty-four hours a day.' His eyes flirted with hers. 'For work, I mean.'

She swallowed and spun round at the sound of more footsteps. She wasn't sure she could cope with meeting another member of the Forbes-Henry family, and this one, with his broad shoulders and stocky thighs, looked like a force to be reckoned with.

'Will!' Milly cried happily. She tucked her arm through his adoringly. 'Tessa, this is my other cousin.'

Tessa sucked her breath in, intimidated by his size and the sheer force of the newcomer's presence. Wow. If Tristan was gorgeous, Will was something else. He was so . . . *manly*. How on earth did he find trousers to fit those muscular thighs? Flustered, she tried to plaster a smile on her face as she held her hand out.

'I'm, er, Tessa Meadmore,' she said, staring at his tanned throat in the open neck of his Oxford-blue shirt. She felt her hand engulfed in a huge, warm grasp and reminded herself that he was most likely a lazy so-and-so who had been born with a platinum spoon in his mouth. 'It's very kind of you to allow us to film inside your beautiful home. I do hope the crew won't intrude on your lives too much.'

'I don't care about the rest of the crew but you can intrude on my life whenever you feel like it,' Tristan quipped, looking her up and down and settling his gaze on her spike-heeled boots.

Will ran a hand through his short, dark-gold hair and gave her a brief smile. 'Shut up, Tris. If you need anything, Miss Meadmore, please just ask. We're all very much looking forward to the reality TV show being filmed here.'

'It's going to be more like a documentary, actually,' she bristled, taking offence at Will's choice of words. He'd been excruciatingly polite but he had managed to make the show sound tacky, like some sort of cheap celebrity exposé. She felt herself flush, remembering that an 'exposé' was exactly what Jilly was after.

Will stared her down, the expression in his deep blue eyes doubtful. 'Really? You must forgive me for sounding cynical. Rufus is an old friend so I guess I'm a little over-protective.'

'You're old friends?' Tessa inquired as subtly as she could.

'We are. School, rugby, that sort of thing.' Guardedly, Will shoved his hands into his pockets.

Jilly's words ringing in her ears, Tessa gritted her teeth and carried on. 'You must be so pleased to hear about Rufus's impending marriage. Have you met Clemmie yet?'

'I've spoken to her on the phone many times. And of course we're thrilled Rufus is getting married.'

'Flabbergasted would be more accurate,' Tristan interjected indiscreetly, pushing a curl out of his eyes. 'He had more girlfriends than me when we were kids and that's saying something. To be quite frank, he's not exactly marriage material, not unless he's had a personality transplant since I last saw him.'

'Tristan!' Will frowned at him furiously. 'I'm sure Rufus would prefer it if you kept your mouth shut about his views on marriage.'

Tristan pretended to look hurt but gave Tessa a broad wink. She scuffed her feet on the floor, feeling her hangover kicking in. She couldn't help thinking she'd royally put her foot in it by trying to pump Will for information. He looked as if he wanted to throttle her.

She was about to politely make her excuses and leave when a petite redhead stomped past the doorway in nothing but a gold thong, a diaphanous orange kimono and four-inch wedges. She was swiftly followed by an older man who, vast gin and tonic in hand, could be heard bleating unconvincingly that the topless picture on his mobile phone was most definitely *not* of his new girlfriend.

Tessa gawped. These two had to be the parents but Caro didn't look old enough. She had a body Sienna Miller would be proud of – she couldn't possibly have given birth to two strapping boys like Will and Tristan, not with those narrow hips. And Jack – he was the man outside the pub who had waved at her as she drove into the village. Remembering his wandering hands, Tessa thought he was on to a loser defending himself to his wife.

'If you don't mind,' Will cut across Tessa's thoughts curtly, 'I really think you should keep your questions about Rufus to yourself. We regard him as part of our family and that means we're intensely loyal to him so there's no point digging around for any gossip. Do excuse me.' Deciding his parents' sex life was a more pressing fire to extinguish in front of this insufferably nosy TV presenter, Will turned on his heel and left the room.

Feeling as if she had been slapped on the wrists, Tessa narrowed her eyes at Will's ridiculously broad shoulders.

'He's under an awful lot of pressure,' Milly murmured sympathetically as she linked arms with Tessa. 'But this is just a normal day in the Forbes-Henry household, I'm afraid.'

Tessa suspected Will was under pressure because he was finally having to acquaint himself with the concept of working for a living.

Tristan gave Tessa a disarming grin as he took her other arm and smoothly led her towards the drinks cabinet. 'And I bet you thought it was the celebrities who were going to give you a headache, Miss Meadmore . . .'

Gil burst through the door and nearly made Sophie jump out of her skin. She dropped the box she was unpacking and winced when she heard something break.

'What on earth is the matter?'

'Plans, plans, I need to find the plans!' He tore past her and started manically sifting through the paperwork on the kitchen table. She watched her shopping lists go flying as he burrowed through the sheets.

'The plans for Appleton Manor! I've missed something major – an entire floor! And there's a party . . . I had no idea the deadline was so tight on this.'

'Darling, everything that arrived in the post went into your business file. It's not like you to miss something like that.'

'I know.' Gil clutched his highlighted hair. 'I don't know how this has happened but now Will Forbes-Henry thinks I'm a total idiot.'

'Let me get you a drink,' she placated, coaxing him into a chair and pouring him a glass of wine.

'But, my God, that house is stunning, absolutely stunning. I can't wait to get my hands on it. It's structurally sound and the rooms are spacious and light. And Sophie, the views! You're going to love it when you see it.'

Her heart clenched as she stared out of the kitchen window. The east wing of Appleton Manor could be seen clearly, the honey-coloured stone warm in the midday sunshine. It seemed close enough to touch, even though it was miles away. She knew Gil wanted to take her to see it but he didn't need to; she already knew the place like the back of her hand. She just hoped some of the people in the village who might remember her had moved on. Or died, she thought hopefully, shocked at herself.

'I know something you don't know!' Gil sang.

Sophie calmly poured herself a glass of wine and waited; Gil was her fiancé and closest friend in the world but he could be really childish at times.

'You were supposed to guess! Oh, if you insist . . . the rumours about Rufus Pemberton and Clemmie Winters getting married at the manor house are true.' Gil nodded. 'And there's more, Soph. There's going to be a film crew there, capturing the whole thing.'

Sophie knew where this was leading. Gil had long harboured ambitions of a TV career and he watched repeats of DIY shows on Sky with slavish devotion.

'I'm going to befriend the TV presenter when she arrives – you know, Tessa Meadmore. I'll offer to give her the lowdown on the honeymoon suite . . . the colour scheme for the ceremony room. I could be a real asset to the programme – an adviser, if you like.'

Despite her misgivings, Sophie gave Gil what she hoped was an encouraging smile. Her fiancé's ego often threatened to get the better of him, but his heart was in the right place.

'Perhaps those plans are in my office.' Gil jumped to his feet and kissed the top of her head clumsily. 'Just think, once the big celebrity wedding is out of the way, we can get married there ourselves!'

Sophie froze. She couldn't think of anything worse than marrying Gil at Appleton Manor. That would just be . . . *wrong*. She pushed open the French windows and headed out for some air, her eyes drawn to the regal house in the distance.

How had she ended up back here? She had left Appleton five years ago with ten pounds in her pocket, an old rucksack and some serious emotional baggage. And now she was back – in a stable relationship, financially secure and with a life most people would envy – in the one place that could bring her perfect world tumbling down around her. She couldn't bear to hurt Gil, she was indebted to him. He was kind and loyal and he had taken her in when she was at her lowest ebb. Most men would have swiftly bolted in the opposite direction after hearing her story but Gil had brushed aside her concerns in that gentle way he had and taken her under his wing.

Sophie hated herself for not being brave enough to speak up before now. She'd had plenty of opportunities but somehow she hadn't been able to bring herself to do it. Fear of losing everything she'd built up over the past five years had turned her into a nervous wreck and Gil had been so thrilled about the move. She was still furious that he had taken the job and rented this house without consulting her, though. He had done it to surprise her, she knew that, and he had also assumed she would have been over the moon that he had landed such a fantastic job. And she was – it was just being back here. Anywhere else but here . . .

Hearing small footsteps on the kitchen tiles, Sophie was reminded that coming back had ramifications for others, not just herself. Crouching down, she held her arms out for Ruby to run into, and buried her head in her daughter's fresh smelling hair. Love threatened to overwhelm her as thoughts of protecting Ruby and keeping her safe rushed to the surface.

At five years old, Ruby had the same caramel-coloured hair as Sophie, that fell in soft waves around her face and identical, delicate features, down to the lightly freckled nose. The only difference was that Ruby had big, round blue eyes, whereas Sophie's were almond-shaped and brown.

'Muuu-uum!' Ruby wriggled free and held out a drawing. 'Look, it's you and me. And Daddy.'

Sophie looked at the childish squiggles and hid a grin. She had been depicted as stick thin, with a smiley mouth and big bosoms – if only. Gil was sporting bright yellow hair and a rather subdued maroon shirt. Sophie scooped Ruby into her arms.

'Gil will love this.'

'That's not Gil, that's Daddy.' Ruby looked petulant. 'My *real* daddy.'

Sophie's stomach lurched. She had recently made the decision to tell Ruby about Gil not being her father because Gil had insisted on it. Having been brought up in a devoutly religious household, he felt it was unfair for Ruby to be lied to and Sophie had reluctantly agreed.

She stroked her daughter's hair, thinking her obstinate expression reminded her of someone. It was quite unnerving.

'He has a red shirt . . . it's his favourite colour. He's got yellow hair, like you and me.'

Sophie clutched her tightly, feeling the blood drain from her face. How did kids have this ability to give you a direct hit to the heart? Wham, just like that. Ruby couldn't possibly know but the likeness was uncanny. She turned the drawing over and gasped.

'Oh my God, Ruby, where did you get this piece of paper from?'

'Some papers I found.' Her face was a picture of innocence. 'Have I been bad?'

'No, darling but . . . These are the penthouse designs from Gil's design pack – no wonder he couldn't find them.' Sophie put Ruby down. 'I'm going to say I gave this to you by accident, OK? You know Mummy doesn't think lying is right but I don't want you to get into trouble, do you understand?'

Ruby nodded solemnly, her eyes suspiciously impish.

Sophie headed for Gil's office, feeling guilty. This wasn't the first time she had lied to Gil, not by a long shot. So why did she feel so treacherous now? Probably because she was back here, home to so many secrets.

She lost her nerve and held on to the wall. She'd never felt as scared as she did right now. When they lived in London, there was no chance of Gil bumping into Ruby's real father. But now that he only lived across the fields . . . Sophie was shaking, the plans fluttering in her hands. It was madness for her to come here, absolute madness. What would Gil do when he found out? He had no idea Ruby was Tristan Forbes-Henry's daughter. But then, neither did Tristan.

Rearranging her features, Sophie pushed open the door to Gil's office and prepared herself to lie to him once more.

Over lunch in the sun-dappled dining room at the back of the manor, Will was desperately trying to talk some sense into his family.

Caro and Jack were too busy ignoring each other to pay any attention, Tristan was engrossed in a sketch he was doing on the back of a newspaper and Milly was talking nineteen to the dozen into her mobile phone, no doubt to her best friend India. David, plugged into his iPod and not remotely interested in joining in the family dynamics, was bobbing his head in time with the music.

Will suppressed a sigh. Fighting like a bear for his family might be the right thing to do but it certainly wasn't going to win him any popularity contests.

'All I'm saying is that I think we need to be on our guard,' he repeated gently.

Caro blew smoke into the air and shot Jack a poisonous look. 'I really don't know what you mean about us misbehaving in front of the cameras, Will. You make it sound as if we're a bunch of unruly children or something!'

'No, I'm saying that there's too much riding on this wedding for any of us to screw it up,' Will said rather more huffily than he'd intended. He couldn't help wishing his mother hadn't been so easily hoodwinked by her previous suitor. Her fragile ego must have needed a major boost because even Caro wouldn't normally have been naive enough to believe the world needed a fashion line made entirely from rubber bands. God, what did it even matter any more? Will thought, rubbing his aching forehead with his fingertips.

'Look, I just want this to work. This TV show is worth a lot of money, not to mention the publicity it's going to bring us. And none of us can afford to mess it up, all right?'

Feeling Tristan giving him a curious look, Will downed another black coffee and wondered if he was doing the right thing by protecting his family from the awful truth. He had allowed them all to think there was more than enough money to play with but the reality was *very* different.

Will's heart sank as he thought about the pile of red bills mounting up in the room he had turned into his office. He had spent the rest of the morning since his run-in with Tessa Meadmore on the phone to their bank manager who, in spite of being a family friend and one of Caro's former lovers, had informed Will that he couldn't extend their overdraft limit any further for fear of losing his job. So Will was going to have to think of something else, and fast. He had already decided to sell the last of his properties in France but after that, they were penniless until Rufus's wedding.

Will found his thoughts drifting to Tessa and he wondered how old she was. Thirty, perhaps? She was younger than he'd expected and considerably better looking. With that wide mouth and dazzling smile, she had reminded him of Julia Roberts – hardly the Rottweiler he had imagined but he still wasn't sure he trusted her. Remembering the shamefully obvious question about his friendship with Rufus, Will felt a rush of contempt for Tessa, deciding he was right not to trust her.

The door opened and they all looked up.

'Oh, it's only *you*.' Caro sounded bored.

Jack's sister Henny came in, looking slightly flushed. She set a tray down on the table and the mouth-watering aroma of freshly baked pastry, bacon and coffee drifted under their nostrils. She was almost knocked flying by Austin, the family's golden retriever, who galloped in, paws soaked from playing in the water sprinkler outside. Exuberantly, he licked flakes of glazed pastry from Henny's sensible lace-up shoes.

'I made an egg and bacon pie for lunch,' she explained.

'Bully for you,' Caro threw back rudely. She looked at the pie as if she had a nasty smell under her nose and belligerently sucked on her cigarette.

Henny bit her lip nervously.

'Here, let me take that. It looks delicious.' Will wished his Aunt Henny knew how threatened his mother felt in her presence. She might bark at her like a fractious child but it was only because she was so insanely jealous of her. As soon as anyone met Henny, they warmed to her; she radiated motherly warmth and selfless generosity. But Caro . . . Caro was about as cuddly as an icicle. As a child, Will had soon learnt to go to his Aunt Henny for hugs and sympathy and that his beautiful, self-centred mother could really only be relied upon to parade herself, half naked, in front of his slavering school friends.

Noticing Henny pouring coffee into the sugar bowl with trembling fingers, Will gently took the coffee pot out of her hands and cleaned up the mess. He had missed breakfast because of his meeting with Gil Anderson, and he piled a plate high with egg and bacon pie before wolfing it down. Henny looked pleased and blushed to the roots of her sandy hair as she took a seat. She nudged David who grinned when he saw the pie and deigned to remove his earphones to tuck in.

'So what was Tessa Meadmore like?' David asked. 'I can't wait to meet her – neither can Freddie.'

Will's mouth set in a firm line. 'I was just saying, I think we all need to be on our best behaviour while the documentary is being filmed, and I certainly wouldn't suggest getting too friendly with her.' He gave Milly and Tristan a pointed look but then broke into a smile. 'Look, I have nothing against her personally but journalists often befriend people and encourage them to reveal their dirty secrets.'

'We don't *have* any dirty secrets,' Tristan pointed out archly, putting the finishing touches to the makeshift sketch he was doing of Tessa. He had captured her proud nose and laughing mouth to a T, in spite of only using a biro. Tristan had no intention of steering clear of their lovely presenter, she was absolutely stunning and he was sure she would be fantastic between the sheets. 'Well, not unless you'd call having sex-mad parents a dirty secret, of course.'

Jack guffawed, stopping abruptly when Caro gave him a sour look before turning her back on him and settling her gaze on the strapping new gardener who was outside wielding a rather phallic strimmer.

'I was thinking more of Rufus,' Will said as he gave the remains of his pie to a grateful Austin. 'We need to protect him as much as possible, not that there's much to say about his childhood anyway. Obviously he used to shag anything that moved, and I'm sure the odd hand job on the dishy prefect at boarding school won't be of any interest . . .' He halted, suddenly remembering Henny and Milly were in the room, and looked abashed. 'Sorry, ladies. But don't anyone tell that presenter I said that!'

'Well, aside from that disgusting piece of information, I don't know anything about Rufus, so I can hardly put my foot in it, can I?' Milly pointed out reasonably. She wasn't going to stay away from Tessa, whatever Will said. She adored him, but she couldn't help but hope Tessa might be like the sister she'd never had, at least until Will's fiancée Claudette came back. Claudette *always* made time for her, as well as buying her fantastically grown-up presents. Milly glared at David who had pie crumbs all over his chin; he was useless as a sibling, far too wrapped up in girls and study to ever listen to her problems. More to the point, Milly thought determinedly, she had to get Tessa and Tristan together to keep Freddie away from her.

'I'm sure you're overreacting, darling,' Caro said, patting Will's shoulder absently as she made eyes at the new gardener in full view of Jack, the young man having no idea he had just become a pawn in a jealous game of sexual chess.

Milly and David started arguing about who was going to be better friends with Tessa and, watching Tristan start a new sketch, Will gave up and left them all to it. He hoped they behaved themselves once filming started, otherwise none of them would have a roof over their heads.

Chapter Three

Waiting at the end of Rufus and Clemmie's driveway for JB to arrive, Tessa lounged on her car bonnet and flicked through the pages of *OK!* magazine. Photos of the glamorous couple moving into their stunning house in the Cotswolds were accompanied by a narrative charting their relationship from the moment they starred in their first film together.

The article went on to say that the much-anticipated documentary was set to take a prime-time slot which should guarantee massive viewing figures and be a competitor for another celebrity-style exposé the network had planned.

Tessa gulped and tossed the magazine into her car. It was bad enough knowing her boss was expecting big things from her without having the expectations of millions of viewers sitting on her shoulders. She quickly gave the outside of Rufus and Clemmie's house a once-over. Filming hadn't started before now as Clemmie had wanted the house to be perfect. If the outside was anything to go by, Clemmie's taste was more classy than Tessa had imagined. The house was as large as expected but the design was quietly traditional and not in the least bit vulgar. It was the only house at the end of a picturesque, leafy lane which guaranteed privacy and seclusion and, no doubt, an extortionate price tag.

Impressed by their exquisite taste once again, Tessa couldn't help wondering how two Hollywood stars would be able to settle in such a tranquil environment. Rufus used to live here, of course, so ensconcing himself in this rural idyll might prove easier than it would for Clemmie, but Rufus's thirst for fame was legendary. However besotted with Clemmie he might be, the idea of him giving up the glitz and glamour of Hollywood in favour of flannel slippers and cosy fireplaces seemed unlikely to Tessa. As for Clemmie, she was a well-respected actress whose portrayal of a rape victim had earned her a Best Actress Oscar and her very own star on Hollywood Boulevard. What could a tiny village like Appleton offer her in comparison?

Tessa checked her make-up in her wing mirror. Both Clemmie and Rufus had agreed to allow cameras to follow them around and film their most intimate moments – they were hardly shying away from publicity. So what were they doing here? It was possible Clemmie was tired of red carpets and flashing lights, or maybe, like Tessa, she was starting to feel a little disillusioned by the very career she had cared so much about.

'*Chérie!*'

Tessa jumped at the sound of JB's cheerful shout and told herself her feelings were temporary. It was just a blip, she was going to get back into her stride, starting today. A spurt of gravel showered her Christian Louboutin slingbacks as JB's flashy Porsche skidded to a halt, followed by a more sedate black van containing Joe the cameraman and his crew of lighting experts and boom holders. Susie, the pretty make-up artist, and Louise, a new hair stylist with a mane of streaky hair, joined them in a clapped-out Golf.

Tessa gave the crew a wave as they started unloading their equipment and mustered up a tight smile for JB.

'Sorry we are late.' Seemingly in a good mood, JB tore a baseball cap from his head as he leapt out of the car. 'Late night,' he explained huskily, trying to tame his wayward dark hair into submission with his fingers. His shirt was almost unbuttoned to the waist, giving her a glimpse of his tanned and rather hairy chest; all he needed was a pirate's hat and an eye patch and he would have been a dead ringer for Jack Sparrow.

Still smarting from his comments the other week, Tessa didn't respond. Judging by JB's unshaven chin and bloodshot eyes, it had been an eventful evening but Tessa decided against asking about it.

After providing details to a PA via an intercom system at the heavy iron gates, they all headed up the driveway together, cables dragging along the gravel.

'What did you theenk of the family?' JB asked as he lit a pungent-smelling cigarette and did up the buttons of his shirt simultaneously.

'Um . . . interesting.'

A slight understatement, Tessa realised as soon as she uttered the words. Milly was adorable and refreshingly honest and Tristan looked angelic but he was undoubtedly a player. He was an outrageous flirt yet he was also witty and easy to be around. After horrible Will had left, Tessa had found herself warming to Tristan more and more and had enjoyed his humour. He would be all too easy to fall for but, as Adam's betrayal came sharply back into focus, she reminded herself that romantic liaisons were to be avoided at all costs. It also would be professional suicide with Jilly snapping at her heels every two seconds.

And I *hate* men, Tessa reminded herself staunchly. She wondered what JB would think of Tristan's offer of a cottage and asked his opinion. She wasn't sure she liked the idea of distancing herself from the rest of the film crew but it could be advantageous to spend some time with the Forbes-Henrys.

'They did *what*?' JB stopped dead and tutted at Joe who crashed into him with his camera. 'You said yes, I 'ope, and took the key before they changed their minds?'

'I said I'd think about it. What's the big deal?'

'The beeg deal?' JB waved his hands expansively. 'The beeg deal is that you 'ave been invited into, 'ow you say, the bosom of the family! You can befriend them and get all the gossip. It's perfect, *chérie*, perfect! Jilly will say the same.'

Tessa knew he was right. It would make it much easier to snoop and get her hands on this gossip Jilly kept going on about – if there was any to find.

'Did you manage to get anytheeng out of Will about Rufus?'

She shook her head. 'I tried but he cut me off, almost as if he was expecting me to snoop. He practically gave me a rollicking in front of the entire family, the stuck-up moron. Tristan was a bit more forthcoming, though. Sounds like Rufus started sleeping around at a young age.'

'Good, good.' JB's dark eyes sparked with interest. 'There might be a story there – photographs, old girlfriends we can talk to, something Rufus 'as tried to bury. Besides, a family like this, they will 'ave something to 'ide, I bet. I might do some snooping myself.' He regarded her with detachment. 'If you're not up to it?'

'Of course I'm up to it,' Tessa snapped.

JB shrugged. 'Just don't get too close,' he instructed, stubbing his cigarette out on the side of his shoe and burying the butt under some pebbles. 'Get them to trust you and tell you theengs but be professional. Whatever you do, don't get attached. It is like women – I love them but I never fall in love with them, I never let myself lose control.' He nodded as if he believed he was imparting words of great wisdom. 'This . . . this is my motto in life; love what you do but always keep your distance.'

'I know how to do my job, thank you very much,' she retorted as she rapped smartly on the front door, wishing it was JB's head under her knuckles. She sent up a swift prayer of thanks as JB cracked his head on a hanging basket. 'Whatever Jilly might have told you, I have no intention of getting close to anyone. I want to do a fantastic job and get the hell out of here and back to London.' She pushed down the feeling that being with the Forbes-Henry family the other week had given her;

that sense of what it was like to be part of a big, loyal gang of people who looked out for you. But they weren't her family and she wasn't going to get sucked in. This was a job, nothing more.

The door swung open and a youngish PA stood aside to let them in, informing them that her name was Annie and that Rufus and Clemmie were waiting for them in the lounge. JB greeted her with his usual panache as the film crew traipsed in, his dark eyes darting around the hallway, absorbing every detail.

They were shown into a spacious lounge decked out in neutral shades of almond and taupe but spoilt somewhat by an abundance of busy chintz and the presence of some self-consciously positioned period furniture.

'Have a seat – anywhere you like,' Rufus called. Reclining lazily on a chocolate-coloured chaise longue, he was clutching a bottle of beer in one hand and caressing Clemmie's neck with the other. His pointy black boots hung off the end of the sofa and his skin-tight black jeans and rock star T-shirt looked out of place in such genteel surroundings.

He was definitely pretty, Tessa thought, trying not to stare as she flipped through her memorised list of facts about him. Rufus Pemberton was a passable enough actor with a string of supporting roles to his name, mostly in action films and the odd romcom. He hadn't reached anything close to the status of fellow Brits Orlando Bloom and Hugh Grant but he was well-known in Hollywood due to his constant partying and reputation as a hell-raiser. With his dark hair and brown eyes, he looked like a cross between Colin Farrell and Russell Brand and he spoke in the Sloaney tones he knew gave him British kudos.

What on earth was Rufus doing in the Cotswolds? Tessa mused, feeling puzzled. As soon as she could conceivably ease it into the conversation, Tessa planned to find out what the move to England was all about.

'It's lovely to meet you, Jean-Baptiste . . . Tessa,' Clemmie smiled as she moved away from Rufus's wandering hands and stood up. Her American accent was soft and deliciously Southern. 'Would you like a drink?'

'That would be . . .' JB stammered, his confident demeanour diminished by her beauty. Her skin was exquisite – smooth and milky white, and the hand that clasped his was small and elegant.

'We're fine,' Tessa assured Clemmie, trying not to show how star-struck she was. Meeting Clemmie Winters was like meeting Jennifer Aniston; she was America's sweetheart, Hollywood royalty and A-list all rolled into one. She wore a well-cut beige dress which screamed designer and exuded class. It showed just the right amount of cleavage, nipped in to hug a startlingly small waist and it finished demurely, just below the knee. Rumoured to have the 'best tits in Hollywood' and one of the most envied bodies around, Clemmie certainly knew how to make the most of her assets.

Her hazel eyes met Tessa's warmly. 'Well, you just let me know if you need anything. And please, sit down. We really want you to get to know us and see how normal we are.'

Rufus raised his eyebrows in amusement. 'Normal? We spend most of our time in Hollywood, Clem . . . we're not normal!'

She laughed with her head back, the full, throaty chuckle reaching her eyes. 'I guess not, honey. But you know what I mean. This is a chance for everyone to get to know us as a couple. We might be famous but like any other couple we bicker and fight and . . .'

'Make love,' Rufus finished, pretending to leer at her chest with eyes that were as dark as boot polish and outlined with smoky kohl pencil.

Clemmie rolled her eyes good-naturedly and swatted him. The film crew finished setting up quietly but there was a buzz of excitement in the room.

As Susie touched up her make-up, Tessa decided she liked

Clemmie. She seemed genuine and down to earth and if she continued to be this open and natural during the filming of the documentary, it was bound to be a success. Tessa considered her discreetly. She knew Clemmie's official age was thirty-three but all actresses shaved years off their official birth date, so it was possible she was even touching forty. She looked young and fresh and her skin had a translucence and smoothness that could of course be down to good genes. Tessa wondered how she could conceivably slip a question about nips and tucks into the conversation but resolved to try as soon as possible.

'It is a pleasure to be 'ere,' JB said, finding his voice at last and relaxing against the sofa as he eyed Clemmie lasciviously. 'The documentary . . . the wedding. It is a special time for you both.'

Clemmie's expression turned dreamy.

'Oh my, I can't tell you how excited I am about it, Jean-Baptiste! As I was saying, it's such a cliché, an American getting married in a traditional British stately home, but I don't care! I mean, have you *seen* Appleton Manor?'

'It's gorgeous,' agreed Tessa, noticing that Rufus was suddenly looking rather bored. She knew men didn't exactly take a hands-on role when it came to wedding preparations but shouldn't he at least look enthusiastic about the thought of marrying one of the world's most beautiful women? Clemmie was charm personified and clearly thrilled to be getting married in England. Tessa couldn't blame her, she wouldn't mind a wedding at Appleton Manor herself if only she could find a man who could tell the truth and didn't already have a long-term girlfriend. She sighed.

'I guess you don't have properties like that in America?'

Clemmie shook her head, her hands clasped together eagerly.

Tessa remembered Jilly's pointed phone call that morning instructing her to ask about Rufus and Clemmie's wedding plans. There had been talk of a winter wedding and Tessa had been tasked with finding out for sure. The documentary was planned to capture the build-up to the wedding, as well as the big event itself, and as far as Jilly was concerned, the longer it was the better.

'So you've decided on a winter wedding?' Tessa glanced out of the window. The sky was clear, blue and cloudless. 'I'm sure Rufus has told you that summer weddings can be glorious in this country but the weather here can be very unpredictable. Winter weddings are so romantic – you never know, you might get snow! Just think, fur-lined cloaks and blood-red roses and, um, candles and log fires . . .'

'Candles and log fires,' Clemmie echoed ecstatically. 'That's why I wanted it in December. What do you think, Rufus?'

Rufus, seemingly engrossed in the rolling Cotswold country-side he must have seen a million times, tore his dark eyes away and looked at Clemmie vaguely. 'Will reckons the manor will need a few more months to be ready for the wedding, but December's fine with me. No rush, is there? We can just chill out and enjoy kicking back for a bit.'

'That sounds wonderful, honey. And I have my heart set on December – so romantic!'

Tessa watched Clemmie. She was utterly besotted with Rufus, that much was obvious. It was evident in the way her eyes repeatedly flickered in his direction and the way her body leant in towards him, yearningly. She virtually lit up like a beacon when he spoke to her and, unless she was a greater actress than Tessa had given her credit for, love shone out of every flawless pore. Rufus appeared to feel the same way; he barely seemed capable of keeping his hands off her for more than a few minutes. They seemed to be very much in love. It was heart-warming and rather unexpected.

'If you don't mind me asking,' Tessa interjected smoothly, 'what prompted the move here?' She smiled genially, earning

47

herself an impressed glance from JB. Patronising sod, she fumed inwardly.

'Of course we don't mind!' Clemmie smoothed her dark hair out of her eyes. 'Well, what can I say? I love this country and I can't wait to settle down here. Hollywood is a truly wonderful place but it's so false, you know? There's so much pressure to look young and to keep working – I've had twenty years of it and I need a rest!'

'Er, twenty years?' Tessa felt a rush of adrenalin and sensed JB shifting in his seat. How old *was* she exactly?

'Oh, you know what I mean!' Clemmie waved the comment away with a show of white teeth and a graceful flutter of her hand. 'It *feels* like twenty years. That's what it's like being in this business. But I meant what I said about needing a rest. Filming ages you, especially when it's something as gruelling as rape scenes.'

The mention of her harrowing role sobered the atmosphere but Tessa wasn't discouraged for long.

'What about you, Rufus?' She turned and gave him one of her hundred-watt smiles. 'What brings you back here?'

'It's my home.' Rufus's expression didn't change but his jaw became rigid. 'And as Clemmie says, Hollywood isn't real. Sometimes you need to take a step back from it and appreciate the simpler things in life.' He slumped back against the chaise longue and closed his eyes.

There was something oddly erratic about Rufus's behaviour. Tessa observed him, noting that he was laidback one minute and fidgeting the next, his body switching from inertness to animation without warning. Drugs? Alcohol dependence? Tessa felt something spark up inside her. Perhaps there was a story here after all. Maybe Rufus Pemberton was more than just a pretty boy who had landed on his feet with his choice of fiancée.

'Does that mean you're turning your backs on Hollywood?'

Tessa was aware she was on dangerous ground. But she also knew a window of opportunity when she saw it.

'Well, I could happily retire here, honey,' Clemmie said as she slithered across the sofa towards Rufus, treating them to a glimpse of sheer, nude stocking and the top of a milky thigh. 'I love the fresh air and the peace and quiet and I just can't *wait* to get married.'

'And I'm happy wherever she's happy,' Rufus said with a touch of defiance. He took Clemmie's face in his hands and kissed her full lips. They were soon necking like teenagers, oblivious of anyone else in the room as their bodies urgently pressed against each other and Rufus's hand slid up around Clemmie's lace stocking top. Frantically gesturing for the film crew to shut down, Tessa motioned for a blatantly turned-on JB to follow her as she headed to the door. Waiting impatiently for the film crew to pack up and averting her eyes from Rufus and Clemmie's writhing bodies, Tessa couldn't help feeling they'd just been intentionally outmanoeuvred.

But based on what she had just witnessed, the documentary was going to be dynamite. And she was equally certain there was a story of some kind bubbling just below the surface as far as Rufus was concerned. And whether she liked it or not, Tessa sighed, it was her job to find out what that story was.

After Tessa and JB had left, Clemmie drew back from Rufus for a moment. Her heart was thumping crazily in her chest and for the first time in years she was finding it difficult to take a full breath. Was her childhood asthma making an unexpected comeback? Or perhaps it was a panic attack. She slowed her breathing to a normal rhythm with an effort.

Rufus stroked her hair softly, trailing his fingers down her neck.

Clemmie gathered her thoughts, needing to make sense of what had just happened. She had warmed to Tessa immediately; there was something about her wide smile and open face that had created an instant rapport between them. But she had to remember that Tessa was a journalist, she was paid to peel back the layers of superficiality and reveal the raw, candid truth beneath. And it wouldn't matter if the truth turned out to be unpalatable; in fact, it would be all the more delicious. Clemmie was aware that, as friendly as Tessa might appear, the likelihood was that underneath, she was as ruthless as a prosecution lawyer.

'What's wrong?' Rufus murmured, running his fingers down the side of her body.

'I don't know. Listen, do you still think this documentary is a good idea?'

'We've been through this, Clem,' Rufus protested laughingly. 'We want people to get to see the real us, don't we? The people behind the make-up and the borrowed lines.'

Clemmie let out a nervous giggle. 'You wear more eyeliner than me!'

'True,' he grinned. 'But this is good publicity for us.'

'Do we need it?'

Rufus avoided her eyes for a second. 'Not now, but maybe one day. I'm as ready to settle down as you are, babe, but who knows what might happen in the future?'

The future wasn't really Clemmie's concern. It was the past she was anxious to protect. Everyone had secrets and hers were buried deep, deep enough to have stayed hidden for a long time, safe from prying journalists' eyes and mucky photographers' lenses. The familiar feeling of shame her memories always threatened to overwhelm her and she fought hard to hold back the tears.

'Clem, you have nothing to worry about.' Rufus put a reassuring hand on her trembling body. 'This is going to be enormous fun, I promise you. Why are you worried about your privacy? There aren't any skeletons in your closet for them to find, are there?'

'Of course not!' She attempted a laugh but stopped as it turned into a grating bray.

Rufus kissed each soft cheek slowly before nibbling the tip of Clemmie's nose and the adorable cleft of her chin. As she turned to butter beneath his caresses, he dipped his hands lower, suggestively sliding them up her thighs and under her dress. Within seconds, he navigated himself between her legs, his fingers practised and his intention clear.

Clemmie gazed into his lovely brown eyes and felt a thrust of emotion, as intense in her heart as it was in her groin. She didn't know whether to revel in the feeling or despise it; all she knew was that she felt helpless around Rufus. She was aware she would do anything to make him happy, even if it put herself at risk, and her gut told her this documentary could be her undoing.

Unable to resist him, Clemmie stood up shakily. She unzipped her dress and allowed it to fall to the floor, maintaining direct eye contact with him.

'Fucking hell,' murmured Rufus as she stood wearing only a pair of frilly, silk panties the shade of candy floss and hold-up stockings. Her waist was slender and her breasts were soft and shaped like teardrops, the nipples hardening as a pink flush spread down her body. Peeling her knickers down with exaggerated, leisurely movements, Rufus could barely contain himself. Suddenly, he remembered why he had proposed to her.

Scooping her up and pressing his hard-on against her hip, he ran the tip of his tongue around each nipple, loving the way she gasped and reared upwards.

'Let's go and screw in that four-poster bed you get so turned on by,' he growled.

Clemmie buried her face in his neck, unable to utter a word.

Chapter Four

A week later, Tessa was quickly unpacking her clothes and stacking her designer shoes in the bottom of a spacious wardrobe. The cottage she had been allocated was compact and pretty and situated to the left of Appleton Manor, with a gorgeous view of the lake and the side of the house. Upstairs, there were two dinky bedrooms and a good-sized bathroom with pale blue panelled walls and fluffy white towels. Tessa had been delighted to discover bottles of Penhaligon's Bluebell products on the window sill. She loved the scent; it was old-school glamour and top-notch quality mixed together – someone around here had class. There were also bottles of Chablis stacked in the fridge and glossy magazines on her bedside table, personal touches she suspected had been provided by Milly's mother, Henny. From what Tessa had seen of Caro, she wasn't the homely kind.

Tessa had chosen the larger of the two bedrooms to sleep in, having fallen in love with the period fireplace and the mint-green walls, and she was using the other, smaller room to store her luggage and clothes.

Checking her watch, Tessa knew she had to get a move on and she pulled on a pair of tailored trousers and a white Joseph shirt that she hoped didn't look overtly businesslike. She needed to fit in with the rest of the Forbes-Henrys, although she wasn't sure she could pull off their rumpled, upper-class chic just yet.

Henny, the recently appointed temporary wedding coordinator, had agreed to meet her this morning and Tessa was hopeful she might be able to get some much-needed gossip about Rufus. She drenched herself with Bluebell eau-de-toilette, dashed down the crooked wooden staircase that seemed to be borrowed from an Enid Blyton novel and grabbed the notes Jilly had faxed her. Jilly wanted sizzling gossip about Rufus as a teenager and, if Tessa could get her hands on any, photos.

Heading for the manor, Tessa couldn't help noticing how beautiful it looked in the glow of the early-morning July sunshine. Fingers of rich sunlight curled round the creamy stone walls, and the Virginia creeper framing the doorway was so glossy, it looked as if the leaves had been individually polished.

Inside the manor, Tessa could hear a rather bossy male voice directing operations upstairs and assumed it must belong to the shit-hot designer she had heard so much about. Poking her head into the library, she found a kind-faced woman surrounded by wedding magazines, fabric swatches and heaps of recipe books. The windows of the library had been flung wide open to allow a gentle breeze to drift through and sunlight bounced off the colourful spines of the books stacked up on the shelves.

'You must be Tessa. Do join me.' With a handsome golden retriever chewing the laces of her sensible brogues, Henny patted the sofa in a gesture of welcome and immediately began pouring out cups of Earl Grey tea.

Tessa took a seat, unnerved when Henny enveloped her in a warm hug. She found herself relaxing against the cushioned body and breathing in the aroma of freshly baked biscuits. For a moment, she was knocked sideways by a deeply buried memory of her own mother. She caught her breath and reluctantly pulled away.

'Wow, that looks like homemade shortbread,' she said, for something to say, glancing at the crumbly pile of pale, sugary biscuits.

'It is. I love to cook. Help yourself.' Henny's cornflower-blue eyes twinkled. 'Sorry about all this mess. I'm trying to put some ideas together for Rufus and Clemmie's wedding – catering, flowers and suchlike. I'm sure Will plans to hire someone much more experienced soon but it doesn't hurt to get a head start, does it? I hope you like dogs, by the way. This is Austin. He's very well-behaved – most of the time. I can't tell you how excited we all are about the documentary!' She paused for breath finally.

'Really?' Tessa didn't want to put a downer on things but as she munched on a melt-in-the-mouth biscuit, she felt duty-bound to enlighten Henny. 'You might not be saying that when the film crew start trampling all over the carpets and wanting to film when you're trying to sleep. And that's before they start demanding endless cups of tea and more of this divine shortbread.'

'Sounds *thrilling*,' Henny said, undeterred, stacking Nigella Lawson cookery books on top of Delia's. Her sandy hair, so like Jack's, looked as if it had been frazzled by the sun and her nondescript brown cardigan had definitely seen better days. But her beaming smile was generous and trusting, Tessa decided as she watched her. Henny was rather like Mrs Tiggywinkle from the Beatrix Potter stories; all bustling kindness and sweet sincerity. Tessa almost felt guilty about her intention to use Henny for gossip but the bleeping BlackBerry in her pocket put paid to her flash of conscience.

'You must be looking forward to the wedding too. With Rufus being such a close family friend and all that.' Tessa smiled winningly and leant back against the sofa.

Henny nodded. 'Such lovely news! It's the only thing that's made Caro unbend about turning Appleton Manor into a hotel. A stroke of genius, don't you think?'

'Definitely. It's one of the most beautiful houses I've ever seen.'

'Thank goodness Will has such a good business head – one of

us needs to be good with money! But Will has always been successful and one of those people who can turn their hand to anything. Even as a child he was *very* entrepreneurial.'

Tessa narrowed her eyes at the thought of rude, bullish Will as an enterprising young boy, wheeling and dealing in short trousers. Even if he wasn't a lazy aristo as she had first thought, that didn't stop him from being obnoxious and obscenely rich to boot. She sipped her tea and said nothing. Why did they all think he was so special?

'Will is rather homesick,' Henny confided apologetically, seeing her face.

'But this is his home, isn't it?'

Henny sipped her tea. 'Oh yes, and he adores it. But Will has lived in France for the past few years, you see, and he feels very much at home there. My mother was French so the three of us spent lots of holidays over there as children. By the three of us I mean me, Jack and our brother, Perry – he lives in France and he's a lawyer. Yes, my brothers always loved their holidays in France as children.' Henny paused, looking past Tessa with a contented expression. 'I can picture them both now, sipping vast bowls of hot chocolate at the breakfast table and munching on buttery pastries. They used to bring half the beach back with them, the monkeys, as well as buckets full of tiny crabs and seaweed.'

Tessa could practically smell warm pain-au-chocolate and salty sea air. She had visited France as a child and had loved every minute of it, and Henny was making her feel deeply nostalgic. Still, she didn't have time to reminisce about family holidays. She was about to ask Henny about Rufus again but the older woman was in full swing.

'Gabrielle, my mother, was terribly exotic-looking – I look nothing like her, unfortunately. I ended up with my father's looks. Anyway, when she was very young, before she met my father, she married a dashing Frenchman. Alain something . . .

incredibly handsome but a bit of a bugger when it came to women.' Henny sighed. 'He cheated on her, several times, and being rather modern of mind, my mother packed up and left. Being French, Alain was shocked when she wouldn't put up with his mistresses and he never got over it. Even though my mother was devastated, she divorced him and fell in love with my father, Jackson Senior. It all happened so long ago now but rumour has it Alain held a torch for her for years, swearing he'd make it up to her, but my parents were killed in a car crash five years ago. And Alain must be dead now too.'

Tessa patted Henny's roughened hand, unexpectedly touched by the story. It was very romantic. Still, she had a job to do. She glanced up at the family photographs lining the walls and caught sight of one of Rufus, Will and Tristan laughing their heads off. Will looked young and carefree in it, far from the stressed-out man she had met the other day.

'Great photo of Rufus,' she started in a playful tone.

'Isn't it? We have tons of them somewhere. Will and he were inseparable as boys.'

'Really? I'd love to see them.' She leant in to Henny conspiratorially. 'Tristan mentioned Rufus was a bit of a cad when he was younger. Naughty boy – did he have tons of girlfriends?'

Henny considered the question, completely forgetting Will's warning. 'Quite a few, I suppose, but no one he was really serious about. Not like Tristan. I haven't a clue how he carried on after what happened. But love can do terrible things to you, can't it?' she asked tremulously. Her hands shook slightly as she set her teacup down. 'I expect you've heard about Bobby, my husband?' She hesitated but, sensing sympathy from Tessa, she continued. 'The cancer was bad enough but I felt so stupid because I had no idea that Bobby had been making such bad investments and then we had to sell our much-loved home. Poor Milly blames me.' She faltered, a sob catching in her throat. 'I can see why. She had to leave her lovely school and all her friends behind which must be crushing at her age. David, my son, has been wonderful but he's older and boys seem to adjust much more easily, don't you think? And in spite of everything, I can't help missing Bobby dreadfully.'

Seeing Henny's eyes swimming with tears, Tessa was alarmed. She tugged a tissue out of her handbag and pushed it into Henny's hands. 'Milly seems fine to me, so please try not to worry.' She only just resisted the urge to smooth Henny's frazzled hair away from her face. But she knew she had to focus her mind on work, otherwise Jilly would be shooting up to the Cotswolds to sack her in person. 'It sounds as though you've had a tough time, Henny. I'm so sorry. At least you have your family around you at such an awful time. Will, Tristan . . . Rufus . . . how lovely to have them all back here with you, and for such a happy event.'

'We never thought Rufus would get married because he was always such a lady's m—' Henny abruptly stopped and dabbed at her eyes with the tissue. She was mortified at having opened up to Tessa so readily. She really hoped Will wasn't going to be annoyed with her – she was only being friendly.

They both looked up as Gil rushed into the library. Resplendent in a red and yellow striped shirt and skin-tight jeans, his manicured hand was outstretched in Tessa's direction.

'Tessa Meadmore! Such an honour to meet you. I can't tell you what a fan I am of *Good Morning UK*. I'm Gil Anderson, by the way – just the lowly designer, ha ha!'

Tessa switched on her trademark smile, and shook his hand politely.

'You *must* give me your opinion on the colour schemes,' he demanded, holding on to her hand and dragging her towards the door. 'I would so value your opinion.'

'Er . . . I'm not really an expert on colour schemes . . .' Tessa shot Henny a desperate look.

Gil was determined. 'Nonsense! You have a great sense of

personal style so you must know your fabrics and shades.' Not giving her a chance to protest and ignoring Henny's feeble attempts to save her, Gil led Tessa up the grand wooden staircase and spun her into the nearest bedroom.

'Gloriously camp or hideously OTT?' he asked, biting his lip anxiously. 'This is totally different from all the other rooms. What do you think?'

Tessa did a slow circle of the room, losing her heels in the plush, jade carpet as she felt the quality of the black, shot silk curtains. It was outrageous but the bold colours dazzled rather than offended and it was decadent and sexy.

'Gloriously camp?' she offered. 'But I think it needs something else . . . handcuffs in the drawer and a whip on the bedspread. This room absolutely *demands* bondage.'

'Oh, you minx!' Gil squealed, clapping his hands together. 'I love it. My fiancée, Sophie – she's just moved to the village – she wasn't sure about it at all but I really feel it works here.'

Tessa hated to admit it but Gil had the Midas touch. Poking her head into some of the other rooms, she couldn't help being impressed. The rooms weren't yet finished, of course, but Tessa could see what Gil was trying to achieve. As he enthused about fabrics in old gold with honey walls, mocha brown silk with midnight blue touches and high-spec baths littered with rose petals, it was obvious he relied on sumptuous fabrics and rich colours to provide cosy havens with mod cons and superb attention to detail.

'We'll try and stay out of your way in terms of the filming,' she told Gil, leaning out of one of the windows to take in a breathtaking view of the gardens. 'We'll film around you and do as many outside shots as possible. If the weather holds, this scenery is going to look amazing on film.' Perfectly tended lawns stretched out in every direction, saved from starkness by a riot of colour in the tapered flower beds.

'Oh, do feel free to film wherever you need to,' Gil assured her with a beaming smile, touching her arm in a familiar fashion. 'I'd like you to think of me as your assistant. Just call on me anytime and I'll provide you with details of the designs and anything else you might need me for. I'd be delighted to do some commentary for you.'

Tessa stared at him. Gil didn't care about her opinion on the rooms at all. He had dragged her up here as an excuse to cosy up and offer his services for the documentary. Tessa met people like Gil every time she fronted a programme. He obviously had dreams of becoming a TV star, hosting his own design show, no doubt, and would be popping up in the background of every shot if she didn't keep an eye on him.

She gave a brief nod in the hope of discouraging him and leant out of the window again. Caro was performing a complex yoga move on the lawn, her slender, freckled limbs arched at an impossible angle. Wearing a nude leotard that left nothing to the imagination, she was enjoying the attentions of a nearby gardener who was struggling with what appeared to be an out-of-control ferret down the front of his trousers. Practically foaming at the mouth, he accidentally lopped the head off one of the prized rhododendron bushes and he and Caro both started to laugh.

Tessa shook her head and managed to sidle away from Gil. The Forbes-Henry family were unbelievable! Extra-marital affairs were clearly all the rage around here, with chequered love lives at every turn. What had Henny meant about Tristan earlier – something about how he had carried on after 'everything that had happened'? As far as Tessa was concerned, Tristan seemed to be the most well-adjusted one in the entire family, so she couldn't imagine it was anything too heart-wrenching.

Back in the library her BlackBerry demanded attention again and, answering it with a sinking heart, she listened to Jilly screeching down the phone. A hardened hack who was married to her job and proud of it, Jilly always peppered her waspish comments with 'kiddo' and punctuated them with swear words.

'No, nothing yet, Jilly . . . but I'm doing my best,' Tessa provided after several 'kiddos' and a couple of strenuous 'goddamnit's. She remembered what Henny had said about photos of Rufus and furtively she stole a glance over her shoulder. The coast was clear . . . Feeling like an intruder, she tiptoed to the cabinet on the far wall and started opening drawers. She swore as dozens of photographs slithered out, some black and white, some coloured – even the odd old-fashioned sepia photo among them.

Tessa gathered them up, noticing one of Will and Tristan taken on a sunny beach, perhaps in France. They must have been in their teens; their arms were flung round each other's shoulders chummily and they were grinning at the camera with palpable mischief in their eyes and the beginnings of bum fluff on their chins. And here was one of what could only be Jackson Senior and Gabrielle in front of Appleton Manor, their flares and platform shoes revealing when the photo was taken. Tessa scrutinised it.

The older Jack was handsome with a very square jaw and hair that looked like a handful of straw plonked on his head (Henny was right about taking after him on the looks front). He possessed the brilliant blue eyes that all the Forbes-Henrys seemed to have inherited. Gabrielle, by contrast, was darker and softer-looking, her hair curling round her heart-shaped face, her expression carefree. The lines etched around her eyes suggested she had spent much of her time laughing and having fun, and the jaunty silk scarf at her neck reflected a style only the French possessed.

Hearing approaching footsteps, Tessa hurriedly flung all the photos into a drawer and dived heroically on to one of the sofas.

'There you are!' Henny reappeared, surprised to find Tessa sprawled out at such a funny angle. 'Those photos of Rufus you asked about? I dug them out for you. Feel free to use them, I'm sure he won't mind. They're very innocent, just a few of him in a nasty private school uniform and some shockingly tight rugger shorts.'

Tessa blushed furiously as she took the pictures, feeling a momentary stab of guilt. She had almost been caught by Henny with her hand in the till, as it were, and she needn't have bothered because here was Henny, kindly and rather naively offering her the goods. Tessa was relieved when Caro haughtily paused in the doorway, still in her yoga gear.

'You must be Tessa,' she purred, holding out her long white hand like a paw.

Tessa wasn't sure if she should shake it, kiss it or drop to her knees in reverence. She plumped for shaking it and, close up, found Caro to be just as breathtaking as she was at a distance. Her freckled white skin and slender limbs were delicate but the ice in her eyes suggested a backbone of steel.

'Thank you for letting me stay in one of your cottages. It's really kind of you.'

Caro shrugged carelessly. 'Glad you like it. Far too poky for me. And I hope you're not bothering our lovely presenter,' she snapped at Henny who, much to Tessa's distress, appeared to be cowering in Caro's presence. 'You're always getting in the bloody way, sticking your nose in where it doesn't belong . . .'

Tessa couldn't help interrupting. 'Henny's has been fantastically helpful, actually.'

Caro raised her thin eyebrows in disbelief. 'Really? She's usually pretty hopeless at everything – apart from cleaning, of course.' She fixed her steely blue gaze on Henny's quivering form. 'Quite right too, seeing as you're staying here for nothing.'

Tessa was aghast. How could Caro speak to Henny like that? It was like punching a teddy bear.

'I'm very grateful to be here,' Henny stammered, her hands shaking badly.

Caro turned back to Tessa, giving her the benefit of a gracious but insincere smile. 'Do feel free to treat the house as your own,' she said crisply. The smile faded and her shoulders became taut. 'After all, everyone else will when it opens as a hotel so you might as well make yourself at home.' With that, she turned and stalked off.

'Sorry about that,' Henny said, scarlet in the face. 'Caro's very uptight at the moment; she hates the thought of Appleton Manor being made open to the public.'

'Don't defend her!' Tessa spluttered. 'She's absolutely vile!'

Henny unexpectedly broke into laughter, buoyed up by Tessa's camaraderie. 'She *is* vile, isn't she? I know I should stand up for myself but she's so dreadful sometimes, I'm left speechless. Thank you for being so kind, Tessa, you've really made my day. Will was so wrong to warn us about you – you're not here to snoop at all.'

Watching Henny scuttle out of the room, Tessa was furious. How dare Will warn the family about her! What right did he have to lord it over everyone, telling them who they could and could not speak to? Pushing aside the feeling that Will had every right to be wary of her, she checked to see that Henny was out of earshot.

Clutching the photos of Rufus to her chest, Tessa couldn't help feeling despicable as she dialled Jilly. But she really didn't have any choice.

Leaning against the wall outside the kitchen, a stricken Caro squeezed her eyes shut with pain. Jack was still cooing into the phone in the hallway, not realising she could hear every word. Caro twisted her hands helplessly. Sometimes she couldn't help taking things out on Henny – she was so loyal to Jack and it wasn't fair because there was no one on *her* side. Feeling utterly destroyed, she wondered if Jack was talking to Sara, the new barmaid at the Appleton Arms. Sara was younger than Caro, *much* younger. Her body was ripe and her skin was plump and fresh. She was the latest in a long, long line of women of all different shapes and sizes who shared one thing in common – their attraction to Caro's husband.

It *hurt*, Caro thought breathlessly, wondering at Jack's ability to puncture her heart with increasing brutality. Anything he can do, I can do better, she reminded herself, head held high. She had already arranged to meet Nathan, the new gardener, in the village later that night.

But where was this going to end? she thought, feeling despair washing over her again. Surely she had been punished enough? They kept up the pretence that neither of them could remember who had cheated first but she and Jack both knew the truth.

Caro bit her lip. Bedding Jack's best friend had been the biggest mistake of her life, a drunken, unsatisfying fumble that had resulted in the best friend running to Jack like a cowardly pussy and telling tales the next day. Typically, Jack had forgiven his best friend but not his wife and he hadn't stopped trying to get back at her ever since. Women had come and gone, each one younger than the last, and the notches on the bedpost were reaching embarrassing levels. And she was just as bad.

These games had to stop, Caro thought in anguish. But listening to Jack's teasing voice as he seduced his latest lover like a pro, she hardened her heart. The only way the games would stop was if one of them declared the other the overall winner.

And Caro was determined to emerge the victor. She just needed to find a prize worth winning – a prize worth losing Jack over.

Chapter Five

Standing in the doorway of Appleton Manor some days later, Tristan was about to head back to his cottage. It was a quiet Sunday and, having just dropped off some paintings for Will to choose between for the new rooms, his head was full of new ideas for a portrait. But maybe there were better things to do than paint on a day like this.

Taking advantage of the sultry July weather, Tessa Meadmore was stretched out on a rug by the lake, wearing nothing but a tiny pair of denim shorts and a bright yellow bikini top. Tristan watched her leafing through a pile of notes with a highlighter pen as Milly chatted to her and tried on her designer sunglasses.

Making a snap decision, he headed back inside and went in search of Henny, guessing correctly that she would be in the kitchen baking.

'Tristan!' Henny emerged from the oven, her cheeks rosy from the heat, a tray of chocolate-chip muffins in her hand. 'Are you hungry?'

'For your food, always. Do you have any of that fantastic homemade lemonade of yours going spare? I need enough for two of us.'

'In the fridge, darling. Help yourself.'

Henny added cubes of butter to a bowl of flour and watched Tristan pour some cloudy lemonade into a jug and stuff two glasses into the pockets of his combat-style shorts. He reminded her of David Larrabee in the Audrey Hepburn film *Sabrina*. She hoped Tristan didn't forget about the glasses and sit on them, like David had.

'Got a date?' she asked slyly, tucking the tail of his pink Ralph Lauren shirt into his shorts in a maternal fashion.

'Just thought Tessa could do with a nice cool drink,' Tristan told her, his smile wide and innocent.

'I see.' Henny wrapped a couple of muffins in a napkin and tucked them under Tristan's arm. She turned back to her bowl and started mixing the cubes of butter with the flour. 'Do you like her?'

Tristan shrugged. 'She's a very attractive girl . . . I'm just being friendly.'

'Of course you are. I meant, do you *like* her, like her.'

'Aaah, who knows, Auntie? She seems like a lovely girl but I don't think I'm ready for anything serious.'

Henny put a caring hand on his arm, leaving a floury print. 'Tris, it's been five years.' She gave him a kindly smile. 'Not everyone's like—'

'Please don't,' Tristan interrupted swiftly. He hung his golden head, knowing whose name Henny had been about to say. The one girl who had made him think that 'long-term' wasn't an abomination, the only girl he could have seen himself settling down with. 'But I know what you mean, Aunt Hen. I just can't seem to get her out of my head, you know? I have tried.' He looked up again, his blue eyes suspiciously bright.

'I know. But don't let one bad experience put you off forever.' She gave him a wry smile. 'Well, two bad experiences, if you include Anna.'

Tristan shuddered at the thought of his ex-girlfriend, Anna. Unbalanced wasn't the word to describe her – hell, psychotic didn't do her justice. What sort of girl threatened to cook one's dog with citrus fruits when their time was up? Anna had been, quite literally, insane and he had been relieved to finally see the back of her five years ago.

Henny turned back to her mixing bowl. 'You need to have some fun,' she advised him, rolling the mixture into balls between her palms.

'You can talk,' Tristan said, kissing the top of her head. 'It's been a year since Uncle Bobby died. You're far too gorgeous to be on your own.'

'Don't be silly!' Henny shooed him away, turning so he couldn't see the pleasure in her eyes. 'Anyway, I'm not sure Tessa's one of your usual lost souls but that's probably a good thing; you need someone who'll put you in your place, not make you come over all masterly and protective. Now, off you go, I've got baking to do.'

She was glad Tristan had noticed how attractive Tessa was; he deserved a bit of fun. And with Tessa's sparkly eyes and sassy attitude, Henny couldn't help thinking Tristan couldn't go far wrong.

Tristan smiled and took the lemonade outside. He didn't want another lost soul, he'd had enough of those to last him a lifetime and all it had brought him was grief. Aunt Henny was right: it was time he had some fun and Tessa might be just the person to have it with. Tristan halted, drinking in the view. He was surprised at how pleased he was to see Tessa. The sun had turned her long chestnut hair the rich colour of molasses and her skin was starting to turn honeyed as it caught the sun. She had a fabulous body and the skimpy, buttercup-yellow bikini top and shorts suited her athletic figure.

Tessa had her head flung back so her hair rippled down her bare back and her body was arched towards the sun in a gesture of worship. The artist in him yearned to paint her so he could capture her long limbs and passionate mouth for all to see, but the other, more lustful side of him longed to tumble her into bed and have those slim thighs and generous mouth all to himself.

Ignoring Milly who, now that school was winding down, was

wearing her other uniform of black leggings teamed with an eighties-style T-shirt and flat ballet pumps, Tristan held the jug aloft.

'Oooh, is that homemade lemonade?' Tessa's moss-green eyes sparkled and Tristan was instantly transfixed by her infectious smile.

Milly watched as Tristan took the glasses from his pocket. 'Only two?' She grinned mockingly. She flipped her white-blond plait over her shoulder, delighted that her plan to pair off Tessa and Tristan seemed to be falling into place without her help. She'd spent the last ten minutes subtly informing Tessa of Tristan's good points but it seemed she needn't have bothered. 'Someone will have to go without a drink, won't they?'

'Yes, *you*.' Tristan gave her a wink. 'Push off, Mills. Haven't you got homework to do or something?'

Milly pouted. 'I've finished my exams now, thank you. All the teachers are screaming at me to make a decision about my A levels but don't worry about me, I can take a hint.' Letting out an exaggerated sigh, she handed Tessa's sunglasses back and left them to it.

'Precocious child,' Tristan grumbled, splashing lemonade into the glasses. 'I hope she hasn't been distracting you.'

'Not at all. I like her.' Tessa pushed her notes to one side and snapped the top on her highlighter pen. 'Incidentally, she was talking about you.'

'Christ, that's all I need. What was she saying?'

Tessa looked coy. 'Not much. She was extolling your virtues, actually.'

'Really?' Tristan glanced after Milly. 'That's odd. She usually tries to scupper my chances with pretty women.'

'If I didn't know better, I'd think she was trying to set us up.' Tessa hid her pleasure at being called pretty by popping her sunglasses on her nose. She wasn't in the least bit interested in Tristan but, God knows, her ego could do with a boost.

'Clever girl, she knows I have excellent taste. What are you doing, anyway?'

He really was incorrigible. 'Reading some work notes.'

Tristan peered at them. 'Christ, what on earth are they? Instructions from the Gestapo?'

'Pretty much.' Tessa gathered them up and fervently hoped Tristan hadn't seen the section Jilly had marked off as 'How Best to Use the Forbes-Henrys'. 'My boss is a bit of a shark when it comes to this stuff.'

'Journalists always are,' Tristan agreed, sipping his drink. Surreptitiously, he breathed in her scent – she was wearing something classy and floral that was vaguely familiar to him but he couldn't quite put his finger on what it was. 'Well, most of them. You're all right, obviously – more like one of us.'

'Hmmmm.' How wrong he was, Tessa thought guiltily.

'Hey, have you met my parents yet?'

'I met your mother the other day,' Tessa said, pulling a face. 'And I've seen your father from a distance.' She didn't want to be rude, but Caro seemed an absolute horror. Jack appeared genial enough but neither of them showed any loyalty to the other.

'Ghastly, aren't they?' Tristan said, sensing her reticence. 'Oh, don't worry, we all know what a pain they can be. My father's all right on his own but when he's with my mother . . . Have you ever seen that old Richard Burton and Elizabeth Taylor movie, *Who's Afraid of Virginia Woolf?* That's them. They fight and they shag other people to wind each other up and every so often they remember they love each other and end up in bed having noisy sex.'

'Wow. Your mother . . . she was a little . . . rough on Henny the other day. It was difficult to watch. Henny's lovely, isn't she?'

'Wonderful,' agreed Tristan. 'Which is why my mother hates her so much.' He admired Tessa's narrow waist and slender thighs, thinking how perfectly proportioned she was body-wise. Her face was slightly off centre but somehow it worked. 'So, did you study journalism at university?'

Tessa nodded, her dark hair falling across her face. 'Well, English and Media Studies then I did a course in journalism before working on a magazine and then getting a break in television. I've been in television for ten years, can you believe that? I started out on GMTV as a roving reporter doing all the celebrity gossip then got headhunted by Sky.' She paused. 'I did various presenting jobs related to celebrities – you know, about their children and slimming habits – but nothing on this scale. Which is why this documentary is so important for my career.'

Tristan studied her. Despite the positive spin she was putting on it, Tessa sounded jaded, almost disillusioned. He wondered what made her tick; surely most presenters would rip their right arm off to front a documentary about a star as famous as Clemmie?

'What about you? Did you study art?' Tessa realised Tristan was dressed in clothes that weren't covered in paint for once and the pink shirt was ironed, the shorts clean. The sun beating down on his golden curls made them look like a halo but she had an idea he was anything but an angel.

'Yes. My father thinks my degree is pointless, but then he thinks everything I do is pretty pointless.' A shadow passed across Tristan's face but his voice didn't contain an ounce of bitterness. 'Will's his favourite, you see. Always has been.'

'Why, is he a bully like him?' Tessa snapped before she could stop herself. She held her face up to the sun, hoping she could blame it for the blush that was spreading across her face.

Tristan's brow furrowed in confusion. 'Will's not a bully! He's a great guy when you get to know him. Admittedly he can be a bit . . . curt sometimes but honestly he's one of the funniest and most loyal people I know.'

Tessa raised her eyebrows disbelievingly. She didn't blame Tristan for defending Will; they were brothers, after all. She just couldn't see why the family thought so much of this man who had shoulders and thighs to swoon over but apart from that seemed pretty short on charm and humour. The whole family seemed to adore him. Still, if she'd had a sibling, Tessa knew she would have made it her business to defend them to the hilt too. Sadly, she was an only child. Well, now she supposed she was technically an orphan.

'Do you have family?' Tristan asked her, keen to understand her.

She shook her head, feeling the familiar tears pricking at her eyelids. 'I'm afraid not. My father died when I was young and my mother scrimped and saved to bring me up on her own and give me a good education. She was the one who encouraged me to get into journalism. She died last year but she would have been so proud of me getting this job.'

Tristan rubbed her arm sympathetically. 'Gosh, I must have sounded really heartless slagging off my parents. They're horrifically flawed but I do love them to bits when it comes down to it.'

Tessa shrugged off her grief and smiled. 'Slagging off your parents is par for the course – everyone does it. Anyway, enough of this depressing talk. Cheer me up, can't you?'

'Cheering women up is my speciality.' Tristan decided to turn the heat up a notch. 'Let's have a look at your work notes.' He grabbed the sheets before Tessa could stop him and twisted his body away from her. 'I want to see what you've got planned for us.'

'Don't!' Panicked, Tessa tried to snatch them back. 'Put those down!'

'Make me!' Tristan held the notes away from her as she

lunged at him. Losing her balance, Tessa fell against him, one of her legs trapped in between his hairy ones and an arm crushed against his pink shirt. Panting, they stared at each other for a moment, both of them aware of the frisson of heat between them.

Tessa noticed a tiny scar on Tristan's forehead and couldn't stop looking at his mouth. I *hate* men, she intoned mentally, and I am here to work.

Tristan almost fell into Tessa limpid green eyes, mesmerised by them as images of emerald-green rock pools popped into his head. Realising he was on the verge of being soppy, Tristan felt the need to break the tension. He dropped the notes and began tickling Tessa mercilessly and much to his delight she shrieked and wriggled against him. They rolled around on the blanket, grappling with one another and giggling as they knocked the jug of lemonade flying.

Tessa felt Tristan's hand in the small of her back, daringly delving into the waistband of her shorts and she ran her finger-tips over his smooth stomach, feeling the muscles tighten under her touch. His obvious attraction to her was hugely flattering and after Adam's betrayal she couldn't help it when her body responded to Tristan's pointed caresses. Breathlessly clinging to each other with warm limbs entwined, they slowly became aware that they were no longer alone.

Springing apart like a couple of teenagers, they found Will standing over them, stony-faced. He was wearing a pair of grey trousers with a crisp white shirt, the sleeves turned back and the neck open.

'Having fun?' he inquired politely, a look of deep disapproval on his face.

'Definitely,' Tristan drawled, giving Tessa a squeeze.

She shrugged Tristan off and did her best to appear dignified, which was rather difficult when she was nearly naked and breathing like a dirty crank caller. She hoped to God her bikini top was still in place but she didn't want to draw attention to herself by adjusting it. She looked up at Will, dazzled by the sunshine behind his tawny-gold head.

'Henny tells me she had a lovely chat with you the other day,' he said, his startlingly blue eyes burning into hers accusingly.

Realising she'd been rumbled, Tessa was at a loss for words. Then she remembered what Henny had said about Will.

'I'm surprised you even let her speak to me,' she retorted primly. 'Isn't that against the law around here?'

Will looked startled for a second but he composed himself. 'Of course it isn't against the law,' he said, his tone cool. 'I'm just looking out for my family.'

'So you keep saying,' Tessa retaliated, tearing her eyes away from the sight of the muscular thighs that were testing the thin, expensive-looking material of his grey trousers. 'Perhaps you should let them make up their own minds. They are adults, after all.' She straightened her bikini top and took a sip of lemonade. God, he was stuck-up!

Will sucked his breath in. This was the second time she had made him sound like some sort of bossy headmaster. He knew his friends and family better than she did and what the hell was wrong with him trying to protect them from a nosy reporter? He clenched his fists. Sometimes he wished he didn't care so much and that he could leave his family to sort themselves out. He was fed up with being told he was over-reacting and he was sick of being judged. And why the hell didn't Tessa put some bloody clothes on, he thought irritably as he glanced down at her tanned shoulders. How on earth was he supposed to concentrate when she was lying there half naked with her long, brown legs everywhere and her flat midriff on show?

'I think this has all been a misunderstanding,' Tristan said smoothly, keen to appease Will and make Tessa smile again. 'Will is absolutely right to want to keep Rufus's private life out of the limelight. He might be a celebrity but he's a real person and he has feelings.'

Tessa just about stopped herself from rolling her eyes. Rufus Pemberton was a rich, pretty boy with a posh education and an easy transition into Hollywood. He hardly seemed *real*. Clemmie was a slightly different matter, Tessa thought in a rare moment of discomfort. But, in time, Tessa was sure Clemmie would probably turn out to be just as self-absorbed as all the other celebrities she had ever met.

'Yes, of course you're right,' she said to Tristan demurely, not meaning a word of it. 'Rufus is a real person with feelings and I will bear that in mind during the making of this documentary.'

Will opened his mouth to say something and thought better of it. This woman was really getting under his skin. She was sarcastic and shallow and all she cared about was her career. Thank God he'd found a woman like Claudette, he thought.

'I'm off to meet Rufus for a pint,' he said shortly. He allowed his eyes to settle contemptuously on Tessa as her ears immediately pricked up. 'I'm sure that's of absolutely no interest to you whatsoever,' he added in an innocent tone, 'since Rufus is a real person with feelings and all that.'

Tessa fumed inwardly. She knew Will could read her mind and could see that she was wishing she could jump into her Audi and follow him. But that would blow her cover in a heartbeat. She couldn't even call JB with Tristan sitting next to her. She gritted her teeth impotently.

Tristan watched Will stride away, guessing by the taut line of his shoulders that he was absolutely furious. He couldn't help thinking Will worried too much; they were all quite capable of looking after themselves. And Tessa was so attractive – she couldn't possibly be as ruthless as Will made out.

'Now, where were we?' His lips were inches from hers.

'I was about to tell you off for being so forward,' she shot back in a prissy tone. She yanked the edges of her shorts down.

'You smell divine, by the way,' he murmured into her neck.

'Thanks. Penhaligon's Bluebell. I forgot to thank Henny for leaving all those goodies in the cottage for me.'

'You should have wafted yourself under Will's nose,' Tristan commented, leaning back on his elbow and chewing a blade of grass casually. 'He might not have been so hard on you.'

'What?'

'Penhaligon's Bluebell, that's Will's favourite scent. He asked Henny to put it in all the hotel rooms. He's a bit of a romantic when it comes to things like that.'

'Does Will think of absolutely everything around here?' Tessa said with bad grace as she rolled on to her front. 'He's like Superman, rushing in to save the family heroically, like some kind of saint! Even though none of you actually needs saving,' she added reprovingly.

Tristan met her gaze with frank blue eyes. 'You've got him wrong, Tessa, I can assure you. Will's always been the one we can all rely on, the one who's there when things go wrong. As for Will thinking of everything around here, you're right about that, he does.' Tristan flicked a blond curl out of his eyes and put his hand gently on her warm back, his fingers calloused from holding paintbrushes. 'One thing you'll learn about me, Tessa, is that I'm pretty focused on my work. I'd love to say I'm the thoughtful type but I'm not. When I'm in love, I'm besotted and you won't find anyone more attentive, but apart from that, I'm painting. If I'm not painting, I'm thinking about painting. And when I'm not doing that, I'm either asleep or having sex.'

She suppressed a smile as he continued.

'My parents are hopeless and Henny hasn't got the guts to stand her ground with anyone. So, yes, Will does think of pretty much everything around here. And even though he's a bit serious at times, that doesn't make him a bad person. In fact, it makes him the absolute opposite of that. Give him a chance, that's all I'm saying. You two would get on like a house on fire if you stopped locking horns for five minutes.'

Allowing Tristan's fingers to trail across her back distractedly, Tessa thought about what he'd said. But she wasn't in the least bit convinced by Tristan's impassioned speech. Will seriously had it in for her and nothing Tristan could say was going to change that. Tessa felt the sun searing hotly into her skin and she didn't protest when Tristan slathered on some factor fifteen, behaving like a perfect gentleman by avoiding any rude bits.

Tessa couldn't shake off the niggling feeling that Will was going to thwart her at every turn, which was going to make life incredibly difficult. More to the point, she thought with trepidation, Will's dedication to protecting his family, Rufus and anyone connected with them could well signal the end of her career.

Will ordered two pints of Guinness and four packets of peanuts and carried everything to a table. He had picked a pub that was out of the way so he and Rufus could chat in peace, and had secured a small area in a private alcove. As he waited for Rufus, he glanced over his shoulder to check they couldn't be overheard. The pub was the old-fashioned kind with pewter tankards hanging above the pumps, dishes of tiny roasted potatoes and lumps of cheese served at the bar, and bar billiards in the corner. Two old couples sat at tables doing crosswords and the barman was relaxing on a stool reading the paper and sipping a pint of bitter. Will was fairly certain he and Rufus could talk without being bothered.

'Mate!' Wearing an outlandish cowboy hat over his dark, teased hair and a pair of Clemmie's huge sunglasses, Rufus joined Will at the table. Pumping Will's hand enthusiastically, he threw himself into the opposite seat and clasped his glass in wonder. 'Oh my God, proper Guinness. The stuff they serve in the States just doesn't taste the same, you know.'

Will chinked glasses with Rufus who suspiciously checked out the two elderly couples and the barman before removing his dark glasses. In silence, they both took a long sip, savouring the velvety taste and licking creamy moustaches off with relish.

Will regarded Rufus fondly. Their friendship might seem unlikely to an outsider but Will trusted Rufus with his life. As a child, Will had struggled with his parents' marriage, living in fear that they would split up and go their separate ways. Jack and Caro's tempestuous union, characterised by passionate rows, bitter sniping and increasingly obvious liaisons with other people made for an unsettling and very insecure childhood for Tristan and Will.

Tristan, fussed over by his mother and bullied by his father, was saved by his art. When things got rough, he would disappear to one of the cottages and lose himself in a world of his own creation, oblivious of time and devoid of any real sense of attachment. For Will, the elder of the two boys, life wasn't so easy. Possessing a strong sense of responsibility and caring deeply for both of his warring parents, he floundered, desperate to reunite Jack and Caro after every altercation, wounded when he discovered either one of them in bed with a stranger. Eventually, he found solace in his friendship with Rufus. He used Rufus's home as a refuge, a safe, comforting bolthole to disappear to when things got out of hand.

Rufus's parents were unexciting, dull even. They might be peers and slightly stuffy but they were also, reassuringly *normal* and, to the young Will, that was all that mattered. When he was in the cocoon of Rufus's family home, he felt safe and settled. Mealtimes, with discussions about the *Times* crossword and idle chit-chat, were uneventful and predictable – in other words, blissful, when compared to the screaming, flying plates and dubious sexual encounters that were de rigueur at Appleton Manor.

'I see you still like eyeliner,' Will commented, eyeing Rufus's black-rimmed peepers with amusement. Aside from the brown Stetson, Rufus was wearing a black T-shirt with the words 'Shag, Marry or Kill?' emblazoned across it and low-slung bullet-grey jeans. 'And you haven't exactly made an effort to blend in with your surroundings, have you?'

'What was I supposed to wear, green wellies and a waxed jacket? What about you? That shirt isn't the kind of thing you'd wear to muck out the cows. If it's not from Jermyn Street, I'll eat my hat.'

'I'm not a famous Hollywood movie star!' Will protested. 'I don't have to blend in. And we don't own a farm, remember? We own an old manor house that's falling into ruin and disrepair.'

'Until Will came charging back to rescue it!' Rufus guffawed. 'Were the olds pleased to see you?'

Will grimaced. 'They were before I told them I thought we should turn the manor into a hotel. Mother's spitting feathers and Dad keeps disappearing to the pub in disgust. Although that might be more to do with the fact that he's sleeping with the new barmaid.'

Rufus took another appreciative slug of Guinness and sat back. 'Isn't it amazing how nothing changes around here? No disrespect to your parents, you know I love them to death, but are they ever going to get fed up with humping anything that moves?'

'I doubt it. But God help me, I still love 'em, whatever they do.' Feeling defensive as he always did when his parents' relationship was under scrutiny, Will adroitly changed the subject. 'Hey, what about you? You've got a reputation for shagging your way around Hollywood. How are you going to do that with a wife?'

'Good point.' Rufus rubbed his chin ruefully. 'It is going to cramp my style slightly, isn't it?'

'What's Clemmie like? I mean, I know what she's like from her films but what's she like as a person?'

'Warm, funny . . . sexy. Everything she seems on film and more. Although she's much sweeter in person – more vulnerable, I suppose.'

'Oh my God, he's in love!' crowed Will. 'I never thought I'd see the day.'

'Shut up!' Rufus wiped his mouth and leant forward. 'Between you and me, I didn't exactly plan to get married.' He shot an apprehensive glance at the barman who had put down his paper to help himself to another pint of bitter.

'What?'

'It's all a bit of a blur,' Rufus confessed, looking sheepish.

'You're going to have to do better than that!'

'We were at a party,' Rufus said, scratching his head, 'and I was really drunk. It was wild, naked girls snogging each other, orgies, drugs, you name it. I got all maudlin and started going on about how much I missed Appleton – I always do that when I get trashed – and Clemmie was going on about coming to visit and I said I'd bring her home to meet the parents.' He wiggled his finger in the creamy top of his Guinness. 'It was a throwaway comment, Will! But Clemmie starting screaming her head off like a banshee and I . . . rather liked seeing her so happy. And I was totally off my head of course – tequila, it does stupid things to you.'

'Wait a minute, are you saying you proposed because you were *drunk*?'

'Shhh!' Rufus squashed his hat down on his head as if admitting it out loud made him feel exposed. 'I think I was drunk . . . I don't really remember . . . maybe a line of coke or two might have been involved. Look, all I know is I woke up on a lounger by the swimming pool with Clemmie wearing my father's pinkie ring on her ring finger. I had a hangover like my brain had been shrink-wrapped and a mouth like Ganhdi's flip-flop.'

'Fuck!' Will stared at him. 'Couldn't you say it was all a big mistake and explain to Clemmie that it didn't mean you wanted to get married?'

Rufus looked vague. 'I didn't want to hurt her feelings. And I'm really fond of her . . . I mean, I *love* her, Will. This would have happened eventually . . . it was just a matter of time.'

Will frowned. He knew Rufus and he knew when he was lying. And he was lying right now. He didn't want to get married; he wasn't cut out for it. So why on earth was he going through with it? Could it be true that he didn't want to hurt Clemmie's feelings, or was there another reason Rufus would put himself through such a spectacle?

Will felt slightly sick as he watched Rufus checking out his reflection in the stencilled glass by their alcove. He had always been ambitious; he had spent his childhood banging on about being rich and famous and hadn't once deviated from his path, despite jeering comments from friends and bribes from his middle-of-the-road parents to 'take a proper job in the City'.

Will sipped his pint thoughtfully. Clemmie Winters was a very famous movie star. Marrying her had to bring Rufus kudos, maybe the publicity and the kind of roles he had always craved. Will was desperate not to judge him but, as a friend, didn't he owe it to him to tell him that he might be making a big mistake?

He leant closer and lowered his voice. 'Listen, mate, you can back out at any time, you know. Don't feel that you have to go through with this if you don't want to.'

'I do want to,' Rufus insisted, laughing. 'What are you getting at?'

'Are you . . . look, I hate asking you this, but are you marrying Clemmie to further your career?'

Rufus caught Will's eye for a fraction of a second before rearranging his features.

'Will, *please*! I'm not that bad! I can't remember proposing and that's the truth but I want to go ahead with this, OK? And it's not for my career. I wouldn't do that to Clemmie. I love her, it's as simple as that – even I wouldn't stoop that low.'

Will drained his glass. Rufus sounded genuine but then he was an actor – not a great one, admittedly, but a passable one. He had been convincing as the Artful Dodger in their school play and he was convincing now. But Will knew his friend like the back of his hand. Over the years, Rufus had stayed in touch, sending outrageous postcards and texts from all over the globe – had even sent some spare tickets to the Cannes Film Festival once. But as loyal a friend as Rufus had always been to him, Will knew he was being untruthful right now. He suspected he saw his engagement to Clemmie as his ticket to the big time, his opportunity to raise his profile and be taken seriously.

'What about you?' Rufus was determined not to hog the limelight for once, mostly because it suited him not to dwell on his relationship with Clemmie. 'Are you still with that bird Claudette?'

'Yes, I am,' Will said drily, wondering what his soignée fiancée would make of being called a 'bird'. 'She's beautiful, funny and one of the sexiest women I've ever met.' A disturbing image of Tessa in tiny shorts and a bright yellow bikini top darted into his mind before shooting out again just as quickly. 'I'm missing her like crazy but she's so caught up in her charity work, she hasn't been able to fly out yet. She's hoping to come out next month, though, for the summer party, and she hinted that she might stick around for a while.'

'So, is she "the one" then?' Rufus prompted, enjoying seeing his friend squirm.

Will nodded. 'I really think she is. She even loves poetry, can you believe that?' He paused, his face sober. 'But most importantly, she's into family, Rufe. She loves the manor house and she adores my family, in spite of all their idiosyncrasies.'

'Wow, she sounds . . . unbelievable. I can't wait to meet her. It's as if you've been swept off your feet or something. But home life and family, they're big things for you so it sounds as if you're well matched.' Rufus let out a laugh as he tore open a packet of peanuts. 'And you were always the cautious one, Will. Going out with girls for years on end before deciding they weren't right for you and then you go and get engaged after five minutes.'

'Eight months!' Will protested rather guiltily. He had to admit, it had been a speedy courtship, especially by his standards. His previous relationships had lasted for at least a year or even two in some cases before he started to realise the girl in question wasn't for him. He wanted to settle down but he wanted to get it right – to find his 'soul mate', if such a thing existed. Jack and Caro's stormy relationship had instilled a deep-rooted desire in both Will and his brother to find 'true love', whatever that may be. Love that wasn't based on competition and one-upmanship, for the most part – love that most certainly didn't involve inviting all and sundry to share the marital bed.

'So, you love her, right?' Rufus asked, throwing a handful of peanuts into the air and catching them in his mouth, a childhood trick that still amused him.

'What?'

'Claudette – you love her?'

Will's brows knitted together. 'Of course I do, we're engaged!'

'You don't sound very convincing,' Rufus said, discarding his peanuts. 'Christ, I can't believe I ate those. My agent would be sending me to a fat farm by nightfall if she was here.'

'God, what a way to live, having to watch every calorie that passes your lips. Hey, does Clemmie want kids some day? Claudette seems very keen on the whole idea.'

'Kids?' Rufus looked stunned. He got to his feet and pulled his cowboy hat down over his eyes. 'Haven't even thought about them. Listen, fancy coming back to mine for some more booze?

81

Clemmie's out at some photo shoot so we'd have the place to ourselves.'

'Great. It'll be just like old times. But no lighting your farts later, understood?'

Rufus cackled and headed for the door.

Following his rather camply dressed friend out of the pub and hoping no one would think they were off to re-enact a scene from *Brokeback Mountain*, Will wondered why he felt so unsettled by the conversation. Shrugging the feeling off, he put it down to the fact that he missed Claudette and hadn't seen her in weeks. As soon as she was at the manor with him, he was sure everything would go back to normal.

Chapter Six

Sophie strolled through Appleton enjoying the blazing sunshine beating down on her bare shoulders. It was the first time she had ventured into the village since she and Gil had arrived and she couldn't help feeling nervous, even though she knew it was unlikely she would bump into anyone who recognised her. After all, she hardly bore any resemblance to the unsophisticated girl she had been then and the older residents of the village were surely likely to have passed away.

But still, the mass of uneasiness swirling round her stomach like an undissolved Alka Seltzer wouldn't seem to subside. Sophie wasn't sure why she felt so jittery. Ruby was at a summer play group until she joined her new school in September and the only mothers Sophie bumped into there were far too young to have a clue who she was and Gil had settled in to his new surroundings as if he was the one who'd grown up here and not her. But she herself was living on tenterhooks, terrified of being recognised by someone and torn between a yearning desire to see Tristan again and the knowledge that she must avoid him at all costs.

Sophie glanced around the village, feeling a sense of pleasure wash over her. Appleton was beautiful. A crooked row of charming antique shops lined one side of the main street, their curved shopfronts with tiny windows delightfully old-fashioned. The old fabric shop was still there, although judging by the luxurious swathes of material and streams of coloured ribbon in the front window, it had been forced to move with the times. There was one of those trendy coffee shop-cum-bookshops on the corner called 'The Snug'.

Sophie caught sight of a quaint little tea shop at the end of the street and removed her sunglasses to get a better look. It was just as she remembered it; the sign saying 'Milk and Honey' on the front showing only the slightest evidence of ageing. Meandering past the small blackboard out front which described the day's specials, Sophie saw that her favourite buttermilk scones with damson jam were still on the menu and felt strangely comforted by their enduring presence. A waft of strong tea and cookies fresh from the oven drifted out of the front door and the aromas gave her a sharp jolt. She felt her heart start to pound as her mind turned to Tristan again.

She and Tristan had spent many a stolen afternoon in this very tea shop all those years ago, excitedly discussing their plans for the future as they drank tea out of floral-patterned, porcelain cups with matching saucers, secretly turned on by the civilised ritual that, for them, was always a prelude to sex.

She turned away to block out the evocative memory and almost knocked someone over.

'Gosh, I'm so sorry . . .' Sophie stared at the woman she had elbowed, feeling her nerves prickling as the colour drained from her face. It was old Mrs North, a nosy battleaxe who used to disgustedly watch Sophie cycle away from Tristan's cottage, as if she had known exactly what they had been up to. She had radiated her disapproval via thin, pursed lips and a primly erect stance and the young Sophie had sensed her reproof and ducked her head low over the handle bars of her bicycle. She had cringed with shame that Mrs North seemed all too aware that she had spent the afternoon being painted before ending up naked in Tristan's bed.

The older, more self-assured Sophie had no intention of feeling embarrassed; she simply couldn't believe her bad luck. Of all the people to bump into . . . Dressed in a shiny frock that looked far too hot for the sultry weather and sporting a hat like a tea cosy, the old lady was peering at Sophie with her head on one side.

Sophie sucked her breath in, scared to speak for a moment. She shoved her huge sunglasses back on in the hope that they would obscure most of her face and that Mrs North would leave her alone.

'I know you!' Mrs North's beady eyes were sharp.

'I-I don't think so,' Sophie bluffed, wishing her voice didn't sound so squeaky.

'Yes. I remember.' Mrs North tapped a painfully thin finger on her dentures, a revolting habit that made Sophie shudder. 'You used to live here . . . you had long blond hair . . . down to your backside like some sort of exotic dancer.'

Sophie put a hand to her artfully streaked hair which, these days, was caramel-coloured and finished just below her chin. 'You've made a mistake, I'm afraid . . .'

'I have not!' Mrs North was indignant and her loud voice drew the attention of a few customers emerging from the tea shop. 'You were a student . . . an art student, was it? Yes, that's right. And you lived with old Mrs Chambers because your parents were dead and everyone thought you were going to get some sort of scholarship. You disappeared mysteriously and no one knew what had happened to you, but I'd remember you anywhere!' She gave Sophie's bejewelled flip-flops and painted toenails a dismissive sniff.

Sophie began to feel panicked. She checked out the surrounding villagers and was relieved to realise she didn't recognise any of them. They were well-shod but slightly self-conscious – burnt-out City types who had scraped together enough money to escape the rat race for a quieter life, she guessed. And not likely to have lived in Appleton five years ago. Relief washed over her.

'I might be old but I'm not stupid,' Mrs North snapped

crossly. 'You looked different then and you didn't have money for this sort of garb.' She gestured to Sophie's silk Whistles camisole and cream cut-offs with her stick. 'But it's you all right. You're that girl who used to sit for Tristan Forbes-Henry – not that you used to *sit* much, I shouldn't imagine.'

Flinching as the barb hit home, Sophie took a deep breath and decided to deflect Mrs North's attack with charm.

'It all sounds thrilling and I wish I could say I was this girl you're thinking of,' she said with an engaging smile. 'But my fiancé and I have only just moved here. He's Gil Anderson, have you heard of him? He's a famous designer, and he's doing up the manor house.'

Mrs North gaped, distracted. 'The manor house? Is it true it's being turned into a hotel then?'

'Very much so. And a very famous wedding is taking place there too.' Sophie nodded knowingly and gave Mrs North a wink. 'You'll read about it in *Hello!* magazine later in the year.'

'Really?' Mrs North looked impressed.

'It was lovely to meet you anyway,' Sophie finished, starting to back away from her while the going was good. 'I must dash. I have things to do and I'm sure you must be busy too . . .' Breaking into a slightly undignified sprint, she headed in the other direction.

Mrs North stared after her, her beady eyes like burnt currants. 'I still think you're that hussy who broke Tristan Forbes-Henry's heart!' she shouted at the top of her voice.

Sophie let out a cry of frustration and thanked God the street was relatively empty. So much for Mrs North being a poor old lady, and as for Sophie being the one who broke *Tristan's* heart! She headed for the new bookshop and stormed inside. Furiously she yanked the first book she came upon from the shelf. Realising she was leafing through 'How to Farm Snails for Eating', Sophie shoved it back on to the shelf and followed her nose to the coffee bar.

'Do you do decaff?' she asked, taking a seat on one of the high-backed stools and looking round the bookshop for the first time. The walls were painted the colour of Tiffany jewellery boxes, which went surprisingly well with the dark wood of the beams slotted along the ceiling and gave it a modern look. An expensive-looking silver machine could be heard chugging away at the back of the coffee bar, letting off the odd blast of steam.

Glancing at the well-dressed woman next to her who was sipping a double espresso, Sophie changed her mind. 'Sorry, scrap the decaff. Can I have one of those, please?' She rubbed her temples with her fingers and muttered under her breath. 'Sometimes, only the real thing will do.'

'I know exactly what you mean,' the woman said. 'Bad day?' She was very attractive and her glossy, chestnut hair and wide-apart green eyes seemed familiar to Sophie.

'Something like that. You know when you bump into someone you don't want to see and you can't get away?'

'Definitely,' Sophie's companion laughed. 'I'm Tessa, by the way.'

'Sophie. Sorry . . . I can't believe I'm saying this, but do I know you?'

'I do the odd thing on TV,' Tessa confessed rather sheepishly. '*Good Morning UK* mainly but you might not have—'

The penny dropped. 'Tessa Meadmore! Oh my God.' Sophie was completely and utterly star-struck. 'I watch you all the time. I can't believe you're sitting here next to me!' She put her hands to her face. 'And I can't believe I'm gabbling away like this. How embarrassing. You must be so bored when this happens.'

'Not at all.' Tessa grinned. 'It's rather flattering. I can never believe anyone actually recognises me!'

They chinked their small espresso cups together.

'Here's to . . . not bumping into people we'd rather avoid,' Tessa said.

'I'll drink to that. So . . . you must be here because of the wedding.'

Tessa's green eyes looked startled.

Sophie hurriedly explained herself. 'It's not common knowledge, don't worry. My fiancé Gil is responsible for the refurbishment at the manor house and he told me about Rufus and Clemmie getting married there.'

Tessa relaxed then looked at Sophie again. Surely this well-dressed, fresh-faced girl couldn't be engaged to the effeminate man in tight trousers she had met the other day? She realised she was staring.

'Er . . . your fiancé showed me round some of the rooms he's renovated at Appleton Manor. He's a really talented designer.'

'He is, isn't he?'

Tessa noticed Sophie's proud expression and realised she cared deeply for Gil.

'Gil is also one of the kindest men I've ever met,' Sophie was saying, gratitude shining out of every pore. 'He's so generous to everyone, even people he shouldn't give a toss about. Like his father. He's a *horrendous* old man.'

'Sounds grim,' Tessa said, feeling sorry for Gil.

Sophie was wondering if she should mention Ruby. It was absurd not to; Tessa was hardly likely to make a connection with Tristan, but for some reason the idea made her feel apprehensive. She decided against it.

'So what do you think of Appleton? The back of beyond – or a charming retreat?' Tessa asked.

Sophie laughed, tipping her head back so that her caramel tresses touched her bare shoulder blades. 'A bit of both. The house Gil found for us is gorgeous and I love the peace and quiet but I know what you mean about it being in the middle of nowhere. And the garden is out of control. Apparently we're allowed to sort it out and I've been meaning to get a gardener but I haven't a clue where to find one. Do you think it's all done on recommendation round here?'

'God knows. But if it is, there's a gardener at Appleton Manor everyone keeps raving about. Nathan, his name is. A bit of a dish, between you and me, although I'm pretty sure he's banging Caro Forbes-Henry.' Gesturing for the bill, Tessa didn't notice Sophie's eyes widen at the news. 'I'll get these coffees – I'll charge them to expenses! Hey, if you like, I can get the details of the gardener for you. I'm sure Henny would give me his number.'

At the mention of Henny, Sophie was all at once overwhelmed with memories of motherly chats over tea and biscuits and afternoons spent baking in the fantastically homely kitchen at Appleton Manor.

'We should exchange mobile numbers,' Tessa was saying. 'Then I can call you once I know about this gardener thing. Besides, us girls should stick together. I really miss all my friends from London, don't you?'

Sophie nodded and fell silent as they speedily keyed each other's numbers into their phones.

'So, what do you think of the Forbes-Henrys?' Sophie inquired as nonchalantly as she could. 'Gil says they're an interesting bunch.'

'You can say that again,' Tessa observed as she headed towards the door. 'Caro's beautiful but she has claws and I haven't really met Jack properly yet. Henny's wonderful, so friendly and sweet, and Milly's great too.'

Sophie closed her eyes momentarily, the memories flooding back to her.

'It's Will Forbes-Henry who's causing me grief,' Tessa grumbled, her face screwing up crossly. 'He's obviously decided he can't stand the sight of me and he's on my case all the bloody time. He's an absolute nightmare.'

'Gil said he was a little intimidating,' Sophie admitted, slightly confused by Tessa's rant. Will was one of the good guys, trustworthy, loyal and astonishingly good-looking. She had no idea why Tessa seemed to dislike him so much. She picked up a book about Kylie Minogue, wondering how she could ask after Tristan without giving herself away – 'Will has a brother, hasn't he? What's he like?' Her tone could be casual, her expression indifferent – but no, it would sound too obvious. She snapped the book shut.

What she really wanted to ask was, 'How is Tristan? Is he happy? Does he have a girlfriend – is he *married*?' The thought rewarded her with a wave of nausea. How was it that she had never contemplated the thought of Tristan being married before now? Because it hurt too much, that was why, Sophie told herself.

'There's another brother too,' Tessa commented, inadvertently coming to her rescue.

'Oh?' Sophie hoped to God she wasn't blushing.

'Tristan, an artist. Do you know his work? It's amazing; he's very talented.' Tessa tucked her hair behind her ear thoughtfully. 'He's been really lovely which is such a relief after the way Will's been sniping at me. At least Tristan doesn't seem to think I'm the devil incarnate.' She let out a heartfelt sigh. 'I've just come out of this really messy relationship, you see, and my boss is on my back constantly about making a good job of this documentary otherwise I might be more interested in responding to Tristan but as it is . . . Oh, I think you dropped something,' she said, bending down and picking up a brightly coloured cloth bunny.

'That's not mine.' Sophie gulped. Could today have been any more excruciating?

'Er . . . are you sure? Honestly, it fell out of your bag.' Tessa proffered the toy with a friendly smile.

'It's not mine, OK?' Sophie roughly pushed Ruby's toy back at Tessa. God, what was she doing? 'I don't know how it got there but it's nothing to do with me.'

'Right. My mistake. I'll just put it here, shall I? And then the rightful owner can collect it.' Tessa gingerly laid the patchwork bunny down on a colourful stack of Marian Keyes novels and held her hands up, rather like someone surrendering a gun at a crime scene.

'Well, it won't be me,' Sophie shot back, giving the bunny a lingering look. Ruby was going to be distraught without it. Why didn't she just own up and say the toy belonged to her daughter? She opened her mouth, on the verge of confiding in her new friend. But courage deserted her and instead Sophie did the only thing she could think of. She pulled open the book-shop door, left her daughter's favourite toy amongst the chick lit and ran for her life. She didn't have to look over her shoulder to know that Tessa was staring after her, baffled, obviously of the opinion that she had just befriended a madwoman.

'No, I don't think you or Freddie should ask Tessa out!' Milly cried heatedly, throwing a book at David. What on earth was wrong with him? He was turning into some sort of sex-starved idiot who couldn't keep it in his pants – or at the very least a sex-starved idiot with aspirations of not keeping it in his pants. He had been needling her for the past half hour and Milly was about to lose all self-control and launch herself across the table at him. She had been sitting in the kitchen reading *heat* magazine and eating chocolate quite happily until David had decided to come in and wind her up.

'Why not?'

David studied himself in the metal lid of Henny's cake tin and started pulling cheesy faces, pointing his finger at his reflection and grinning like a buffoon. He was wearing a black T-shirt that made his lily-white skin look as pale as a ghost and a pair of tight blue football shorts that should have been thrown out a decade ago. Milly pushed her heavy blond hair out of her eyes in frustration.

'I think you should give up perving over Tessa because you look about twelve and you've got enough spots to start your own pharmaceutical company, OK?'

'Ooooh, bitchy!' David whistled and narrowed his eyes. 'Got your period or something? Or are you just worried that Freddie might actually succeed in sweet-talking Tessa into bed?'

Milly reddened uncomfortably. David was right on both counts. She had raging PMT which had made her mood vile and hair greasier than a piece of fried cod. And as for Freddie, she was dreading him meeting Tessa face to face because for all she knew teenage boys might be Tessa's Achilles heel. Milly shovelled a piece of Dairy Milk in her mouth and thought back to the other day when Tristan had brought lemonade out to Tessa. From their banter and flirtatious eye contact, they seemed to have chemistry and it was obvious Tristan fancied Tessa like mad. But Tessa had seemed very focused on work. Which hopefully meant that even if she wasn't interested in Tristan, she wouldn't give Freddie a second glance either.

David examined his bitten-down nails speculatively. 'Frankly, I think you're on to a loser where Freddie's concerned. He's never going to notice you. He likes models, not immature schoolgirls.'

'Why don't you just fuck *off*!' Milly screamed at him, feeling her heart plummet. How did brothers know exactly how to stab you right where it hurt? David was an expert at working out the thing that would freak her out the most and then twisting the knife constantly until she cracked.

'That Gil Anderson drinks more coffee than that group of builders did,' Henny said, bustling in with a tray of empty coffee mugs. 'He asked me this morning if I could do him a "little cappuccino with chocolate sprinkles", the cheeky so-and-so. He must think we have one of those expensive machines in here. Which reminds me, I must ask Will about getting one,

92

we'll need it when the hotel opens.' She set the tray down, sensing the animosity in the air. She felt exasperated as her two children glowered at each other across the kitchen table. 'What's going on? Are you two fighting again?'

'David's being a wanker,' Milly offered sulkily. 'And I wish he'd just piss off and leave me alone. Why don't you go and get a tan or something, freak boy? You look like a bloody albino.'

Henny put her head in her hands briefly. Since they had moved to Appleton, Milly had been unbearable. Her language was appalling and she was developing a chip on her shoulder the size of Africa. Henny had no idea how to control her.

'Can't you two just get along?' she begged, directing her gaze at Milly. 'David's just at a loose end because Freddie's on holiday at the moment and—'

'Oh, you would take his side, wouldn't you?' Milly stormed, leaping up from the table. 'What a fucking *surprise*!' She grabbed her magazine and her Dairy Milk and flounced out of the kitchen, leaving Henny gaping and David shaking his head in mock disapproval. Seeing his mother's face crumple, he jumped up and gave her a hug.

'Hey, don't take it so personally, Mum! She's just hormonal and missing her stupid friends from that posh boarding school and taking it out on everyone. It's just a phase she's going through – a very obnoxious one, I grant you. ' David gave his mother a kiss on her soft, rosy cheek. 'And to make matters worse, I'm fairly certain she's in love with Freddie who doesn't even know she exists.'

Henny sniffed, grateful that at least one of her children didn't seem to think she was Cruella de Vil. 'Do you really think it's just a phase?'

'Sure to be. And I probably pushed her too far anyway. I'm so bored at the moment now that our exams are over. And with Freddie being away on bloody holiday, the lucky sod.'

'Thank you for being so sweet to me.' Henny eyed her son kindly. 'Milly was right about one thing though, David.'

'What's that?'

'You *are* rather pale, darling.' She gave him a push. 'Slap on some factor fifteen and get those legs out. It'll dry your spots out too.'

For a second, David looked offended, running a hand over his spotty chin in a wounded fashion. Then he glanced down at his pale, hairy legs and grudgingly started to laugh.

Driving back towards her house after the incident with Tessa, Sophie felt like a prize idiot. She had made an utter fool of herself *and* she had run away like a bloody coward. She felt sure Tessa was someone she could trust – maybe not with the full story but she could have at least confided in her that she had a daughter.

Sophie rubbed her throbbing head and took in a few deep breaths of fresh air as she drove past the turning for Appleton Manor. She screeched to a halt, sending stones flying into a hedgerow.

Was she seriously contemplating going down there to have a look? Yes, she was. In for a penny, as they say . . . Sophie reversed her car and headed down the narrow lane. Seeing Appleton Manor looming into view and feeling her heart crash against her ribcage, she lost her nerve and took the first turning on the left. It was an unmade road that ran round the perimeter of the manor grounds and the car bumped and jerked over verges which had been baked solid by the relentless July sunshine.

Realising she would end up next to Tristan's cottage if she wasn't careful, she put the car out of its misery and clumsily mounted a rigid mudbank which brought the car to a sputtering stop. She stepped out and saw that she was yards away from a beautiful willow tree. If she had her bearings right, the willow tree hung over the secret place she and Tristan used to escape to. She couldn't believe it, after all this time . . .

She headed towards it, ducking under branches and batting away midges that danced crazily around her head. She crouched down as she came to the secret spot but kept her distance, not daring to get any closer. There it was, the cool, leafy haven she and Tristan used to hide in, running into it breathlessly like children, safe in the knowledge that no one would ever discover them.

Sophie felt overcome with dizziness as a vivid memory swam into her mind and for the first time in years, she indulged herself and sank into it as if she was disappearing into a forbidden rock pool.

She was lying on her side under the willow tree, leaning on one elbow, naked apart from some carefully positioned sweet peas. Her long hair was draped coyly over one breast, the generous slope barely concealed by her locks, and the other breast was exposed, the pale pink nipple pointing skywards. She was giggling as Tristan, naked and covering his dignity with his sketchbook, swiftly outlined her shape with his pencil. He was laughing and he kept telling her to lie still for one minute longer so he could capture the exquisite curve of her hip.

Rippling with expectation and desire, she hadn't been able to stop giggling, and as the baby-pink sweet peas had fallen away from her body, Tristan's eyes had darkened with lust. He had tossed his sketchbook aside, gathered her up in his arms and kissed every single, bare inch of her.

Sophie felt light-headed at the thought of his paintbrush-calloused fingers roughly caressing her skin, teasing her until she couldn't take any more. She had revelled in the security of his embrace, loving the feel of his arms around her, his fingers entwined in her long hair . . .

Feeling the familiar throb pulsating in her groin, Sophie squeezed her thighs together and arched her back as she sat in the shadows. Tristan had been capable of turning her into a squirming, helpless mess and she had loved every second of it. She guessed she had been one of his 'lost souls' – orphaned, abandoned, searching for someone to rescue her. And, like a strong, dashing lifeguard holding out the proverbial water float, he had done just that. For months she had been deliriously happy. If only Tristan had been content enough with saving her to hang up his lifeguard shorts for good, they might have still been together.

Hearing the snap of a twig underfoot, she shrank back into the shadows. Catching sight of someone shouldering his way through the low branches, Sophie gasped and clapped her hand over her mouth. It was Tristan. Frozen with fear, she watched him part the willow fronds. Did he look any different? She peeked through the branches, blinded by the brilliant sunshine every two seconds as a gentle breeze lifted the leaves and obscured her view.

His hair was slightly longer at the neck, the bohemian curls giving him the look of a fallen angel. Even in the dim light beneath the willow tree, his hair shone like polished gold and Sophie hated herself for wanting to reach out and touch it. He turned towards her for a heart-stopping second before sitting down. Once she was sure he couldn't see her, she greedily drank in the sight of him.

There were a few more lines around his navy-blue eyes these days – worry lines or were they laughter lines? The thought of him laughing with someone else, his wide mouth guffawing the way it did when something really tickled him, tore her apart momentarily.

Beneath the paint-streaked jeans and yellow shirt, Tristan's physique looked the same, lean but strong-looking. She watched as his pencil started to move across his pad, the strokes hesitant at first then gaining momentum. She wondered what he was drawing. Absurdly and completely without ego, she hoped he might be drawing her again. But of course he wouldn't be! He had forgotten her easily enough when she had been around; he was hardly likely to remember her after such a long absence.

Was he drawing Tessa Meadmore perhaps? Sophie almost lost her footing. Tessa had said Tristan was paying her attention. God, it didn't bear thinking about. The thought that she might be Tristan's latest muse almost threatened to suffocate her.

She watched Tristan look up every so often, as his fingers moved rapidly over the page. His expression changed as she observed him, wistful in the beginning, turning sorrowful for mere seconds before descending into something thunderous and dark, his eyebrows knitting together furiously.

She jumped as he swore loudly and, with a jerky hand, tore the page from the pad. He looked anguished but it was so brief, Sophie thought she must have imagined it. He got to his feet and stuffed the page into his pocket as if he were humiliated by it. Taking one last look at the dense, lush haven, he turned his back on it and stalked away.

Silent seconds ticked by. When it was safe, Sophie got to her feet. She felt unsteady on her legs and her steps were weak and uncertain. So this was how it felt to see him again. A torrent of emotions raged within her – anger fought with regret, agony threatened to overcome sadness. She felt curiously elated but oddly flat at the same time.

How could he have ruined what they had, how could he have callously tossed aside her love for him the way he had?

Sophie wiped unexpected tears from her cheeks and headed back to her car. The worst thing about the encounter with Tristan was that it had proved to her something she had suspected for the past five years. She was still in love with him. Even after everything that had happened, her feelings hadn't changed. What about poor Gil? What about Ruby? What a *mess*.

God, she needed someone to talk to, Sophie thought as she kicked at the parched mud with her flip-flops. She felt so alone.

Grabbing her mobile phone and not giving herself another second to think, she dialled Tessa's number. She would tell her about Ruby. Furthermore, she thought, as she strengthened her resolve, she wasn't going to interfere in Tessa's love life, even if it meant denying her feelings for Tristan. It would take a monumental effort but it wasn't Tessa's fault Tristan had fallen for her and she wasn't going to make someone else miss out on being happy just because she couldn't forgive him. She'd learnt her lesson: friendships before relationships. She didn't want to end up isolated and alone because of a man like she had the last time.

'Tessa? It's Sophie, the nutter from the bookshop? Listen, I know you'd probably have me committed but I really need a friend. I . . . I'd love to tell you about my daughter Ruby if you have time for a chat.'

Hearing Tessa's warm voice immediately suggesting a time, Sophie let out a jerky sigh of relief.

Chapter Seven

'I won't be a minute!' Tessa called, leaning over the twisty wooden staircase in the cottage.

'The film crew are waiting!' JB shouted up in an unnecessarily loud voice.

Moody bugger, Tessa thought tetchily as she grabbed some skyscraper Gina sandals and shoved her feet into them. Working with JB was unpredictable to say the least – he was either leaping around enthusiastically or he was sullen and snappy. She had no idea what was going on inside his head but she was beginning to wonder what on earth he was doing on a job like this.

Tessa forgot about JB as she checked out her reflection. The pink Gina sandals weren't exactly practical and she wasn't entirely sure they went with her beige Joseph suit, but they were drop-dead gorgeous and she needed the confidence boost today. She and JB were meeting Clemmie and Rufus at the manor. Clemmie was finally being introduced to the family and had agreed to being filmed wandering around, making wedding plans. Will had insisted that Gil be allowed a few weeks' grace to get the lion's share of the decorating out of the way. Tessa could see the sense in it but couldn't help feeling frustrated at Will for slowing everything down.

She added a slick of red lipstick and brushed her already gleaming chestnut hair for the umpteenth time. Good enough, she decided as she headed downstairs.

Seeing that she had a text from Sophie on her BlackBerry, she grinned. They had become firm friends over the past few weeks and Tessa had even met Sophie's adorable daughter, Ruby, who had shaken her hand with great seriousness before talking her into wearing a fluffy pink tiara over lunch.

Sophie had explained away her reluctance to talk about Ruby by saying that she hadn't been sure about how to bring it into the conversation. She confessed rather shamefacedly that Gil wasn't Ruby's father and that she didn't want to talk about it, and she had gone on to extol Gil's skills as a stepfather. Tessa had an idea Sophie was finding village life rather difficult – she seemed so lonely on her own in that big house. Treating her the way she would one of her good friends in London, Tessa had spent as much time as possible at Sophie and Gil's house, grabbing lunch there two or three times a week and texting whenever she had a minute.

'Come on, JB, we're late,' she said with a twinkle, knowing damn well it was her fault but not caring because JB was so prickly this morning. Navigating the pebbled pathway to the manor at the same time as sending a text message, Tessa was lucky she didn't break her ankle in her spiked heels.

'So what's brought on this mood?' Tessa asked him, enjoying the feel of the afternoon sun on her face as she discreetly switched off her BlackBerry so that Jilly couldn't contact her for a few hours.

Tessa suspected JB's mood was woman-related; JB had worked his way through most of the single girls on the film crew, a few of the married ones and the odd barmaid since he had arrived. He had probably run out of totty to chase, Tessa decided, thinking he and Jack would get on famously. 'Filming is going fantastically well so you surely can't be stressed about that.'

JB shrugged as they made short work of the beautifully clipped lawn and gave a curt nod to Nathan the gardener who was wearing a pair of khaki combats and a black vest top which showed off his bulging biceps. Nathan waved back and JB scowled.

'Bloody poof.'

'A man can wave without being gay, you know, JB,' Tessa informed him, rolling her eyes. He was so arrogant, he even thought men fancied him!

Striding through the hallway of the manor, Tessa could see that Gil had discreetly tweaked the furnishings, removing the odd personal photograph and tidying away some of the more unappealing family heirlooms. It made a huge difference and made the grand hallway seem even more impressive and welcoming. Remembering that they had arranged to meet in the formal sitting room in the west wing, Tessa tiptoed towards it so as not to make holes in the stunning walnut flooring and pushed the door open. Seeing Caro and Jack already in attendance, she started to introduce JB to the family.

Caro, wearing the slinkiest emerald-green leotard Tessa had ever seen and not much else, sashayed over sinuously, a provocative smile playing at her lips. Her nipples poked through the leotard as she simpered at a goggling JB, almost taking his eye out.

'*Enchanté, monsieur,*' she cooed, flicking her flame-red hair out of her eyes. '*Je suis* . . . er . . . *très heureuse* to . . . er . . . meet . . . *vous!*'

Tessa hid a smile and watched JB's eyes flicker as he gritted his teeth. One thing she had learnt about him was that he detested people speaking bad French, but she watched in astonishment as JB bent down low over Caro's pale, delicately freckled hand in a gesture of reverence.

Henny shot a look at Jack, who was lounging on a sofa drinking a Bloody Mary out of a pint glass.

'*Enchanté, madame,*' JB murmured, brushing her skin with his full lips in a faintly suggestive manner. '*Parlez-vous français?*'

'Oh, just *un peu,*' she responded girlishly, holding on to his hand. 'We have French ancestors, you see. Jack's mother Gabrielle was French.' She gestured helpfully towards a glorious portrait hanging over the fireplace, of a woman in a white evening gown and long white gloves. The expression in her eyes was enigmatic but her mouth was curved upwards in a genuinely happy smile.

Still holding on to Caro's delicate hand, JB's eyes slid to the portrait. He seemed transfixed, although whether it was by Gabrielle's exotic beauty or by Caro's gushing attentions was anyone's guess.

'We've spent such a lot of time in your wonderful country.' Caro smiled fetchingly. 'It's so . . . er . . . *très belle* there, *n'est-ce pas?*'

'I couldn't agree more,' he said softly.

Caro simpered. 'It's my favourite place in the world, in fact. I'd—'

'Careful, darling,' Jack chimed laconically. 'You've practically unzipped the poor chap's trousers – mentally, that is. Do remember your manners, sweetness.'

'Shut *up*, Jack.' Caro flushed deeply. She threw him a scornful look and snapped open a bottle of water. 'No one cares what you think.'

'Really?' Jack answered mildly, sipping his Bloody Mary with great dignity. 'No one will mind me telling you to brush up on your French, then, darling. JB might be too polite to mention your atrocious accent but to be honest, it grates on my nerves. I've been meaning to tell you that for years.'

Caro glowered at him, clenching and unclenching her fists. JB turned away, his expression unreadable but not before giving Jack an approving look, almost as if he had recognised a kindred spirit.

The awkward moment was saved by the arrival of Clemmie and Rufus who swept in looking every inch the Hollywood movie stars. Clemmie was wearing one of her trademark dresses

– clingy, feminine and sprigged with cherries. Leaving a heady cloud of Chanel No. 5 in her wake, she oozed star quality. Beside her, Rufus was the perfect foil in black designer jeans and a grungy white T-shirt printed with skulls.

'Your home is simply beautiful,' Clemmie started in awed tones. 'I can't tell you how delighted I am to be here.'

'You are so *welcome*.' A smiling Jack leapt up and grasped her hand. 'I'm such a fan of yours . . . it's lovely to meet you.'

'Why, thank you!' Clemmie kissed both his cheeks, leaving juicy imprints of her cherry-red lipstick behind. 'You English are *so* kind.' She moved forward to embrace a stiffly unresponsive Caro. 'Goodness me, you're *gorgeous*. I wish I could carry off red hair. And you're so *slim*! Unlike me – I upset all the designers in Hollywood with these enormous hips of mine.'

Clemmie patted her tiny hips comfortably while a mollified Caro offered to show her around the manor. Clemmie linked arms with her and allowed herself to be led away, making discreet but admiring comments as she went.

Tessa applauded Clemmie's ability to win people over with such genuine warmth and sincerity. It might be the result of years of giving sycophantic hangers-on the brush-off but it worked, even on the likes of Caro who wore her frostiness like a pageant crown.

Rufus shook Jack's hand heartily. 'Long time no see, Jack.'

Jack gave him a hug. 'Rufus! Good to see you again.' He stood back to get a better look. 'Christ, you've lost your rugby physique, haven't you! I could snap you in two and I'm an old codger.'

'Old codger, my arse,' Rufus grinned. 'You're in great shape.' He lowered his voice, putting his mouth close to Jack's ear. 'And still pulling birds, I hear. You wily old fox, you.'

Tessa grimaced as she checked her notes. Why did some men feel it necessary to congratulate another on what essentially constituted being a slut of the highest order? To her surprise,

Jack inclined his head awkwardly, almost as if he agreed with her unvoiced sentiment.

'I'm getting a bit long in the tooth for all that,' he replied almost sadly. 'Believe or not, I'd be happy to settle down in front of the fire with my pipe and slippers these days.' Seeing Rufus's stunned face and realising he might have toppled himself off some sort of dubious pedestal, Jack rushed on. 'Hey, congratulations on your impending wedding. Clemmie seems absolutely charming. Ravishing, in fact.'

'She is, she is,' Rufus agreed, turning at the sound of other people arriving.

Gil burst in wearing what could only be described as a Hawaiian shirt from hell. Smoothing down his freshly high-lighted hair, he dashed over to introduce himself, his flowery shirt tails flying out behind him. He proceeded to twitter and trill like a demented budgie at a bemused Rufus, who didn't know whether to snigger or help Gil into a chair so he could calm down. Tessa, who was prepared to give her new friend's fiancé the benefit of the doubt, nonetheless secretly felt he was a bit of a prat.

Gil was quickly followed by Milly who, Tessa noted, had teamed her off-the-shoulder silver top with the shortest black skirt she could find and was consequently flashing an indecent amount of toned, brown thigh. Her friend India was in tow – Amazonian in height and sporting a long, ginger ponytail and a somewhat alarming fake tan. At a loose end now that their GCSEs were over, the girls had obviously decided it was about time they met up with the resident celebrities.

Everyone wanted to get a look at them, Tessa realised as Milly's brother David sloped in, looking healthier than normal with a slight tan and fewer spots on his chin. He was accompanied by Freddie Penry-Jones, who was all floppy black hair and leather wristbands. She watched Freddie work the room like a pro, introducing himself to Rufus and the film crew before seamlessly moving on to Jack, his mouth lifting into a wicked grin as he high-fived him.

Having been informed by Tristan that Freddie was a small-time drug dealer, Tessa was taken aback at his immaculate manners. Not that she had met many drug dealers in her time – they might all be as polite as Freddie, for all she knew. He turned the spotlight of his gaze towards her, his dark blue eyes slowly making their way down her Joseph suit, lingering on her breasts before travelling down to her waist, his eyes continuing their descent to the tips of her painted toenails.

She couldn't help laughing at his audacity and he smiled back at her, pleased to be the cause of her mirth. Tessa caught sight of Milly over Freddie's shoulder and felt surprised when she was treated to a glacial look that would have put Caro to shame. Confused, she turned back to Freddie.

'Freddie Penry Jones,' he said, his upper-class voice softer than expected. 'So naff having a double-barrelled name, don't you think? Can't be helped, though. There's no need to introduce yourself, you're Tessa Meadmore. I'm a huge fan. No honestly, I mean it. I have posters of you on my wall at home.'

'That's very sweet,' she replied, aware she was blushing. What was she thinking? He was only a child! Eighteen – not quite young enough to be her son but not that far off.

'Seriously,' Freddie told her, giving her another smouldering look. 'I can't understand why *FHM* haven't put you on their Top 100 Sexiest Women list.'

Enjoying the harmless banter, Tessa let her eyes wander over him, taking in the tanned throat outlined by the unbuttoned, white linen shirt and the dark jeans and pristine trainers. 'You're quite the charmer, aren't you?'

'Only where you're concerned . . .' Freddie sneakily moved closer. 'You're the epitome of the perfect woman, as far as I'm concerned.'

In amusement, Tessa raised her eyes to the ceiling before

becoming aware that Milly had ditched her earlier frostiness and was now baring her teeth at her with all the ferocity of a trained-to-kill Dobermann. Comprehension dawned. Milly wasn't here to see Rufus at all. She might have come with her friend India, who was purring over Rufus like an underage sex kitten, but Milly obviously only had eyes for one person. And no wonder. With his crushed blueberry eyes, his overlong black hair and the pop star clothes, Freddie had to be every teenage girl's wet dream. Apart from his sideline as a drug dealer, of course, but perhaps she was thinking like an adult there. To a young girl, that probably just gave Freddie an irresistible air of danger. If the white-hot glint in her eye was anything to go by, Milly had a crush on Freddie; a whopping, great big crush that occupied every waking thought and no doubt had her lying awake at night, shivering with unrequited lust.

Tessa felt Freddie's eyes on her and gave him a discouraging shake of her head.

'Your compliments are lovely, but you must know I'm far too old for you. You really should be with someone more your own age.' She gestured vaguely towards the girls.

Freddie made a derisive noise with his tongue. 'What, like India, the fatuous bimbo? Or Milly, who's like my kid sister? No thanks! Besides, David fancies India and there's a code between men, you know? I'm into proper women with a bit of class and experience. Like you.'

'Sometimes the right person is under your nose and you don't even realise it.' Tessa wondered at herself; the role of big sister was coming to her more easily than she might have imagined. She had no experience of being a sibling and caring what happened to them – the feeling had sprung from nowhere.

'What do you mean?'

'That . . . friendships can often turn into romances,' she finished obliquely. Freddie didn't seem cruel; he was probably unaware that Milly saw him as anything other than another big brother. She let him down gently. 'And I'm deeply flattered by your sweet comments but I'm afraid my interests lie elsewhere.'

Leaving Freddie puzzled and with a slightly dented ego, Tessa headed over to Milly who, it seemed, was taking out her frustration on her mother.

'God, Mother, do you have to follow me everywhere?' Milly folded her arms defiantly. 'I'm sixteen not six, remember?'

'Of course I remember, darling,' Henny said hesitantly. 'I was just wondering if anyone wanted any drinks.'

Milly was in no mood to be forgiving. 'God, Aunt Caro's right,' she blurted out rudely. 'You're always getting in the bloody way!'

Recoiling as if she'd been shot, Henny went scarlet and scuttled away like a tormented kitten.

'Do you have to be so mean to her?' Tessa asked Milly with as much patience as she could muster. 'She only wants the best for you.'

'What's it got to do with you?' Milly snarled at her, her expression mutinous.

'Absolutely nothing. I just think you should give your mother a break now and again. She's kind and thoughtful and she loves you dearly. I wish I had a mother like her.'

'No, you don't,' Milly stormed, eyeing Tessa's sandals jealously before turning tortured eyes towards Freddie, who was chatting to Rufus and making furtive hand gestures. Meanwhile India's eyes were out on stalks and she was arching her back for all she was worth, sticking her chest out towards Rufus like a beauty queen.

Tessa suppressed a sigh and watched the film crew setting up, hindered by Gil who was so hell-bent on getting in shot, he had tangled himself up in camera leads and microphones, much to the exasperation of the cameramen.

'What a dickhead,' Milly sniped.

Taking a leaf out of Clemmie's book, Tessa decided to go for a charm offensive.

'By the way, Freddie's lovely.'

'What?' Milly looked gripped with pain.

'Lovely, and way too young for me,' Tessa told her firmly. 'Not my cup of tea at all.'

Milly couldn't hide her elation. 'Really?'

'Really. He's a nice boy but he needs to grow up a bit. And when he does, he'll probably realise the perfect girl for him has been right under his nose all along.'

'D-do you think so?'

'I *know* so.' Tessa squeezed her hand sympathetically. 'Just give it time.'

Milly looked absurdly grateful and Tessa basked in the glow of her role of wiser big sis.

Suddenly she clutched her head – JB would go nuts if he knew she was befriending the youngest member of the Forbes-Henry clan with such enthusiasm. She wondered where he'd got to and, clutching Jilly's notes about the family (she never went anywhere without them for fear of them getting into the wrong hands), she went in search of him.

JB was in the hallway, looking disinterestedly at some framed photographs on the wall, the obligatory cigarette clamped between his lips.

'I'm not sure you're supposed to smoke in here . . .'

JB cursed and dropped his cigarette into a vase of yellow roses with a sizzle. 'Caro Forbes-Henry is very attractive, *non*?'

Exasperated by his lack of manners, Tessa fished the cigarette butt out of the vase. 'Very. Hideous French, though. I would have thought you'd have been mortified to listen to it.'

'Oh yes, her accent was *exécrable*, so bad. But she is very beautiful so . . .'

Tessa raised her eyes to the ceiling.

'Do you theenk Caro 'as – what do you English say – the 'ots for me?'

'As we English say, I think you're in there,' Tessa said tartly. Feeling discomfited at the sight of Henny approaching, sporting an uncharacteristically tight-lipped smile, she moved away from JB.

'Sorry, Henny, that was so rude of me . . .'

The older woman waved her apologies away. 'You have no need to say anything. I've seen Caro do this too many times before to get upset about it. It's Jack I'm worried about. He never used to care and he's always given as good as he got, but lately,' her eyes clouded over with concern, 'lately, it's as if he's given up. I think he might finally be hurting and there's not a thing I can do about it.'

Tessa squeezed her arm sympathetically, not sure what to say.

'Goodness, there I go again!' Henny visibly pulled herself together. 'You must forgive me, I always seem to unburden myself to you, don't I? I guess that's why they hire you to interview celebrities, you get them talking about themselves!' She brightened up and beamed at Tessa. 'I came to see you to say that Will has asked to see you in his office.'

'Has he really?' Tessa felt her heart thud into her Gina sandals. Great, this was all she needed, a meeting with grumpy old Will interrogating her about the documentary. It felt as if she'd been summoned to the headmaster's office, for heaven's sakes!

'Top of the stairs, first right,' Henny told her obligingly, not noticing Tessa's look of horror. 'I think he just wants to catch up and see how things are going, that sort of thing.'

'How *very* kind of him,' Tessa muttered with a grimace, climbing the first stair as if she'd been banished to death row. Will was causing her no end of bloody headaches and she wondered what exactly she'd done wrong now.

'I can't tell you how excited I am to be getting married here,' Clemmie told Jack as she wobbled on the gravel in her high heels. She wasn't sure at which point Caro had slipped away from showing her round the house or when Jack had sidled up and taken her place, but she was enjoying his company.

She gave him a sneaky sideways glance. There was something very attractive about Jack's slightly bleary green eyes and his laidback humour. Clemmie suspected he was a bit of a ladies' man – his flattering questions and genial smiles were slightly too practised to be off-the-cuff but he had been gallant and respectful towards her and nothing short of a gentleman. He liked a drink, that much was obvious. His hands shook slightly and alcohol was probably responsible for prematurely fading his good looks. But that was his business.

Clemmie held her face up to the fading evening sunshine for a moment, luxuriating in its warmth before reminding herself that her plastic surgeon would kill her if she went back with a single wrinkle. She hurriedly bent her head before she caused any lasting damage.

'What do you think of the motor, then?' Jack said, proudly running his hand around the curve of the bonnet of the Rolls-Royce Phantom.

'I think it's breathtaking,' Clemmie admitted in an awed voice, slowly walking round it to get a better look. The car was in perfect condition; the sweeping Air Force blue wings and doors were clean and flawless and the windscreen gleamed so brightly in the sinking, golden sunshine, it almost blinded her.

'Go on, jump in!'

Jack held a door open in invitation and helped her in, averting his eyes as she scooped the skirt of her dress over her knees. Leaping into the driver's seat next to her, he ran his hands over the steering wheel, his green eyes bright with pleasure.

'Isn't she a beauty? I don't usually let other people touch her, let alone sit in her.'

'Thank you.' Clemmie ran her fingertips over the spotless dash in wonder. The car smelt manly – of leather, wax and Jack's spicy aftershave. The combination of smells reminded her of her youth. A lifetime ago, she had peered out of windows like these at the film studio, dreaming of being famous. 'I can understand why you love her so much.'

'Not everyone appreciates a classic car,' Jack said as he turned the engine over, his ear cocked. 'Hear that? Smooth as velvet – she never lets me down.' He glanced at Clemmie. Not only was she absolutely ravishing, she seemed delightfully down-to-earth. Her milky skin was delectable, as pale as Caro's but freckle-free, and her dark hair emphasised the creaminess of it. The clingy dress outlined every curve of her body but it was the direct eye contact and ready laugh that made him think she was worth talking to.

Clemmie let out her famous throaty chuckle. 'The words of a man who doesn't trust women.'

Jack raised an eyebrow. 'You have met Caro, haven't you? I'd be stunned if she hadn't advised you of all the gory details of our countless affairs; dignified silences aren't Caro's style. We have a somewhat . . . *unconventional* marriage, I suppose you could say.' He breathed in Clemmie's scent, a waft of Chanel No. 5 tickling his nostrils.

'She mentioned it to me just now, actually,' Clemmie admitted, leaning back in her seat. Her dark hair fanned out against the headrest made Jack visualise her lying back on snow-white pillows. 'You must love each other, though, otherwise neither of you would still be here.'

Jack grunted. He stared through the windscreen, his eyes darkening with confusion. Why *was* he still here? Did he still love Caro? He hardly knew any more. He didn't know what love felt like – he had lost sight of his emotions. He felt enraged and impotent, but that was all. Life seemed almost intolerable at the moment, as dramatic as that sounded. He felt flat . . . sort of dead inside.

'Your sons seem charming,' Clemmie commented out of the blue. 'I just met Will and we bumped into Tristan the other day. He's lovely.'

Jack gave an ill-tempered shrug. 'Will's made a real success of himself with his property business in France. The same can't be said for Tristan.'

'But he's an artist. An incredibly talented artist!'

'Is he? He's not exactly ambitious.'

'Does he need to be? His talent speaks for itself.' Clemmie turned to face Jack, wondering why his tone had been so dismissive. 'What do you want him to do, show his paintings in the Louvre, or something? Honey, just because he didn't paint the Mona Lisa doesn't mean he's not successful or that his work isn't sought after. Rufus paid a fortune for one of Tristan's paintings in New York last year and it's tripled in value since then.' She gave Jack's hand the briefest of touches. 'I do hope Tristan doesn't know you feel this way about him, honey, he'd be absolutely crushed. He probably hero worships you.'

Jack said nothing. He savoured the fleeting feel of Clemmie's soft hand over his before she withdrew it; it had been a tender gesture, one that unexpectedly made his chest flutter. When was the last time a woman had touched him in such a caring, understanding way? Sex was overrated, Jack realised with a shock, and it counted for nothing over sentiment and intimacy. His foggy mind drifted back to Tristan.

Why was it that his son couldn't do enough to impress him? Why did Tristan's very presence irk him so much? He knew that girl Sophie had made him go off the rails, firstly with drink and then, shortly after, with women. There had been a time when Tristan's cottage had resembled a sex den with a revolving door, pretty girl after pretty girl traipsing in and out, all convinced they could be the one to heal him.

Was he jealous of his own son? Jack felt repulsed. Or did his cavalier attitude to the opposite sex remind him of himself and therefore highlight a heartache which was much closer to home? He had never fathomed it out, but for the first time in his life, he felt slightly ashamed that his heartfelt favouritism had been detected outside the family and had been, ever so gently, chastised.

'Do you want children?' he asked Clemmie gruffly, surprised to find himself thinking she would make a great mother. He imagined her pregnant, ripe and full and still beautiful, less 'Hollywood' and more 'Motherhood'. Whatever that meant. God, he was turning soft in his old age.

'Oh yes, Jack, I can't wait! It's going to be idyllic having children with Rufus, sending them to English schools, helping them with their homework, hanging all those little Christmas stockings over the period fireplaces you have over here.'

Jack took in her wistful expression and the slightly glazed look in her eyes. He seriously doubted her cosy, rose-tinted dream would ever be realised. From what he remembered about Rufus, he wasn't exactly the settling down type. But then, what did he, Jack, know about any of this? He couldn't have predicted the farce that his marriage had become and yet here he was, living it out every day in painful technicolour.

'You do know Rufus is a bit . . . immature?' he offered cautiously. He liked Clemmie far too much to see her made a fool of. 'You know, when it comes to kids and all that stuff?'

Clemmie looked startled. 'We've never really discussed it, but I just assumed . . . I mean, we're getting married so he must . . .'

Jack happened to look out of the car window at that moment, although he instantly wished he hadn't. Caro, her russet head bent towards JB's dark one, could be seen in an upstairs window, her mouth willing and open to receive his kiss. Jack

113

tried to make sense of the churning feeling in his stomach, which could no longer be blamed on too many Bloody Marys. It was difficult to know what had changed but he had no choice, he had to acknowledge he was unhappy. Miserably, depressingly, woefully unhappy. And he didn't for the life of him know why.

Was he finally tiring of the games? He ran a hand through his faded blond hair. Perhaps. Or perhaps he was simply too old to be mucking around and scoring points. His marriage to Caro had never been straightforward. He had loved her deeply in the beginning, she had been like an unbroken horse, challenging, unpredictable and utterly glorious. He remembered the way her back used to arch when she climaxed on top of him; her long, red hair reaching the small of her back and tickling his fingers, her pale eyelashes fluttering like butterfly wings as she came. Back in the days when Jack had been enough for her, that was.

And then she had betrayed him. Jack's lips tightened at the memory and he pushed it away again, as he had done over and over, unable to confront it, unable to understand it. Now Caro had become hard and her looks were beginning to fade, not so much through age but through regret and revenge. And as for being unpredictable, Jack swallowed a terse laugh. These days, he could plot Caro's next move almost before she had thought of it herself. He'd known as soon as he saw JB that Caro would pursue him. He pictured his wife's slender limbs wound round that good-looking bastard in some dark corner, as she cooed at him in terrible French and gasped in delight at any hint of encouragement he might deign to offer her.

But why did that bother him so much? Jack was genuinely stumped. It seemed as if she'd taken a step too far this time but he couldn't put his finger on why that was. Shagging gardeners was one thing but there was something about the way Caro was flaunting her obvious intentions to bed JB in front of him that

114

felt sordid and cheap. Was it because it was being shoved down his throat on his own doorstep? Or was it just the deliberate, mocking way she was degrading herself for all to see? Jack didn't know, nor was he sure he cared any more. He just didn't seem to have the energy to fight back – not this time.

'Er . . . Jack?' Clemmie broke into his thoughts apologetically. 'I think I might be needed for filming shortly . . .'

Jack visibly pulled himself together and twisted towards her in his seat. 'How rude of me, I'm so sorry.' He shook all thoughts of Caro from his head. 'Hey, do you want to have a drive of her? You seem to appreciate a classic car like this.' He dangled the keys at her enticingly.

'Oh no!' Clemmie looked horrified and she shrank back. 'I-I wouldn't dream of it.'

'Go on!' Jack urged her, starting to get out of his seat.

'No, really.' Clemmie had turned pale and she clutched Jack's hand with her own which felt cold and child-like. 'I should explain . . . I don't drive, you see. Haven't for y-years.' Her voice quivered.

Jack looked dumbfounded. 'You don't drive? Do you mean you *can't* drive, or you just don't?' His expression became mocking. 'You mean you *don't* drive because you get chauffeured around in limos all the time.'

'Not really but it's not something I like to talk about . . .'

Clemmie was wringing her hands anxiously but the gesture barely registered with Jack, who was in full flow.

'God, you Hollywood types! You're just not like normal people, are you? You're all so spoilt; you can't even function like normal human beings any more!' He sneered at her, his earlier rage at Caro manifesting itself cruelly in Clemmie's direction.

Clemmie's eyes filled with tears. 'I can't . . . it's difficult to explain, Jack . . . but it's not what you think . . . I wish I could tell you.' She folded her dress between her fingers in agitation.

Jack shrugged carelessly. This was the last time he'd offer to let anyone drive his car again. Bloody women, they were more hassle than they were worth!

Clemmie blinked and a tear slid down her cheek. Brushing it away bravely, she leapt out of the car. 'I need to g-get back,' she stammered. She gave him a beseeching look, as if willing him not to judge her too harshly, before hurrying away in her high heels.

Clemmie clutched frantically at the door of the manor, fearing she might collapse. Jack's comments about driving had brought everything back to her with horrific precision and the familiar, cloying sense of guilt threatened to crush her like a ten-ton weight. It was too much to bear, too overwhelming. How was she ever going to forget what happened?

Hearing her name being called for make-up, Clemmie swallowed down a sob. Making a monumental effort to regain her composure, she let go of the door and took a deep breath. Certain her cheeks must be grey with shock, she pinched them until she felt the blood rush to the surface and she smoothed her dress down carefully.

Holding her shoulders back and her head high, Clemmie headed towards her waiting public. She was an Oscar-winning actress and she had a part to play. And, ever the professional, Clemmie knew exactly what was expected of her.

Staggered that Clemmie had rushed away from him in such a terrible state, Jack gazed after her until she disappeared inside the house. He found himself running his hands around the rim of the steering wheel in profound discomfort. What on earth had possessed him to attack her like that? For all he knew, Clemmie had a perfectly reasonable explanation for not wanting to drive his car and he had jumped to conclusions without even giving her a chance to speak. And he was guiltily aware that he had lost his temper and directed his anger at

Clemmie instead of at Caro, which was grossly unfair. He had bullied her and she didn't deserve that.

The thought of her wide hazel eyes clouding over with dismay before unexpectedly filling with tears tugged at Jack's consciousness – another new sensation. He saw Clemmie as a rare, fragile bird, one that he had practically obliterated underfoot. He cursed himself. They had been getting on so well, too.

Jack was vexed at his bad behaviour. He really needed to get a grip, he decided as he got out of the Rolls-Royce. His blood-shot eyes squinted as the late evening sunshine boldly played across his face. He needed a stiff drink. And after that, he needed to figure out what the hell to do about Caro.

Chapter Eight

Tessa stood outside Will's office feeling rebellious. Clenching Jilly's notes in her hand, she wondered whether to leg it in the other direction. How dare he summon her like this!

The door was slightly ajar and, feeling childish, Tessa couldn't help peering through the gap before going in. Forewarned is forearmed, she told herself determinedly, hoping no one would catch her. The office was light and airy, with walls painted golden-brown like freshly baked bread. The windows were wide open and a fan was whirring in the corner, the breeze lifting the edges of tidy stacks of paperwork which were prevented from flying round the room by a heavy book. A large maple-wood desk dominated the room, flanked by a couple of battered old brown leather armchairs.

Will was predictably positioned behind the desk, bent over some papers, but somehow he looked different. His broad shoulders were taut with tension and his tawny-gold hair was sticking up at the front as if he had been clutching at it.

'Jesus *Christ*,' he muttered under his breath.

Tessa frowned and shuffled closer to get a better look. Instead of the impeccably dressed man she had witnessed previously, Will was wearing a crumpled white linen shirt and faded shorts, his feet bare beneath the desk. Brow furrowed, he was poring over some paperwork and lifting up what looked like red bills.

What on earth was he doing? Tessa wondered as she watched him worriedly leaf through the pile. He was disgustingly rich, wasn't he? And it wasn't just Will; from what everyone had said, the entire family was loaded. Perhaps this was just a stack of bills Jack and Caro had forgotten to pay. Still, she had never seen Will looking so anxious before . . .

Abruptly, Will looked up and caught sight of Tessa loitering by the door. Immediately, he shoved the paperwork into a drawer, locking it smartly for good measure.

She stiffened. What did he think she was going to do? Rifle through his drawers? She swallowed, squashing down the unpalatable memory of doing just that recently.

'Are you going to stand there all day or are you coming in?' Will inquired coldly. His dark blue eyes were flinty as he gestured for her to take a seat in one of the leather armchairs.

'You . . . asked for me?' she said with exaggerated politeness, only just stopping herself from using the word 'summoned'. Taking in her surroundings from the lavish silk curtains to the ornate tiles in the fireplace, Tessa realised she must have been mistaken before. Will couldn't possibly be worried about money, every inch of the manor house reeked of good taste, and good taste cost serious money. Even Will's makeshift office looked as if it deserved a four-page spread in *Homes and Gardens*.

She felt her hackles rise beneath her expensive suit and she crossed her legs, glad she had chosen to wear the Gina sandals. What girl couldn't project confidence when she was wearing four-inch heels?

'How's the documentary going?' Will countered, ignoring her shapely brown calves and sexy ankles. He wasn't going to pull any punches about why he'd asked her to come and see him, and he definitely wasn't going to be deterred from his goal, however long Tessa's legs looked beneath the short skirt of her suit. 'I trust your film crew are being as discreet as possible. As grateful as we are for the publicity, I wouldn't want anything to affect the hotel being completed on time.'

Seething inwardly, Tessa ignored him and instead gazed around his office, allowing her eyes to take in every detail. There were some poster-sized pictures of stunning French countryside, including a huge one of the Loire Valley and a framed copy of Byron's poem 'She Walks in Beauty' took pride of place over the period fireplace. An obvious choice, Tessa thought snippily and not one of her personal favourites. She tore her eyes away. In keeping with the rest of the house, the walls of Will's office were adorned with family photographs and several that Tessa assumed were of Will's fiancée, a striking girl with glossy bobbed hair who looked as if she'd stepped off the cover of French *Vogue*. Tessa wondered why this irked her so much. How typical of Will to have a perfect French fiancée. She pictured them swanning around Appleton Manor together without a care in the world. Rich, privileged and effortlessly upper class.

Incensed at her rudeness, Will wondered why he'd bothered to ask Tessa to his office in the first place. He had wanted to see how the documentary was going but, truthfully, his gut told him she was here to cause trouble somehow. He had thought it before he had even clapped eyes on her and everything she'd done since she'd arrived had convinced him he was right. His family might be besotted with her, he thought irritably, but he wasn't fooled by Tessa Meadmore one bit.

Will watched her proud nose in profile as she scrutinised every inch of his office, noting the way her wide mouth curved upwards as her eyes alighted on the signed poem from Claudette. Will had mistakenly thought he might be able to maintain some degree of control over the documentary but from what he had seen, Tessa and her crew turned up whenever they pleased and shot whatever they fancied. They humped their heavy equipment across the period floorboards and shone heavy lights on priceless paintings with a complete lack of consideration as well.

Well, not priceless paintings as such, Will conceded wryly.

Anything worth selling had already disappeared to auction houses and Tristan had obligingly provided portraits for each brightly coloured square of wallpaper as yet another hurried sale took place. Tristan, his mind totally focused on his creations, didn't question Will nor did he wonder where the old paintings were disappearing to. He simply produced further work whenever he was asked to and for once Will was grateful for his distractedness – although he had an uncomfortable feeling that Tristan's mind was focused very much on Tessa Meadmore right now.

She had finally completed her belligerent appraisal of his office and was now coolly fixing her moss-green eyes on him. He waited, exercising admirable self-control in his opinion.

'Of course my film crew are being discreet,' she said finally, her hands tightly clasped around the stack of notes she had brought with her. 'We're a professional crew and we've filmed documentaries like this before.'

'Have you?'

Will raised his eyebrows at her and Tessa reddened under his stare. Had he been checking up on her? How aggravating he was! It was bad enough that Jilly and JB had her on trial, she didn't need this arrogant aristocrat thinking he could put her down as well. Tristan came from the same background yet he did nothing of the sort.

'Your family have been very helpful,' she said sweetly, knowing it would rile him. She was briefly distracted by the sight of Will's tanned rugby player thighs beneath his desk. He really was very masculine, she thought with surprise . . . Seeing him regard her with something close to dislike, she put the thought of Will's thighs firmly out of her head.

'So I hear.' He sat back in his chair, staring at her. 'I trust you've been respecting their boundaries as far as Rufus is concerned. I know you think I'm being over-protective but Rufus has had a dreadful time with journalists in the past, especially British ones. Surely even you can admit that they can be vicious at times. And, as you're probably aware, my family really aren't used to dealing with the press.'

That much was obvious, Tessa thought, guiltily remembering the way Henny had innocently handed her the photographs of Rufus as a teenager.

'I'm a professional, Mr Forbes-Henry,' she replied smoothly. 'The last thing I want to do is take advantage of your delightful family.'

'It's Will . . . there's no need to be so formal,' he said in a tight voice.

'Mr Forbes-Henry – Will, whatever,' she replied. She couldn't help feeling a small sense of victory as she sensed him bristling on the other side of the desk.

Feeling at a disadvantage in the low armchair, Tessa got up and tossed her notes on to the chair.

Walking slowly round his office on her spike heels, her back taut with tension, she examined some of Will's family photographs. She focused her attention on a photograph of a much younger Caro wearing a black lace evening dress whose neckline plunged almost to her freckled navel. Beside her, Jack looked very handsome in a dinner jacket, his blond hair slicked back and his green eyes unusually clear and sparkly. He had his arm round Caro's shoulders in a proprietorial manner, his tight smile suggesting he was holding on to her for dear life.

'My parents are outrageous, aren't they?' Will ventured. Realising his words could be misconstrued, he rushed to gloss over them. 'Well, unconventional is perhaps a better word to describe them. They love each other very much, but I'm afraid they do fight rather a lot. Actually, while you're here, I did want to ask if you could avoid filming them if you can help it. I know Clemmie and Rufus are the stars but I guess the family might appear now and again in relation to the manor house. The thing is, my parents . . . well, they're going through some . . . some issues at the moment.'

If by 'issues' he meant Caro bedding the hunky gardener and Jack chasing after every twenty-year-old in a skirt, Tessa supposed Will was right. She was surprised he was so defensive of them; surely it wasn't his fault if they behaved like a couple of teenagers on heat? Or was this just another example of him being a complete and utter control freak? Her mouth curled contemptuously.

'My family are very important to me, whatever they might get up to,' Will confessed, not noticing her look of derision. Tiredly, he ran a hand through his tawny hair, making it stick up even more. 'It's amazing to know that whatever else happens in your life, they're always going to be there for you, you know?'

Tessa turned away from him, suddenly choked. Her eyes stung with tears and she bit down on her lip hard to stop them from spilling over. She didn't have any family, not now her beloved mother was dead. She would never experience the strange, unspoken devotion the Forbes-Henrys shared, the unwavering trust and respect they seemed to have for one another, and the closeness that was difficult for outsiders to penetrate. Will's fiancée Claudette seemed to have managed it; they all talked about her as if she was the best thing since sliced brioche, Tessa thought, catching sight of a ravishing picture of Claudette wearing an off-the-shoulder cashmere jumper. Grudgingly, she supposed they had made her feel very welcome. But it didn't make up for her own loss nor did it assuage the sense of loneliness that being without a family gave her.

Staring at the photographs enviously, Tessa felt a rush of resentment for Will. He was so privileged, so lucky to have such an amazing family. After everything she had gone through, it didn't seem fair somehow. Logic told her it wasn't Will's fault but at that moment, it felt like it.

'What about you . . . do you . . . er . . . do you have family?' Will asked in a reserved tone, sounding to Tessa as if he was just making conversation.

'Me? Have family?' Tessa laughed at the question, her voice sounding slightly hysterical. She pushed down the sob in her throat. 'No, thank God! My father upped and left decades ago and my mother died last year. Which made things much easier, actually, because I travel around so much with my job, it would be difficult to have too many ties. Families affect your choices, don't you think? You have to consider them when you're offered work and they're always on at you for something or other . . . No, I'm much better off as I am.' She had no idea what she was rambling on about; she just knew she couldn't bear to appear in any way vulnerable in front of Will.

'Really?' Will studied her. He wasn't sure he believed her. The words sounded plausible enough but Tessa's breathy tone and slightly wet eyes suggested she was feeling something else entirely.

Seeing uncertainty in Will's navy-blue eyes and detesting the thought of him pitying her, Tessa hammered on. 'Look, family isn't important in my life, OK? It's my career that matters to me. I just want to do my job to the best of my ability and . . . and make as much money as possible along the way.' She stopped, catching her breath, wondering at her ability to lie so slickly. Perhaps all her years as a journalist hadn't been wasted after all. Will was looking at her as if she was a slug he had found in his lobster ravioli, but it was better than having him think she was weak. Wasn't it? Tessa wondered why she had the overwhelming urge to curl up under Will's desk and sob uncontrollably, the way she had after Adam's betrayal.

Will regarded her coldly. So he'd been right about her from the start: Tessa was a hard-nosed journalist who didn't care who she trampled on to get to the top – including his family, evidently.

God, he was lucky he was engaged to someone like Claudette, Will thought fiercely. Tessa might be spectacularly good-looking but she was just about as far away from his idea of a perfect woman as she could possibly get. He had nothing against career women; Claudette was involved in a high-profile charity in Paris which was why she wasn't able to join him in England yet, but at least she had her priorities straight about the things that mattered.

Tessa flinched under Will's hard stare but pressed on regardless. 'I just want to get this documentary completed as soon as possible so I can move to the States. I could really hit the big time there.'

Will gave her a look loaded with scorn. 'How wonderful for you! Making it big in America – well, that has to be the epitome of success, I should imagine.'

'I'm surprised you even know what success feels like,' she shot back. Will looked taken aback and he leant forward, his hairy, bare forearms almost obscuring his paperwork.

'Meaning?'

'This house, the grounds – you didn't build this yourself, did you? Or pay for it?'

Will looked astonished.

'I didn't think so. And all these period features that people pay a fortune for must have been here before you were even born.'

Will's eyebrows knitted together. 'Of course they were! This house has been in the Forbes-Henry family for hundreds of years but I honestly can't see what you're getting at.'

Tessa rolled her eyes. 'Oh, forget it! I just don't think someone like you has any right to judge me for wanting to have a successful career. Not everyone can fall back on the family millions, you know.'

The family millions? Will stared at her open-mouthed. Tessa obviously saw him as some sort of lazy aristocrat who hadn't done a day's work in his life. Will was so enraged by the injustice of it all he didn't know what to do with himself. They glared at each other furiously and Tessa thought Will might be about to climb over the desk and slap her.

She was saved by the arrival of Tristan who lolloped in like an excitable, golden puppy.

'There you are, Tessa!' he managed as he bent over with his hands on his knees and caught his breath. 'I'm so unfit! They're looking for you everywhere, so I volunteered to come and find you. Little did they know I had an ulterior motive.' He straightened up and snuck his arm round Tessa's waist, giving it a cheeky squeeze. 'Lordy, I just got stuck talking to that designer, Gil Anderson. He knows his stuff and all that but I've never seen such tight trousers in my life.'

Listening to Tristan talking at a hundred miles an hour, Tessa scooped up her notes, not noticing as one slid to the floor. Unable to look Will in the eye for a second longer, she dashed out after Tristan.

Will bashed his fist down on his desk. He accidentally dislodged the book holding down his paperwork and within seconds the breeze had sent his papers spiralling into the air. Letting out a howl of frustration he leapt up and started gathering them to his chest.

Managing to locate most of his spreadsheets, Will frowned as he looked at the unfamiliar sheet of paper on top of the untidy stack. He realised Tessa must have accidentally dropped some of her notes before she left the room.

'How Best to Use the Forbes-Henrys,' Will read out loud. Scanning the contents with increasing horror, he sat back thoughtfully. Tessa was indeed everything he had thought she was – and more and worse than that, she intended to milk his family for all they were worth. Milly, Henny, Tristan – every single one of them.

Henny balanced a tray of homemade lemonade on her palm and pushed the kitchen door open with her not inconsiderable bottom. She was still reeling from Milly's malicious comments but she kept trying to tell herself that her daughter didn't mean it. She was a teenager, that was all, and she was doing what every other girl her age did – blaming her mother for everything. Henny would prefer to think it was this rather than the unthinkable – that Milly was turning into Caro and that by bringing her back here to live, Henny was responsible for creating a monster in Caro's likeness.

Speaking of the devil . . . Henny realised she could hear Caro's high-pitched voice in the corridor that led to what used to be the servants' quarters. She could hear her giggling and whispering something that sounded suspiciously like 'Bad boy!' in dreadful French. Caro must be flirting or, knowing her, worse than that, with that sly-looking director – JC or JB or whatever he called himself.

Feeling outraged on Jack's behalf, Henny set the tray down firmly and headed for the voices. Caro was crushed up against the wall with her hands entwined in JB's dark hair and he was kissing her thoroughly, his hand expertly slipping the emerald-green leotard from Caro's milky-white shoulder. Sensing they had an audience, JB drew back, his dark eyes flashing, a cocky smile playing at his lips.

'I'm *so* sorry to interrupt,' Henny said sarcastically, sounding anything but.

Caro narrowed her eyes at Henny's tone and calmly slipped her leotard back on to her shoulder. There was nothing she could do about the scarlet rash spreading across her breastbone, nor about her prominent, swollen nipples, but she didn't care.

'So you should be,' Caro told her, flicking a flame-red curl out of her eyes. 'You can't just go barging in on people like that, Henny. Have some respect, please.'

'No harm done,' JB said, seemingly unruffled by the diversion. 'I was about to leave anyway. I will be in touch, *chérie*, and we can get down to business,' he told Caro with heavy intent. 'Serious business.' He gave Henny a shameless wink before taking his leave.

Henny faltered. Jack was her brother and the reason she had a roof over her head. Was she really going to stand by and watch Caro make a fool of him on his own doorstep?

'Cat got your tongue?' Caro mocked, her hands on her bony hips.

'You can't . . . you can't do this to Jack,' Henny gasped. 'He doesn't deserve it.'

'Doesn't he? What would you know about it?'

Henny flinched away from Caro's sneering tone and the blazing contempt in her eyes. She was appalled at herself for being so pathetic but she wasn't brave enough to stand up for herself, or for Jack.

'You're a wretched excuse for a human being,' Caro crowed, incensed that Henny would even dare to challenge her.

Perfect Henny with her perfect bloody marriage, what the hell did she know about being married to a man like Jack? Caro's fingers curled into a ball. Did Henny have the first idea how much it hurt her when Jack cheated on her, how much it tore her heart into tiny little pieces, even after all this time? She tossed her red hair insolently. 'I have every right to be happy, and JB makes me happy.' At such an early stage of the relationship, she didn't know anything of the sort but that was her story and she was sticking to it.

'Caro, you must stop doing this to yourself,' Henny pleaded, trying to appeal to Caro's better nature, if she had one. 'You're hurting yourself as much as Jack. Can't you see this can only end badly?'

'This is nothing to do with you, Henny! And if you know

what's good for you, you'll keep your mouth shut, OK?' Caro pushed past her and shot down the corridor.

Hearing a crash as her tray of homemade lemonade went flying, Henny gripped the edge of a nearby table for support as tears streamed down her face.

Chapter Nine

Tessa was beginning to feel thoroughly fed up. The interview was going well but it was rather slow and so far, she hadn't produced any questions that had been even slightly demanding for Clemmie to answer. A vision of Jilly's beady eyes rolling skyward at what she called Tessa's 'soft, Parkinson-style' interviewing technique reminded Tessa it was about time she pulled something more impressive out of the bag.

The strong lighting and suffocating heat was making her eyes feel prickly but she resisted the urge to rub them and ruin the heavy layers of eye shadow Susie had artistically applied. She could feel Joe shifting position behind her with his camera and she felt under pressure to make sure they weren't wasting film.

'So what made you want to become an actress, Clemmie?' Tessa asked. She glanced at Rufus who was flicking through the *Sun*. He was in an amiable mood today, his sunny disposition evident in the scrambled-egg yellow T-shirt he wore rather than his usual black. It was August already and something akin to a tropical heatwave had hit Appleton. Ice creams were in high demand at the local village shop and they were doing a roaring trade in bottled water and over-priced suncream.

Tessa noticed Rufus looking outside again longingly as if he would rather be anywhere but here, and she didn't blame him; she'd rather be sunbathing herself. The film crew had been following Rufus and Clemmie around relentlessly and for

Rufus, at least, it was apparent the novelty was rapidly wearing off.

Clemmie shook her dark hair out, and it settled around her shoulders in old-style Hollywood waves. 'I think I always wanted to act.' She smiled, stretching luxuriously until she almost popped out of the strapless coral-pink sundress that clung adoringly to her curves. It was obviously a designer classic, bearing no visible stitch marks whatsoever, the fabric discreetly expensive. 'I used to drive past that big Hollywood sign in awe when I was younger and I'd tell myself that no matter what had happened to me, and no matter how I'd been judged, that one day I'd be somebody.'

'Does that mean you craved fame rather than artistic credibility?' Tessa ventured quickly, cringing as Clemmie's hazel eyes narrowed with disappointment at the underhand attempt to twist her words.

Tessa felt hot in the white Stella McCartney dress Jilly had instructed wardrobe to send up from London. It was stunning but it felt like a bribe – something to whet her appetite so she did as she was told and ferreted out the truth like a pig sniffing out prized truffles. She suppressed a sigh. Sometimes she felt torn in two; part of her hated the way celebrities were manipulated and exploited by the press and the other part of her wanted to ask the sort of questions she knew any member of the general public would ask in her place.

'No, it doesn't mean I craved fame above credibility,' Clemmie replied crisply. 'It simply means I wanted to feel as if I'd made some sort of difference in the world. It means that I wanted to be like the idols I'd admired since I was a little girl and I went after that dream.' She leant forward; giving the cameras an eyeful of creamy cleavage. She placed a small, white hand on Tessa's knee. It felt cold and somehow disapproving and Tessa felt a trickle of sweat run down her spine.

'And as much as I hate to push my Oscar down anyone's

throat,' Clemmie said in a voice that was deadly quiet but undeniably commanding, 'can I just remind you that fame and money mean nothing compared to an accolade of that kind. If all I was interested in was fame, I wouldn't have put myself through the trauma of playing a rape victim which, I can assure you, wasn't much fun. I would have taken more commercial roles and hung out at the paparazzi night spots instead.'

From the corner of the room, Rufus let out a cheer that wouldn't have been out of place on a rugby field. He flicked his thumbs up at Clemmie before refocusing his attention on his newspaper.

Tessa gulped, feeling the tension in the room. She cast her eyes down to avoid Clemmie's steely gaze and consulted her notes for assistance. She could feel JB's eyes boring into her and was half inclined to turn and ask him if he'd like to take over.

Christ, he was aggravating! Tessa felt as if the entire film crew were sitting back and waiting to see whether or not she could survive this moment. She thought for a second before lifting her head confidently to camera.

'And that, viewers, is a lesson to any would-be actresses out there. With the current trend of reality TV and the creation of overnight celebrity, it should be remembered that having lasting success in Hollywood takes grit, determination and enduring talent.' She finished with a glance back at Clemmie that she hoped radiated genuine admiration. There was a long pause before Clemmie graciously – professionally – conceded with a smile that would no doubt convince their audience they shared a mutual respect for each other.

'And . . . cut!' shouted JB, waving a hand at the cameraman who held his own hand up to indicate his agreement. JB gave Tessa a snappy little nod before barking orders at the team, who rushed around gathering up leads and dismantling lighting equipment.

'Hey, I hope that was OK?' Tessa started, feeling the need to clear the air between herself and Clemmie. She knew she had to occasionally ask questions that wouldn't be well-received but at the same time, if Clemmie didn't trust her or feel any kind of connection, the interview was going to feel flat and clumsy.

Clemmie relaxed as the harsh lighting dimmed and the film crew backed away. 'There's no need for you to apologise, honey,' she reassured Tessa, her smile reaching her eyes this time. 'I know you have to ask these questions. I'm the one who should say sorry – I was a little defensive there! But this whole fame thing is such a double-edged sword and I don't think there are many actresses who like being accused of pursuing celebrity over professional achievement.' Her expression was self-deprecating, her palms turned upwards to indicate frankness.

'I'm sure you're right.' Tessa wondered at Clemmie's ability to initiate effective and appropriate body language in every scenario – except ones that made her feel personally threatened for some reason. Was that the real Clemmie she had seen, perspiring ever so slightly, her eyes registering momentary panic before her extraordinary talent kicked in and saved her from revealing her true self?

'Please remember that I'm just doing my job and at times I'm going to be asking you things which might annoy you or make you want to slap me.' Tessa smiled back, equally candidly.

Clemmie laughed, charm personified. 'Ask me anything you want to, honey. I know it's all part of the job.' If she had taken offence at anything Tessa had said or done, it was now dead and buried. She sashayed over to Rufus who kissed her rampantly, sliding his hands over her silk-clad bottom as she sat on his lap and lifted the newspaper out of his hands.

Tessa couldn't help liking Clemmie immensely. She was so warm and down-to-earth in spite of the crazy, superficial world she lived in and she won over every single person she came into contact with. Still, Tessa couldn't help wondering why she was so on edge when she was being interviewed. Tessa shook herself. Why did she care what made Clemmie tick? Why couldn't she just get on with her job without analysing everything and wondering if she was upsetting people all the time?

'You rescued that – just,' JB growled in Tessa's ear, his accent strong. 'But she almost made you look like a bloody fool, you know that?'

Tessa put her hands on her hips with some aggression, fed up with being criticised by him. Who did he think he was, anyway? She felt disadvantaged by his imposing presence but, undeterred, she squared up to him.

'I'm the journalist here, remember? And you're the director. I can handle myself, thank you very much. You stick to direct-ing and I'll stick to what I do best. Then we'll get on just fine, OK?'

JB looked as if he was about to explode so she headed for the door, leaving him mouthing at her redundantly. Checking her phone messages, Tessa's heart sank when she saw three from Jilly.

Between Will, her boss and JB, her life was becoming quite depressing, Tessa thought as she threw her notes on to the back seat of her Audi and jumped in. The exchange with Will the other day had been horrendous and, more worryingly, she had mislaid an incriminating sheet of Jilly's notes. She couldn't handle the thought that she might have accidentally left it in Will's office so she kept telling herself she must have dropped it somewhere else.

Tessa decided to head back to her cottage and discard the Stella McCartney before trawling through the internet again to see if she could find anything incriminating about Rufus and Clemmie. Jilly's journalistic antennae were going into overdrive because she was sure there was scandal afoot. In fact, as Jilly charmingly put it, 'she could feel it in her water'.

Driving through the windy lanes towards Appleton Manor

with the roof down, Tessa wondered what lay behind her lack of passion for this particular job. She found herself unable to focus most days, confused by her apathy and distracted by the slightest thing.

Indulging herself for a moment, Tessa allowed her thoughts to drift to the novel she planned to write. Until now, she hadn't had much of an idea about the sort of story she wanted to create but something Henny had said about her glamorous French mother Gabrielle and her wild love affair with Alain whatsis-name had sparked Tessa's interest. Going the long way to the manor house, she started to sketch an idea out in her mind. A gorgeous woman with wild blond hair and pansy-coloured eyes, caught up in a passionate affair with her lover in Paris, and a grief-stricken husband vowing he would always love his departed wife. Leaving her car by the main house, Tessa strolled across the grass, happily allowing her mind to drift . . .

She pushed open the door of her cottage and almost had a heart attack. Sitting in an armchair with a glass of white wine in her hand, her ubiquitous laptop powered up and twinkling like a Christmas tree, was Jilly.

'There you are, kiddo.' Jilly sat back and regarded her shrewdly, her dark eyes like burnt currants. 'I wondered where you'd got to. JB said you finished filming a while ago.'

He's such a grass, thought Tessa as she tried to make sense of what was happening. Her boss. Was here. In Appleton. Jilly, who never ventured beyond W1.

'I was just passing, so I thought I'd pop in and see how you were getting on. Take a seat, Tessa – it's your cottage after all.' Jilly pointed to the armchair opposite, her stubby fingernails painted with her usual carmine polish. For a woman who lived on the edge, she was a creature of habit when it came to her personal appearance.

Wordlessly, Tessa did as she was told. In spite of the fact that it was eighty-five degrees outside, Jilly was dressed in one of her favourite navy Nicole Farhi suits, tailored to fit her lean frame like a glove, and a pair of contrasting Chanel heels.

'Sweet place,' Jilly said, her razor-sharp blond hair barely grazing her shoulders as she took a quick look around. 'And handy for you to nose around the manor house, I should imagine.'

'Very,' Tessa said, with a sinking feeling. She knew this couldn't be a passing visit. Jilly was here to check up on her. Which meant that Jilly didn't think she was cutting it . . . which meant she was in for an extremely hard time. Now probably wasn't the moment to mention that her notes about the Forbes-Henrys had gone missing, she guessed, letting a shaky breath out and doing her best to look unruffled.

'So, what have you found out, kiddo? JB tells me the interviews with Clemmie and Rufus have gone quite well so far.'

Tessa knew Jilly far too well to take this as a compliment. 'They have but there have been a few hairy moments. Today, for instance, Clemmie seemed to overreact a bit to a few of my questions and she even dangled her Oscar in front of me, metaphorically speaking. Which I took to mean she was rattled,' she explained when Jilly looked unimpressed.

'Oh?' Jilly sipped her wine musingly. 'It's Rufus we're really interested in though, isn't it? People have tried to dig up the dirt on Clemmie and no one's been able to find a single thing.' She gave Tessa a disparaging look. 'So I hardly think you'd be able to succeed where everyone else has failed, do you?'

Tessa pulled out a sheet she had printed off the internet at the bookshop. 'No, but don't you think that's weird?'

'What?'

'That no one can find a single thing about Clemmie that's remotely scandalous. That's got to be unheard of in this day and age, hasn't it?' Tessa pointed to the sheet in her hand. 'Clemmie said something today, she said "I'd tell myself that no matter what had happened to me . . . no matter how I had been judged, that one day I'd be somebody." *No matter what had happened to me . . . no matter how I'd been judged*, Jilly. And she's said things like that before. So I looked her up and this was what I found.'

Jilly impatiently snatched the paper from her and scanned it at high speed. 'What's the big deal about this? Clemmie landed the part of a lifetime aged twenty – everyone knows that. It's hardly the discovery of the century, Tessa.'

Tessa slapped her hand on the arm of the chair. 'That's the whole point! There's nothing that relates to Clemmie before she hit the big time. Nothing about the high school she attended or plays she might have showcased her early work in. There are no exposés from former boyfriends or dirty photographs lurking in the background.' She shook her head. 'Scandalous in Marilyn Monroe's day, I know, but it's par for the course to start off in *Playboy* in this era!'

Jilly rolled her eyes at the cliché.

Tessa wasn't going to give up without a fight. She knew Jilly wanted her to focus on Rufus but there was something about Clemmie that didn't fit. 'It's still odd, Jilly. What did Clemmie do before she became famous? Did she work in restaurants or bars? Was she a filing clerk with dreams of becoming an actress?' Her voice became impassioned. 'How many women achieve the impossible and land a lead part, first time? Not even kids who go to RADA do that!'

Without batting an eyelid, Jilly pointedly screwed the sheet of paper up into a tiny ball and tossed it over her shoulder. 'You're barking up the wrong tree, kiddo. It's Rufus we need to focus on. He's a good-looking kid with a just-about-passable talent to his credit, so he's bound to have done something heinous to get his foot on the ladder. Forget all this nonsense about Clemmie and focus on the task in hand, OK?'

Tessa blinked. She was stunned that Jilly had dismissed her so curtly. But hearing one of her negative, carping diatribes in this

137

peaceful environment rather than their busy London office suddenly made her indifference towards the documentary seem completely understandable.

Oblivious of Tessa's lack of enthusiasm, Jilly was in full flow. 'Now, what I'm interested in is this idea that Rufus was a total womaniser as a teenager. I need you to pursue that, to see if you can find any of his ex-girlfriends who might be prepared to do the dirty on him. Imagine one of them rolling up at the wedding shouting, "It could have been me!" Priceless . . .'

'I'm sure Clemmie would be over the moon if that happened,' Tessa said drily.

Jilly gave her a funny look. 'I'm sure Clemmie would get over it, Tessa. Hollywood marriages have a shelf life like sushi, you know that. Anyway, what about drugs? Do you think there's any chance Rufus is involved in those?'

Tessa shrugged. 'His behaviour is quite erratic at times and he was deep in conversation with the local drug dealer the other week. But it's small-time stuff – pot, not coke or anything heavy.' She tried not to show how bored she felt. Did any-one really care if Rufus had a drug problem? Shovelling down amphetamines with their daily toast and marmalade was as mundane for a celebrity as snorting lines with a thousand-dollar note.

'Hmmm.' Jilly was out of her chair and pacing round the room. 'We need to do better than that. Would Rufus have an affair, do you think? Is it worth putting out a honey trap?'

'A honey trap?'

'You know, where someone chats someone up, just to see if they take the bait or not and then—'

'I know what a honey trap is, Jilly,' Tessa said through gritted teeth. 'I just can't believe you'd even contemplate such a thing. Isn't that taking things too far?' As she said the words, Tessa thought she wouldn't put it past Jilly to suggest that *she* should be the honey trap.

Looking up, she saw Jilly contemplating her gravely. 'No way, Jilly! You've got to be kidding. There's no way I'm doing something like that!'

'OK, OK, keep your hair on.' Jilly threw herself into the armchair with bad grace. 'Christ, it's hot in here. I don't know how you put up with it.' She held up a sheaf of notes. 'And where the hell is the front sheet for these?' You haven't lost it, have you?'

Tessa leapt out of her chair and wrestled the notes from Jilly. It was inexcusable that she was here checking up on her like this! She had barged into her cottage unannounced, she was practically pimping her out to their resident movie star and now she was rifling through her notes like a second-rate detective, demanding to know where things were.

'Well?' Jilly voice became harsher than fingernails scraping down a blackboard. 'You know you can't let information like that out in the open, kiddo. You're supposed to be a professional, not a fucking novice.'

Tessa cast her eyes round the room wildly. The page had to be here, it simply had to be. Catching sight of something sticking out of her briefcase, she swooped down on it and yanked it free. It was here! About to triumphantly waft it under Jilly's nose, Tessa stopped dead. She hadn't even used her briefcase since she'd arrived; she carried her notes around loose or she used a clear folder.

So how had it got there? Had she left it in Will's office that day after all? With a slow realisation, Tessa understood that Will must have found it and returned it. He was on to her. He was going to make her life even more hellish from now on, Tessa thought dispiritedly. Maybe she should introduce him to Jilly. They'd get along like a bloody house on fire.

'My notes are all here, Jilly,' she said, dropping into her chair wearily. She had never felt more disillusioned than she did right now. 'I'll see what I can find out about Rufus, and I'll do my very best to find someone who can march into the church and ruin the happiest day of their lives – how does that sound?'

'Good girl,' Jilly drawled, totally missing the sarcasm in Tessa's voice. 'I knew I could rely on you. Now, before I phone Wilkins to drive me back to London, do you have any more of this delectable white wine in the fridge?'

'Bloody hell, these people really *piss* me off!'

Clemmie serenely smoothed Crème de la Mer body lotion over her pale feet and didn't react to Rufus's comment. She was sitting at her heavily lit dressing table which dominated almost half of one wall of their bedroom. The room wasn't as large as the open-plan affair in LA which had floor-to-ceiling windows and a Bose stereo system built into the headboard of the bed, but it had a romantic four-poster bed decked out in exquisite Gingerlily mulberry silk sheets from Harrods and a picture window which afforded them a stunning view of Appleton. And that was something you couldn't put a price on, she thought with pleasure, drinking in the glorious view bathed in pinkish evening light. She stole a glance at Rufus. They probably made an incongruous couple, her reclining in a scarlet kimono she had been given on a promotional tour of Japan, and Rufus clad only in jeans and cowboy boots, but even though they didn't exactly encapsulate the image of a country couple at home, Clemmie couldn't help relishing the sense of cosy familiarity it gave her.

She jumped as Rufus swore again loudly. His dark flowing hair was a mess, probably because he kept clutching at it as he pored over a story in the *Sun*. He had been pontificating about the injustice of something for the past ten minutes – unusual behaviour for a man who tended to find it hard to drag his eyes away from Page Three – and his brown eyelinered eyes were sparkling with new-found animation as he let out another indignant exclamation.

'Who pisses you off, darling?' Clemmie said indulgently as she tipped more lotion into her hands. The body lotion cost over two hundred dollars a bottle which was absolutely obscene in the scheme of things, but it smelt like heaven and made her skin feel as if she was seventeen again so these days she swallowed the cost and enjoyed it.

'These criminals!'

What on earth had got him so rattled? Clemmie set the bottle down as Rufus sat up and slapped the newspaper with some force.

'They get shut away for doing the most horrendous things and then they get to walk free, like nothing happened.' He turned accusing eyes towards her as if it was her fault such things were going on in the world.

Clemmie shrugged. 'Surely they've served their time if they've been to prison, honey?'

'Yes, but you know what the bloody legal system's like these days! They get sent down for ridiculously short sentences and then they get let out early for good behaviour. Good behaviour – that's a joke! How can you be well-behaved in prison? By not killing anyone else accidentally?'

'Is that what they did then, kill someone accidentally?' She twisted her body away from him.

Rufus didn't notice the tension in her shoulders.

'Yes! These kids killed someone when they were young and now they're out of jail and able to start a new life without anyone knowing who they are or what they've done. Do they have a right to do that after what they did to this poor woman?'

Clemmie felt her skin prickle all over. She got up and retied the belt of her kimono. 'I don't know, hon. It's not for us to decide what happens when someone does something wrong. But you said it was an accident . . .'

'So what?' roared Rufus, tossing his newspaper aside like a

teenager. 'I just don't think people should be able to literally get away with murder.'

'Manslaughter,' Clemmie offered tentatively.

'What?'

'I think it's called manslaughter when you kill someone by accident.'

Rufus narrowed his eyes until he was all dark lashes and sweeping eyeliner. 'I'm not *stupid* you know.' He did toffee-nosed haughtiness better than anyone she knew.

Clemmie regarded him. 'I know you're not stupid,' the words came out slowly, 'but I never knew you were so judgemental.' She couldn't believe it of him; Rufus was so laidback normally. Clemmie remembered the day they had met on the set of the film they were both in, a romantic comedy that involved their characters seducing each other as part of a con before falling head over heels in love. An unoriginal script but a box office smash, saved by some genuinely touching moments and their undeniable on-screen chemistry.

They were soon a couple for real, spending every day together and being photographed wherever they went. Clemmie had been smitten with Rufus, at first swept away by his good looks, his swoonsome British accent and his ability to make her laugh. As their relationship developed, she realised she was under his spell completely, caught up in his zest for life and his huge appetite for adventure. Their engagement had made Clemmie happier than she had ever thought possible, and the decision to move to England and spend time in a romantic country house had sealed the deal as far as she was concerned.

Rufus stood in front of her, his bare, hairless chest exposed, his hands on his slim hips, and Clemmie was overwhelmed with love for him. But suddenly she saw him in a different light; he was a mere *boy*, she thought, shocked. Rufus might be in his thirties but he was immature, unprepared for the reality of life. He lived in a world of great wealth and fame but he was spoilt and childish, as if everything had come easily to him, just as Jack had said.

Unexpectedly, Clemmie found herself comparing Rufus to Jack Forbes-Henry. Maybe Jack had let himself go and most likely he was emotionally stunted beyond repair, but there was something *manly* about him. That was it; Rufus was a boy and Jack was all man – virile, chivalrous and bold.

She remembered the day at Appleton Manor when she had sat back in that fabulous old Rolls-Royce Phantom of his. She had felt so relaxed and free – until Jack had carefully questioned Rufus's commitment to the relationship. Had he been trying to warn her that Rufus might not deliver on his promises? Or were they simply the words of an embittered old man who was so jaded by love, he couldn't see the real thing if it kicked him up the butt?

Feeling chilly all of a sudden in spite of the evening sunshine, Clemmie's fingers tightened around the neck of her kimono. Jack wasn't a lost cause. He knew what real love was, otherwise he wouldn't be so devastated by Caro's appalling behaviour.

Aware she was tiptoeing into dangerous territory, Clemmie dared to voice her growing fears. 'What if our children did something like that, Rufus? Killed someone by accident, made a mistake. Would you turn your back on them? Would you throw them out of the house without a thought and never let them darken the door again?'

'*Our* children?' Rufus's voice grated uneasily, the words sputtering out jerkily. 'What children?'

Clemmie rounded on him. 'You know I want children! We may not have discussed it in detail but there have been so many conversations about settling down here in England and starting a family. Are you saying you don't want that?'

'Of course I want that.' Rufus stared at her, chewing his lip.

Clemmie felt oddly mesmerised by his reaction. Inside, she was fuming, she felt as if she might erupt into a savage rant about how he had led her on and let her down, promising something he couldn't deliver. But on the outside, she felt detached and she couldn't help noticing the way his Adam's apple bobbed in his throat when he felt trapped. Or when he was lying, she realised with a flash of insight.

Her stomach lurched with disappointment and loss. Rufus might not ever be mature enough to be a father.

Mortified to find tears running down her cheeks, Clemmie abruptly turned her back on him.

Rufus sidled up behind her and slipped his hands down the V of her kimono.

'Aw, don't get all moody,' he cajoled, his fingers circling her nipples with languorous movements. He squeezed her full breasts with intent and ground his pelvis against her bottom, his erection prodding at her belligerently.

She smacked his hand away smartly and spun round. 'I'm not "getting all moody", as you put it,' she advised him curtly. 'I'm just not interested in sex right now, OK?'

'Why the hell not?'

Rufus wasn't used to rejection and the crotch of his black jeans still bulged expectantly.

'I think you need to think about what you want out of this relationship.'

'What the fuck does that mean?'

Clemmie was shaken by his challenging tone but she stood her ground. 'Just that. I think you need to decide if you really want to be with me and live this life together. I've been clear about what I want, and I need to know you're clear about what you want.'

Rufus put his hands on his hips, seemingly about to rage back at her. Changing his mind, he stuck his head in the wardrobe and grabbed a black T-shirt. Pulling it over his head and ducking down to look in the mirror, he began teasing his dark hair into unruly spikes.

'What are you doing?' She watched him apply a liberal dose of hairspray.

'Figuring out what I want.'

His tone was aggravating, distant and cocksure.

'And what's that?'

'A pint of Guinness,' he told her, grabbing his keys from the bedside table.

'Hey!' She was at his side in seconds, her face stained with anger, her kimono gaping open and giving Rufus an unadulterated view of a perfectly formed, creamy breast. 'Don't you dare walk out on me!'

Rufus wondered if Clemmie had ever looked as desirable as she did right now. Anger had pulled her Texan drawl to the fore so her words oozed out like butterscotch, and her flushed cheeks and heaving, naked chest only added to the erotic image. Ferociously turned on but stubbornly determined not to give in, Rufus turned away from her as if she left him cold. And they said he couldn't act.

'Watch me,' he snapped arrogantly.

Stalking out, he left Clemmie staring after him, aghast.

At the pub, Rufus took a seat at the bar and ordered a pint of Guinness. He wished he'd worn his cowboy hat. Not only did it partially disguise his identity, it also made him look like a Guess model in his not-so-humble opinion. He checked no one was staring at him and sipped his pint morosely.

He and Clemmie had never rowed before and they had certainly never got to the stage where one of them had stormed out like this. The talk of children had seriously unnerved him but he knew he only had himself to blame. Clemmie had made her feelings on that subject clear and although she could be accused of not pushing him for a definitive answer, Rufus knew he was guilty of deliberately not offering one. The truth of the matter was that he didn't know if he wanted kids or not. Proposing had been unexpected enough and marriage was equally alien as a concept; the idea of children was a conundrum his brain simply couldn't untangle for the time being.

'Fancy some company?'

Turning at the throaty voice, Rufus found a tall girl at his side. She had ginger hair down to her bum and she wore skinny jeans with a cropped pink T-shirt that revealed a flat stomach and a sparkly belly button chain. Her heavily fake-tanned face was vaguely familiar to him but he couldn't quite place her.

'Er . . . have we met?'

'I'm India. I was at Appleton Manor the other day when you were doing some filming. I'm Milly Forbes-Henry's friend.'

Of course she was. He barely remembered Milly – full of teenage promise, if memory served him correctly, but with rather too much puppy fat and attitude for his taste – but India, with her long legs and knowing eyes, had made more of an impression on him. He had met far prettier girls than India but Clemmie's rejection of him had left his erection and his ego irrevocably deflated. He needed a boost.

Rufus slid into flirt mode smoothly, effortlessly turning on the Hollywood charm he was so well-known for.

'I should warn you, I'm in a terribly grumpy mood so I can't promise to be very good company.'

India looked unabashed and she gave him one of her hundred-watt grins. 'Don't worry, I'll cheer you up. And that's a promise.' She settled her tiny bottom on the stool next to him.

'Aren't you a little young to be in a pub?'

India's slanting eyes twinkled at him. 'I know the owner. Besides, I look young, but I'm not.'

'Really?'

She smiled. She wasn't going to let on that her sixteenth

birthday was still a few weeks away. 'Now, are you going to buy me a drink or not?'

Rufus was attracted to her confidence and he couldn't help smiling back at her. 'That depends. What do you drink? Something girly like vodka with cranberry?'

India chuckled. 'No thanks. I'll have what you're having.'

'A Guinness? Are you sure?' Rufus had never met a girl who drank Guinness before. Pleased, he ordered another pint. He still felt uptight about the incident with Clemmie but now that India was here, he was slowly starting to unwind. He watched her sip her pint delicately, enjoying the way she licked creamy foam from her upper lip in a way that was both ladylike and lascivious at the same time.

He didn't have time to dwell on his row for much longer as India turned the tables on him and fired questions at him relentlessly. He answered them laughingly, occasionally dazzled by her bluntness but nonetheless enjoying himself enormously.

'What was it like working with Brad Pitt?' she demanded, referring to the small part in an action movie he had shagged a female producer to get.

'Intimidating. The guy's a hero – a brilliant actor and a handsome bastard.'

'Too right. Have you ever shagged someone to get a part?'

'Yes. For the aforementioned Brad Pitt movie.'

'Wow!' India was impressed. 'You didn't have to shag Brad Pitt, did you?'

'No.' He grimaced. 'But that would have been preferable. The lady in question nearly suffocated me with her enormous thighs.' He shuddered comically.

'Eughhh! Are Clemmie's breasts real?'

Rufus's mouth twitched. 'They're . . . out of this world and that's all I'm prepared to say. Next question.'

'Is she good in bed?'

'Don't ask if you don't want to hear the truth,' Rufus murmured, feeling a momentary stab of disloyalty about Clemmie who was probably sobbing at home. 'She's ... dynamite. A class act.'

India's face was the picture of worldly innocence. 'Class doesn't automatically guarantee a good blow job.'

Rufus let out a scream of laughter. 'What do you know about blow jobs at your age?'

She gave him a sideways glance that seared into him and made his groin stir as if it had been fired up with jump leads.

'Plenty, actually.' India stretched, drawing his attention to the thrilling sight of her nubile, bra-less breasts jiggling freely in her tight T-shirt. She screwed her nose up as she thought of another question. 'Do you have a stunt double for your nude shots?'

'Absolutely not! I'm like Mel Gibson, I do all my own bum work.'

'Mel Gibson? He's so *old*.'

'Careful, you're giving away how young you are.'

India ignored him and drained her pint. 'My round.' She leant over the bar, giving him a view of her denim-clad bum cheeks, and put her order in. She shot a look at Rufus, her eyes registering his interest in her body matter-of-factly. 'Didn't I say I'd cheer you up?'

'You did,' Rufus told her with a wide smile. 'And you have.'

The sight of India's tanned breasts straining to break free from her cropped T-shirt was enough to put him in a sunny mood, let alone her nonchalant manner and obvious flirtatiousness.

Turning his stool to face her, Rufus pushed any thoughts of his fiancée from his mind and focused on India. She might be jailbait and not up to his usual standard, looks-wise, but she was here and in spite of her laid-back manner, she obviously thought he was a god.

Rufus had a feeling he and India were going to be very good friends indeed.

'Are you serious? Your boss just turned up unannounced then tried to pimp you out to Rufus?'

Sophie burst into a peal of laughter as Tessa giggled and poured out chilled glasses of Sancerre. She was sitting at Sophie's dining table which was set up for lunch at one end and littered with Gil's design drawings, Ruby's sketches and various colouring pencils at the other. They had taken to having lunch together a couple of times a week, and after Jilly's impromptu visit, Tessa had felt in need of some of Sophie's no-nonsense humour.

She admired Sophie's gorgeous linen trousers and Chloe top, feeling slightly dowdy in her jeans and flip-flops. 'Jilly is awful. She genuinely wants me to find someone who can ruin Clemmie's wedding day. I mean, what sort of person does that?'

'Frankly, someone appalling! It's no wonder you're feeling disillusioned with the whole thing,' Sophie said reassuringly as she threw some tiger prawns into a bowl of spinach and dressed everything with some olive oil. 'And this JB sounds like a nightmare too – who made him king of the castle?'

'God knows. He can't decide whether to tell me off for getting too close to the Forbes-Henry family or to wind me up about "losing my touch", the arrogant bastard.'

'*Bastard*,' Sophie agreed equably.

Tessa smiled and chinked glasses with her, her mood improving by the second. She was glad she'd found a friend in Appleton; even though her friends from home were keeping in touch and phoning regularly, she missed having proper, face-to-face girly chats with them. Sophie had the same sense of humour and she could always be relied upon to listen to her woes and cheer her up.

Tessa sat back and looked round the house Sophie and Gil were renting. It was large but homely and it felt comfortably lived in. Ruby had a little play area by the back door of the kitchen which had teeny pink seats like the chairs Tessa remembered from school and a wooden doll's house with cute furniture and tiny people in gingham frocks. In the main living area, Sophie had added richly coloured cushions and throws in mocha browns and midnight blues to contrast with the dove-grey and cream walls, and some small framed sketches added character.

'Is this how you and Gil met?' Tessa asked as she admired an ink sketch of a pansy that had Sophie's signature next to it. 'You have an amazing flair when it comes to all this arty stuff. Wow, you actually did all these sketches?'

'Yes, I did. Nothing fancy, just a hobby. I worked for Gil for a while at his London-based firm before Ruby was born.'

'This could be more than a hobby – you're really talented. It's a shame you didn't go to art school.'

Sophie put two bowls of salad on the table and hoped her hair would hide her blushes. Tessa wasn't to know but she *had* attended art school years ago in Appleton, for a while at least. She changed the subject. 'Why would JB be concerned about you getting too close to the Forbes-Henry family? Why would that even happen?'

Tessa shrugged. 'Part of this kind of job involves getting in with the family. After all, we're trampling all over their house and it helps to have them on side.' Her face clouded over as she remembered her run-in with Will the other week. 'I honestly don't know why JB's getting so het up about it. Will Forbes-Henry is giving me such a hard time, hell will freeze over before he and I get cosy.'

'Really?' Sophie looked puzzled. 'But Will's very fair most of the time.' She bit her lip. 'I mean, that's what Gil told me anyway, but he could be wrong, of course.'

150

Tessa rolled her eyes. 'Oh, don't worry, everyone seems to think Will is some sort of hero, it's just me that can't stand him. It's really aggravating; even Milly thinks the sun shines out of his backside and she's notoriously hard to please.'

Sophie hid a smile. She remembered meeting a young Milly years ago and Tessa was right, she wasn't easily won over.

'At least Tristan's lovely,' Tessa sighed. 'He's funny and flirtatious and he's really taking my mind off everything at the moment.'

Sophie bristled; she couldn't help it. Any mention of Tristan sent her into a tailspin. And the thought of Tristan flirting with Tessa was enough to put her off her tiger prawns. She put her fork down.

'If only I wasn't so focused on work,' Tessa continued carelessly, wondering why Sophie seemed to have lost her appetite. 'I'm just not interested in men right now. I mean, Tristan's fun and all that and great for my ego, especially after the bastard I was seeing before I came here shat on me from a great height. But boyfriend material?' She screwed her nose up. 'I think not.'

Sophie picked up her fork again. 'Isn't Tristan the one who has tons of girlfriends? I'm sure Gil mentioned that he had a bit of a reputation.'

'I have no idea,' Tessa said, giving her a sideways glance. Why was Sophie acting so strangely? She seemed nervous and her hand was moving jerkily over her salad. 'I don't even know Tristan that well so I can't say I've paid much attention to his previous love life.'

Sophie smiled widely, returning to normal. 'And why would you? That sounds like Gil and Ruby.' She jumped up to greet them and was almost knocked flying as Ruby rushed into her arms. Her cheeks were flushed and she was wearing pink shorts and a strappy white top. With her mop of blond hair, she looked like a miniature angel; all she needed was a teeny harp and a golden halo.

'Tessa!' she cried, clearly pleased to see her again. She climbed on to her lap, showing her a picture of a dragon with bulging eyes she had painted at summer school. She smelt of fresh air and radiated childish good health.

Wearing a peach-coloured shirt and his favourite tight white jeans, Gil kissed Sophie before giving Tessa a sunny smile. 'How lovely to see you again, Tessa. I hear that filming is going well.'

'Yes, it's going very well, thank you.'

'And you do remember that I am more than happy to offer my services if you'd like details about the hotel renovation?'

Sophie nudged him. 'Gil!'

'What?' He looked at her quizzically, not sure what was wrong with the question.

'Gil says dragons aren't blue,' Ruby pouted.

Gil looked pained. 'I just thought green might have been better . . .' he started.

Ruby looked put out. Tessa was about to shoot Gil a withering look before she realised he wasn't being critical, he just didn't know how to deal with children. Personally, she thought Ruby's painting was rather accomplished for her age – childish, naturally, but full of imagination and the dragon was a surprisingly good shape.

Gil, however, was already preoccupied with the manor house renovation again. 'Now, I need to finish the penthouses. The sunken baths haven't arrived yet, can you believe that? And I must remember to order the rose petals to float in them for the summer party . . .' He grabbed a notepad and started scribbling his thoughts down.

Ruby pulled a face at Gil and Tessa was suddenly jolted. There was something about Ruby's haughty look, the snub nose held high in the air and the blue eyes dancing with disdain that reminded her of someone . . . Try as she might, though, the face evaded her. Tessa shrugged the thought off. She must have imagined it.

'I see you've hired Nathan,' she said, watching the gardener make short work of a troublesome hedge with his phallic strimmer.

Gil stopped scribbling on his notepad and stared. 'What? When?'

'You told me to hire a gardener,' Sophie reminded him mildly, pouring a glass of milk for Ruby. 'He's supposed to be excellent.'

'Right. Yes. I suppose it makes sense. Don't let him in the house though, will you?' Gil wiped his forehead with a flowery silk handkerchief. 'He's got a . . . a bit of a reputation, that's all.'

'Tessa told me.' Sophie gazed out at Nathan's rippling muscles. 'Don't worry, Gil, he's not my type.'

'Right. Of course not. No need to worry then.' Frowning as Nathan stripped his vest top off to reveal a bronzed torso, Gil turned away. 'See you later, Tessa, and remember what I said about filming. I'm available, any time.'

'I'll remember that,' she said, catching Sophie's eye.

As Gil left the room, they both got a serious attack of the giggles.

Chapter Ten

'Now, shall we have a raspberry meringue or one with passion fruit?' Henny asked as she lifted the perfectly whipped creation from its tray and placed it on a crystal cake stand.

Milly shrugged morosely. She had been at loggerheads with her mother for weeks now and even though she could tell that her mother was making an effort to still the waters between them, Milly couldn't seem to back down. Wearing shorts and a baby-pink halter-neck top, she was sitting at the oak kitchen table, surrounded by books to help her with her A level choices and her brain was aching with the effort of it.

'Passion fruit it is then.' Henny grimaced, starting to slather cream all over the meringue and coax it into place with a palette knife. She broke into a broad smile as she caught sight of Tristan pulling a mock-moody face behind Milly's back and chided him silently. He was sprawled across a battered old sofa at the end of the kitchen, with Austin across his knees. Bathed in sunlight from the open back door and kept cool by a vast fan, Tristan's golden head was lit up like a beacon as he devoured a well-thumbed Jilly Cooper. In spite of lunch being less than an hour away, he was consuming tortilla chips with equal gusto.

'Is Tessa coming then?' he asked with his mouth full.

'As soon as she's finished filming,' Henny confirmed. 'I couldn't believe she has to work on Sundays but it seems that director JB is a bit of a taskmaster.' Her mouth twisted bitterly as she remembered the way JB had casually winked at her after manhandling Caro. She and Caro hadn't spoken about it since but judging by the way Caro kept disappearing without explanation, her affair with JB was in full flow. Henny couldn't put her finger on why she was so worried about this particular indiscretion but she couldn't help thinking Caro had gone too far this time. Jack was playing games of his own but to Henny's knowledge he had never been disrespectful enough to conduct an affair on his own doorstep. She hoped her brother was all right.

'Tessa!' Henny caught sight of her in the doorway wearing a mint-green wrap-around dress and flip-flops. 'Do come in. You look beautiful in that dress, so summery. You remind me of a mint julep.'

'Thanks, and thank you for inviting me to lunch. It's great to be away from the film crew for a bit. We're living in each other's pockets at the moment.' Tessa could see a couple of lamb loins with peppered crusts cooling in the corner and the delicious aroma was making her mouth water. She wondered why Henny was wearing such an unflattering floral overall and made a mental note to herself to give her a lavish makeover as soon as she could squeeze it in. 'Can I do anything to help?'

Henny flapped a hand covered in cream in the direction of the table. 'Thank you, darling, but no, everything's under control. Have a seat and sorry about all the books all over the place.' She felt rather than saw Milly scowl at her and she could have kicked herself for sounding as if she was nit-picking about the mess.

Taking a seat next to Milly at the table, Tessa immediately felt the stresses of the morning slipping away. JB, no doubt fired up by Jilly's recent visit, had been sniping at her all morning, having the audacity to stop the filming session with Clemmie eight times to query Tessa's choice of questions. She felt thoroughly compromised by his presence, not to mention embarrassed at being shown up in front of Clemmie who, thankfully, had been as gracious as ever and had shown herself to be unbelievably patient and sympathetic throughout.

Tessa hadn't been sure about accepting Henny's offer of lunch; after all, Will might show up and that would be awkward. But turning it down would have sounded ungrateful and she didn't want to offend Henny who had been nothing but kind and friendly towards her.

She took a good look around the homely kitchen, feeling herself unwinding as the welcoming sight and smells drifted over her. The kitchen was vast, with a fireplace occupying an entire wall and a double oven and Aga dominating the L-shape next to it. Shiny but much-used copper pots hung from hooks on the side of the fireplace and strange-looking cooking utensils sat in fat cream pots dotted along the scrubbed wooden worktops. There was a smell of passion fruit and baking scones in the air, and on the worktop next to the Aga, Henny's pile of cookery books were stacked, post-it notes poking out of several pages, covered in personal comments and ideas. It was a proper, family kitchen, and completely unfamiliar to Tessa who had never experienced anything like it.

She was suddenly poleaxed by a suffocating wave of loneliness. Since her mother had died, she hadn't sat down and enjoyed a family lunch of any description; gourmet brunches in Putney with her glamorous friends weren't really the same thing.

'Help me choose my bloody, *bloody* A levels,' Milly beseeched, letting out a dramatic sigh. 'I'm about to top myself.'

Tessa shook herself out of her reverie and tugged Milly's school prospectus towards her. 'Shouldn't you have chosen them already? And between you and me, they're really not worth topping yourself over, hon.'

'But it's such a nightmare! I picked French, Physics and Maths because they're easy and I'd get the best grades in those subjects. I was going to read French at university, you see, like David plans to.' The scattering of freckles across Milly's nose had turned amber from the sun and her platinum hair swung loose around her shoulders.

Milly frowned up at the ceiling at the sound of something heavy breaking, followed by Gil screeching at the top of his voice. 'That designer drives me nuts. How he's managed to convince anyone to marry him is totally beyond me. Have you met his mysterious fiancée yet?'

Tessa burst out laughing. 'Why is she mysterious?'

'No one's met her or seen her so we all think he's telling porkies,' Milly said darkly, tapping the side of her nose the way she had seen people do in films.

'She does exist and she's absolutely ravishing, actually. I'm good friends with her, we have lunch a few times a week.'

'That's put paid to my other theory then.' Milly didn't elaborate but she winced as Gil's voice permeated through the house like a banshee. 'How anyone is supposed to concentrate with that racket going on is beyond me.'

'You should definitely do French,' Tessa approved, blushing as Tristan tore himself away from his book to blow her an exaggerated kiss. 'You'd ace it. But what's the problem with choosing your A levels anyway?'

Milly twiddled a lock of hair between her fingers contemplatively. 'I might want to read English instead now, you see. So I'm thinking of swapping Physics for English Language and Lit but it means I have to read all these dull Shakespeare plays and bloody awful poems.' She gestured to the musty-smelling pile of books she had commandeered from the manor library.

'Shakespeare plays aren't dull,' Tessa said, astonished. She picked up *The Tempest* and flicked through it. 'I loved doing Shakespeare at school. And poetry can be wonderful. Granted, it depends on the poet but there are so many great ones out there. A good English teacher can make all the difference too.'

'You're so right,' Henny murmured as she spooned passion

fruit purée over the cream-topped meringue. 'Mine was fabulous. He made Shakespeare come alive for me and I developed the most enormous crush on him after he read Benedick's part in *Much Ado About Nothing*—'

'Too much information, Mother!' Milly interrupted, making loud vomiting noises.

'I was about to say,' Henny turned her bright blue eyes in Milly's direction, 'that people are divided into two camps where Shakespeare is concerned. Those who get him and those who don't. And those who don't will insist that he's boring and verbose and full of flowery prose. I agree with Tessa, you just need a good English teacher to show you the beauty of the words.'

Milly shot her a sour look. 'I *get* Shakespeare,' she muttered as she took *The Tempest* from Tessa unenthusiastically. 'I never said I didn't *get* him.'

'Why the change of plans?' Tessa inquired, hoping to diffuse the tension between Milly and Henny. She noticed that the open page of Milly's diary was covered with love hearts and 'Emilia Penry-Jones' scrawled across them in pink pen. The one-sided love affair with Freddie was obviously still going strong.

Milly closed her diary hurriedly, her fingers fumbling with the lock as she blushed. 'I've decided not to major in French because I want to be a journalist now.'

Tessa reeled with horror. 'What? Why on earth would you want to be a journalist when you could be anything you wanted to be! You're so clever – you speak fluent French, you find maths easy. You could be a . . . an astronaut or a . . . a bilingual . . . something or other . . .'

Milly gawped at her as if she was mad. 'I thought you loved your job! You've inspired me, I want to be like you.'

'Do you?' Tessa said feebly, wondering if Milly would feel the same if she'd seen JB putting her down like some inexperienced

158

ingénue – or witnessed her creeping around the manor house like a spy from a James Bond movie, trying desperately to find something to get Jilly off her back.

Christ, how awful that Milly wanted to change careers because of her! It made Tessa want to shake her hard until she changed her mind back to doing something less . . . less seedy and soul-destroying.

Milly glanced at Tristan who was making eyes at Tessa over the top of his Jilly Cooper. Milly's eyes danced mischievously and she lowered her voice marginally. 'How are things going with my dishy cousin? Have you done the deed yet?'

'The deed?' Tessa echoed, trying to ignore Tristan who was sucking tortilla chip dust off his fingers in a highly suggestive manner.

'You know . . . *sex*,' Milly said impatiently, rolling her eyes.

Tessa frowned. She and Tristan had spent some time together but they had barely kissed, let alone anything else, and she couldn't see it happening any time soon either. She stole another glance at him, watching the rays of the sun turn his cap of longish blond curls golden. She was still sticking to her decision to steer clear of men but Tristan was handsome and funny and he massaged her ego in the most delicious way.

But was she seriously considering starting something up with him? Tessa didn't think so. She couldn't possibly, she had far too much on her plate and, besides, she just didn't feel that way about him. Both Henny and Sophie had also hinted at Tristan having some sort of chequered love life and she had been hurt quite enough over Adam not to want to get her fingers burnt again.

'Your cousin is . . . lovely,' she said diplomatically, not wanting to squash Milly's enthusiasm for match-making, knowing it was probably because she had such a thumping great crush on Freddie. 'He's very . . . handsome.'

Milly seemed satisfied with her answer and changed the

subject. 'I reckon India's had sex but she won't admit it.' She almost helped herself to Tristan's crisps but, remembering her good intentions about losing weight in case she got caught on camera, she made a monumental effort to get excited about an apple. She bit into it with small, white teeth, her expression disgruntled. 'India's being all secretive at the moment which usually means she's up to something. She keeps hanging round some smelly old pub in the next village because someone mentioned seeing Rufus in there with Will ages ago.'

'Are they still good friends?' Tessa asked tentatively. 'Will and Rufus, I mean?'

'I think so.' Milly shrugged, dipping into *The Tempest* with more determination. 'I don't know much about Rufus, to be honest, or his relationship with Will. I know they used to play rugby together but Will never talks about Rufus because he's worried we'll tell you about it.' She grinned endearingly at Tessa whose smile faded. 'So I can't help you there, I'm afraid. I used to think Rufus was gorgeous before I met him, but now I wonder if he wears make-up. Men wearing make-up is such a turn-off.' Her mind flitted around like a butterfly as she forgot the conversation and focused her attention on *The Tempest*. 'Who's this Caliban nutter?'

'Caliban is a figure of fun, a sort of comic wild man,' Tessa explained, feeling antagonistic towards Will all over again. She also couldn't help noticing how vulnerable Milly looked when she wasn't giving off attitude. 'The Duke, Prospero, enslaves him and torments him for trying to rape his beautiful daughter, Miranda. Yet he has some of the most eloquent and moving speeches in the whole play so he's actually more of an integral character than you might think.'

Listening with a rapt expression, Milly turned back to the first page. Forgetting about her apple, she fell silent as she starting reading the play properly.

'I bet this is much more fun,' Tristan grinned, holding up his novel. 'Although I guess it wouldn't get you a degree in journalism. Shame. I could write an excellent essay on this. It would be very naughty, all about buttery caverns and willies like conga eels.'

Henny shot him a disapproving look and poured Tessa a glass of homemade lemonade. 'Ignore him.' She glanced at Milly who was reading *The Tempest* with more interest than she had ever shown for English before.

'Help me with these lamb loins,' Henny said softly, beckoning Tessa over to the Aga. She pushed a chopping board towards Tessa and stole another look at Milly. 'You're really good with her, darling. If I told her it'd be a good idea to study English, she'd probably become a mathematician instead.'

Tessa was full of sympathy. 'Sorry, Henny. I can only think she's swayed by the glitz and glamour of my job. Such as it is.'

'No need to apologise,' Henny told her, arranging slices of perfectly roasted pink lamb on a huge platter. Her voice sounded as if it might crack. 'Milly's as obstinate as her father was. And anyway, I'm just glad you're getting through to her. She doesn't seem to have many positive influences in her life, what with India as her best friend and Freddie as *amour de jour*.'

'Oh, you know about that?'

Henny heaped Tessa's slightly chunkier lamb slices on to the platter and wiped her hands on a tea towel. 'Of course!' She lowered her voice again. 'Milly thinks she's very sophisticated and clever but she's more like me than she'd care to admit – she wears her heart on her sleeve, always has done. David reckons Freddie doesn't even know she exists but I think he's a nice boy underneath all the charm and posturing. And very handsome, in a pop star kind of a way, with those dangerous blue eyes and floppy black hair. I can see why Milly's head over heels.'

Tessa looked sceptical and wondered whether or not to enlighten Henny about Freddie's after-school activities.

'Oh, I know all about the drug dealing,' Henny informed her briskly. 'Please don't be shocked. I happen to know most of his stash ends up with a couple of old boys Jack knows from the next village. They're rich, bored and still trying to prove they've got life in them by smoking dope and having drunken parties. Young Freddie is harmless enough; he just needs to grow up a bit. If he was dealing in something stronger than pot, I'd be concerned, but I honestly don't think it's going to progress beyond that.'

Tessa nodded in agreement. She was beginning to realise there was more to Henny than she had first thought. She was as sweet and good as she appeared but she was also far smarter than she let on.

'It's strange to think of Rufus getting married before Will,' Henny mused rather abruptly and Tessa could see where Milly got her butterfly mind from. Milly and Henny really were very alike; Milly just didn't want to acknowledge it. She watched Henny add a generous slab of butter to some new potatoes and chop mint into the bowl. 'Rufus was always the one who had four girlfriends on the go when they were kids whereas Will didn't have many and then never more than one at the same time. We were quite taken aback when he proposed after such a short courtship but Claudette is perfect for him – beautiful, charming, chic.'

'I've seen photographs of her,' Tessa nodded, feeling nauseated.

'So you know how glamorous and lovely she is. They seem to have so much in common, too. Claudette loves the same food and poetry and everything else. I think the love of France helps,' Henny volunteered, nudging her frizzy blonde hair out of her eyes and revealing a sunburnt forehead. 'Will and his grandmother Gabrielle had such a wonderful relationship, you see, and they used to jabber away in French together all the time. And Claudette is so *good* for Will, she gets him to relax away from work and have fun.'

Tessa couldn't help feeling inadequate in comparison to the absent Claudette; Henny was making her sound like an absolute goddess.

'Even *I* like Claudette,' Milly announced crushingly as she looked up from her book, 'and I hardly like anyone. Apart from you, of course.' She gave Tessa a winsome smile.

'You and Claudette are disgustingly chummy,' Tristan remarked. 'But I think it might have more to do with that Gucci handbag she gave you than anything else.'

Milly stuck her tongue out. 'Shut up. Claudette's like a sister to me. She makes time to listen to me which is more than *you* lot ever do.' She turned to Tessa. 'You're great too, and don't listen to Tris, he's the only one who doesn't get excited when Claudette visits. I can't understand it; how can one person take a dislike to someone when everyone else raves about them?'

Tessa understood the notion completely.

'Claudette can make the summer party, after all,' Will informed them cheerfully as he ambled into the kitchen, his broad shoulders seeming to take over the whole room. He was wearing baggy navy shorts and a cobalt-blue polo top that accentuated his tan and he looked reasonably relaxed for once. He shot Tessa an impassive look but, to her immense relief, made no reference to the notes she had left in his office.

'That's wonderful news, darling,' Henny said vaguely, handing him a saucepan of sugar snap peas. 'Drain those for me, would you? I've got some of that mouth-watering Shropshire blue you love so much and a big slice of cheddar to have with some pear slices and chutney.'

'I love it when you spoil me.' Will grinned, dumping the sugar snap peas in a bowl. He squinted at a menu Henny had pinned to the fridge. 'What's this? Ideas for Clemmie and Rufus's Christmas wedding breakfast?' His eyes slid to Tessa briefly then back to the menu. 'Why is there a question mark next to the sorbet?'

'To sorbet, or not to sorbet,' Milly intoned solemnly.

She sniggered and Tessa couldn't help joining in. She was amazed when Will chuckled loudly and elbowed Milly like a kid; she hadn't detected even the slightest glimmer of a sense of humour before now.

Henny waited patiently for their giggles to subside before answering. 'Well, yes, actually, that is the question. Is sorbet still trendy these days, or is it terribly old-fashioned? Or is it just . . .'

'Wanky?' Milly suggested helpfully. 'And don't say trendy, Mother, it makes you sound like an old fuddy-duddy.'

'Oh, I do beg your pardon,' Henny retorted with more than a hint of sarcasm. 'But I *am* an old fuddy-duddy, so I shall say what I like. And while we're laying our cards on the table, young lady, I don't want you to say wanky. It makes you sound like your friend India and she's not exactly known for her manners.'

Milly did a double take. 'Bloody hell, who gave you some balls?'

'I'm . . . I'm not sure.' Henny looked as if she might have unnerved herself with her comeback and she turned away and started heaping buttery potatoes around the lamb slices. 'But I'd still prefer it if you didn't say wanky, darling.'

Milly was so stunned she didn't even answer her back.

'Well, that told you, didn't it?' Will tweaked the book out of Milly's hands curiously. 'I thought you hated Shakespeare, Mills. You told me Romeo was a whingeing turd who deserved to die.'

Milly giggled. 'Romeo was *such* a dweeb. But I've decided I'm going to be a journalist and Tessa reckons I should get to grips with literature so I'm giving it a go.'

Will gave Tessa a tight-lipped smile and handed the book back. 'A journalist. Interesting. I wonder where you got *that* idea from.'

'I didn't suggest it,' Tessa defended herself hotly. 'I told her to be an astronaut or something bilingual— oooh!' She nearly jumped out of her skin when Tristan started kneading her neck with firm, magical fingers.

'You should come over to the cottage later,' he purred, his voice as velvety as his fingertips. 'I can show you some of my work.'

'Oooh, come and see my etchings!' Milly chorused, falling about with mirth.

Will didn't join in the laughter this time. He stared at Tessa and Tristan stony-faced, his fingers clenched round his glass of lemonade so tightly, it looked as if it might shatter in his hand.

Going as red as a fire engine, Tessa gibbered incoherently. To her chagrin, Tristan joined in Milly's guffaws. 'She knows me so well! No, seriously, do come over later, Tess. I have some new paintings I'd like your opinion on and I could show you round the grounds first.'

Tessa gulped, feeling everyone's eyes on her. What was she supposed to say? Milly looked delighted at the thought of her spending time with Tristan but Will looked utterly murderous. Tessa supposed she was expected to turn Tristan down but something in Will's eyes made her backbone quiver back to life. 'That would be lovely,' she managed finally. 'I'm looking forward to it already.'

Will slammed his glass of lemonade down on the table so hard, it splashed out over Milly's books.

'God, Will, you're so clumsy . . .'

Milly started mopping up the mess with a tea towel as Caro wandered into the kitchen in a teeny turquoise bikini that revealed her preference for Brazilian waxes. Her thin, freckled limbs remained milky-white and untouched by the sun and Tessa wondered if she wore total sun block all over. Or perhaps the bikini simply allowed easy access for her latest flame – JB, from what she could surmise from the film crew gossip. Poor

Nathan was presumably now on the back burner and relegated to weeding duties.

Tessa half expected Caro to walk past bow-legged but she was as elegant and fresh-looking as ever, her ankles as delicate as a racehorse in a pair of silver slingbacks.

'No lamb for me, I'm on a diet,' Caro announced expansively, stretching luxuriously like a self-satisfied cat.

'A diet? What, a *French* one?' Jack muttered with some malevolence as he followed her in, wearing a black towelling dressing gown and a pair of sunglasses. He was clearly hung-over and his hands were shaking like mad. Watching Caro undulate smugly across the kitchen, he lost his temper and tore off his sunglasses. Snatching the damp tea towel from Milly and balling it up in his hand, he tossed it across the room at his wife. 'I think you dropped your skirt, darling,' he snarled at her.

Caro gave him a saccharine smile and lit a cigarette. 'Dropping skirts is more your forte, isn't it?' she mocked. '*Darling.*'

Jack exploded. 'I'm only human, Caro, and you're pushing me to the goddamned *limits* this time . . .'

'And lunch is served!' Henny said in an overly bright voice as she timidly spun round, brandishing the huge platter of lamb.

'I didn't show you the lake properly,' Tristan declared later on as he let Tessa into his cottage. They had been for a long but undemanding stroll around the manor house grounds after lunch, designed to work off some of Henny's sumptuous food. Austin had come along for the ride, trotting at their heels and occasionally charging off to find rabbits before flopping down in the shade with his pink tongue hanging out. The manor looked magnificent as the sun had slipped rosily behind it, bathing the house in a warm glow and making the beautiful Virginia creeper blush as its leaves were bathed in golden-pink light.

Tristan had behaved like a perfect gentleman as he showed her round a lovely woodland glen at the back of the property, chatting easily about the house and the gardens. Nathan had created some magnificent flower beds in the main garden in front of the driveway, displaying his usual flair with a mixture of sophisticated blooms which gave off heady fragrances, and pretty, wild flowers with delicate, pastel-coloured petals. Tristan had spoilt Nathan's display somewhat by snapping off one of the fragrant yellow roses to tuck in Tessa's hair but she could hardly complain about such a sweet gesture.

All in all, it had been a lovely afternoon and Tessa was pleased she had agreed to join Tristan for the walk. She did her best to push the image of Will's piercing navy eyes out of her mind as they ambled round the gardens but she couldn't help wondering if he might pop out from behind a hedge at any second to keep an eye on them.

'You can show me the lake later,' she told Tristan as she followed him into his cottage.

'My family are certifiable, aren't they?' He led her past a much tinier kitchen than the one in her cottage and put up a warning hand. 'Watch out, this beam is really low and every-one cracks their head on it when they come in here for the first time.'

'I think your family are lovely.' She ducked under the beam and hid a grin as she noticed a small bathroom with a visible toilet, the seat firmly up. Tristan winced and rushed in to slam it down. Tessa didn't know why he had bothered; it was what she would have expected in a bachelor pad. She did hope he wasn't overly concerned about impressing her.

'Thank God Henny's living with us again. I'm about as much use as a chocolate saucepan in the kitchen and, as you can imagine, my mother is absolutely hopeless when it comes to domestic stuff. It's not really her forte.'

Tessa climbed over a pile of untidy, mismatched shoes

where the odd welly boot sat next to a well-worn flip-flop. A coat rack groaned with waxed jackets and padded body warmers, looking as if it might fall to the ground at any second.

'This is my studio,' Tristan stated with some pride. 'Isn't it incredible? Look at the way the light falls across the floor, even at this time of night.'

Tessa nodded; the carpet was suffused with pink-gold light. She glanced around the room. What looked like a genuine neo-classical sofa with cream and pink tapestry and a gilt frame with carved floral details sat in the centre of the room. It was draped with richly coloured velvet throws and cushions and was no doubt the backdrop for the plethora of canvases which were slotted into specially made wooden units.

'Sorry about the mess,' Tristan apologised, frantically gathering up tubes of oil paint and different sized notepads and juggling them in his arms. 'Fuck, I'm such a messy bastard!'

'Don't mind me.' Tessa smiled, pausing by the window to drink in the view. The cottage had an unadulterated view of the lake, with its pretty stone bridge and the stretch of ivy-green water, which glittered like a highly polished emerald.

'Make yourself at home,' Tristan called as he disappeared into the kitchenette. 'I'll get us some drinks.'

There were paintings all around the studio, an explosion of colours, with iris blues, clarets and saffron yellows sitting side by side, but somehow the muddle of colours worked. The paintings were vibrant, bold and eye-catching, some so utterly ravishing they took Tessa's breath away.

She picked up a small canvas that was lying on the window sill. It was a painting of a young girl with blond hair flowing down her back. The girl was nude and she was lying down, posing from the tips of her toes to the crown of her head. Her face was in profile and her neck had an elegant arch that seemed both feminine and sensual. Whoever the girl was, she seemed at ease with her sexuality and her fair colouring looked beautiful against a background of burnt sienna.

Tessa put the canvas back and took a sneaky look at some other paintings. There was the odd landscape but mostly Tristan seemed to be intrigued by people and there were a variety of head portraits as well as a few more nudes. Some of his subjects were quite ugly. Tristan was obviously more interested in the contours of light and shade the bodies provided than how attractive they were. For some reason, Tessa found this very appealing, the first sign that there was more to Tristan than good looks and clever hands.

There was a dignity to the slope of an old man's jowl and an achingly tender appreciation of a middle-aged woman's post-childbirth belly. Tessa caught sight of a sketch of a young boy, the arrogant jut of his chin matched by the sparkling deter-mination in his eyes. Bloody hell, was it a young Rufus Pemberton? Not more than twelve years old and wearing mud-splattered jodhpurs and a dishevelled polo shirt, Rufus personified breeding and privilege but steadfast ambition could be detected in his dark brown eyes, even then.

The sketch was rather naive and crude compared to Tristan's later work; he could only have been nine or ten at the time of the drawing, but he had nonetheless managed to capture Rufus's upper-class confidence to a T.

Tristan gave his subjects character. Rather than flat canvases depicting random people, his subjects were alive with personal-ities, background and substance. Increasingly impressed, Tessa noticed a stack of paintings at the back of the studio which were covered in a white sheet and set apart from the others. The end of one of them was poking out and she recognised the girl from the other painting.

'Won't be a minute,' Tristan yelled, sounding flustered. There was a smash, followed by a muffled pop. 'Troublesome cork . . .'

Tessa tiptoed over to the stack of paintings. She lifted the sheet. It was definitely the same girl – the one she had seen that first day in the library at Appleton Manor. In this painting, the girl was lying on some grass with some strategically placed flowers covering her modesty. Her smile was knowing but she still managed to look soft and innocent, her chin lifted to the air again, showcasing what seemed to be a near-perfect profile – the nose was smallish and upturned and the full lips were the colour of dusky rose petals; the colour most women spent a fortune on make-up to achieve. The cheeks had just a hint of bloom about them, but the result was achingly natural; the dappled sunlight bore testament to the lack of artifice on her face.

Was she real? Tessa wondered. Was this the girl who had messed with Tristan's head? The girl Henny had referred to when she said that 'love had done terrible things' to Tristan? And if so, what had happened between them to destroy their love affair?

Tessa pulled another canvas out. There she was again, naked, sublime, her skin silken and flawless – could it really be that translucent? Was it down to the finesse of Tristan's paintbrush or perhaps the rose-tinted view he had of his subject? There was canvas after canvas, tightly packed against one another but all depicting the same beautiful girl against different back-drops, her skin taking on a hue of colour determined by her surroundings.

Whoever she was, Tristan hadn't easily tired of her image, Tessa thought as she gazed at a jaw-dropping painting which was a simple study of the girl's breasts and her long, long neck. His exquisite brushwork had captured the youthful curve of her bosom, the breasts heavy and ripe-looking against the elegant line of her throat. The strawberry-tipped nipples protruded proudly, lustfully, as if the mere act of capturing them on canvas had fuelled her desire. Tessa felt her insides stirring at the sight of it, and imagined the painting had been finished shortly before wild, passionate sex. She had the vaguest idea the girl from the painting was familiar but she dropped the idea, knowing she would remember if she had met such youthful beauty in person.

Feeling voyeuristic and hearing Tristan's approaching footsteps, she hurriedly pulled the sheet down over the canvases. Her toe caught the edge of a small portrait that looked as if it had been shoved out of sight and she pulled it free, studying it with interest.

In stark contrast to the gloriously joyful, sensual paintings she had just seen, Tessa was intrigued to see that this one depicted a plain girl with strange, crazed eyes. The colours in the picture were dull and depressing, most unlike the rest of Tristan's work. Before she had time to shove the painting back, he had returned.

'Champagne!' he announced, holding up a bottle with the end smashed off. 'Sorry about the presentation – it might be worth checking for glass when I pour it out. Christ, what have you got there?' He handed her a rounded, old-fashioned champagne glass and peered at the portrait. 'Oh my God, that's Anna.'

'Love of your life?'

'Total nutter.' He shuddered, pouring frothy champagne into their glasses. 'I don't like to talk about her, but let's just say the term stalker was made for this particular ex-girlfriend. Poor Austin hasn't been the same since she threatened to stuff oranges up his bum and roast him in the Aga.'

'You're not serious!'

'I'm deadly serious. And so was she. Some people just can't take no for an answer. I lost count of the times she threw herself at me. I made it clear I couldn't stand her but she just kept coming back for more.' Tristan pulled a face. 'Honestly, she was the most unhinged girl I've ever met. Mental. Milly nicknamed her The Psycho and she used to do these amazing impressions of her – scarily accurate, actually.'

171

'Why do you keep the portrait of this Anna if she was so awful?'

Tristan gave a rueful shrug. 'Ego, I suppose. It's a good painting. It has light and shade, it's a strong image but rather unnerving at the same time. Oops.' He realised he'd overfilled Tessa's glass and attempted to mop it up with a paint-stained rag.

'I thought you were supposed to be a dab hand at all this seduction stuff,' Tessa teased him as she wiped her fingers on her dress. 'Haven't you had dozens of girlfriends besides this loony Anna? Or rather, hundreds?'

He took a gulp of champagne and settled himself on the sofa. 'Oh dear, my appalling reputation has reached your ears already. I can't deny it, I love women but that doesn't mean I'm any good at soppy gestures.' He whipped a notepad out of his pocket and started on a rapid sketch of her. 'And I told you . . . with me, it's all about the art.' His fingers moved nimbly as his eyes flickered from her face to the page.

Tessa poured them both another glass of champagne each and took a seat a few prim feet away from him. Really, these little glasses held practically nothing at all but somehow she already felt rather woozy. 'I remember you telling me that, about you being all about the art.' She nodded at the easels dotted round the studio and the pristine brushes which had obviously been carefully cleaned and dried before being put away in see-through plastic boxes. 'I can see what you mean.'

Tristan ripped the page of his sketchpad and passed it to her. He had flattered her tremendously; her features looked far more balanced than they did in reality and her figure had taken on a Lara Croft-worthy hourglass shape. She had pronounced cheekbones, according to this sketch, as well as an impossibly slender waist.

'If only I really looked like this.'

'You do,' he insisted earnestly. 'I said you had interesting bone structure. Your colouring is lost with pencil as the medium, of course, but watercolours could pick out the chestnut tones in your hair and the moss colour of your eyes beautifully.' He held a tube of earthy green paint up next to her face, as if trying to capture the exact shade of her iris. She intrigued him, her unusual features made him long to do a proper study of her – that slightly crooked, proud nose and wide mouth would be complex to capture but it would be immeasurably pleasurable to do so.

Tristan eyed Tessa languidly. She was undeniably sexy and he found himself increasingly drawn to her. She thought he had flattered her with his sketch but the artist in him couldn't help but admire the slender curve of her waist and the beautiful arch of her ankle. Bedding her would be deeply satisfying. A practised lover with countless experiences to draw on, Tristan sensed a freedom in Tessa that promised sensual abandon between the sheets.

Would she prefer to go on top, riding him urgently like a jockey, or would she hurl herself down on all fours, dirtily, begging him to take her? He hadn't a clue what her preferences were but as he clumsily opened another bottle of champagne, he believed anything was possible. And the very idea was an instant turn-on. In fact, he could feel his boxers bulging at the thought of it.

But could he fall in love with her? he thought as he poured champagne all over his fingers. Bleakly, he caught sight of a painting of . . . of *her* that he had left out on the window sill. He still couldn't say her name. She had left him incapable of *feeling* – and incapable of imagining his heart singing again. He had tried; Christ, he had slept with more women than he could remember. But it didn't matter. He had lost the love of his life and he had lost his muse.

'Whoa there, mister, careful with the champers! We want to drink it, not waste it.' Basking in his compliments but aware that Tristan had drifted off into private thoughts, Tessa began to question whether he really liked her or not. Was he simply trying to get her into bed? Was she simply a distraction from the woman in the paintings, a ghost from the past who haunted him, maybe even *taunted* him and made it impossible for him to do anything beyond indulging in mindless sex?

Tristan, seemingly aware that he had mentally left the room, dropped the paint tube and leant forward. 'You must understand, Tessa, you're creative. In a different way of course,' he allowed, noticing her incredulous expression, 'but you seem very committed to your job so you understand what I'm getting at, don't you? It's all-consuming when you do something like this . . .' He ran a finger along one of his canvases, not appearing to notice he was stroking an old lady's wrinkled buttock. 'It takes you over, occupies every waking thought and some of your dreams. It's like an obsession.'

'I used to feel like that about my job,' Tessa confessed regretfully. 'But I'm afraid I'm beginning to think I've lost my edge. JB tells me so nearly every day and my boss seems to think I'm a hopeless waste of time.'

'Nonsense!' Making a decision, Tristan poured out the rest of the champagne. Henny was right, it was about time he had some fun. He urged Tessa to drink before refilling her glass. 'You seem very professional. And much nicer than that JB chap. Aside from the fact that he's shagging my mother, he loves himself far more than any woman could.'

She laughed then stopped. 'Do you care?'

'What about?' He reached out and caressed her eyebrow with his finger.

Tessa faltered. It was an intimate gesture but there was something careless about the way he had done it, as if he touched women without thinking. She tried to concentrate as his finger dropped disturbingly to her shoulder, the tip stroking her with agonisingly slow movements.

'About Jack and Caro – your parents, I mean. Sleeping with people the way they do. Does it bother you?'

Tristan let out a heavy sigh and his finger fell away. 'I've grown up with it. When I was little, I thought everyone's parents behaved like that. It was only when I went to school and met my friends' parents that I realised mine were different.' He considered her with bleary eyes. 'I could pretend it's made me the sad old commitment-phobe that I am but that would be a lie. After all, look at Will. He might be apprehensive about marrying Claudette – oops, don't tell him I told you that – but deep down, he knows what he wants.'

'What about you? What do you want?' In her drunken haze, Tessa was surprised to hear that Will might be feeling nervous about marrying his flawless fiancée.

Tristan considered her. 'What do I want? I know . . . more champers.' He planted a kiss on her head and felt himself falling against her.

Tristan really was *very* attractive, Tessa thought as she relaxed against him in a warm fug of alcohol. Did she care if he was only able to indulge in mindless sex? It was probably exactly what she needed. She held the empty bottle close to her eyes. Wasn't that another empty bottle over there? Could they possibly have drunk that much already?

Tristan stood up unsteadily. He wasn't quite as strapping as his brother but so what? Will was out of bounds, and bloody rude to boot. And Tristan was so *funny*; she giggled happily, her eyes crossing from all the booze as she watched him dance around on the spot like an idiot. He was fun and he was looking at her as if she was the sexiest thing on two legs. Tessa suddenly realised she was beyond squiffy and most likely verging on paralytic. At that moment, Tristan chose to kiss her, planting his lips juicily over hers, his hands in her hair. For several minutes, they snogged, their tongues joyfully delving into each other's mouths as they rolled around on the floor. Breathlessly, they pulled apart. Tessa tried to get up but lost her balance and slid down the side of the sofa until her head was almost in Tristan's lap.

'Easy, tiger,' he cackled, although Tessa heard it as 'teasy eiger'. God, she must be plastered. She felt his fingers massaging her neck playfully and she leant against him feeling deliciously uninhibited. 'I attract lost souls,' he was saying. 'Always lost souls. People without parents, tragic people, tragic *women* who need me to save them.'

'I don't need you to save me,' she told him indignantly, hoping he wouldn't stop stroking her neck. It was making her knees go wibbly. 'Not unless . . . I was drowning or something.' She pointed out of the window towards the lake and looked up at Tristan.

His fingers paused and she frowned, put out. Tristan's mouth broke into a grin. 'Are you thinking what I'm thinking?'

'Probably not,' she said, her head lolling against him. Not unless he was thinking of smearing paint over every last inch of her naked body before making hot, frantic love to her against his easel . . . 'Hey! Where are you going?'

Tristan had jumped up, grappling with his shirt as he attempted to pull it over his head. Abandoning this idea, he ripped it open and buttons pinged in every direction. 'Skinny-dipping!' he whooped, tearing his deck shoes off and heading for the door.

'Come on!' she heard him shout in the distance.

Not giving herself a second to think, she held on to the sofa for dear life as she got to her feet, kicked off her flip-flops and fumbled with the tie at the waist of her dress. Running out after Tristan in her bare feet, she found she was too drunk to undo the knot, so she stopped, gathered the bottom of the dress up and wriggled out of it that way.

* * *

176

Standing outside making a phone call to Claudette, Will was gobsmacked at the sight of Tessa shimmying out of her clothes as she streaked down the garden. He was even more surprised to see that beneath the demure mint-green dress was a sexy body and some very inappropriate underwear.

Wordlessly, he watched her tear across the lawn wearing only a lime-green bra which barely contained her bobbing breasts and a matching thong which showed off her flat stomach and toned thighs.

God, her body was better than he had imagined. Not that he had any business imagining Tessa naked, Will hurriedly reminded himself, but still, that slim waist flaring out to curvaceous hips, and those long, long legs . . . Will swallowed. There was something so wonderfully *free* about the way she was running down to the lake, her dark hair flying out behind her and her eyes sparkling with radiant abandon. He wasn't sure he had ever seen Claudette like that – although he reminded himself it was early days.

Still, could he really see his soignée girlfriend running with such uninhibited delight, her cheeks stained with exertion and her hair all over the place? Claudette was sophisticated and self-aware . . . classy – in fact, she possessed all the qualities he generally admired in a woman.

So why was his throat going dry at the sight of this amazing girl dashing down the lawn in her garishly coloured undies? Why was he suddenly wishing Claudette would do something as impulsive and crazy as skinny-dipping in the manor house lake the next time she came to stay? Will gulped. Just for a moment, he hadn't been sure if he had wanted Claudette to be more like Tessa, or if he simply wanted Tessa.

Feeling as if he had no place observing the intimate moment but apparently rooted to the spot, he watched Tristan hurl himself into the lake stark bollock naked, shortly followed by Tessa who merrily unclipped her bra to reveal glorious brown breasts that seemed to defy gravity as she ran. As she dive-bombed Tristan with a yell of exhilaration, Will was nonplussed to find his stomach exploding with jealousy and his shorts straining to contain a gigantic erection.

Fucking hell, he must be missing Claudette more than he thought, Will said to himself, turning away from the sight of Tristan's hands disappearing under the water. Unfortunately, he couldn't miss the sounds of Tessa shrieking in delight as she splashed around in Tristan's arms and, once again, Will was gripped by a wave of jealousy that threatened to overwhelm him.

What the hell was the matter with him? Tessa is a ruthless, over-ambitious journalist, he reprimanded himself steadfastly. She hates family; according to the notes he'd found, she was using his shamelessly, and she was everything he despised in a woman. Wasn't she? He turned back towards the lake, almost afraid to look.

Tessa was screaming with laughter as Tristan inelegantly tried to re-create the lift from *Dirty Dancing* and her tiny lime-green thong was soaked and practically transparent. Will frantically tried to get things in perspective. His reaction to Tessa was lust, it was as simple as that. What he had with Claudette was quite, quite different, a proper relationship with shared interests and similar values. And they had *great* sex, he reminded himself honestly; fun, exciting sex. All the time. Whenever they were together. And not working.

Will prayed for his erection to subside but it didn't seem to be responding. Nor did he seem able to remove the image of Tessa naked but for her ridiculous lime-green thong from his memory – seemingly, it was branded there for eternity. The sooner Claudette got here, the better, he told himself grimly as he adjusted his shorts and minced stiffly into the manor.

* * *

Unaware they had been seen, Tristan goggled at the sight of Tessa's tanned breasts dangling tantalisingly in front of his face and accidentally dropped her into the water. Tessa re-emerged, spluttering, with her hair slicked back from her face, and she swatted him round the head for almost drowning her. They started to kiss again but soon found they couldn't stop laughing so instead they clutched at each other and roared until tears ran down their faces.

'You're funny,' Tristan gasped when he could catch his breath.

'Funny-looking?' Tessa hiccoughed as she peeled a piece of green slime from her chin. She scrabbled around under the water. Her thong seemed to have slipped off and she was never going to find it amongst all the greenery.

'*Funny-looking!*' Tristan cracked up, holding his sides and almost slipping under the water again.

Tessa collapsed into giggles and held on to him. This was so much fun! She didn't even care if they had sex after this. Downing champagne before streaking down the lawn in her knickers seemed to be exactly what she needed after all the pressure from Jilly and the worry over losing her job. Shrieking with delight as Tristan took advantage of the dense lake and goosed her, Tessa flung her arms round him and unceremoniously shoved him under the water.

Chapter Eleven

'So kind of them to invite us, isn't it? It's going to be a wonderful day.'

Gil glanced at Sophie who had gone rather pale, and topped up her glass of white wine. He had had a stressful day at the manor trying to make sure the penthouse bathrooms went according to plan and he hadn't finished work until seven o'clock that evening. Sophie had been enjoying the late evening sunshine on the patio, stretched out on a padded lounger. She already had an enviable tan, a gorgeous golden-brown colour that complemented her caramel-streaked hair and white bikini.

'You'll be able to see the manor in all its glory, darling, and I'll be able to showcase my designs on national television! What could be better than that?'

'A party?' whispered Sophie, clutching at the arms of her lounger. 'At Appleton Manor?'

'Isn't it thrilling? They do it every year, apparently.' Gil frowned as he watched Nathan tear off his sweat-soaked vest and wipe his bronzed brow with it. He didn't know any gardeners who worked this late. Nathan seemed to love his work. He was painting the fence at the back of the garden, slightly hindered by an over-exuberant Ruby who was trying to help. Gil took a sip of wine, thinking it was time she was in bed. 'This time, Will is turning the party into a business event, and inviting people who might want to use the hotel as a conference centre, which is such a good idea! I think it's going to be an enormous success.' He pouted. 'And you did promise to come and see my designs at the manor very soon.'

With trembling fingers, Sophie struggled mindlessly with a bottle of suntan lotion, a strangled gargle escaping from her throat. She *had* promised Gil she would give him her opinion on his designs; how could she have refused him?

'I know I moan about Will,' Gil went on, smoothing down his outrageous jade and white checked shorts, 'but I have to confess that I really admire him. He's such a lovely man, so trustworthy and strong. You feel that he's the type of man who wouldn't let you down, do you know what I mean?'

Sophie gave him a feeble nod and let the bottle of suntan lotion slide to the ground. What was she supposed to do now? She couldn't possibly turn up at Appleton Manor on Gil's arm. For a start, it would mean letting on to Gil that she knew the Forbes-Henry family. Naturally, he would demand to know why she had kept her connection to them a secret.

Feeling panic trickle down her spine, Sophie began wringing her hands in despair.

'Darling, are you all right?' Gil sat up, concerned. His hair was too long for someone his age but, vainly, he liked it swept over one eye. So useful when he wanted to flick it out and make sexy eye contact, and especially important if you wanted to connect with people behind a camera lens. 'You look positively drained. Have you been overdoing it?'

'Maybe. What with the move and the decorating and keeping Ruby amused . . .' Sophie hated being so untruthful to Gil. It was becoming a habit and it didn't sit well on her shoulders. She thrust her sunglasses on to her nose, certain her face must be white with shock. Why hadn't she seen this coming? She knew the Forbes-Henrys held a summer party in August; she had attended a few herself in the past.

'You poor thing,' Gil clucked, splashing iced water into a glass for her. 'I hope you're not worried about this party. It's going to be a unique opportunity, not least because of all the exposure I'm going to get. Just think, I'll be in the same documentary as Rufus Pemberton and Clemmie Winters! Who would have thought it, little old me, mingling with the rich and famous!'

Sophie gave him a watery smile. Trust Gil to be more excited about the thought of being on television than anything else! But she supposed she couldn't blame him; he had been talking about hosting his own show from the day she had met him. This might finally be his ticket to the 'big time' and after all the support he had given her in the past, she couldn't begrudge him the success he craved. He deserved it.

'That's such good news,' she said, trying to sound encouraging. 'I'm really pleased for you.' A thought struck her. 'What about Ruby? I don't know if I want her going to a party like this . . .'

'Not to worry,' Gil reassured her. 'Children are *definitely* not allowed. Well, children of Ruby's age, anyway. This is an event for adults, and I wouldn't want Ruby getting under my feet when I'm at work.'

Sophie wasn't sure Gil liked Ruby getting under his feet, period, but she wasn't about to bring it up. Gil had been so good to them and she didn't want to sound ungrateful. After all, it wasn't that he was impatient around Ruby, more that he didn't have a clue how to deal with her.

At least she didn't need to worry about Ruby bumping into Tristan, Sophie thought with a rush of relief. She had no idea how Tristan would react, but she had a feeling it wouldn't be a pleasant moment. He would either be furious that she had kept the truth from him or, more likely, incandescent with rage that she had been stupid enough to get pregnant in the first place, especially when he had already moved on to some other girl.

Would he accuse her of lying and saying that Ruby was his so that she could get her hands on his money? Sophie shuddered at the thought. Tristan's money was of no interest to her; it never had been. No, Ruby and Tristan must never meet, it was as simple as that. It might not be fair to Ruby to keep her from her real father but how would her daughter feel if Tristan rejected her? It was too horrible to think about.

But keeping Ruby out of Tristan's way didn't solve the issue of how Sophie was going to avoid attending the party herself.

Could she feign illness? Sophie wondered, as she watched Nathan handing Ruby a tiny brush to paint the fence with. She could cook seafood for dinner the night before and pretend to be ill. She had reacted badly to a dodgy moules marinière once before . . . It was plausible. Knowing Gil, he would find the sight of her bent over the toilet bowl absolutely stomach-churning and it wouldn't be difficult to persuade him to go without her.

Just as she began to brighten at the thought of her splendid plan, Gil grabbed her hand.

'You *must* come to this party, darling. I'd be terribly anxious without you. We've stuck together through thick and thin, you and me, haven't we?'

Sophie's stomach flipped over. 'Yes, yes, we have.'

Gil's eyes resembled a puppy's as he covered her hand with his. 'That's why I love you, Soph. I always know I can rely on your support. We make a great team, don't we? It's you and me against the world!'

'You, me and *Ruby* against the world,' she corrected him reproachfully.

'You, me and *Ruby* against the world,' he echoed, giving Ruby a distracted wave.

Sophie felt a flash of irritation. Ruby might not be Gil's biological daughter but he'd spent every day with her since they had brought her home from the hospital. In the early days, Gil had seemed a doting father, enchanted with Ruby's pink, scrunched-up face and dainty fingernails. But as she grew older

– and increasingly like her real father in both looks and behaviour – the more Gil seemed to find her difficult to engage with.

Sophie believed the age-old argument of nature versus nurture was the root of the problem. Or was it just good old-fashioned ego? If Ruby displayed more of an interest in the things Gil was passionate about or shared any of his quirky personality traits, Sophie was sure he would be delighted to spend time with her. She seemed to enjoy art, which should have been something they could have fun with, but Gil had little idea about children's imaginations and their need to express themselves. No doubt he had been forced to be sensible as a boy, Sophie thought, knowing what a strict upbringing he had had. Gil's father was an uptight vicar, a dreadful bigot whose judgemental attitude shocked Sophie to the core. Poor Gil had spent his childhood petrified of inducing his father's wrath and consequently was ill-equipped to deal with an exuberant Ruby.

Gil changed the subject. 'By the way, I have some very important news to share with you.'

'Er . . . what's that?' Sophie didn't like the expectant look in his eyes. The last time she had seen him look this way was when he told her he'd accepted the job in Appleton and rented this house without consulting her first. She knew he hadn't done it selfishly. She had always supported his career and he had been convinced she would be blown away by a lovely stint in the Cotswolds.

Sophie braced herself.

'I've booked our wedding!' he declared, beaming.

Sophie almost fell off her lounger; she was speechless.

'I know we hadn't set a date, darling, but working at Appleton Manor and seeing Rufus and Clemmie making all their plans made me come over all Mr Darcy, so I thought I'd surprise you!'

Rufus and Clemmie . . . Appleton Manor . . . Sophie was

aghast. He hadn't . . . Gil wasn't seriously suggesting he had booked the manor for their wedding . . .

'Christmas Eve.'

'What about Christmas Eve?'

'I've booked our wedding for Christmas Eve. At the manor house!' Gil looked beside himself. 'What could be more romantic than a Christmas wedding?'

Sophie felt the colour drain from her face. What in God's name had he done?

'Isn't it the *best* idea?' Giving Nathan an irritated glare, Gil was soon happily outlining his thoughts for the wedding, from the classic, hand-tied bouquet of lilies he thought Sophie should hold, to the sleek, ivory sheath he could see her gliding down the aisle in.

'Why the rush?' Sophie interrupted hoarsely. 'I don't understand . . .'

Gil broke into a beatific smile.

'I thought it was about time I made an honest woman of you, my love. It will be so romantic. We've been engaged for ages now, so why not make a commitment to each other? We love each other, don't we? We're sure of our feelings, aren't we?'

She turned her face away. Gil was her best friend. He was steady, reliable and caring and he had always been there for her; in fact, he had been there for her when no one else had been. But he wasn't Tristan, he never could be. Which was a good thing, right?

Sophie cast her eyes down, feeling tears pushing at her eyelids. When Gil had proposed, she had accepted, swept away by his excitement, hopeful it would be a long-term arrangement that she would get used to in time. He had been vague about making things official and had seemed happy that the diamond on Sophie's finger meant they were committed to one another. Gil had given her so much and she loved him for it. Their relationship could hardly be described as the romance of the century but she cared about him deeply and she did love him – in her own way. She had an idea their engagement had been mutually beneficial because it seemed to have pleased Gil's father greatly. Seeing his only son living in sin with his girlfriend and her child had caused the vicar no end of headaches but in light of a 'proper commitment' being made and the promise of a wedding at some point, Gil's father had relaxed visibly.

Sophie realised she had bitten her lip so hard it was bleeding. Hearing Ruby let out a playful chortle, she was gripped by fear once more. Christ, and she had imagined avoiding the summer party was all she had to worry about, she thought, pushing her sunglasses up into her hair.

'Darling, you are pleased, aren't you?' Gil looked distressed. 'I thought this was what you wanted . . . what we both wanted. Eventually. They have this darling chapel in the grounds that I think you're going to love . . .'

Sophie closed her eyes. She could draw him a map to the chapel with her eyes shut.

'I've invited the Forbes-Henry family and they're all dying to meet you,' Gil gushed, putting on a pair of big, black sunglasses Victoria Beckham would have fought him for. 'I wonder if Tristan might bring your new friend Tessa. You know, as a date?'

'H-his date? What do you mean?' Sophie thought she might faint.

'Oh *yes*!' Gil tapped the side of his nose smugly.

'Don't *do* that!' Knowing she had sounded unnecessarily sharp, Sophie forced herself to smile brightly. 'What do you mean about Tristan and Tessa?'

'They're having a *thing*,' Gil confided with a naughty glint in his eye. 'One of my design team was working very late at the weekend and he saw them having a scandalous frolic in the lake the other night – a sexy skinny-dip, by all accounts.'

Jealousy tore through Sophie like a hot blade through butter.

Her insides were aflame. The thought of Tessa naked and wet, in Tristan's arms with her lips on his, was more than she could bear. She felt nauseous, suffocated, as if she was drowning, and she had forgotten how awful it felt.

Vividly, Sophie was transported back to that painful day more than five years ago when she had walked in on Tristan.

She had heard voices as she approached Tristan's cottage, but that was nothing new. He worked constantly in those days, painting anything that caught his eye, staying up all hours to work on something he couldn't put aside. The radio often blared out while he painted – not that he seemed to notice the music – or Will might pop by for a chat – one of the only times Tristan would take a break and crack open a beer.

Sophie had been bubbling over with happiness as she sped up the pathway. She had been in London on an art course but, deciding she could no longer ignore her throbbing breasts and inexplicable nausea, she had bought a pregnancy test and headed into the toilets in Selfridges. Biting her nails as the minutes passed, she had been elated to see two pink lines boldly emerging and had rushed out of the toilets with a joyous shriek.

Grabbing the first train home and forgetting all about her course, she remembered imagining how Tristan would react to her news. He would be pleased, surely. The pregnancy hadn't been planned, of course, she hadn't even completed her college course and he was a struggling artist in those days, fortunate by way of his background but not exactly cash rich.

But they had discussed marriage many times. They might only be in their early twenties but it had seemed like the natural step after such an intense love affair. And discovering that there was part of Tristan growing inside her had filled her with a euphoria she had never thought possible.

A *baby*! She had paused, rubbing a hand over her still-flat tummy, wondering how she would look as it grew. It had felt frightening and fantastic at the same time and she hadn't known for sure if she was ready. But with Tristan at her side, deep down she had felt that they would manage. They loved each other – this would only make their relationship stronger.

As she had approached, she had realised that the voice in Tristan's cottage didn't belong to the radio, or to Will. It was a female voice, a deep, confident, female voice.

Sophie had sucked her breath in, feeling uneasy. She didn't recognise the voice but she couldn't help thinking the throaty laughter and rasping tones sounded awfully intimate.

Should she turn back and leave Tristan to it? She trusted him; there was no need for concern. But at the same time . . . she had big news to tell him and she couldn't wait to see his face when she told him they were going to have a baby. And there was the small matter of a strange girl being in his cottage in the middle of the night, a night when Tristan knew she was meant to be miles away in London . . .

Pushing open the door of Tristan's cottage with a thumping heart, Sophie had told herself to stop being so stupid. She trusted Tristan implicitly and she knew their relationship was strong enough to survive the odd night apart. She had ducked under the low beam by the front door that seemed designed to announce the arrival of strangers. She remembered wondering if the girl with the sexy voice had bumped her head on the beam on the way in or if she was already familiar with its unusual height . . .

Sophie tiptoed to the edge of Tristan's studio, hardly knowing why she felt the need to hide her presence. Oddly, the laughter that had been ringing out so confidently had halted abruptly and the only discernible sound was . . . the girl sobbing hysterically. Sophie froze. What was going on? Petrified this girl was another of the 'lost souls' Tristan seemed so incapable of resisting, she had summoned up the courage to peek into the studio.

Tristan was sitting on the sofa with the sobbing girl, his sketchpad on his knee, a pencil poised over the page. His body language seemed tense but he was sitting close to the girl as if he knew her well. In a daze, Sophie noticed that the girl had tears streaming down her cheeks but that her eyes seemed bright and curiously alert. She wore a low-cut dress that finished at thigh length, her bare knees almost touching Tristan's.

Sophie let out what she imagined must have been an audible gasp but the two figures in front of her didn't react. Clapping her hand over her mouth, Sophie suddenly figured out who the girl was, recognising her from a portrait she had seen in Tristan's studio once, months ago. Tristan had been at pains to hide the portrait but had finally admitted the plain girl was Anna, an ex-girlfriend, but he had seemed reluctant to elaborate further. It had struck Sophie as odd at the time that he kept the portrait at all but Sophie had told herself she was being silly.

Biting down hard on her lip, she had watched, utterly mesmerised, as Anna's tears seemed to cease and her arms wound their way seductively round Tristan's neck. Her body arched towards him, her mouth wet with anticipation and her breasts straining to break free from the cheap dress. Although her cheeks were stained with tears, Anna's eyes were strangely triumphant. Triumphant? Or simply brimming with confidence that Tristan would reciprocate?

How right she was and, for Sophie, that had been the worst thing. For a heart-stopping second, she watched as Tristan did nothing to push Anna's ardent lips away.

Not waiting to witness what was about to happen next, Sophie had turned and dashed for the door. Sobs of pain tearing from her throat, she had run. She had run away from Tristan, away from the family she had learnt to love as her own and away from Appleton. And she had taken Tristan's baby with her, vowing to herself that no one would ever hurt her again the way he had.

'Tristan's rather a handsome chap,' Gil cut across her reverie, 'but I don't think he's the marrying kind.'

'Sorry?'

'Flighty, if you can use that word about a man,' Gil continued in pompous tones, oblivious of Sophie's stiffening frame. 'I do hope Tessa hasn't fallen in love with him because I think she might end up disappointed.' He leant forward and tapped Sophie's thigh. 'Between you and me, I think Will is a better bet but by all accounts they detest each other, which is a shame. And of course he has this gorgeous French fiancée who is due to arrive at any second.'

Sophie nodded wordlessly. After all this time, why did her heart feel as if it could break in two? Watching Ruby paint the fence with intense concentration, she was struck again by her likeness to Tristan and she couldn't help thinking it was a double-edged sword. It was chilling to see the odd look that reminded Sophie of him so much but it was also heart-warming to witness the infectious smile that reminded her of happier times.

'I'm just popping in for a drink, if that's all right?' Nathan paused by their loungers, his rock-hard pecs like two solid orbs attracting the sun.

'Don't get paint on anything, will you?' Gil said rather snippily.

'I won't,' Nathan promised, flexing his muscles as he wiped his paintbrush on a rag. 'I'll be in and out before you know it – excuse the pun.' He gave them a wink.

Gil leapt off the lounger. 'I'm going in to get some more water,' he spluttered, snatching the jug from the table and hurrying into the house.

Sophie wasn't listening; she was watching Ruby with her heart in her mouth, painting a crude portrait on a fence panel. It was clumsy and childish but Nathan's face was instantly recognisable from the self-assured brush strokes Ruby had undoubtedly inherited from her father.

Sophie watched her, transfixed, her stomach plummeting as she wondered how much longer she could keep up this ridiculous charade.

Clemmie wished she'd cried off sick and postponed the interview. It had only been a week since the terrible row with Rufus but something in their relationship had shifted since that point and Clemmie couldn't stop thinking about it.

Listlessly, she walked alongside Tessa in the orchard at the back of their house, which sported rather long, wayward grass studded with fruit trees. They hadn't had time to hire a gardener to address the weeds and misshapen lawn littered with russet red apples and slightly dented pears, and there was a wild honeysuckle plant growing in a tangle along the stone wall surrounding the property. Its heavy flowers hung in clusters like pink and cream bells, giving off a heady scent, and attracting bees, moths and butterflies to it like kids to candy.

Swatting away a group of buzzing midges, Clemmie fervently hoped she wouldn't get bitten. She watched Rufus pick up a big, ripe apple and shine it like a cricket ball on his black denim groin. He bit into it, giving her a broad, unconcerned grin.

Thankfully, Tessa seemed to have picked up on the fact that Clemmie wasn't up to talking and rather than asking fresh questions, she was running through previous interviews they had conducted, checking that they were happy with the content before they were included in the documentary.

'That sounds fine, honey,' Clemmie murmured, feeling as if she might embarrass herself by sobbing like a child at any second. The sun on the top of her head felt warm but she shivered, and goosebumps appeared on her bare arms.

Since Rufus had walked out, Clemmie had been as miserable as hell. She had been stunned when he had refused to talk about their future and had left her sitting there like a fool while he went to the pub. Had her rejection of him been the final nail in the coffin? His ego was legendary and before that point they had never exchanged cross words like that, nor had she ever pushed him away. She had spent half an hour after his departure convinced he would come home, his arms full of flowers and his eyes brimming with apology. How wrong she had been.

Not only had Rufus not appeared in the half hour after the row, he hadn't come home all night. She had spent hours lying in bed waiting for him, her eyes wide open and tears dripping on to her pillow as her imagination ran riot. He was a player, she knew that. And even though she didn't think he had cheated on her since their relationship had started, she believed he was childish enough to need the ego boost after the awful row. She had committed the cardinal sin of rejecting his advances, something she had never done in the time they had been together. Feeling ill or tired or simply not in the mood, she had never declined and she had matched his high sex drive stroke for stroke. And she wasn't ashamed to admit that she had enjoyed every minute of it; they had a passionate, varied sex life and it was a very important aspect of their relationship.

But his casual reaction over the issue of children had left her cold and she had been unable to go along with it this time. But Clemmie knew what a monstrous ego Rufus possessed and she could well imagine how slapping him away might have inadvertently pushed him into another woman's arms. And it was unlikely he would be short of admirers, even here in the back of beyond. There had to be any number of nubile girls who would surrender their Gucci handbags if he so much as looked at them. Clemmie felt her skin crawl at the thought of Rufus's hands on someone else's body.

'I won't include that interview we did the other day if it makes you feel any better,' Tessa was saying kindly as she took in Clemmie's pasty complexion and slightly uneven steps.

'I-it doesn't matter,' Clemmie stammered as her high heels slid on Rufus's discarded apple core and almost tripped her up.

God, had she turned into one of those women who loved their partners so much, they were willing to put up with any old crap? One of those women she had said she would never be, not after what had happened to her before. What she did know was that she was floundering totally out of her depth. When Rufus had returned to their home the day after their row, he had acted as if nothing had happened. And by the evening, things seemed to be completely back to normal between them – he was making jokes and laughing at something on the TV and she was doing her best to move on and be the bubbly, loving person she normally was.

Only when Rufus had slipped his hand between her legs when they were in bed later that night had she finally relaxed. His warm, thrusting fingers had brought her pent-up tension to a shuddering release and as she felt his mouth on the back of her neck, she had felt reassured that he still wanted to be with her. Clemmie wished she could be stronger but where Rufus was concerned, she was helpless. She had to believe he had simply drunk himself stupid in the pub and then slept on a bench somewhere rather than imagining the hideous possibility of him cheating on her. He had come back and, not only that, he had been as jovial and attentive as he had always been to her. Surely that had to mean nothing had happened?

Clemmie felt her insides turn molten as Rufus turned and gave her a look of burning intensity. It was a look she was familiar with, the one he had given her at lunchtime before lifting her floral skirt, pushing her silk panties to one side and plunging himself into her with a husky groan. She returned his look, wishing Tessa would disappear so he could push her down on to the long, dry grass and make love to her. She needed constant reminders from him that he still wanted her but she knew she had to trust him because otherwise they were done for. The issue of children remained unresolved but Clemmie was willing to let it slide and tackle it later on. Right now, she didn't want to rock the boat; she just wanted Rufus to tell her how much he loved her and prove it.

'Um . . . do you have any childhood photographs?' Tessa asked tentatively. Seeing the state Clemmie was in, she would rather have ripped her own toenails out than ask that question but Jilly had left seven messages on her BlackBerry asking her to fax something over to her that day. She glanced at Rufus, who was gleefully booting apples into the air with the pointy toe of his black shoes. He seemed fine, not particularly communicative but then he wasn't prone to mindless chatter. By comparison, Clemmie looked as if she could dissolve into tears at any second. Tessa wondered if they'd had a row; the air between them seemed taut with tension.

'Mine are at my parents' house,' Rufus informed her helpfully. 'They're due back from one of their many holidays shortly so I'll give my mother a ring when they're back and get someone to drop them over to the manor house.'

'That's really kind of you, thanks.'

He gave her a keen stare. 'You won't find anything interesting in them, though. They're mostly of me looking like an arrogant tosser in some awful clothes, sporting an array of exotic hairstyles. Hideously embarrassing but hardly newsworthy, I can assure you.'

'Right, not to worry. My boss just wants me to gather background information on both of you.'

'I-I don't have any photos here,' Clemmie stated nervously, stopping dead in front of a drooping tree laden with pears. 'They're all back in LA, I'm afraid.'

Tessa was at pains to be polite and helpful as she tried to ignore the alarm bells going off in her head. 'Would a PA be able to send them over or something? Just a few of you as a child would be fantastic if you have some, so we can build up a picture of both of your lives before you met, that kind of thing.'

Clemmie walked alongside her haltingly. 'There might be . . .

but I'm not a sentimental person, you see. My parents are dead and I didn't get to keep many photographs of myself.' Her fingers pleated the skirt of her floral sundress manically. 'I was quite an ugly child too, all goofy teeth and big hair. Not like Rufus, he was adorable as a boy. Maybe that was why my mother didn't keep many pictures of me!' Her laughter sounded harsh and it petered out far too soon.

'What a shame,' Tessa said lightly. 'Photographs are wonderful memories, I always find.'

'Yes.' Clemmie gave her a brief nod. 'I can't promise anything because I'm almost certain I don't have anything you could use. But I'll see what I can do.' She walked away, grabbing Rufus's hand with something close to desperation.

Tessa felt torn once more. It was too much of a coincidence that Clemmie didn't have any childhood photographs and there had to be a good reason why her childhood remained such an enigma. A good reason that could set Hollywood aflame with gossip if only she could get to the bottom of it. But did she want to?

Tessa left Clemmie and Rufus alone, not before time as she saw Rufus slip Clemmie's dress from her shoulder. Why they felt the need to get it on in front of all and sundry was anyone's guess but she couldn't help feeling sorry for Clemmie.

Tessa felt the familiar weight of disillusionment settle across her shoulders and wondered who she could talk to about it. Sophie was always really supportive but Tessa didn't feel she could keep going round there and moaning all the time, especially not with Gil eavesdropping in the background. He had been nothing but pleasant in her presence but she wasn't sure she trusted him, not when it came to her TV career. Could she speak to Henny about it, perhaps? The thought of melting into Henny's warm comforting embrace and talking things through was incredibly tempting, Tessa decided as she headed back to her car. It would be just like talking to her own mother, being listened to and comforted, without being judged or criticised.

Tessa ignored her beeping BlackBerry by shoving it in the glove compartment of her car. Could she talk to Tristan about work? Probably. After all, they had touched on the subject the other night and he had been sympathetic and understanding about it. The trouble was, they had fun together but so far they hadn't done that much talking and since their drunken kiss the other night, they had thankfully acted like good friends, but nothing more. The night in the lake had been a fantastic stress reliever and Tessa remembered laughing so hard, she had thought she might wet herself. Afterwards, they had wrapped themselves in towels and fallen asleep on Tristan's studio floor like two exhausted kids. But she didn't feel that close to him. They were friends and he was good-looking and funny but she wasn't attracted to him in that way, she knew that now for a fact.

Sighing, Tessa realised she longed to spend another Sunday with the Forbes-Henry family, sharing a delicious family lunch cooked by Henny, with Jack and Caro sniping comically at each other as Milly made acidly witty comments to a placid and unbothered David, followed by a walk around the grounds of the manor with Austin for company. Perfect. As long as Will wasn't there to spoil everything.

Tessa did her best to push any thoughts of the Forbes-Henrys out of her head. Gritting her teeth, she tried to focus her efforts on finding a photo of Clemmie as a child.

Chapter Twelve

'I must go, *chérie*,' JB murmured as he checked his watch absent-mindedly. He was sure he was late for a meeting with Tessa but, strangely, time always seemed to drift by when he was with Caro. Disturbingly, it appeared to be happening more and more.

They were locked away in the room Will had named 'Loire', which sat at the back of the house and had cool forest-green walls. A wide window looked out over a picturesque view of the chapel and a well-tended fruit orchard, and the room also featured a kinky four-poster bed with silk tassels dangling from each corner.

When he had first set eyes on it, JB had wondered if the tassels were there for bondage purposes and whether this was intentional or not. JB could bear testament to the fact that they were more than up to the job.

He winced at thumping sounds from the floor above, no doubt courtesy of Gil and his team putting finishing touches to the penthouses which Will was so keen to showcase at the summer party. The drilling was grating on JB's nerves but at least it lent some form of cover for his noisy tryst with Caro.

'Turn that fucking drill off!' he heard Jack scream from the other side of the door, his stomping footsteps indicating his fury.

'Probably hung-over,' Caro sniped acerbically, twisting her head round in the direction of his voice. 'Austin whining for a dog biscuit sends him crazy when he's been at the Scotch, let alone an electric drill.'

JB felt an uncharacteristic flicker of guilt towards Jack. After all, the man was mere metres away from his adulterous wife and her lover. It was such a unique feeling for JB, he almost managed to convince himself it was something else. But still, when he had been introduced to Jack, JB had recognised a kindred spirit, a man who appreciated women, who drank to excess and lived to excess – things close to JB's own heart. And he could tell Jack had a sense of humour and, in spite of his lecherous ways, a streak of integrity.

JB lit a cigarette and passed it to Caro before lighting one for himself. Seeing Jack had scared the shit out of him. There was an edge of cynicism to Jack's voice and a despairing look in his eye that spoke volumes about the dissatisfaction in his life and the intense regret over his failing marriage. Meeting Jack had made JB wonder if he might end up that way if he carried on philandering but it had been a fleeting concern and not one that prevented him from responding to Caro's obvious advances. JB rationalised the affair by reminding himself that he was a red-blooded male, that it was Caro who had chased him and not the other way around, and that he, JB, could not be held solely responsible for Jack's misery.

Besides, he thought, as he caught sight of one of Tristan's ravishing paintings of Jack and Henny and their absent brother, proudly flanked by their parents, he had his own reasons for bedding Caro. He was aware his liaison with her meant he was taking his eye off the ball professionally, but needs must. He turned his piratical dark eyes towards her and reminded her that he had to be somewhere else.

She said nothing but slowly slid the sheet away from her body, exposing her naked, freckled skin and small breasts.

'Your family . . . you love ze French?' he murmured as he traced a finger down her collar bone. A spark of desire flashed in his eyes as she responded the way he knew she would.

'Will adores Frenchwomen . . .' Caro purred as she ran her

fingers down her rake-thin body, teasing her dark nipples to points. 'And I, for one, rather like Frenchmen, it seems.'

JB was distracted by her provocative display of self-arousal. 'Your 'usband Jack, 'is mother was French?' He squeezed her small breast with his hand and rubbed her nipple lazily with his thumb, his eyes alert and watchful.

'*Oui*,' Caro said breathily. She jerked against him, the steady pressure of his thumb driving her wild. 'Gabrielle . . . she didn't like me very much because she adored Jack and thought he was too good for me.' She was playing the relationship down dramatically; Jack's mother had detested Caro and had barely been able to stay in the same room as her, but she wasn't about to tell JB that. She didn't want him thinking she was difficult to get on with. 'Oh, don't stop, JB!'

JB bent his head obediently and grazed her skin with his mouth. 'She is dead now? Gabrielle, I mean?'

'Car crash,' Caro panted, her head thrashing around wildly on the pillow as JB's hot tongue left a trail down her stomach. 'Jack was beside himself with grief when his parents died. He was so devastated, he shut me out completely.' Again, Caro failed to add that she had found Jack's devastation incomprehensible, having no idea what it was like to actually get on with one's parents. Nor did she add that she had been ill-equipped to cope with his loss and, as such, she had been the one to shut Jack out, not the other way round.

Turned on to fever pitch, Caro woozily wondered if she should get one of those CD things to learn French with. Jack would kill her for only bothering to do it now that she had a lover she wanted to converse with, but what the hell. That was one of the problems with Jack, she thought, trailing her fingers down JB's bronzed chest. He never bloody *listened* to her. Whereas JB, by comparison, spent hours listening to her opinions on everything, positively encouraging her to talk about herself and her life. He seemed fascinated by her, flatteringly so, and feeling hard done by that her family didn't take her seriously, she found that having a captive audience was something she craved.

Determined to get his attention once more, Caro spread her legs and touched herself. She gasped in mock ecstasy, one eye open so she could watch JB's reaction.

JB let out a deep groan and leant over her, putting his hand round her throat as he kissed her roughly. As he knew she would, she responded eagerly, tangling her fingers in his dark curls and wrapping a yoga-toned thigh round his waist. She matched and, at times, even outdid his voracious appetite for sex, something deliciously unexpected in an otherwise predictable affair.

JB lay back as Caro began to kiss his chest, feeling her sharp fingernails digging into his side. He had met many women like Caro in his lifetime, older women who exuded confidence on the surface but who were dreadfully insecure underneath. Women like Caro had something to prove. And that made them dynamite in bed, in JB's opinion. But Caro had proved to be better than most. Expecting a quick shag with no regrets, JB had been staggered to discover that there was more to Caro than met the eye.

Blowing curls of blue smoke into the air, JB considered her, wriggling downwards, the intent gleaming in her eyes. He saw himself as something of a connoisseur when it came to sex. He had slept with hundreds of women and as far as he was concerned, he knew an amateur from a pro. He was confident he could arouse the most celibate of women in the right circumstances and he knew how far he could push it in terms of exploring the kinkier joys of sex. He lay back as Caro's flame-red hair tickled his thighs. But often, he found women lacking; they invariably thought they were fat (he didn't disagree but if they were so upset about it, why didn't they steer clear of butter for a while?), they found certain positions degrading and, at times, they simply lay there like a wet fish and let him do all the work. But every so often, one came along who taught him a thing or two and Caro was one of them.

JB let out a howl as Caro took him in her mouth expertly, her knowing hands cupping his balls, squeezing them with the exact amount of pressure needed to send him wild. Her eyes letting him know that for the next few minutes, she was in charge. Fine by him . . . he closed his eyes as Caro's tongue worked her magic.

'*Mon Dieu!*' he yelped suddenly, unable to control himself.

Caro flung herself back against his shoulder and coiled her arms round his neck. However smug her expression might be, he knew if he looked into her pale blue eyes, they would be hopeful, intense even, unconsciously communicating her need to be loved and her desire for reassurance.

JB stared up at the ornate coving framing the ceiling and tucked his arms behind his head. Caro wouldn't get either of those things she so desperately yearned for from him. He was fond of her – rather more than expected, in fact. She was fun and she had her uses but he intended to keep himself detached.

Caro tore herself away from him and shrugged her small, ice-blue dress over her head, believing she had JB wrapped round her little finger.

JB smirked. For all her bravado, JB knew he held Caro's fragile ego in the palm of his hand and that, on a whim, he could crush it beyond repair.

Realising he was planning to do just that at some point, JB was perturbed to find himself squirming slightly. He berated himself for losing his nerve. Fascinated, he watched Caro wander to the door. Her dress finished at mid-thigh – a difficult length to pull off – but with her lithe limbs and the matching blue killer heels holding her erect and proud, she managed it with ease. The silk dress was cut low at the front which only the most flat-chested of women could get away with and it exposed her graceful white neck. Carelessly flaunting the rule about not showing her chest and thighs at the same time, Caro carried off the outfit with panache. She wasn't classically stylish, not like Frenchwomen were, JB decided, but she had her own brand of brash, provocative chic he found rather endearing.

'I'll leave through the back way,' JB told her as he grabbed his boxer shorts. The 'Loire' room had a convenient double door which led out on to a balcony with steps down to the garden. They often used it so he could make his escape through the manor gardens, not that the subterfuge felt entirely necessary. JB avoided Caro's eyes as he yanked his jeans on. He was annoyed with himself for scrutinising her so openly, he wouldn't want his detached interest in her to be misread as something more meaningful.

'See you later, lover boy,' she cooed, blowing him a kiss and making much of the fact that seconds ago her pouting lips had been wrapped round his dick.

Shutting the door behind her, Caro was startled to find Jack sitting in an armchair on the landing facing the bedroom door. His stance seemed casual but his eyes blazed at her with such force that she started.

'Jack . . . w-what are you doing sitting there?'

His lip curled. 'Listening to you and that arrogant French *shit* screwing each other senseless.' He hated her for looking so beautiful. The ice-blue dress enhanced the colour of her eyes and complemented her vibrant hair and it made him want to tear it from her body.

Caro felt her stomach dip queasily. This wasn't in the rules. She and Jack never followed each other around or got involved in each other's affairs. Granted, she never usually did the deed on their doorstep, but since when had Jack ever cared enough to comment on her indiscretions?

'Is that what your problem is?' she mocked him, her hands on her bony, jutting hips. 'You can't bear the fact that I meet JB at the house?'

Jack stared at her coldly. 'You don't "meet" JB, Caro, you *fuck* him. Don't you dare dress it up to be anything else.'

She coloured and bit down hard on her lip. He was right, of course, but his words made her feel like a cheap whore. Jack had always had a way of exposing her vulnerability and she hated him for it.

'But since we're on the subject, tearing your clothes off and riding the bloke bareback in the family home is very tacky, Caro.' His mouth twisted bitterly. 'Even for you.' His green eyes clouded to dark olive as he stood up. He seemed to be finding it hard to articulate. 'I always thought we had an understanding, you and me,' he said gravely, his hands held out helplessly in front of him, 'but you seem to have moved the goalposts without telling me. I've never flaunted my affairs in front of you, *never*. But this . . . this is taking things too far. This changes everything.'

'Why do you *care*?' she shouted at him suddenly. 'This is what we do, this is how we live, Jack! You and me, this is what we've become.'

'Is it?' Jack shook with anger as he grabbed her arm, his fingers biting cruelly into her flesh. 'I think it's what *you've* become, Caro. You're making a fool of yourself with this bloody Frenchman. He doesn't care about you! He's using you. I have no idea for what – amusement, perhaps. Who knows? And you're falling head over heels for him.'

'As if!' Caro tossed her head proudly. Her chest rose and fell as her breath became more ragged. She felt close to tears but she had no idea why. She knew she had to defend herself. '*I* know our motto, Jack, even if you don't. "Never get serious, always keep your distance and, above all, leave your heart out of it." And that's exactly what I'm doing.'

Jack sneered at her. 'You're kidding yourself! I've never seen you throw yourself at someone like this before. Not since Jamie—'

'Don't talk about Jamie!' Caro shrieked, losing her cool. 'We said we'd never talk about Jamie, *ever*. How dare you—'

'Oh, I dare, Caro,' Jack said, yanking her closer, twisting her arm against his chest until she feared it might break. 'I dare because I'm fed up with acting like the bad guy in all this. You turned our marriage into a farce when you slept with my best friend and I've been bearing the brunt of it ever since. I'm sick of it! Sick of it, DO YOU HEAR ME?'

'You've slept with most of Appleton,' Caro whispered, her face white with shock. Jack had never spoken to her like this before. She hated it and she hated the look on his face. It was revulsion, despair and torment all messed up together and, in spite of her defiance, it ripped at her insides like a cut-throat razor.

'I slept with all those women to block out your fucking betrayal,' Jack hissed, letting go of her arm in disgust. 'And you know it.'

'Ja-ack,' she wheedled, running her finger coquettishly down his chin. She shimmied closer and pressed her body against his, not even thinking she might still have JB's scent all over her. 'You know we're meant to be together. We love to make each other jealous . . . it's our *thing*.'

Jack couldn't help himself; he slid his hand down her back, the heat from her skin and her lack of underwear whacking him in the groin like a vicious penalty kick. He knew what she was playing at and the pass she was making at him was predictable and downright offensive. But, as ever, he couldn't resist her and the heat of her body writhing against his was sending him into a tailspin.

'We're as screwed up as each other, we sleep around, we get jealous and we make mad, passionate love.' Caro guided his hand to her bottom and, helplessly, Jack kneaded it and let out an anguished groan. 'This thing with JB means nothing . . .'

Over her shoulder, Jack squeezed his eyes shut. The blatant

insincerity in her voice reached in and tore at his heart. Why couldn't Caro admit she was falling for JB? Or perhaps she simply didn't realise she was, he thought in agony. That hurt like corrosive acid in his emotional wounds and the needling pain threatened to overwhelm him. As a waft of French cigarettes and sex drifted under his nostrils, it was all Jack could do not to hurl Caro away from him. Instead, he called on every last vestige of dignity he had left in him and carefully, pointedly, he let go of her.

'I can't carry on like this,' he said gruffly. 'I don't know what's changed for me, but I can't do this any more. I want you, Caro, but it has to be all or nothing.' His eyes were tormented but as clear as his feelings. 'No more affairs, no more lies and no more than two of us in this marriage. If you still want me, that's how it has to be.'

'What?' Caro let out a grating laugh loaded with nerves. 'Just the two of us? You'd be bored stupid within weeks.'

'No, I wouldn't,' he said, holding her gaze with admirable steadiness. 'I'm too old to chase barmaids and flirt with school teachers. I want us, but only on those terms.'

Caro's mind was racing. 'Really, Jack, I never expected you to go all faithful on me!' She swallowed, playing for time. Could she give JB up for Jack? She didn't care about Nathan or any of the other boys from the village she dallied with, but JB – there was something different about him, some sort of connection that told her their relationship could be special. He was so interested in *her* and he loved to hear her talk. He cared about her, Caro sensed it. But if it meant losing Jack . . . There was so much history between them, so much passion. Could she walk away from that for ever? She moved closer to him, prepared to do whatever it took to get a reaction out of him.

Jack stared at her, appalled at being forced to witness her weighing up her options. Was he right? Did Caro care for JB more than she claimed? Instinctively, he knew she needed to hedge her bets. He could read her like a book; Caro would have to know she still had sexual power over him and she would try again and again until he gave in. He took a step backwards, needing to put some distance between them. He shook his head.

'No.'

'No? *No?*'

'You have to make a choice, Caro,' he told her in a voice that sounded far calmer than he felt. He could see how hurt she was but, somehow, it no longer mattered. He had to show her he meant business. 'It's him or me.' He let out a terse laugh. 'How dramatic I sound! That should appeal to your sense of occasion, at the very least.'

'You can't love me very much to turn me down,' she jeered, her voice shaky with pain.

'I love you too much not to,' he responded quietly.

Caro froze. She couldn't bear him to push her away like this. It hurt so much. But she needed something more than Jack's love; she needed someone who couldn't live without her, who couldn't throw her past in her face and demand that she change. There was nothing for it, she realised. It had to be JB. Whether he liked it or not, JB had to be the prize worth losing Jack over.

As she dashed away from him with a sob, Jack stood rooted to the spot, devastated. Her silence could only mean one thing. He had lost her. Hearing a floorboard creak behind him, he turned to see Will standing there, his horrified expression telling Jack he had overheard some of what had been said.

'I wasn't . . . I didn't mean to . . .' Will held up a fistful of CVs in a less than steady hand. 'I was on my way to interview a housekeeper and . . . shit, Dad, I'm so sorry.'

'Don't,' Jack choked, unable to bear the look of compassion in his son's eyes. 'I wish you hadn't had to hear that. I'm so sorry, son.'

Will pulled him into an awkward embrace. Feeling his son's

arms around him and the sympathy radiating from him, Jack almost lost it. He drew back.

'I need to know one way or the other if we can survive this,' he gulped, giving Will a brave smile. 'Your mother can be a nightmare but I love her. God knows why but I do. But it has to be a normal marriage, no more mucking about. Somehow, though, I don't think she can manage that.'

Will didn't know what to say but he couldn't help thinking his father was right.

'Especially now I've rejected her,' Jack said, scratching his head. 'Twice. That's tantamount to murder in your mother's eyes.'

'She slept with your best friend,' Will returned reasonably. 'Tit for tat, I'd say.'

'True.'

'No wonder Uncle Jamie disappeared without trace one day.'

'I forgave him,' Jack confessed, looking uncomfortable with his confession. 'Isn't that daft? I forgave him but not her. Why is that? Shagging one's best friend's wife is the height of ill manners, wouldn't you say?'

'Terribly inappropriate,' Will agreed heartily, glad to see his father's sense of humour hadn't completely deserted him.

Jack might be able to see the funny side of his dilemma but his nerves were shot to pieces. 'Fancy a drink? I feel a session coming on.'

'I'd love one but I've got to do all these bloody interviews.' Will glanced down at the CVs unenthusiastically. 'Although why we're bothering to hire a housekeeper is beyond me. We'd still need a general manager temporarily but Aunt Henny runs this house like clockwork; she could do this job with her eyes shut. We could pay her a proper salary which would probably make her feel far more like she was contributing and I for one would feel reassured to know she was in charge and not some stranger . . .'

'Hmmm.'

Will gave his father a thoughtful sideways glance. 'Dad, if you don't want to go ahead with this hotel idea, tell me. I know Mother hates it and wishes I'd bugger off back to France before all the riff-raff arrive and start using all the good silver. And with everything else that's going on . . .'

Jack shook his head vehemently. 'Seriously, Will, take no notice of your mother. Whatever she thinks, I believe this is the best thing for the family. It was a stroke of genius to turn this place into a hotel – and thank God you have the finances to pull it off.'

Will opened his mouth and closed it again. Now was not the time to enlighten his father about his dwindling bank balance. 'I just want the family to have a business we can all rely on. Especially now that you're practically past it.' He grinned to soften the blow.

'Watch it,' Jack told him with a glint in his eye. 'I might be old but I'm still your father and you need to show me some degree of respect. It's the rules.' He cast his eyes to the floor, his shoulders slumping. 'It's probably not the most advisable thing to do now, Will, but I'm afraid I need to go and get absolutely plastered.'

Will watched him from the banisters and let out a heartfelt sigh. It wasn't every day you got to witness your parents' marriage break down, even if he had seen it coming for years. Was his mother really willing to risk everything for some guy she barely knew? It seemed particularly ill-advised when JB had a reputation as a womaniser but, remembering her recent, terrible investment, Will realised logic didn't feature when his mother was obsessed with a man.

He made a face at the CVs in his hand. He had half a mind to cancel the interviews he had lined up so he could get drunk with his father but, as ever, the burden of family responsibility weighed heavily on Will's shoulders. Doing the 'honourable' thing as usual, Will headed downstairs to ask people turgid questions about where they saw themselves in five years' time.

Rufus checked his watch again. He was sure he had said two o'clock. Where the hell was she? He tweaked a curtain back furtively to have a look outside and cursed as his coiffed hair got caught on the gauzy material. He tugged it free and with a derisive snort looked round the room he had rented. This wasn't the glamorous location he had imagined, but he supposed it would have to do.

Rufus grimaced. The night of the terrible row with Clemmie, he had got so drunk in the pub with India he had barely been able to say his own name. His mind had been thinking one thing but his body quite another, so the evening hadn't gone as planned. Any hopes of dragging India upstairs to one of the pub's bedrooms had fallen by the wayside when he'd passed out on the table. The next time they'd met up, India had only managed to join him for an hour before very reluctantly dashing home, mumbling something about having to get up early for work in the morning. Rufus had almost called the whole thing off but India had bombarded him with so many lurid text messages since then, he couldn't resist meeting up with her again. But this time, he meant business.

The pub he'd chosen, the Brayford Arms, was in a small village twenty miles east of Appleton and it wasn't the most salubrious of establishments; the torn, musty curtains had seen better days and the carpets were matted and worn. But it was run by an old couple who were unlikely to have seen any of his movies and even more unlikely to read *heat* magazine, a publication that often pictured him with Clemmie on his arm and in which he regularly won the coveted spot of 'Torso of the Week'.

Rufus had almost ruined his hair by sporting a huge baseball cap with a wide brim which covered his dark eyes. He had worn an old grey sweatshirt, shorts and trainers but vanity had made him bring a change of clothing. Disguises were one thing but he had a reputation to uphold so as soon as he was inside the dreadful room, he had changed into his uniform of a funky black T-shirt, his favourite black Diesel jeans and pointed boots.

Rufus had hired the honeymoon suite on the understanding that it would at least be superior to the other rooms in the hotel in terms of décor. Big mistake – the room was actually an old-fashioned, lace-festooned nightmare, a room Dickens's grotesque character Miss Havisham could happily move into. Each piece of furniture was badly made and fake 'period'; the four-poster bed consisted of a rickety white frame and frothy drapes of discoloured lace, and the naff Chippendale copy dressing table proudly displayed a glass tray with a set of silver hairbrushes, frizzy blond hairs trailing from one of them.

Rufus shuddered. The room gave him the bloody creeps. He half expected to find intricate cobwebs looped across the timbers and a crusty old wedding dress in the wardrobe. God-damnit, where was she? He threw himself on the peach lace bedspread petulantly and allowed himself a few seconds' thought about Clemmie as he waggled his pointed black boots at the ceiling. She was becoming increasingly insecure around him, demanding to know where he was going and where he had been. She wanted to make love morning, noon and night – not a problem for someone like him who could get an erection at the drop of a hat, but he was aware that it was Clemmie's desire for reassurance that was behind her ravenous sexual appetite, rather than desire for him. And, frankly, it was becoming rather wearing.

Rufus sipped a glass of rose-pink champagne and wrinkled his nose in distaste. He had never liked champagne and this limited edition version had come with an extortionate price tag and a fancy pink-edged label. But considering how downmarket the hotel was, he knew he needed to take other steps to impress. Experience had taught him that over-priced bubbly invariably did the trick – not that there would be many bubbles left soon, he told himself sulkily as he watched them dissolve in the flute.

He idly checked his phone, rolling his eyes when he saw three more text messages from Clemmie. Each one was more explicit – and, therefore, more desperate – than the last. He frowned. He supposed he couldn't blame her for not trusting him; after all, he was betraying her right now, wasn't he? But was he betraying her because of her neediness, or was she needy because she suspected him of betrayal? Rufus knew which answer sat more comfortably on his conscience so he settled for that one.

There was a tentative knock on the door and he leapt up off the bed and put his ear close to the door.

'Who is it?' he whispered, beginning to feel turned on by the cloak and dagger nature of it all.

'It's me . . . India. Open the door, for God's sake!'

He opened the door and yanked India into the darkened room.

'Ow! What do you think you're doing?' She rubbed her arm with exaggerated hurt and looked at him as if he was nuts. Rufus was acting like some sort of paranoid freak and she was already in a horrible mood. Having found out that day that she had flunked her GCSEs spectacularly, achieving F grades in all but one subject, India had spent the morning listening to her mother droning on about how a measly C in Geography wasn't going to get her very far. India had no idea why she had been so inspired in her Geography lessons – perhaps her desire to see the world had sparked some sort of interest – but to make matters worse, Milly had, of course, aced every single one of her exams and wouldn't shut up about how she was going to be the next Tessa Meadmore.

Knowing Rufus was the last person she could talk to about her exam dilemmas, considering she had told him she was 'practically eighteen', India pushed her worries aside and gave him a dazzling smile.

'I can't risk anyone seeing you here with me,' he replied, staring at her. She was wearing a frumpy, shapeless mud-brown dress which hid her body completely and her feet were covered by flat sandals in a less than fetching shade of mushroom. Her ginger hair was pulled back into a neat bun at the nape of her neck and she was wearing old-fashioned NHS spectacles with heavy lenses which made her blue eyes look enormous.

'Wow, pink champagne,' she said, suitably impressed. 'Sorry I'm late, I had to get three buses to get here. Oh, what a shame, you started without me. I hope there are still some bubbles left.'

Rufus ignored her. 'What the fuck are you wearing? How did you know this room was missing a real life Miss Havisham?'

'A real life who?' India looked mystified.

'Never mind.' Rufus faltered for a moment, wondering if he could seriously start up any kind of affair with someone for whom decent literature was clearly an enigma. On reflection, India might not know her Dickens, but he was sure she knew her *dicks*. He silently laughed at his own joke.

Unabashed, India grinned back at him. 'I borrowed these clothes off my mum. You told me no one could recognise me. It's a disguise, see?'

She kicked off the hideous sandals and removed the glasses and Rufus watched in wonder as she undid the neat bun and let her long, ginger hair fall down her back. He felt his groin snap to life as she slowly unbuttoned the horrible brown dress – underneath it, she was wearing a figure-hugging red dress which was as subtle as a kick in the balls. It had cut-outs at the sides which showed an expanse of brown, taut flesh and fragile straps that Rufus longed to snap from her wide brown shoulders. Not being the deepest of individuals, he soon found that India's lack of literary awareness was forgotten in light of her blatant lack of disregard for underwear.

'Better?' she taunted him as she twirled on the tips of her

painted toenails to give him a three hundred and sixty degree view of her body.

'Much.' Rufus pulled her towards him. 'You seem to be a bit of an expert at this. Do you often meet older men in hotel rooms?'

She gasped at his touch and shook her head, her gingery-blond tresses shaking from side to side. It wasn't just that she fancied Rufus, it was what he represented. With him, she could see a glittering, Hollywood lifestyle ahead of her, full of riches and success. India was all about the glamour and she knew that if she could just entice Rufus away from Clemmie – and not just as a secret fling – she was well on her way to the lavish, indulgent life she deserved. She didn't think her mother would be so upset about her only having one GCSE if she managed to get Rufus to propose to her, India thought triumphantly.

Rufus kissed her, gently at first but when she responded ardently to his lips, with more force. Teeth clashed, tongues met and hands dived beneath clothes to caress bare flesh. Rufus was delighted at how keen India was and found her boldness a massive turn-on. Clemmie was spectacular in bed, particularly at the moment when she seemed hell-bent on showing him every single sexual trick she had ever learnt, but there was something erotic about India's selfishness; it was as if she was focused on her own pleasure just as much as his. And compared to Clemmie's recent, overly generous attentions, Rufus couldn't help feeling oddly enthralled at finding himself with someone as self-absorbed and as greedily sexual as he was.

Pushing India away from him, he removed the straps of the dress from her shoulders roughly and flung the dress to the floor. Beneath it she was, as expected, totally naked, apart from a pink diamanté 'I' on a chain. She stared back at him confidently, watching his eyes travel from her small, youthful breasts to her flat stomach and beyond.

Christ, she was as bald as a coot down there, Rufus thought

excitedly, his erection jumping madly in his jeans. He sank down on to the bed, his breath ragged. On the dressing table, his eyes caught sight of something unsettling. Attached to India's handbag was a key ring with 'Justin Timberlake' emblazoned down the side of it. He felt uneasy when he clocked the pink diamanté necklace again – it was unsophisticated and not something he would have expected her to wear. As she advanced upon him purposefully, he halted her with the toe of his pointed boot.

'Who bought you that necklace?'

'Milly. It was an early birthday present.' India could have kicked herself. The last thing she wanted to draw attention to was her age; it was the only thing that might have Rufus running for the hills.

He narrowed his heavily smudged eyes. 'A birthday present? Just how old are you?'

'Old enough.'

'What does that mean?' God, she was exasperating! She had told him she was 'practically eighteen' which had almost made him change his mind about starting up with her but was she telling the truth? He narrowed his eyes and watched her but she gazed back at him innocently, her shaven groin taunting him.

'I'm old enough to know what I want,' India told him curtly, obviously bored with his questions. 'And I want you. Do you want me?'

'You know I do.' He groaned as he watched her play with her nipples in the most distracting way.

'Then shut up,' she murmured as she moved closer. 'I'm eighteen and that's legal, so what's the problem?' She felt his hands on her waist and leant towards him until her perky nipples grazed his chin.

'You can't tell anyone about us,' he warned her as he ran a finger up the inside of her thigh.

She quivered and jerked against him. 'Not even Milly?'

'Definitely not Milly.' Rufus suppressed the urge to reprimand her for being so immature. What did she think this was, some sort of joke? She needed to understand how serious he was. He might be willing to play with fire but he most emphatically did not intend to get his fingers burnt.

'This isn't just about me being older than you, India, this is about who I am. I'm famous, and photographers, reporters – let's just say they'd pay you handsomely for gossip like this. Therefore, no one can know about us, not your parents and not your best friend. Do you understand me?'

India's head dropped backwards as Rufus left a trail of kisses across her stomach and moved up onto her left breast. Keeping something like this from Milly was going to kill her, they were close and they told each other everything. But if telling Milly meant losing Rufus . . . India let out a squeak as Rufus took a nipple into his mouth and sucked on it hungrily, just as he slid a finger inside her. Her knees felt like jelly and she grabbed Rufus's shoulders to stop herself toppling over. So it was true what all these stupid romance novels said about good sex – she just needed to be with a real man instead of some spotty adolescent who didn't know one end of a clitoris from another.

India felt her insides turn molten as Rufus leant down and gently kissed her smooth crotch. This was probably going to be the best sex of her life and if he wanted her to swear she wouldn't tell anyone, she would.

'I won't . . . tell . . . anyone,' she managed shakily as his finger probed deeper.

'Good.' Rufus knew he had been right about India when he had first clapped eyes on her. He felt sure he could trust her and once he had her totally under his spell sexually, he knew she would do anything for him. Rufus decided to hammer the point home while he had India's full attention.

'And I am due to marry one of the biggest movie stars in the world in a few months.' He found her G spot and fingered it

215

hard. 'And this . . . *fling* isn't going to change that. Are we clear?'

India, torn between giving in to the delirious head rush she was experiencing as she reached her first proper orgasm and taking in the enormity of what Rufus was saying, looked jolted. Feeling waves of pleasure mounting inside her, she nonetheless allowed herself a moment to get her thoughts in order.

Rufus could think what he liked, she thought, almost fainting as her body rippled with desire. She would play by the rules and she would keep their affair a secret, even if it meant hiding the truth from Milly. She would wear absurd disguises and she would turn up to whatever disgusting hotels Rufus chose. India grimaced at the décor in the old-fashioned honeymoon suite, knowing she deserved better, but she could put up with it if it meant she would get her own way in the long run.

However, if Rufus thought she was going to settle for being his shag bunny for the next few months while he floated around in the background with Clemmie choosing buttonholes and writing wedding vows, he was very much mistaken. By the time she had finished with him, he wouldn't even be able to remember Clemmie's name. And as for marrying her – India let out a scream as she came all over Rufus's hand in a flood of wetness.

'Shush!' He laughed, flattered that she seemed to fancy him so much. He put a hand over her mouth to stop her crying out again, not realising he was turning her on even more.

India's eyes gleamed in the semi-darkness of the room. That might have been her first orgasm but it sure as hell wasn't going to be her last. She knew she could easily get addicted to the feelings Rufus was stirring up inside her but it was about time she showed him what he could have on tap. And although she wasn't going to advertise the fact just yet, sexually, there wasn't a single thing she was going to say no to. That had to keep him interested for the next few months. He could do whatever he liked to her, whenever he liked. And she'd bet her life that

Clemmie, as fabulous as Rufus claimed she was in bed, drew the line at certain things.

Whipping his belt free and yanking open the buttons of his jeans in one smooth movement, India grabbed the half-full glass of champagne from the bedside table and tossed it into Rufus's lap.

'I hope that's vintage,' she said mockingly as she slowly lowered her long hair over the rearing head of his penis until it was trailing along the top. 'Now, let's see if we can blow those bubbles away . . .'

Chapter Thirteen

At Appleton Manor a week later, Clemmie was completing another short segment of filming with Tessa. There was a buzz of excitement in the air as the summer party neared. Invitations had been sent, flyers had been distributed and that very morning a gleaming ivory sign had been erected at the front of the manor house with 'The Appleton Manor Hotel' printed across it in bold lettering.

Outside the manor house, David, safe in the knowledge that he had scored his place at Bristol University, was topping up his tan, stretched out like a lanky stick insect. Freddie, who had unsurprisingly failed all three of his A levels but was reeling from the unexpected and rather searing monologue he had received from his father that morning, was chain-smoking from the shock of it all. Calmly unruffled by the certainty of failure until his intelligence had been brought into question, Freddie was sulkily doing his best to ignore David who was rather sanctimoniously advising him that it was high time Freddie knuckled down and took his education seriously.

Unable to track India down on her mobile yet again, Milly had cautiously donned a funky purple bikini before reclining on a towel on the other side of the lake. She drooled longingly over Freddie's tanned biceps from behind her dark glasses.

Watching them enviously from the open French windows of one of the now completed penthouses, Tessa and Clemmie wished the interview was over so they could get outside in the fresh air, Tessa to strip down to her undies in the sun and

Clemmie to escape outside to fret about Rufus in peace. The penthouse was beautiful, with luxurious ruby-red armchairs sitting either side of a gorgeous brickwork fireplace, and the bathroom was to die for with a double jacuzzi tub, a monsoon shower with jets tilted at the most interesting angles and rows of the Penhaligon toiletries Will was so fond of.

'So your Christmas wedding will feature white and purple flowers, hundreds of tiny lit candles and Venetian crystal centrepieces with diamond bases?' It seemed incongruous to be discussing Christmas on such a stiflingly hot day but Tessa had been instructed by Jilly to get the lowdown on Clemmie's wedding details, 'because, kiddo, that's what the public wants to know about'. Tessa sighed, feeling sorry for Clemmie having to answer such mundane questions. She had already been forced to quiz her on how many different types of flowers she and Rufus might have, how many tiers their cake would feature with what different flavours and frostings and how much their exclusive, diamond-encrusted wedding rings would cost.

Clemmie, wearing a delicate, strapless lemon sundress and matching mules, seemed distracted. 'Er . . . yes, I think so. The, um, evening ceremony is going to be held in the ballroom and Gil says he can create a star-studded canopy or something for the ceiling. Isn't that right, Gil?' She twisted in her chair.

'That's right. A celestial sky in inky, midnight-blue decked out with hundreds of Swarovski crystals and twinkling stars,' Gil called delightedly from the sidelines. Clutching a swatch book of coloured fabrics and wearing a scarlet T-shirt, he stood behind Joe the cameraman, looking ever so slightly unhinged, his excitement at being referred to by Clemmie almost sending him over the edge. Feeling Joe nudging him backwards as he gestured for his lighting man to tilt the hot lamps towards Clemmie more, Gil moved to one side, transfixed by Clemmie's star quality.

'And the menu features a lobster terrine with a champagne jelly,' Tessa continued almost apologetically as she consulted her notes, 'and individual chocolate and plum soufflés with brandy milk ice cream. Sounds delicious.'

Clemmie smiled but it was tinged with weariness, as if she could barely manage to hold it together. 'Yes . . . er . . . Henny Forbes-Henry came up with some wonderful ideas so I've handed them over to my wedding team in LA. If we stick to Henny's menu I think the food will be to everyone's expectations.'

Tessa was keen to wrap the questions up, realising Clemmie had had enough. 'And finally, is it true you plan to ship purple dragonflies over from Florida to hang in glass baubles from a Christmas tree?' She had read this in a tabloid magazine at the weekend and was sure it wasn't true but it had animal lovers in such a tizzy, she didn't think she could get away with not asking Clemmie to comment on it.

'Dragonflies? In glass baubles?' Clemmie repeated, looking flabbergasted. 'No, of course we're not going to do anything as ridiculous as that! That would be inhumane and seeing as I love animals, I wouldn't dream of doing something like that and certainly not for this bloody wedding. Good God!' Ripping off her microphone and tugging it free of her clothes, she put her hand up to the camera defensively as if to ask them to stop filming.

Tessa nodded at Joe who was already lowering his camera and gesturing at his lighting team to pack up. Furious that JB had once again missed a filming session, she wondered where the hell he had got to. He was no doubt with Caro somewhere but his increasingly frequent absences made his continuous taunts about her having lost her touch harder to stomach. His unprofessional attitude seemed out of character and Tessa wondered what Caro had done to put him under her spell because JB didn't strike her as the kind of man to be deterred from his job.

One advantage of JB being absent, however, was that Tessa had full control of the interviews (Jilly's interference aside) and seemed to have earned the respect of the film crew for handling everything so well. Without JB there to snarl orders and criticise her and anyone else who fell short of his expectations, filming was much smoother and more relaxed. Which didn't excuse the way she had made Clemmie feel and she rushed to make it up with her.

'Clemmie, I'm so sorry to have to ask you about such stupid things,' she said quickly. 'The dragonfly thing – it was in a magazine and I was instructed to get a comment from you about it.'

'Honey, it's not your fault.' Clemmie shook her head, her dark hair like a cloud around her shoulders. Her honeyed Texan tones were as rich as maple syrup on hot pancakes but her voice was filled with distaste. 'I can't believe the papers write this rubbish but I'd rather have a chance to deny it than have people think I'd do something as cruel as shipping dragonflies over to string them up on a Christmas tree. What do they take me for?' She looked thoroughly ted up, her mouth drooping at the corners and her body cowed.

Catching sight of a gushing Gil heading straight for them, Tessa whipped Clemmie away, but Gil was determined and he hurried down the stairs after them.

Ever the pro, Clemmie paused on the landing and took Gil's sweating hand in hers. 'Thank you so much for letting us film here,' she told him, her eyes shining with genuine warmth. 'I know how incredibly busy you must be, getting everything finished for the grand opening.'

'You are *most* welcome,' Gil said breathlessly. 'And may I say how splendid you look in that outfit?' He bowed over her hand in an attempt at gallantry but ended up head-butting Clemmie's hand. He turned as red as his tight T-shirt but Clemmie gave him a distant smile before drifting away, barely seeming to notice. As Tessa went after Clemmie, she heard Gil answering his phone, his face lighting up like a sixty-watt bulb when he realised who his caller was.

'Jilly! How lovely to hear from you . . . what's that you say? Oh, what *fun*!'

Wondering why on earth her boss would be calling Gil directly, Tessa rushed after Clemmie who was wandering around the manor hallway like a lost soul. Was she ill? Tessa wondered. She had bloodshot eyes, possibly from lack of sleep, and her normally rosy cheeks lacked colour underneath all the blusher she was wearing but it was her jerky manner that worried Tessa.

'Are you all right?' Tessa didn't know if it was the sad look in her eyes or the slightly unsteady way she was wobbling on her heels, but Clemmie seemed as fragile as a newborn foal at the moment.

Clemmie nodded. Seeing Henny approaching, she plastered a smile of greeting on to her face, once more proving she was worthy of her Oscar.

'Oh, there you are!' Henny greeted her happily, waving a card covered in pink roses at her. 'I didn't know if you wanted to have a quick chat about the wedding invitations. Tristan finished that purple flower you commissioned him to paint for your special invitation company and it looks beautiful. Come and see and I'll bring us all some tea.'

For a second, Tessa wondered if Clemmie was about to lose her temper but instead she said nothing and inclined her head graciously, her shoulders drooping just a little.

Giving Clemmie a sideways glance, Tessa hesitated for a moment. 'Actually, Henny, would it be possible to have something refreshing like . . . some white wine? I could really do with a drink after the week I've had.'

Clemmie caught her eye and with a slight smile nodded. 'I don't usually indulge but that sounds lovely.'

Henny bustled off to fetch a bottle and glasses, returning in a jiffy. 'Here we are!' Her frazzled sandy hair seemed even more out of control than normal, with random strands sticking out at all angles. Her rather tight beige blouse was buttoned up the wrong way and she seemed flustered as she poured Sancerre into huge crystal glasses, great splashes landing on the tray.

'Er . . . let me,' Tessa said gently, removing the wine bottle from her. 'Is something the matter?'

'Yes, you seem terribly upset,' Clemmie said, worriedly exchanging a glance with Tessa.

Henny sat back against the cushions and began pleating her faded blue cotton skirt with frantic fingers. She seemed unwilling to unburden herself but seeing the kind faces in front of her, she gave in.

'I'm just *so* worried about Jack,' she confessed finally. 'He won't talk to anyone and he's sinking bottles of whisky quicker than you can say Johnny Walker.' Her expression became fierce. 'It's all bloody Caro's fault! Starting up this stupid affair with that . . . that *man*.' She couldn't bring herself to utter JB's name. 'I thought he was trouble and I tried to warn Caro but she wouldn't listen. She's such a selfish little madam. Jack's absolutely devastated because he thinks Caro's about to leave him.'

'This is the third session of filming JB's missed,' Tessa informed them grumpily as she handed out glasses of white wine. 'I wouldn't mind but as soon as he deigns to turn up, he starts bellowing in every direction and wanting to do things his way.'

'Men!' Clemmie exclaimed, taking a sip of wine. She stared ahead of her but felt their eyes on her and made an effort to explain her unexpected exclamation. 'I just mean they can be a law unto themselves. Poor Jack, though – he's such a sweet man. Do you really think his marriage to Caro is in trouble?'

'I do.' Henny downed her wine rapidly. 'I don't care about

Caro, as awful as that sounds, but Jack is my brother and he's been so wonderful to me, especially since Bobby died. It's unbearable to see him so grief-stricken.' Her voice broke.

'Oh, Henny!' Tessa grabbed a bunch of tissues from the table and thrust them at her, feeling useless.

Henny took some gratefully. 'I know I must sound terribly dramatic but I always thought Jack and Caro would stay together. I know they row and cheat on each other all the time but it was part of the game. But this is wrong . . . this is *serious*. Caro seems so . . . bloody-minded at the moment. It's almost as if she's decided JB is something special, someone she could leave Jack for.'

Tessa snorted. She couldn't see JB running off with Caro somehow. It wasn't the age gap or even that she thought JB would give Jack's feelings any kind of consideration. It was that JB seemed so in control of himself, she couldn't imagine him losing his head over any woman. Run off with Caro? She couldn't see it. Tessa was distressed to see tears running down Clemmie's face now too and she plucked another wad of tissues from the box to stem the flow.

'Oh no! Clemmie, please tell us what's wrong.'

Henny looked appalled to see Clemmie in such a state and almost upset her wine glass.

'I'm so sorry, I really didn't mean to let my guard down like this.' Clemmie looked down at her lap. Her narrow, exposed shoulders in the strapless yellow dress made her seem even more vulnerable. 'Can I say something? Off the record, I mean?'

Realising Clemmie's comment was directed at her, Tessa blushed. She couldn't blame Clemmie. Nothing tended to be off the record for people in her profession. But Tessa was beginning to think she was a friend first and a journalist second these days. Maybe Jilly was right. She had lost her edge after all.

'I know you have to ask and I understand why but it makes me feel really sad. I'd much rather you could see me as someone you could confide in than an untrustworthy hack.'

Clemmie shook her head. 'Tessa, I don't think that! I just . . . need to know I can speak freely without my words ending up in a magazine. It's happened so many times before, you see.' She gazed at them miserably. 'It's Rufus. He's been acting really strangely lately. It's . . . I can't even put my finger on it . . . but he's not himself.'

'In what way?'

'He's attentive, affectionate and nothing seems to have changed there.' Clemmie dismally took another sip of wine. 'But he keeps disappearing and I have no idea where he goes. If I ask him, he gets so annoyed with me so I try not to do it. But there are so many times I can't get hold of him and I send him text after text and he doesn't respond. He seems irritable and moody and almost . . . *guilty*, as if anything I ask him is accusatory, even if it isn't. What do you think? Please be honest with me.'

Tessa started to feel uncomfortable. Did Clemmie have any idea that she was making it sound like Rufus might be having an affair?

Henny was obviously thinking the same thing. 'I feel dreadful saying this to you when you seem so unhappy but since you've asked us to be honest, is it possible Rufus is, you know, up to something? With someone else?'

Clemmie buried her face in her hands, her cloud of dark hair providing momentary privacy from the world. 'Oh my God! Of course he must be . . . I thought it at the start but since then I kept telling myself I was being horrible, not trusting him that way. You're right, Henny! There isn't any other explanation.'

'There's always another explanation,' Tessa said with more conviction than she felt. 'Rufus still wants to get married, doesn't he? Maybe this isn't as bad as it sounds. Sometimes the worst situations can turn out to be innocent.'

'Can they?'

The plea in Clemmie's voice was painful to hear, Tessa thought. As for the look of utter terror in her eyes as she contemplated losing Rufus, well, it was almost impossible to witness.

'We'll help you through this,' Henny told Clemmie, patting her hands as she caught Tessa's eye rather guiltily. 'Whatever is going on, we're here for you and we're all going to stick together, aren't we?'

Tessa nodded silently as Clemmie dissolved into grateful tears.

'What about this one, darling? This is so *you*.' A few days after being told he had a presenting slot on Clemmie and Rufus's documentary, Gil had taken Sophie out to celebrate in the only way he knew how: shopping. He planned to buy her a new dress for the summer party and had taken her to an exclusive boutique in Manchester where every dress was a 'one-off' and cost a fortune.

Sophie sighed as Gil held up a cream dress made of linen which had feminine ruffles on the skirt and a narrow bodice. She had intended to ask Tessa to come dress shopping with her but since she had found out about her skinny-dip with Tristan, Sophie felt a bit awkward around her. They still sent each other texts and spoke on the phone but thankfully Tessa was busy filming and hadn't been able to come over for lunch. Sophie felt bad about it but she wasn't sure she was ready to hear Tessa waxing lyrical about what a good kisser Tristan was – or, worse, how good he was in bed. She forced herself to give Gil her full attention.

'The ruffles are very "of the moment",' he was saying, 'and I think the cream would look fabulous with your colouring.' He put a finger to his chin thoughtfully. 'The only problem is that it will probably crease like buggery . . . Something to consider, I think? But not a deal breaker by any means.'

Sophie drifted off again for a minute. How on earth could she face Tristan? What would she say? Sophie clutched her stomach as her breakfast muesli swirled dangerously and threatened to make an unwelcome reappearance. She closed her eyes as she imagined the look on Tristan's face. Would he look stunned to see her? Would he look guilty? Contrite? Totally unconcerned? Worst of all, *bored*?

'I also like the chocolate brown,' Gil was saying bossily, as he held up a strappy sundress with a full skirt and a matching bolero. 'I think you should try both of them on, darling, so we can get the full effect. I'll be wearing my cream Armani trousers with my emerald shirt and it would be lovely if we could complement each other, but it might not be possible if we plump for the brown one. Sophie, are you listening to me?'

'Sorry, Gil. I'll try them on.' She headed for the changing rooms, watched by a beady-eyed assistant who was taking sucking-up to a whole new level. Taking her jeans off listlessly, Sophie listened to Gil who was chattering on incessantly on the other side of the door.

'Isn't it splendid news about me being offered my own design slot on the documentary? I don't know if Tessa put in a good word for me with her boss but the offer from Jilly came out of nowhere and I intend to make the absolute most of it. Do you have the cream one on?'

'Almost,' Sophie muttered as she struggled into it. It was frilly and far too fussy for her taste. 'It's such good news about your TV slot, Gil. I'm so pleased for you.' She could actually see him being a big hit with viewers with his over-the-top delivery and his years of design expertise. She pulled the door open and paraded in front of her fiancé and the kiss-arse assistant.

Barely hearing the cries of, 'Oh yes, darling, that's the *one*!' and 'Oooh, madam, it's as if it was *made* for you!' Sophie stared at her reflection. Should she just tell Gil about Tristan and worry about the consequences later? Maybe it would be better. She turned to him tentatively and thought hard about what to say. 'I lied . . . I have been here before and I know all the Forbes-Henrys, some better than others . . .' No, that sounded horrendous. 'I probably should have said something before but Tristan is Ruby's father and I was once very much in love with him . . . ' Even worse.

On the other side of the door, Gil misunderstood her anxiety for indecision. 'You can have any dress you want, my angel. Just say the word. Don't let me railroad you into making a bad choice.'

The assistant looked affronted at the suggestion that any of her designer threads would result in a 'bad choice' then hurriedly rearranged her features.

'It's not the d-dress,' Sophie stammered, clinging to Gil's arm for stability, the way she had always done. It was no good; the innocent look in his wide blue eyes stopped her from taking action. She couldn't hurt him, she simply couldn't do it.

'Try the chocolate one on, my love. I think it's going to look exquisite!'

Suddenly, Sophie needed to get out of the shop. 'Let's just take the chocolate one,' she said, handing it to the assistant who was delighted to have sold the more expensive dress.

'But you haven't even tried it on yet,' Gil protested touchily, 'and we'll clash if I wear my emerald green.' He handed over his credit card with bad grace and started muttering under his breath about wearing his fawn-brown Galliano shirt instead.

Sophie wasn't proud of herself. And she was still faced with either feigning illness to avoid the party or dealing with the prospect of coming face to face with Tristan. And Gil discovering the secret she had kept from him for the past five years. She had less than forty-eight hours to prepare herself for the biggest confrontation of her life. And it didn't feel like nearly enough time.

'So when's Claudette turning up?' Tristan said as he took a step back and squinted critically at his canvas. He grabbed a tube of paint and squirted it on to a board before scraping it off into a bin. It was too late to be painting; the light in his studio was terrible at this time of night but he was woefully behind on his latest commission – a portrait of the spoilt, toad-faced son of a local peer.

'She plans to get here on the morning of the party,' Will replied, cracking open two bottles of beer and handing one to Tristan. 'Cutting it a bit fine but she has work commitments, unfortunately.' He gave his brother a knowing grin. 'But I know you're not a fan of Claudette's, Tris, so you don't have to pretend to be excited or anything.'

Tristan looked sheepish, pausing with his paintbrush in mid-air. 'Is it that obvious? Sorry, I thought I'd done an excellent job of hiding it.'

'Not exactly. It's fine, though. I mean, we can't always like each other's girlfriends, can we?' Will took a slug of beer and strolled over to Tristan's stash of completed canvases. 'Or fiancées, in this case.' As a matter of fact, it bothered Will greatly that his brother seemed to have taken an instant dislike to his fiancée. Claudette was the one woman he could see himself spending the rest of his life with and it irked him that Tristan hadn't warmed to her. Particularly when in the past he had always valued his brother's opinion of his girlfriends.

'You've got a point about the women in our lives, Will.' Tristan wiped his paint-stained fingers on his already ruined polo top and tipped the cold beer down his throat. 'I mean, you can't *stand* Tessa and I think she's amazing.'

Will turned and narrowed his eyes. 'Is Tessa your girlfriend, then?'

'Sadly not.' Tristan peeled the label off his beer bottle, avoiding Will's gaze. 'I tried to fall in love with her, I really did. I thought she could be the one, you know? After everything that happened with . . . *her*. Tessa's just so funny and bubbly and honest, I genuinely thought it could work.'

'*Honest?*'

Tristan found the obvious doubt in Will's voice exasperating. 'Yes, Will, *honest*. Christ, I seem to spend most of my time convincing the pair of you to give the other one a chance!'

Will almost choked on his beer at this. Tristan was convincing Tessa to give *him* a chance?

'Anyway, we're not talking about you and Tessa because there is no you and Tessa. You can't stand the sight of each other and that's that.' Tristan grabbed a rag and wiped a small smudge from his canvas. 'It's a shame because you've both got totally the wrong impression about each other and you're acting like a couple of children, but who cares? I certainly shouldn't.' He stared past Will unseeingly. 'I'm just gutted because Tessa and I had . . . let's just say a bit of a moment but it didn't actually lead to anything.'

'When you say a "bit of a moment", are you referring to the infamous skinny-dip in the lake?'

Tristan sat up straight. '*Infamous* skinny-dip? Infamous would indicate that the . . . thing in the lake was something everyone knows about.'

'Seen by many and talked about by absolutely *everyone*,' Will corrected with a twinkle. 'I was unfortunate enough to catch the entire thing whilst on the phone to Claudette.'

'You could have looked away, for God's sake!' Tristan burst out laughing. He reddened slightly as he remembered the scene. 'Bloody perv.'

Will protested. 'I did look away! I just wasn't expecting to see Tessa charging down the lawn in her undies, that's all.' Not that it mattered if he looked away or not; the sight of Tessa's bronzed limbs and skimpy underwear had disturbed him more than he would care to admit. He pushed the persistent image away.

'What a sight,' Tristan sighed, enjoying the replay in his mind. 'Aah, it was great fun. But not the romantic moment it should have been. Just . . . a brilliant laugh, really. Tessa is an incredible girl when you get to know her. Seriously, Will. I know you've taken a dislike to her because you think she's this hard nosed bitch who only cares about getting her story, but I can assure you she's not.'

Will rolled his eyes and decided to spare Tristan the details of the notes he had found. What was the point of hurting his brother when there now didn't seem to be any danger of Tristan falling in love with Tessa? Maybe he shouldn't worry too much about Tristan's opinion of Claudette; if he was that easily taken in where Tessa was concerned, perhaps he wasn't such a good judge of character after all.

'Think what you like,' Tristan shrugged, guessing Will thought his view of Tessa was inaccurate. 'I've spent time with her and got to know her properly so I can safely say I know Tessa better than you do. She's actually very disillusioned with her job and her boss threatens to sack her every day, did you know that? Thought not. She's seriously contemplating changing careers and she's actually much more vulnerable than you might imagine.'

Will started. This didn't sound like the brash, cocky girl who'd stalked around his office belligerently before coolly firing off a diatribe about how her career meant everything to her. Before he had a chance to digest Tristan's information about Tessa, Tristan was speaking again, his tone sober.

'I had thought Tessa could be the one to get me over . . . the other one . . . but sadly, she's not. We're great friends but romance is most definitely not on the cards, I would say.'

'Her name is Sophie,' Will told him gently. 'You have to learn to say her name again, Tris, or you'll never move on.'

'You're right and I know you are.' Tristan made an effort. 'Sophie. There. I said it. And I didn't even add *the bitch* on the end.'

'Wow, that's progress. Although I see you're still keeping all of her portraits for posterity.' Will pointed to the stack of canvases partly hidden by a sheet. 'And don't you dare say it's because they're a "good representation of your work", Tristan.'

Tristan looked shamefaced. 'Christ, you know me so well. Look, I know I have issues as far as . . . *Sophie* is concerned, all right? But what else can I do?' His face contorted. 'She was the love of my life . Nothing can equal the pain she caused me when she left, nothing. I don't think I've ever recovered from it.'

Will lifted one of the canvases out, thankfully one of the more discreet ones of Sophie swathed in a piece of material. Each brushstroke lovingly caressed the canvas and every angle of her body demonstrated Tristan's feelings for her. Will frowned, wondering if his feelings towards Claudette had ever been that strong. Did he feel as if his life was over when she wasn't around? Did Claudette occupy his every waking and sleeping thought until he could no longer function? Will wasn't sure she did. In fact, he suddenly felt that Tristan's feelings for Sophie's ghost, the mere wisp of a memory, were far more powerful than his feelings for the real, flesh-and-blood woman he was planning to marry.

'By the way,' Tristan said, changing the subject, 'some woman from the Gas Board came here looking for you the other day. Said there was some enormous bill to pay and if it wasn't, she was going to have to take action.'

'Fuck!' Will exploded. 'When is this ever going to end? I'm paying out money hand over fist and there never seems to be enough. We're so into a zero balance now, it's not even funny.' He stopped short, aghast that he had spoken without thinking.

Tristan put his beer down. 'So we do have money worries, then? I thought as much.' He squeezed Will's big shoulder affectionately. 'Why didn't you say so before, bro? You mustn't keep taking responsibility for everyone all the time. What was it – Mother doing something stupid with our inheritance?'

Will nodded and put his head in his hands. 'I'm sorry. I really had no intention of worrying you with any of this.' He lifted weary eyes to meet Tristan's. 'But it's bad, Tris. Really bad. If the summer party doesn't generate enough interest in the hotel, we're done for and we'll have to sell the manor.'

'Shit.' Tristan looked shell-shocked. 'Look, I can get another commission easily and I'll give you all the money from it, OK? You really mustn't take this shit on yourself all the time. We're a family, we all need to muck in. I know we're hopeless with money but it isn't down to you to bail us out every time we fuck up.'

'Thanks. Any commission money would be a massive help and you can get it all back if the hotel takes off.' Will let out a slow, grateful breath. 'I've already sold all my properties in France, you see. This hotel project is eating money like you wouldn't believe and what with Gil splashing out on the most expensive baths and bedframes in the world . . . And another thing, this documentary could be make or break for us. Why do you think I've been so bloody paranoid about it?'

'You should speak to Tessa about it. She'd understand, I promise you—'

'I don't trust her, Tris. I know you've said that she's not as ruthless as she appears but I haven't seen a single shred of evidence to support that view.'

'You just don't want to see it,' Tristan said wisely, pointing his paintbrush at Will. 'For some reason, you don't want to get to know Tessa and it's going to be your downfall.' He started painting again, his eyes focused on perfecting the chubby cheeks of his subject. 'If I didn't know better and you weren't so nauseatingly in love with Claudette, I'd think you had a thing for this girl.'

'Don't be ridiculous,' stormed Will, slamming his beer down. 'Nothing could be further from the truth. Tessa is the absolute opposite of everything I want in a woman. Shit, I suppose I'd better go and call the Gas Board before they cut us off.' He turned back briefly. 'And not a word to anyone else about the money issues, Tristan. The fewer people who know about it, the better, especially Tessa, do you understand?' With that, he turned on his heel, already worriedly flicking through his BlackBerry for the Gas Board number.

Paintbrush poised thoughtfully, Tristan stared at Will's retreating back.

Chapter Fourteen

Tessa awoke with a start and sat bolt upright in bed. No, she definitely wasn't mistaken, she could hear something. It sounded very much like someone had broken into her cottage and was steadily making their way up the stairs.

Getting out of bed carefully, she grabbed the nearest thing she could find as a weapon and crept towards the door. Yanking it open, she let out an ungodly scream and held her weapon aloft. Tristan, standing barefoot in front of her in a pair of blue and white striped shorts and a white T-shirt, held the over-sized canvas he was clutching aloft like a shield.

'Jesus Christ, woman!' he yelled in a high-pitched voice. Regaining his composure, he lowered the canvas and leant against the banisters with a hand held dramatically to his chest. He started to laugh. 'What were you going to do with that – Jimmy Choo me to death?'

Tessa glanced at the high-heeled shoe she was wielding like a dagger and collapsed against the doorframe. 'It was the only thing I could find!' she said, feeling foolish. She swatted him with the shoe. 'Bloody hell, Tristan, you scared the shit out of me. What the hell did you think you were doing, creeping up the stairs like that?'

'It was a surprise,' Tristan explained, rolling his eyes. 'I didn't mean for you to charge at me like that, shrieking like a banshee and trying to brain me with a designer mule. I could have fallen down the stairs and broken my leg or something. You should be ashamed of yourself. Nice nightie, by the way.'

Tessa glanced down at her diaphanous pink baby-doll nightie and went scarlet. Thank God she'd worn the matching panties. She was still more or less topless in front of Tristan, though, and she ducked behind the bedroom door for cover. 'Er . . . I think I need more clothes . . .'

'Don't mind me.' He grinned nonchalantly. 'I'll stick some coffee on and then I need your opinion on this.' He pointed at the canvas and disappeared downstairs with it.

Tessa sighed and quickly pulled on some shorts and a T-shirt. She heard what sounded like Henny shrieking at the top of her voice outside and leant out of the window to see what was going on.

'Will you all please get in line!'

It was the day of the summer party and frantic preparations had started early, with delivery vans depositing crates of champagne and wine at the crack of dawn and a marquee being noisily erected beside the manor house. Henny was flapping around like a demented budgie, feebly shouting orders at a higgledy-piggledy line of waiters and waitresses who kept tugging at their neckties. She was struggling to keep the male representatives of the waiting staff focused, mainly because they were far more interested in the sight of Caro sunbathing nude behind them next to the lake. Stretched out gracefully on a bright red towel, her skin milky-white as ever, Caro was clearly enjoying the attention she was getting from the adolescent waiters who were gaping at the sight of her small, exposed breasts and savagely trimmed, red pubic hair.

Tessa privately thought Caro needed to eat something; her thin frame was bony and skeletal these days. She looked sensational in the skimpy outfits she wore but naked, with all her ribs showing and her collar bones protruding like a coat hanger, she looked positively anorexic.

Downstairs, Tristan handed her a huge mug of black coffee before removing the covering from his canvas with a flourish.

'What do you think? I've been working on it for ages but I thought it might cheer Will up if I gave it to him today.'

She stared at the canvas, mesmerised. The portrait was of the entire Forbes-Henry family, sitting on one of the big, squashy sofas in the library. Milly and David sat in front with Henny behind them, Caro and Jack stood regally at the back with Will and Tristan at either side. It was simply stunning.

Tristan shuffled the portrait forward to make the most of the early morning sunshine trickling through the doll's house windows of the cottage. He had been modest in his depiction of himself, rather playing down his golden beauty, but he had captured the rest of the Forbes-Henrys perfectly: Caro's translucent skin, emphasised by the rich russet tones of her hair; Jack's faded but glamorous blondness and seductive green eyes; Will, his tawny blond hair falling over one exceptionally blue eye; and then there was . . .

'You've included Claudette,' Tessa said, gazing at the soignée brunette with bobbed hair and a perfect dusting of mocha freckles, who sat to the left of Will.

Tristan chewed his lip distractedly. 'I wasn't sure if I should include her or not but she is Will's fiancée so I thought she should be there.' He frowned at the canvas. 'She's ravishing, obviously, but I still can't help thinking she's not right for Will. Oh well, I suppose if the worst comes to the worst, I can paint her out, can't I?'

'Tristan!' Tessa shook her head at his cheek. 'As infuriating as your brother is, he doesn't seem the type to change his mind that easily, so I reckon Claudette is here to stay.'

'We'll see.' Tristan looked unrepentant and glanced at his watch. 'Aren't you supposed to be giving Henny a makeover or something?'

'God, yes!' Tessa frantically grabbed a holdall and headed upstairs with it. 'I'll see you later,' she yelled down to Tristan, 'and I still need your help with dresses – you promised!'

237

'I'll pop over later,' Tristan called back.

After finding Henny in floods of tears after another run-in with Caro a week ago, Tessa had found herself promising to make Henny look special for the party to boost her ego. She was regretting it now because she had woken up late and barely had time to sort out her own outfit but a promise was a promise.

She flung toiletries and make-up into the bag and wound the plug and cord around some heated rollers. Dashing downstairs, she ran outside. Almost losing a flip-flop and a foot under an enormous tractor-like lawn mower, Tessa jumped back, relieved that she'd spotted Nathan in time. He was riding the machine like a great tank, keeping it painstakingly rigid to achieve perfectly straight lines like a cricket lawn. Stripped to the waist with his muscles glistening in the sun, his khaki trousers and black boots made him look like Action Man.

'Whoa, watch out!' He waved at her cheerily, then grabbed the steering wheel before the lawn mower went off course.

Tessa marched up to Henny and grabbed her arm. 'Come on, I'm doing your makeover right now.' She had arrived in the nick of time; Henny looked slightly hysterical. 'The waiting staff can wait. Didn't Jack say he was going to train them, anyway?'

'Fat lot of use he's going to be,' Henny retorted, clutching her frizzy hair as the waiter at the end of the wonky line desperately tried to cover his bulging erection with his tray of glasses. 'Bloody Caro, lying there like a porn star! She really is the limit. Jack took one look at her from the window and got stuck in to the whisky. And it's not even midday!'

'Hi there.' Tessa nodded politely at Caro who'd lifted her head up to peer at them. 'Er . . . lovely day for it.'

Caro's mouth curved upwards smugly. 'Isn't it?' she cooed, staring right at Henny, her lip curling at the sight of her stained dress and flat moccasins. 'Good God, I do hope you're going to

238

sort yourself out, Henny. I know you're practically the hired help anyway but you jolly well don't have to look like it.'

Rather the hired help than an ageing *slut*, Henny thought with unexpected venom, but she didn't have the guts to say it out loud. 'At least I have clothes on,' she offered instead, going pink at her own audacity.

Caro said nothing to this but deliberately opened her bare legs in what could only be seen as a gesture of defiance. Her privates were on show for all to see, leaving the waiters pointing in delight and the waitresses swatting them jealously.

'She's an absolute disgrace!' Henny spluttered. Her rosy cheeks turned an ugly scarlet and she didn't know where to look.

'Ignore her,' Tessa soothed. Leading Henny towards the kitchen, Tessa wondered why Caro seemed so hell-bent on upsetting everyone around her. It obviously wasn't enough to sleep with JB under Jack's nose. 'She's trying to wind you up, Henny. From what I've seen, the best way to deal with Caro is to ignore her – she just wants a reaction.'

'You're absolutely right, darling. I just seem to rise to it every time.' Henny slumped down into a chair, running pink-stained fingers through her sandy fringe. She'd been up all night baking meringues and chopping strawberries for the Eton Mess she planned to serve later and she was absolutely exhausted. 'Caro just has this way of getting to me, that's all.'

'I know.' Tessa gave her a sympathetic smile, her mind already full of ideas for making Henny look so fabulous, even Caro wouldn't be able to criticise her. It was going to take some seriously hard work but she wasn't leaving until Henny looked perfect. She plugged in the heated rollers and grabbed a bottle of frizz control spray. 'Now, you're going to have to trust me, all right? I'm going to be spraying and putting all sorts of potions on you but you're just going to have to let me get on with it. And then we're going to choose a dress for you. And when I've finished with you, Caro won't be able to think of a single horrible thing to say. And all the dishy men will be swarming around you,' she added for good measure.

Henny looked rather frightened by the array of beauty products on display as Tessa heaved everything out of the bag but thinking about a day free of insults from Caro, she knew she was going to go along with whatever Tessa suggested.

'Do your worst,' she said, clutching the sides of her chair as if she was on a plane that was about to crash-land in the sea. 'Make me beautiful, or at the very least passable – *please*.'

Tessa advanced on her with the frizz control spray, a look of crazy determination in her eyes.

'So you think you'll be here at about two o'clock?' Will asked in French, glancing at the antique clock on the wall as Claudette babbled at him down the phone. 'I think my Uncle Perry might be on the same flight as you – he's the lawyer, you know, the one who lives in Aix-en-Provence? But he was in Paris for business at the weekend. Yes, yes, I'm looking forward to seeing you too, of course I am.'

His phone glued to his ear, Will peered into one of the bedrooms, grimacing as he saw Gil's team slapping honey-coloured emulsion on to the walls. Still, Gil had pulled out all the stops to get the rooms finished on time, even managing to get two more completed than Will was expecting.

'I am so sorry about the delay,' Gil said, looking vexed. His hair was standing on end and flecked with cream emulsion and he was looking uncharacteristically dishevelled. 'We've been working through the night but this paint was only delivered at seven o'clock and it's been a *nightmare* . . .' Realising Will was on the phone, he put a finger to his lips and tiptoed backwards like a mime artist.

Will tried not to raise his eyes to the ceiling. 'Yes, Claudette, I'm still listening to you. I'm just checking the hotel rooms at the same time. What did you say? God, yes, they look amazing. You won't recognise the place when you get here.'

It was true. Baths were full of floating rose petals, beds were covered in sumptuous cushions and throws, and curtains were swagged with ties to show off the stunning views of the grounds. The windows of the penthouse had been left open to showcase the spectacular vista and Gil had cleverly added personalised touches in each room so that as well as the Penhaligon toiletries and Tristan's incredible portraits on offer, each room boasted piles of classic novels, the odd mini bottle of Veuve Clicquot or a large organic candle on a bedside table.

'It's just that such a lot is riding on this,' Will murmured to Claudette as he admired a gigantic sleigh bed Gil had insisted on purchasing. It might have blown their budget out of the water but it reeked of luxury and today Will couldn't be happier with the way the hotel rooms looked. He headed down to the dining room to check that all the crockery had been left out for the waiting staff. 'And my parents are misbehaving like you wouldn't believe . . .' Catching sight of his father sloshing at least five inches of whisky into a pint glass, Will finished his call and just managed to grab the glass before Jack downed it.

'I was looking forward to that,' Jack sulked, looking like an obstreperous child.

'You've had quite enough,' Will scolded him, tipping most of the whisky out of the open window. Seeing his father's crestfallen face, he took pity on him and handed him the remaining inch. 'Knock yourself out with that but please don't drink any more, all right? Today is incredibly important and I need you to be on your best behaviour – you *and* Mother.'

Jack necked the whisky with a thunderous expression. 'I'll do it for you, son, but your mother can go whistle. She's out there sunbathing in the nude like a bloody hooker, and she's invited that French twat to the party, for fuck's sake!'

'Go and get ready,' Will placated, propelling him towards the door. 'And leave Mother to me. I'll make sure she doesn't let us down.' Rather grimly, he grabbed a throw from the back of one of the dining-room chairs and prepared to do battle with his mother. If she made a show of herself today, he would never forgive her, he thought despairingly.

'What do you think?' Tessa spun Henny round to give him the full effect.

Tristan gaped. 'Where's Aunt Henny and what have you done with her?'

'Doesn't she look amazing? The hair took some time but I really think it was worth the effort.'

Henny was in Tessa's bedroom in her cottage, standing in front of a full-length mirror in absolute awe. Her frizzy hair had been tamed into submission with tons of different products before being twirled into heated rollers and then pinned up into a loose chignon. But that wasn't the only change in her appearance.

'My skin . . . Tessa, how did you make it look like this? It's never looked this soft and dewy before.'

Tessa tactfully chose not to mention that she had been tempted to resort to taking a sander to Henny's weathered cheeks and vaguely gestured to her beauty kit. 'A bit of this, a bit of that,' she declared airily. 'It's incredible what a face pack and some foundation can do.'

'You look wonderful,' Tristan commented, still unable to associate the glamorous woman in front of him with his homely Aunt Henny. 'I've honestly never seen you looking this good. And where did you get this dress from? It's taken ten years off you, not to mention about a stone in weight. Oops, I didn't mean that the way it came out, it was meant to be a compliment.' He grinned engagingly.

Tessa shoved him. 'Gorgeous, isn't it? And to think you were going to give this away, Henny!' She fingered the pale green silk dress which had a square neckline, a belted waist that made Henny look as if she was more hourglass-shaped than she actually was. A full skirt hid her rather wide hips and white high-heeled sandals and a clutch bag finished off the look.

'Bobby bought it for me, but I didn't think it suited me and then I thought I was too fat to squeeze into it.' Henny kissed Tessa's cheek. 'Thank God you made me buy those magic knickers and that push-up bra!'

Tristan looked pained. 'Christ, girls, too much information! Anyway, Auntie, I need to help Tessa with outfits now, not that she needs it.'

'Of course, darling, and I'm horrifically late now anyway.' Henny took one last look at her unfamiliar reflection and headed for the door. 'Thank you so much, Tessa. I feel like a million dollars. See you both later!'

Tristan smiled at Tessa. 'You did a nice thing,' he said, squeezing Tessa's hand. 'A really nice thing. She looks so happy and I reckon her self-esteem must have trebled in the past few hours.'

'That was the general idea.' Tessa blushed, feeling an unexpected surge of pleasure that she had been responsible for Henny's sunny mood. And all because of some heated rollers and mascara. She noticed that Tristan was looking exceptionally handsome in a beige suit and a crisp white shirt, a look not everyone could pull off with such aplomb. She was definitely over her crush on him but she was delighted he had turned out to be such a good friend.

'Getting Aunt Henny to look like that was no mean feat, I can imagine,' Tristan said with a naughty laugh. 'It's all right, I'm allowed to say that. She's my aunt and I adore her. Are you filming today?'

She shook her head. 'The crew are going to be here to capture Rufus and Clemmie's arrival and get some shots of the manor but I'm not needed for any interviewing so Henny said I should just come as a guest.'

'Great.' Tristan flung himself on the bed and tucked his hands behind his head. 'Now, show me all your frocks.'

Three hours later, everything was in place for the party. The formerly wayward waiters and waitresses were lined up in a poker-straight line, wielding champagne and canapés. The weather couldn't have been more perfect; there wasn't a puff of cloud in sight and the sky was azure blue. How long it would hold was anyone's guess – August being just as unreliable a month as the other eleven in England – but for now it felt pleasantly hot, if a little lacking in breeze. The jazz band Will had hired for the day was in full flow, and a jaunty version of 'My Funny Valentine' could be heard throughout the grounds.

Will caught sight of his mother wearing a short, peacock-blue dress which showed an expanse of thigh and an indecent amount of pale, freckled back. For once, she looked like mutton dressed as lamb and the heavy eye make-up and garish lipstick she wore did nothing for her. She was floating around with a drink like Lady Bountiful, in spite of the fact that she hadn't lifted a finger to help with the preparations. Jack, wearing a smart, navy blazer with an off-white shirt and beige slacks, stalked past Caro clutching a vast, neat whisky, his expression dark, but seeing Will pulling a face at him he smiled sweetly at Caro until his face nearly cracked.

Will bit his lip and checked his watch for the hundredth time. Was anyone even going to turn up? Distractedly, he pushed his hand through his hair, making it stick up comically. At one o'clock precisely, he let out an audible sigh of relief as a stream of cars pulled into the driveway of Appleton Manor.

'Mum . . . Dad . . .' He chinked glasses with them, pretending not to notice the murderous looks they were giving each other. 'Let's have a toast to the Appleton Manor Hotel.'

'The Appleton Manor Hotel,' Jack and Caro chorused, pacing round one another warily.

Will resolutely ignored them. He had more important things on his mind right now.

Chapter Fifteen

Tessa left her cottage once she saw some guests arriving. The grounds of the manor house resembled a polo match, with men dotted around in neutral, summer suits and women in brightly coloured dresses and hats, the heels of their designer shoes leaving holes in the clipped lawn. Champagne, soft drinks and delectable canapés were being circulated and people were making full use of a marquee that had been erected as protection from the searing sunlight as much as for keeping the drinks cool.

The village had come out in force for – and hopefully in support of – the hotel venture, with the new bookshop owners nervously introducing themselves and other villagers greeting one another politely. Even nosy old Mrs North was in attendance, sporting one of her nasty polyester dresses in a girlish shade of apricot, her painfully thin frame hardly looking strong enough to support her.

Tessa glanced down at her own outfit, a shocking pink strapless dress that nipped in her waist and made the most of her full bust, and hoped to God Tristan hadn't stitched her up. It was an eye-catching dress but perhaps more suited to a London party than a country do full of toffs. Tessa's heart sank at the thought of looking out of place. Tristan had encouraged her to wear her Gina sandals with the dress and she was wobbling around all over the place in them, but as she drew closer she could see that she wasn't the only one wearing designer shoes or a dress with a four-figure price tag.

She caught sight of Will wearing a navy suit that made his eyes look bluer than ever and a white shirt which was open at the neck, revealing a glimpse of tanned chest. His tawny gold hair needed a cut and kept flopping into his eyes.

Catching sight of his irate expression as he took a phone call, she bolted past him; the last thing she wanted today was another confrontation with Will Forbes-Henry.

'Lovely to see you,' Will murmured to another guest for what felt like the two hundredth time. He shoved his BlackBerry in his pocket and downed his champagne in one gulp.

'Problem?' Henny inquired at his elbow.

'Kind of. Claudette phoned . . .' He did a double-take as he looked at her properly. 'Wow. You look . . . lovely. What . . . who . . . ?'

Henny smiled prettily, touching a hand to her hair. 'It was all down to Tessa. She gave me this amazing makeover and did my hair and make-up and everything. She really is an absolute gem, so *sweet*. I haven't felt this good since . . . gosh, before Bobby died.'

Feeling overwhelmed at seeing her taking such pride in herself, Will didn't know what to say. He couldn't believe Tessa had taken the time to do such a lovely thing for his Aunt Henny; it had obviously boosted her self-confidence because she was greeting guests like a pro and already assuming the role of housekeeper without preamble.

'Claudette phoned?' she prompted him, privately thrilled that her new look was having such a remarkable effect.

'Yes . . . I was just going to come and find you. The French are doing one of their blasted strikes over pay today so all the flights out of Paris have been cancelled. I'm afraid Claudette can't make the party and—'

'Neither can Perry,' Henny finished, her face crumpling with disappointment. 'Oh, poor you, darling, I know you were dying to see Claudette. And what a shame about Perry. I haven't seen him for months and I had hoped he might be able to get Jack out of his depression.'

'I know.' Will fiddled with his BlackBerry, not sure why he found the situation so distressing. 'Claudette said she'd try to get here in the next couple of days so maybe Uncle Perry might be able to do the same.'

'Let's hope so, darling. Oh, look, Rufus's parents have arrived, we must go and say hello.'

They headed over to Lord and Lady Pemberton who were greeting the rest of the villagers warmly, secretly elated that their son was marrying a Hollywood movie star but doing their best to hide it.

'Will, how lovely to see you!' Lady Pemberton gave him a kiss on the cheek, hugging him tightly as she stood on tiptoe. 'Goodness, I always forget how tall you are!' She was a small woman with a forgettable face, saved by wide, green eyes and even white teeth. 'The manor house looks wonderful, Will, really beautiful. You must be so proud.'

'Just wait until you see inside,' he told her with a smile. 'It's not the manor you're used to seeing. Our designer Gil Anderson has done a sterling job.'

'Oooh, yes, I wanted to speak to him about decorating our drawing room . . .'

'Has Rufus arrived yet?' Lord Pemberton interrupted heartily, his ruddy complexion already turning redder in the searing sunshine. 'I can't wait to meet his bride-to-be again. What a charmer!'

'Indeed.' Will smiled and stepped out of the way as JB and the film crew took up their places near the entrance. He was still in two minds about allowing them to film Rufus and Clemmie at the party but Rufus had convinced him it would be brilliant publicity for the hotel when the documentary was shown in the New Year. Their rumoured arrival had certainly attracted enough onlookers; the lawn was positively heaving with expectant guests. Will just hoped the crowds weren't so focused on their resident celebrities that they forgot to look around the manor and make a booking.

He watched Milly, her blonde hair loose, wearing an inappropriate blue mini dress that made her look years older than she was. Ridiculously over-excited, she was chatting to a guest and drinking a glass of orange juice. She laughed uproariously like a crazy woman, and Will decided the drink must be liberally laced with vodka. Milly's sidekick India was nowhere to be seen but having a reputation for being the consummate party girl, Will had no doubt she would turn up at some point.

He was jolted when Tessa appeared at Milly's side wearing the sexiest pink dress he had ever seen. It flattered her shapely figure, leaving her tanned shoulders bare, and her glossy chestnut hair trailing down her back. Her brown legs looked fantastic beneath the skirt and she was wearing the outrageously high sandals she had sashayed around his office in.

Will tore his eyes away from her with difficulty and found himself glancing vaguely down at his empty glass. Heading to the marquee, he realised he badly needed a top-up.

'Darling! So wonderful to see you,' Caro brayed insincerely at one of Jack's more recent exes. They air-kissed with noticeably mutual loathing but kept up the pretence of impeccable manners in front of the crowds.

To her left, JB, wearing an expensive, well-cut suit, was puffing on a cigarette rather sexily as he bawled out the camera crew. Used to Tessa's rather more gentle guidance of late, the cringing crew couldn't seem to put a foot right.

'What the 'ell are you doing?' JB roared as the boom holder tripped over some lighting cables. 'You are all acting like bloody amateurs!'

Joe the cameraman clenched his fists crossly when JB laid into Susie the make-up artist for some insignificant misdemeanour or other, fully prepared to step in if things turned nasty.

'*Arsehole*,' Jack muttered into his whisky, his green eyes dark and malevolent. He was holding his glass so tightly it looked as if it might shatter in his hand and his jaw was rigid.

'Ignore him,' Tristan said smoothly, cupping a hand under his father's elbow and steering him in the other direction. After Will's shocking confession about money the other day, Tristan had resolved to take more responsibility for the family and that included keeping his parents from scrapping in public. 'Come on, Pa, I thought you were going to try and play nicely with Mother today – for Will's sake, if nothing else.'

Jack bristled as Caro drifted past in a flash of bright blue silk. 'She's dressed like a bloody twenty-year-old,' he commented truculently. 'I don't even know if I can get through to her any more. She doesn't want me; she wants a bloody gigolo half her age.' He glanced at Tristan in surprise; he wasn't used to opening up to his youngest son.

Tristan was about to defend his mother when, without any warning, she did the most appalling thing. In full view of all the onlookers, she sauntered up to JB, spun him round to face her and kissed him openly, her hips grinding against his, her hands possessively gripping his buttocks.

'What the fuck!' Jack bellowed.

Shaking Tristan's restraining hand from his arm he stormed up to Caro and pulled her and JB apart. Growling at JB viciously, which caused some of the more daring camera crew to break into a ripple of applause, Jack took Caro to one side and pushed her unceremoniously against the newly erected hotel sign.

'Darling, do stop manhandling me like some sort of loutish brute,' Caro said, the colour high in her cheeks as she struggled free of his grasp. 'Everyone's staring.'

'Everyone's staring because you're behaving like a *slut*!' Jack bawled at her, unable to control himself. He was shaking with anger and he couldn't stop clenching and unclenching his fists. He had never felt more like striking Caro in his life.

'It was only a kiss,' Caro said silkily, her blue eyes sparkling with excitement. It had been a spur-of-the-moment decision to snog JB in front of everyone but she was glad she had done it. It had been a huge thrill and it was about time Jack realised she was playing hard ball this time.

Truthfully, she hadn't really thought about the consequences when she had stuck her tongue down JB's throat but Jack's rejection the other day had stung. She couldn't bear the fact that he had the willpower to push her away; surely that meant he didn't love her any more? Or more likely it proved that he didn't love her *enough* and in Caro's world that wasn't going to cut it. More than that, she had made a decision. JB was replacing Jack.

'It wasn't just a kiss,' Jack said bleakly, feeling all the fight in his body desert him just when he needed it the most. He couldn't help it. Caro had just stepped over the line in a way he could never forgive her for. He turned desperate, booze-addled eyes to hers. 'Enough. OK? This ends here.'

In spite of the sizzling heat, Caro started to shiver. 'What does?'

Jack took one last sad look at his wife. 'Our marriage,' he stated in a low voice. He was astonished by his own calmness but suddenly it felt like a relief to utter the words out loud. 'You've won. That's what you wanted, wasn't it? To win? Well, congratulations, Caro. You win the first prize – whatever that is. JB maybe, or was it just getting one over on me and proving a point?' He shook his head. 'I just hope it was all worth it.' He stepped away from her and turned on his heel, stumbling slightly as he headed for the marquee.

Caro was paralysed. She could feel everyone's cold eyes on her.

'What are you all staring at?' she burst out, glancing wildly around her. The music had halted and guests were standing like statues, their champagne flutes poised in mid-air. Caro looked around for some support but could only see Henny looking as frosty as a frozen margarita and, beside her, Milly gazing at her in abject horror. JB seemed to have disappeared, the cowardly bastard, so Caro couldn't even rush to his side for safety.

'I think I need to go . . . to go and powder my nose,' she managed in a small voice, walking unsteadily towards the manor house. Reliving the look of utter dejection and defeat in Jack's eyes, she let out a cry of misery, her walk turning into a run as she dashed away from all the staring eyes.

'Sorry about that,' Will ventured into the silence, clearing his throat and gesturing for the band to start playing again. As if a magician had waved his wand, music filled the air and conversations started again, Caro's inappropriate behaviour no doubt the favourite topic of conversation.

Feeling utterly let down by his mother and hoping to God the local press wouldn't feature the showdown in the papers tomorrow, Will gestured for a group of guests to come and see the inside of the manor house.

Tessa found JB down by the lake, smoking moodily and kicking loose stones into the water. They broke the tranquil, mirrored surface of the water with solemn plopping sounds.

'Are you all right?' she ventured, knowing a cautious approach was in order. The sight of JB's white knuckles and rigid neck gave away how tightly coiled he was underneath the pseudo-calm exterior.

JB glanced over his shoulder. '*Oui*,' he returned tersely. He turned his dark eyes back to the glittering water.

'That was a bit . . . embarrassing, wasn't it?'

'Was it?' JB seemed to have no intention of communicating properly.

Tessa observed his profile, the arrogant sensual tilt of his nose and the full mouth. He was one of the most selfish men she had ever met in her life but she couldn't help wanting to try to reach him somehow. It was almost as if, just beneath the surface, a human being glimmered, someone whose bark was worse than their bite. Someone who was desperate to hide his vulnerability.

'Caro is . . . unpredictable,' he offered abruptly, his mouth curving into a rather cruel smile. 'But that is all part of her charm, *non*?'

Tessa frowned. There was something odd about JB's tone, something that didn't quite sit right. Had he, in spite of all of his warnings to her, done the unthinkable and got too close to a member of the Forbes-Henry family? On paper, it seemed unlikely; Caro was high-maintenance, bitchily insecure and as tiring as a toddler. Besides, Tessa couldn't see JB having tender feelings for a woman some ten years his senior.

'She is . . . an enigma . . .' JB said, sounding wondrous, as if he wasn't quite sure what he was saying.

Tessa gawped at him. 'Oh my God, you've fallen in love with her!'

JB swung round aggressively. 'What? In love? Me? Do not even suggest such a thing!'

'You have! You're in love with her; I can see it in your eyes.' Tessa couldn't prevent her next comment spilling out; weeks of sarcastic taunts from JB had left her ego reeling. 'After everything you said to me at the start of this documentary, you've done the very thing you warned me against! You're way too close to Caro and it's affecting your professional judgement. That's why you haven't turned up for filming over the past few weeks and why you think you need to come in now and scream at everyone to remind them that you're in charge. You've got a bloody cheek behaving like such a prima donna, especially when you're the first one to put other people down.'

JB regarded her furiously, his dark eyebrows leaping up and

down in the most alarming manner. 'You are wrong,' he hissed at her. 'You 'ave no idea what I'm feeling but I can assure you, falling in love is the last theeng that is going on here. Caro is nothing to me, do you understand?'

Tessa stared at him disbelievingly.

'And do not *ever* criticise my work!' he roared at her, sounding like a temperamental actor. With that, he stomped away from her, expletives tearing from him in several different languages as he stormed back to the manor house, barging into Tristan who was approaching Tessa.

'What on earth is the matter with *him*?' Tristan asked Tessa in amusement, watching JB sending a waiter flying with his elbow. 'He looks like a madman!'

'He *is* a madman. Honestly, I haven't a clue what's going on in his head. I thought he might have fallen for your mother but he's just told me in no uncertain terms that hell would freeze over before that happened. Where's Jack?'

Tristan pulled a face. 'Last seen heading off towards the chapel with a bottle of whisky. And who can blame him? I think I'd want to get blind drunk if someone did that to me.'

Tessa caught sight of Will striding towards them and rather thought she might need to get drunk herself. 'Fancy another drink?' she said, taking Tristan's arm and ushering him towards the marquee.

At the top of the driveway leading to Appleton Manor, Sophie was having a panic attack. Tristan was probably only a few metres from her and she was totally, totally unprepared for their meeting. She had spent the last two days in a state of sheer panic, alternately talking herself out of going to the party before reminding herself not to be such a wet blanket, then losing her nerve again and thinking of increasingly absurd excuses to get out of going.

Fortunately, Gil was so caught up with plans for his slot on the documentary he had barely noticed any change in her behaviour. Ruby had also provided a welcome distraction for Sophie over the past few days, painting all day long as she hummed to herself, lost in her own little world of bizarre, brightly coloured creatures and occasionally recognisable people.

'You look *glorious*, darling,' Gil told her indulgently, thinking she might be nervous about her outfit.

Sophie tugged at the chocolate-coloured dress. She was more than nervous about her outfit – buying it without trying it on had been a huge mistake. As Gil fondly imagined she was still the trim size eight she had been before Ruby was born, the bodice was too tight around her rib cage and she could barely breathe. Glancing at Gil in his skin-tight Galliano shirt which drew attention to the beginnings of some unsightly man boobs and his rather snug brown trousers, she couldn't help thinking they must both look as if they were too vain to wear their correct sizes.

'We look like the bloody Beckhams,' Sophie grumbled. 'Except that my boobs are a lot smaller than Victoria's.'

Gil preened. 'I think we both look very nice, darling. We look like the young, trendy, loved-up couple we are.'

Sophie was beginning to feel rather hysterical; it was almost as if she was in a bad dream. 'Why don't you go and chat to Nathan?' she suggested. She felt guilty for pushing Gil on to Nathan but she couldn't risk bumping into Tristan with Gil at her side. Thankfully, Gil did as he was told for once and strolled towards the gardener who was looking like a Calvin Klein model in a pair of black jeans and a grey T-shirt which clung to his muscles.

Taking refuge under the majestic oak tree that had stood by the manor house for as long as she could remember, Sophie spotted the back of Tristan's head nearby. She felt her heart begin to thump madly in her chest. She could see Tessa, looking breathtakingly pretty in a to-die-for pink dress, throwing her head back with laughter at something Tristan was saying and her insides curled up jealously.

Sophie haltingly emerged from the shade of the tree and stood rooted to the spot as Tristan caught sight of her behind Tessa. Shading his eyes from the dazzling sunshine to get a better look, his face turned absolutely white with shock. It couldn't be . . . not after all this time . . .

'What's the matter?' Tessa asked, twisting round to see why Tristan was looking as if he'd seen a ghost. She followed his gaze and saw what, or rather who, he was stonily transfixed by. 'That's only Soph . . . oh my God . . .' Tessa gasped audibly. She didn't know if it was the flood of sunlight turning Sophie's caramel tresses golden-blond or the contrast between her fairness and the lush green of the backdrop behind her, but suddenly everything seemed to fall into place.

Why hadn't she seen it before? Tessa wondered as she gaped at Sophie. The hair was different – shorter and darker. Her figure was slightly fuller and she had a more sophisticated look these days, but there was no getting away from it, Sophie was the girl in Tristan's paintings. The girl that Tristan had been head over heels in love with, and who had, according to Henny, left Tristan heartbroken and a changed man.

Tessa was frankly astonished that having viewed so many of Tristan's portraits, she hadn't seen the likeness before. She had been rather drunk, of course, so perhaps she hadn't been paying proper attention, but still.

'She never said . . . I didn't know, Tristan,' Tessa mumbled, feeling the need to let him know she hadn't guessed the truth.

'It's all right,' Tristan said in a monotone. 'It's not your fault.'

'But she's my friend . . . she never said a word . . .'

Looking absolutely gobsmacked, Will joined them. He glanced from Sophie to Tessa with animosity. 'You knew, didn't you? You knew she was here and you didn't say anything.'

'That's not true!' she defended herself hotly.

'Shut up, Will,' Tristan implored him, his voice cracking. 'This has nothing to do with Tessa, so just back off and leave her alone, can't you?' Seeing Sophie . . . *his* Sophie, standing mere feet away from him, her brown eyes huge in her face, had left Tristan poleaxed. She looked different . . . older, more stylish, but it was her. As bold as brass, in the flesh, standing in front of him as if she wasn't the one who had run off and left him with a broken heart.

She was still so beautiful, Tristan thought, aching inside. That bone structure, the long, swan-like neck, the deliciously feminine curve of her shoulders . . . His fingers twitched at his sides. He yearned to touch her creamy skin. Sophie stared back at him helplessly, beseechingly, her anger towards him forgotten as she drank in the sight of him. It felt so *good* to see his handsome face for real instead of just in her dreams.

'I knew it!' Nosy old Mrs North pushed herself forward, her eyes beady and her head tilted inquisitively, like a bird. 'I said it was you! You tried to deny it but I knew I was right!' She looked round with a self-satisfied smirk.

Tristan and Sophie stood gazing at each other, oblivious of anything else around them. But Mrs North wasn't finished. 'I knew you were that hussy who broke his heart!' she said, waving her stick in the air.

The spell was broken. Tristan and Sophie blinked at each other and all the old feelings rushed bitterly to the surface. He marched up to her, his face hostile.

'I think we need to talk,' he said grimly. 'Don't you?'

Chapter Sixteen

Stealing a glance in Gil's direction, Sophie was relieved to see him talking animatedly to Nathan, completely oblivious of the drama going on around him. She was grateful; she didn't want to hurt him. But she needed to have it out with Tristan. He was standing by the edge of the lake, the tension in his shoulders visible through his white shirt. She joined him silently. She wasn't sure she should be the one to smooth things over between them. Surely Tristan was the one who needed to explain his behaviour, not her?

How odd, she thought painfully as she stared across the lake; she could see Tristan's cottage from here. It had been the setting for so much of their time together, heady days spent talking, laughing and making love. Hours had passed as Tristan painted her nude and she had adored the way he studied her and perfected every nuance of her body. Ironically, the cottage had also been the backdrop for the final, dramatic scene that had ended their relationship.

She turned away from it distastefully, overwrought with memories.

'What are you doing here?' he asked her in a hoarse voice. His eyes searched her face for answers.

'I . . . live here,' she answered jerkily. God, it was hard to look him in the eye. Was it possible to love someone and hate them with equal ferocity? she wondered, fiddling with the folds of her dress. She was torn between an urge to kiss his wide, sexy mouth, and an urge to spoil his angelic good looks with a vicious black eye.

Tristan looked shaken. 'Here? You live *here*, in Appleton?'

'Yes. For now, anyway.'

'When did you move here?'

'A few months ago.'

'What? Why haven't I seen you before? Have you been avoiding me?'

Sophie let out a short laugh. 'Yes. Does that really surprise you?'

'I guess not.' He looked down, raking his fingers awkwardly through his golden curls. 'I mean, why would you come and see me? After all, you left without a word five years ago so why would it occur to you that I might want to find out what the hell happened to you?'

He lifted his eyes to hers and she flinched, puzzled. She could see fury there too, and burning accusation. She shook her head dumbly, not sure what was going on.

She had the right to be furious, surely? He had kissed his ex-girlfriend Anna, believing he could get away with it because she had been away. Sophie's stomach tightened. No doubt it hadn't ended there, either; the determined look in Anna's eyes had told her that she was after more than a quick snog. And Tristan wasn't known for his abstinence. She swayed slightly. The thought of Tristan's hands touching Anna's skin instead of hers sent her into a head spin.

Tristan was incredulous. The defiant way Sophie had met his eyes! How dare she stand there in front of him like that, belligerently, as if *he* was the one at fault! What had he done wrong, for fuck's sake? Love her too much? If that was the crime he was supposed to be guilty of, he would put his hands up and beg for her fucking forgiveness.

Had he loved her too much? Tristan stared at Sophie. Perhaps he had suffocated her with the intensity of his feelings. There was a chance his attempts at taking her under his wing when she'd first arrived in Appleton had been perceived as heavy-handed or controlling, he supposed, but it hadn't been meant that way.

At the time, Tristan had been convinced they were on an equal footing and that Sophie felt exactly the same about him as he did about her. But loving someone had been new to him and he hadn't known how to handle it back then. He had been a player, a playboy who loved sex and hated commitment. And Sophie had burst into his life and changed all that. Suddenly, sex had meant something, it had involved *feelings* and he hadn't been prepared for that. He had thrown himself into it wholeheartedly and with the best of intentions but had his clumsy adoration of her made her flee from him?

He twisted away from her, needing to think. Both her arrival into his life and her departure had shaped who he was today; both had changed him irrevocably.

Tristan remembered the day Sophie had left with absolute clarity. He had been up half the night trying to finish a commission for a new gallery in London that had expressed an interest in his work. It was around the time his career had really taken off; three galleries in New York had started showing small pieces of his work and the National Portrait Gallery was willing to run a week-long exhibition of his 'Women in Love' portraits.

He had been working like a man possessed to complete a half-finished portrait of Sophie that would form part of his exhibition collection. It was a stunning piece, a sensual depiction of her with a sheet slipping away from her curvaceous body, her long hair caressing the cleft of her bottom. It was one of his most beautiful portraits to date and, working furiously on it, he had been aggravated at being interrupted by Anna, the ex-girlfriend he had hoped to avoid for the rest of his life. His heart had plummeted to the depths of his stomach when she sashayed into his studio, her low-cut dress and obvious musky scent making his senses lurch unpleasantly.

'What do you want?' he had asked her warily, feeling the need to keep his distance. His relationship with Anna had been ill-fated from the start – doomed for disaster. Knowing his weakness for limping puppies, she had ingratiated herself with him with sob stories, slithering into his life and his bed with practised lies and impressive acting skills. She had proceeded to become clingy and intense, phoning him non-stop and demanding his attention.

Once Tristan had figured out that Anna was unbalanced, bordering on certifiable, he had at first gently let her down but as the weeks passed and she still turned up unannounced in his bed, expecting him to send her flowers in spite of their terminated relationship, he had been forced to be crueller to her. Terrified she would jinx his new relationship with Sophie, he had cut her off without compunction, hoping his cruelty might turn her off and that she would meet someone new and move on. Having been blessed with silence from her for months, Tristan had assumed Anna had forgotten about him. It seemed he was mistaken.

'Don't be like that, Tris,' Anna had pouted. 'Haven't you missed me?'

He had sighed impatiently; keen to finish his painting before Sophie arrived in the morning. 'I'm busy, Anna. What do you want?'

She had laughed, strolling around his studio jauntily, chattering incessantly about how fantastic her life was now. Tristan had done his best to ignore her, focusing on trying to capture the exact, rosy shade of Sophie's skin. Mixing a touch of Venetian red to a buttery, golden shade of ochre hadn't seemed quite right . . .

'It's just . . . we had so much fun, didn't we, Tris?' Anna's voice had turned whiny, the grating tone alerting Tristan to danger. Tearing his eyes away from his portrait reluctantly, he had lowered his paintbrush. All he could think about was how to get Anna out of his studio as quickly as possible, without her going psycho on him and ruining any of his work, the way she had on one occasion when he had sent her away from his cottage.

Anna had laughed throatily. 'I know you're busy but I have a favour to ask you.' She lowered herself on to his sofa and patted the velvet throw. 'Come and sit with me, Tris. I won't bite, I promise!'

Dreading being so close to her, Tristan had ignored his gut instinct and had gingerly taken a seat next to her. The events that followed had left him reeling. Anna had proceeded to burst into hysterical tears, throwing herself against him as she had jerkily muttered something about her mother dying of cancer.

Claiming her mother was a huge fan of his work, Anna had asked him, through much sniffing and sobbing, if he would do a portrait of her with the utmost urgency, convincing him that it was her dying mother's last wish.

Mistrusting of her but ultimately soft-hearted, Tristan had conceded, figuring he could do a quick sketch of Anna and get rid of her. It would waste valuable minutes he should be spending on his portrait for the gallery but he could catch up if he worked into the early hours. Anna had seemed satisfied and had moved closer, 'into the good light', she had murmured in an oily tone.

Tristan remembered feeling uncomfortable in her presence and concerned that Anna would be displeased with the sketch. After all, he could only be true to his subjects, regardless of his relationship with them, and Anna had always been plain with unremarkable features. Overtly sexy, perhaps, but the crazed look in her eyes put paid to her looking anything more than a femme fatale with a serious temper.

He needn't have worried; the real reason behind Anna's visit was soon obvious. Throwing herself at him – literally – she had wound her arms round his neck and pushed her tongue into his mouth. Her serpentine touch had left him paralysed. Dropping his sketchbook in shock, he had realised Anna had lied to him: her mother wasn't dying; the dreadful untruth had been a ruse to get close to him once more and make a move.

Frozen for a moment as her wet lips ardently pushed against his, Tristan had stared into her wide open eyes, repulsed. She seemed triumphant, her body pushing against him urgently, clumsily, as if she no longer knew where she was.

He had been shaken to the core; Anna was ill, she had to be, this wasn't normal behaviour by anyone's standards. He wanted to help her, hated the thought that he might be responsible for sending her over the edge, but what could he do? Hearing her giggle into his ear like a child, Tristan had no choice but to push her away. He remembered how he had wiped a paint-stained hand across his mouth to remove the last vestiges of her saliva, desperate to rid himself of her touch.

Livid at being rejected once more, Anna had turned on him, hissing evil words into his face before tearing out of his cottage like a demented banshee. Tristan had never seen Anna again. He had no idea where she had ended up, nor did he care. He had more important things to deal with because he had never seen Sophie again after that night either. He had stayed up all night finishing the painting and had waited, with tired, prickly eyes, for her arrival. He had waited and waited but she hadn't shown up and eventually he had left for London to deliver the portrait by hand. As the hours went by and there was no word from Sophie, he had become more and more concerned. In those early hours, had he thought for one minute she had left him? Never.

It was only later that this had occurred to him. Days had passed, every minute more brutal and lonely than the last. He had been bewildered, helpless. Nothing had made sense to him and he had spent hours rehashing his last conversation with Sophie, trying desperately to spot clues that would explain her disappearance.

Will had been a rock during that time, Tristan remembered, staring across the lake with eyes blurred with tears. He had helped by phoning every hospital in the area to see if Sophie had been brought in there after an accident. She must have lost her memory, be hurt, Will had suggested, crossing through another number in the Yellow Pages. He had repeatedly reminded Tristan how much Sophie loved him and that she would never leave him. He had rushed round the village interrogating anyone he could find and had even made a nuisance of himself at Sophie's art college in the months that had followed her disappearance, handing out flyers with a photocopy of one of Tristan's paintings on it and asking questions.

When these efforts had produced nothing concrete, Will had taken another tack and had sat late into the night with him for weeks on end, getting drunk with him and lending a grief-stricken Tristan the proverbial shoulder to cry on as he continually broke down. Eventually, knowing he had no other choice left, Will had forced Tristan to face up to Sophie's loss firmly but with infinite kindness.

Thank God for Will, Tristan thought fervently. The first days without Sophie had been agonising; the first weeks physically painful. He couldn't recall whether he had been more tormented at the thought that she was alive somewhere but had chosen to be without him or that she was dead, which would at least mean she still loved him.

Tristan came back to the present with a start. Sophie wasn't dead. She was standing here next to him, alive and as serenely beautiful as she had always been. She was older and the long hair had gone, and her clothes were stylish and they reeked of money but her skin remained velvety soft-looking and her amazing mocha-brown eyes were unchanged with time. He caught a waft of the timeless Oscar de la Renta perfume she always wore, the powdery, spicy scent taunting him with memories. It was intoxicating and before he could stop himself, he breathed it in like a junkie. What was she doing here? And why did she seem to think he had wronged her?

Sophie might have seen that painting he had done of Anna all those years ago but they didn't even know each other. She wouldn't know about the kiss – how could she? She was in London at the time; she had attended part of her course before disappearing, her classmates had said so.

So what could possibly have made her walk away from their relationship without even leaving him a note or saying goodbye? The million-dollar question, thought Tristan. Since Sophie had left him, he had trusted no one and he held himself back. He used women when he needed them but gave nothing of himself. And Sophie was the reason why.

Tristan turned to her, with every intention of screaming at her, demanding to know what he had done to make her hate him so much. Instead, he found himself falling into her incredible eyes. Forgetting all the hideous memories and the heartache, all he could think about was how much he had loved her and the way she had made him feel.

'It was us against the world,' he said softly, not even thinking before he spoke. 'Do you remember how we used to say that to each other?'

She nodded, her hair falling forward into her eyes.

Tristan gave her the ghost of a smile. 'We'd snuggle up on the floor of my studio and make love all night. And we'd tell each other that no one could touch us, that nothing could tear us apart.'

Sophie fought to keep her hands by her sides. All she could think about was how much she wanted to kiss him. She wanted to crush her lips against his until it hurt and she wanted to feel his arms around her, his hands touching her everywhere. She wished she could go back to those innocent days when the anticipation of him putting down his paintbrush and covering her body with his had been just as erotic as the act of him capturing her on canvas in the first place.

'I loved you so, so much,' he said, his voice breaking. He felt for her fingers blindly, forgetting how much he hated her. His heart leapt as her fingers slid into his, slotting together perfectly, the way they always had.

'I loved you more,' she said tremulously, using one of their old jokes. She could feel herself melting against him, the feel of his hand in hers almost more than she could bear. When he rubbed his calloused forefinger into her palm, she felt as if her heart might break. The sensation unsteadied her but she gained control of herself. 'No, seriously, Tristan. I loved you more.' She snatched her hand back. 'I must have done.'

'You have to be kidding me.' His voice was flatly disbelieving.

She laughed and the sound grated on his already shot nerves. 'I don't think so. And I shouldn't have touched you just then. I wouldn't want you to get any ideas about us getting back together.'

'*Really.*' Tristan narrowed his eyes at her, feeling fury bubbling to the surface. Who did she think she was?

'I'm getting married,' she said in a cold voice. 'To Gil Anderson. On Christmas Eve.'

Tristan's head spun. His Sophie . . . getting married . . . She couldn't be. Not that he wanted her back – she had crucified him once and once was more than enough, but *married*? To *Gil Anderson*? Tristan couldn't get his head round it. 'But . . . but why did you leave in the first place?' He grabbed her hand again. 'Why are you acting as if I'm the one who's done something wrong?'

Sophie whipped her hand away, unable to stand the feel of him on her again. 'Don't act the innocent, Tristan! We both know what you did.'

He suddenly felt as if he didn't know her at all. She was so unlike the unsophisticated girl he had known before. And he had liked the other Sophie a whole lot better than this new one.

'I thought you were *dead*,' he snarled at her, finally snapping. 'Did you know that? You left without a fucking word and I thought you'd been killed because I couldn't believe you would put me through all that pain unless it was an accident.'

Sophie gaped at him. What the hell was he talking about? Spinning away from him, she did the only thing she seemed to be any good at and ran.

Tristan scratched his head, totally confused. What on earth had just happened? He had never been sure how he would react if he ever saw Sophie again but he was baffled by the way *she* had reacted to seeing *him*. Catching sight of the chapel, he walked towards it, remembering his father was in there downing whisky like Communion wine.

He found Jack slumped in a pew at the front, dusty sunlight swirling around him like a mass of bees on a flower. His blond head was almost on his chest and his legs were splayed out carelessly. Tristan flopped into the pew next to him.

'Thought you might need some company.'

Jack flicked bloodshot eyes in his direction and grunted.

'I know you were probably hoping for Will, but I'm afraid I'm going to have to do.' Tristan leant his elbows on the pew in front and fixed his eyes on the altar which was covered in a heavy red cloth and two bronze candlesticks. 'I've just seen Sophie.'

'Sophie? *Your* Sophie?'

Tristan took the half-empty bottle of whisky from his father and swigged from it. 'Not *my* Sophie, no. She made that patently obvious. She's going to marry Gil Anderson. On Christmas Eve, by all accounts.' He drank some more, needing to deaden the pain of Sophie's return and blot it from his memory. He felt as if his heart had been drop-kicked by Jonny Wilkinson and it hurt like hell. Glancing at his father's stricken face, he could see he felt the same. 'I wouldn't worry about JB,' he commented mildly. 'I shouldn't imagine he's capable of loving anyone more than he loves himself.'

Jack focused his gaze bleakly on the exquisite stained-glass window above the altar. It was a rather sensual representation of Adam and Eve. They were naked, their dignity covered by the curve of each other's bodies and some carefully placed tendrils of hair. Jack wanted to warn Adam that loving Eve would be the most heady and most damaging experience of his life but he knew it would be pointless; Adam had been just as clueless as the rest of them. 'I gave your mother an ultimatum, you see. I told her she had to give JB up or our marriage was over.' He barked out a bitter laugh. 'I was sort of expecting the worst but I had imagined she might just whisper it to me in passing one day. Not grab the arsehole's backside and clean his tonsils in front of everyone.'

'You probably should have told her that banging JB was the best thing she'd ever done and she would have been back like a shot; Mother's always hated being told what to do.'

Jack's eyes crossed drunkenly as he downed at least five fingers of whisky in one gulp. 'Couldn't play games any more, son. Don't have the energy. I just want a woman, a good woman who won't muck me around.' He blinked away the tears that were threatening to spill out on to his weathered cheeks. 'All I want is to love someone with all my heart and for that someone to love me back just as much. Nothing complicated, nothing out of the ordinary. Is that too much to ask, Tris? Is it?'

Tristan shook his head, wiping his eyes on his shirt sleeve. Wasn't that all he wanted? To love someone with all his heart and for that someone to love him back just as much? Lost in thought, he nursed the bottle of whisky in his arms.

Jack stared at him, recalling a conversation he had had months ago with Clemmie in his Rolls-Royce. He had slagged Tristan off, he remembered, comparing him to Will and saying that he hadn't made a success of himself because he lacked ambition. Guiltily, Jack recalled the gentle way Clemmie had touched his hand and said something about hoping Tristan didn't know how he felt about him because he'd be crushed. The kindly reproof in her eyes had pierced him straight through the heart.

Jack felt hollow. Clemmie had been absolutely right to reprimand him and he blamed himself for thinking his youngest son should be punished because he reminded him of Caro. But he knew now that he had been lying to himself all along. The truth was far more revealing. 'I think I owe you an apology, Tris,' he sniffed. 'For favouring Will. I mean, making you *think* I favoured Will.'

Tristan raised his eyebrows. 'But you do, Dad. Everyone knows that. S'OK, I've lived with it for years.' He picked at the label on the bottle of whisky, his eyes downcast. 'I used to feel hurt about it, you know, when I was a kid, but now I just feel the occasional twinge.' He held his fingers up to show how infinitesimal the occasional twinge was.

Jack had never felt more like a shit than he did right now. He was a terrible father. 'I used to think you were flighty like your mother, never happy with what you had, always thinking you deserved better than we gave you.' He put up a hand to silence Tristan's outraged defence. 'I know that's not true. The truth is, I think I was more worried that you reminded me of *me*. You were a player but you were sensitive and I thought you were going to get hurt. I thought you needed toughening up so I was hard on you, very, very hard on you. I was terrified that you'd inherited my insecurities and that you might end up like me, regretting what you've made of your life and never having a normal relationship.'

Tristan was stunned. He had waited years to find out what he had done to induce his father's wrath.

'I thought I was doing the right thing,' Jack said despairingly. 'I thought I was protecting you . . .'

'And I still got hurt anyway,' Tristan observed. 'So you needn't have bothered.' Feeling his father collapse next to him, he grabbed hold of him fiercely. 'Dad, I still love you, you idiot! It's one of those stupid, unconditional things kids do. It doesn't matter, it really doesn't matter.' He flung his arms around Jack and held him.

Jack was so overcome, he sobbed like a baby. 'I don't deserve you,' he kept saying as he snorted and left great wet blotches all over Tristan's white shirt. Tristan held him until his shaking shoulders started to relax. He wasn't sure why he was finding it so easy to forgive his father's bullying but seeing Sophie seemed to have put everything sharply into perspective.

'And I wish I'd seen what a bloody good painter you are, Tris,' Jack said in a gruff voice. 'I could retire early if only I'd thought to accept the pieces you tried to give me all those years ago.' He clasped his hands around his throbbing head. 'Fucking hell, my hangover's kicking in already.'

Tristan gently patted his hand. 'Yes, I think you might need to do something about that, Dad. The drinking, I mean.'

'I know, I know. I'm not going to rehab though.'

Tristan let out a roar of laughter. 'Who do you think you are – Amy Winehouse?'

'Who?'

'Never mind. We'll all help you – *I'll* help you.'

'Thanks, son.' Jack sat back and put the whisky bottle to one side. 'We're a right pair, aren't we?'

'It's a wonder either of us ever gets a shag,' Tristan agreed. They looked at each other and laughed. Suddenly, things didn't seem so bad after all.

'Oh look, there's Clemmie.' Milly nudged India. 'She always looks so beautiful, doesn't she?'

They were supposed to be handing out the glossy brochures and miniature bottles of Penhaligon's perfume to promote the hotel but so far they had spent most of the day people-spotting and acting like the fashion police. And there had been many crimes for them to snicker over: Mrs North's horrid polyester dress, Gil's too-tight shirt and lack of support bra . . .

'Do take one of these lovely brochures,' Milly said sweetly, shoving one at a passing guest, who was too polite to say he already had three. 'And some of this lovely Penhaligon's scent for your wife.'

The guest thanked her, thinking it best not to mention he had a boyfriend, not a wife, and hurried away, his pockets bulging full of perfume bottles.

'Bugger it, I've still got tons of these left,' Milly grumbled. She fanned her hot face with one of the brochures. 'At least they're keeping us cool. And Will says we can have as many of these perfume bottles as we like.'

Glaring at Clemmie with some venom, India didn't answer. Knowing how much her best friend coveted designer clobber, Milly hid a smile and mentally totted up the cost of Clemmie's cornflower-blue prom dress and silk slingbacks. She couldn't believe Clemmie and Rufus had arrived so late; most of the guests had been shown around the new hotel and local reporters had rushed off to write glowing reports about the 'newest glamorous jewel in the Cotswolds' crown', assuming Clemmie and Rufus weren't going to put in a appearance. They were going to be gutted in the morning . . .

'I bet that's an Ungaro dress,' Milly said longingly. 'It's so feminine.'

India looked sullen. 'It's a stunning dress but she always looks so prim and proper.'

'I think she's gorgeous! I'd love to look like her.'

'She never shows any flesh.'

'That's because she's classy,' Milly said sarcastically, noticing that India was showing even more flesh than she normally did in a sawn-off denim skirt teamed with a revealing pink bustier top. She caught sight of a new gold chain with what looked suspiciously like a real diamond hanging from it.

'Where did you get that?'

'It was . . . a birthday present,' India said evasively, fingering the Tiffany diamond. It had been delivered to her house with a card scrawled with an 'R' and India had been beside herself. As far as she was concerned, it was the start of her path to fame and fortune. Desperate to appear nonchalant in front of Rufus, India couldn't resist pulling her top down slightly to show off more cleavage. Rufus looked hot; he was wearing tight white jeans and a black shirt, teamed with a heavy silver belt with a skull on it. Remembering their last meeting at the B&B at the edge of Upper Slaughter, which had been the dirtiest, most erotic experience of India's life, it was all she could do not to throw herself into his arms and wrap her legs round his waist.

Milly was peeved. Whoever had bought India the necklace had expensive taste and it made her pink diamanté effort seem paltry by comparison. She slopped another inch of vodka into her orange juice as neither Will nor Tristan seemed to be around.

India smirked as Rufus took advantage of Clemmie being photographed with a fan to give her a surreptitious wink.

Milly didn't notice. 'I can't believe we're going back to school in a few weeks.' She looked dreamy at the thought of immersing herself in hundreds of Shakespeare plays.

India's academic failure swam before her eyes. 'You're a right swot these days,' she said bitchily, 'doing fifteen A levels and mooning over bloody university brochures.'

Milly frowned. 'It's *four* A levels actually, and wanting to be a journalist doesn't make me a swot. '

'Whatever.'

'Look, I know what it's like when you don't know what career you want to get into. I could help you with your A level choices, if you like.'

India pulled a face, not caring that Milly was trying to make amends with her. She couldn't stand the sight of Clemmie's arm around Rufus's slim waist and Milly was the nearest person she could lash out at. 'No thanks. Just because David's off to uni and you think you're going to be the next Tessa Meadmore doesn't mean I'm going to turn into some geek as well. Frankly, I'd rather marry someone famous and live in LA.' She flipped her ginger hair over her shoulder defiantly.

Milly smiled brightly at another guest as she handed them a brochure then laughed. 'Yes, but that's why you need to get an education, Ind. Because the chances of some bloke whisking you off to LA and paying for your life are pretty remote, aren't they? Especially in Appleton.' She was taken aback when India threw a dirty look at her and turned away to chat to a girl called Alicia from the next village. Milly scowled at them. India had been secretive for the past few weeks, disappearing for hours and never answering her mobile. Milly was convinced she was up to something but it could just be that she had a new best friend, she thought, narrowing her eyes at Alicia's pale, slender back. Either that or she had done something to upset India. It was as if India suddenly saw Milly as immature and silly and as if all their old jokes were meaningless.

Miserably, she watched India and Alicia wander off towards the drinks marquee together. There was only one thing for it, she was going to have to get paralytic. Seconds later, she forgot about her vodka and orange when Freddie joined her, looking suave in dark blue jeans and an Oxford-blue shirt. She beamed at him.

'Milli Vanilli, you look adorable!' he said, flinging a casual arm around her bare shoulders. 'I love this strappy dress thing. How did you know blue was my favourite colour?'

Milly almost fainted. She blushed at his touch but made the most of it, revelling in the scent of his expensive-smelling aftershave and the roughness of his leather wristband grazing her cheek. She didn't want to tell him that she had picked the dress because it reminded her of his crushed blueberry eyes, although unfortunately it made her beastly big boobs look gargantuan. She took another gulp of her drink for courage.

'Good turnout, isn't it?' he said, surveying the throng of people. His fingers caressed her shoulder lightly, unthinkingly. 'Christ, look at my dad with his silly new wife. Do you think everyone sees him as an old fool?'

Milly gulped, knowing if she tried to speak it would come out as a squeak. She watched Freddie's father circulating with his incredibly young blonde wife on his arm, her heart soaring as Freddie's fingers carried on their magical caresses.

'Hannah chases after everything in trousers, including me one time, not that I've told my father, of course. But I'm her stepson – that's illegal, isn't it?'

Milly gave him a soppy smile. This had to be the most heavenly day of her life. She felt him lean closer and her skin quivered. She desperately hoped he wouldn't notice her trembling like a virgin. She *was* a virgin, of course, but she didn't want him to know that. Freddie seemed wildly experienced, so she didn't want him thinking she was unsophisticated. Thank God he had failed his A levels. She knew it wasn't a very charitable thought but she couldn't help feeling delighted that Freddie would be sticking around for the next couple of years, especially since David was off to study French at Bristol University in a few weeks.

Milly suspected the school was very much aware of Freddie's extracurricular activities but overlooked them because his rich father Hugo made such extravagant contributions every year. Still, Freddie's father didn't have enough influence to bribe an entire board of examiners so Freddie had little choice but to go back and start again.

Freddie pushed his floppy black hair out of his eyes and watched Clemmie talking to a very dull vicar with an animated expression. 'She certainly knows how to work a crowd, doesn't she?'

'She's lovely,' Milly agreed, finally finding her voice. She couldn't believe Freddie still had his arm around her and even though her mane of hair was trapped uncomfortably beneath it, she didn't dare move a millimetre.

'For a film star, she's frightfully down-to-earth, isn't she?'

'I know. She's always so friendly, even to me. I'm not sure about Rufus though.'

Freddie jerked his head in Rufus's direction. 'What? You must think he's a bit of a hunk!'

Milly raised her eyebrows. 'He loves himself. Not my cup of tea, to be honest.'

'Really?' Freddie looked sceptical. 'He must be every young girl's wet dream.'

She buried her burning cheeks in her drink. If only he knew *he* was the one who interrupted her dreams on a regular basis.

'I think he has the hots for you,' Freddie observed, tickling her ear jokingly with his fingertips.

'What! No, he barely notices I'm alive!'

'As if! He's not blind, Mills, and you're female, so trust me, he will have noticed you.'

The delicious sensation of his fingertips brushing her earlobe was so wonderful, Milly's surprise at Freddie's assertion that Rufus fancied her barely registered. She gazed up at his eyelashes lovingly.

Freddie flicked his dark fringe out of his eyes like a rock star. 'Seriously, I've seen him looking over at you. And once, he even asked where you and India hang out. I'm not sure if he realises how young you both are, of course.'

Milly frowned. Freddie must have got it wrong about Rufus but she wasn't remotely interested either way. She wished he would do that thing with his fingertips again and edged her head closer in the vain hope she might encourage him. Disappointingly, Freddie removed his arm from her shoulders to shove his hands in his pockets as Rufus approached them.

Milly felt bereft. Damn Rufus for coming over just at that

moment! She looked up at him, feeling rather star-struck at first but as he moved closer, she realised he was wearing eyeliner. And roughly a can of hairspray.

'Help me out,' Rufus said, smiling easily. 'I'm being chased by one of the old dears in the village.'

Milly sighed. So he had only come over to speak to them because he didn't want to mingle with the elderly. He was such a poseur in his white jeans! He was handsome but compared to Freddie, Rufus didn't stand a chance. A line from *The Tempest* came into her head, something Miranda had said about her beloved Ferdinand: 'I might call him/A thing divine; for nothing natural/I ever saw so noble.'

Milly knew *exactly* where Miranda was coming from. She felt a surge of gratitude towards Tessa for introducing her to Shakespeare. She really couldn't get enough of him and was currently working her way through a collection of his complete works, a weighty tome that would frighten the life out of all but the most ardent of fans. Milly's only regret was that she hadn't discovered it earlier.

Rufus nodded briefly at Freddie before fixing his heavily eyelinered eyes on Milly in a way that suggested he thought he was rather magnificent. 'Are you enjoying the party?'

'Er . . . yes. You?'

Rufus made a big show of rolling his brown eyes. 'It's annoying when you've got a camera shoved in your face the whole time.' He gave Joe, the cameraman, a pointed look but it didn't make any difference; the camera remained glued to his face, the red light indicating that it was capturing every word. Seemingly forgetting that he was supposed to be aggravated by the presence of the film crew, Rufus turned his best side to the camera lens and struck a pose. 'Still, Clemmie and I signed up for this, so I guess we're going to have to see it through.'

Milly struggled to think of something to say. She glanced at

Freddie for help and was taken aback to see him glowering at Rufus in a most unfriendly manner. She struggled momentarily, her powers of conversation seeming to have deserted her in her hour of need.

'You must be looking forward to the wedding,' she managed eventually.

Rufus looked rather uncomfortable at the mention of his forthcoming nuptials. 'Well, Clemmie's dealing with all of that. Women like to get involved in all the details, you know? Fabric, flowers, shit like that. I think she'll be happy enough if I turn up and say "I do"!' He laughed loudly, as if he found himself very amusing indeed.

Contemplating him over her vodka and orange, Milly decided Rufus was a tosser. He didn't seem the least bit interested in Clemmie and he clearly wasn't pulling his weight in the wedding department. And, inspecting his white jeans more closely, she was sure he had socks stuffed down his crotch.

'It's more of a girl thing, isn't it, the whole wedding vibe?' Rufus asked her, casting a look over his shoulder as if searching for someone more exciting to talk to.

'I haven't really thought about it,' she said primly, despite the fact she had mapped out her wedding to Freddie in minute detail, right down to her hand-tied bouquet of deep blue Dutch irises with baby's breath and bridesmaids' dresses in shot silk the colour of Freddie's eyes. 'But if I did, I'd want my husband-to-be to do more than turn up and quote the one line he's bothered to learn.' Not liking the slightly lascivious way Rufus was eyeing her legs, she shot him a cross look and hoped the camera had caught every second of their conversation.

Rufus stiffly made his excuses and to Milly's delight Freddie resumed his position with his arm round her shoulders.

'I told you he fancied you,' he said, his mouth tight around the edges.

Before Milly could reassure him that Rufus didn't fancy her

in the least and was just performing for the cameras, David rushed up to them breathlessly.

'I've just been talking to the most awfully pretty girl,' he gasped, tucking the tails of his black shirt into his jeans in an attempt to smarten up. 'She's much better looking than India, a proper redhead with freckly skin. And she's really intelligent too. Alicia, her name is. Isn't that beautiful? Al-ee-seeya . . .'

'Yes, we know how to pronounce it,' Freddie said impatiently. 'That Hollywood moron Rufus was just bloody chatting your sister up.'

'I doubt it, Fred, she's only sixteen!' David looked unper-turbed and grabbed two glass bowls of Eton Mess from a passing waitress, the heavenly scent of strawberries and fresh cream drifting under their noses. 'Hmmm, these look delicious. Girls love strawberries, don't they? But seriously, what on earth would a guy like Rufus see in Milly?'

'I'm standing right here, David,' she huffed moodily, feeling her cheeks turning red.

'I just meant that you're a bit young for him, that's all.' Juggling the glass bowls, David hastily raked his fingers through his greasy fringe and hoped his breath was fresh. He'd munch on a Polo mint as soon as he had a free hand. 'Can you believe I've met someone so totally gorgeous weeks before I leave for uni? It's such a bummer! I must get her phone number . . . see you later . . .'

Freddie tutted and tightened his grip on Milly. 'Don't worry, Mills, I'll look after you. David's obviously thinking with his dick at the moment but I'll make sure Rufus keeps his distance.'

Milly was speechless. Bizarrely, Freddie seemed to be feeling protective of her but she couldn't see that he had any cause to; Rufus was far too in love with himself to be thinking about someone like her. Nor could she ever see herself going out with anyone who could wear skinny jeans better than she could, she thought with a giggle. Still, if it meant Freddie putting his arm round her possessively, the way he was now, Milly was more than happy for him to think that Rufus was about to drag her into the bushes and ravish her.

Milly wasn't the only one who was astonished by Freddie's over-protective behaviour. Freddie himself was having a hard time understanding why he suddenly felt so responsible for David's little sister. He had always thought of Milly as impossibly cute but terribly childish at the same time, so he had no idea why he felt the need to act as her bodyguard all of a sudden.

I'm doing this for David, he told himself. He's preoccupied with this new bird, so I'm doing him a favour and looking after his baby sister, that's all. He caught sight of Tessa walking past rather unsteadily in a beautiful pink dress and 'fuck me' heels. 'Wow!' he whistled, totally knocked sideways by the sexy dress. 'Talk about sex on legs!'

Gloom descended upon Milly's sunny mood like a big black rain cloud. Freddie clearly wasn't over his crush on Tessa, even though she'd obviously given him the brush-off. She stiffened defensively as she caught sight of her mother approaching.

'I hope there's nothing suspect in that,' Henny said, sniffing Milly's glass suspiciously.

'Do go away, Mother. I'm not drunk, OK? I'm perfectly capable of looking after myself and not causing a scene. And why are you dressed up like a dog's dinner?' she added nastily, taken aback to see her mother actually looking very pretty for once.

'Milly!' Freddie removed his arm from her shoulders and frowned at her as if she'd just slapped a puppy. 'You look amazing, Mrs H.' It was his pet nickname for her. 'As pretty as a picture. You're turning heads wherever you go today.'

'Thank you, Freddie,' Henny said, wondering why Milly was so dreadful to her all the time. She caught sight of an older man in a smart blazer. Without thinking, she said, 'He's rather

279

dashing, isn't he? He reminds me of Bobby a bit, although Bobby was dark, not silver-haired.'

'That's Barnaby Wellham-Cooper,' Freddie said, giving him a wave. 'He's a widower – his wife died a few years back, I think. My father went to school with him. Terribly nice bloke.' He gave Henny a naughty grin. 'Isn't it about time you started dating again, Mrs H?'

Flattered for a moment, Henny instantly felt her hackles rising as Milly let out a scornful laugh.

'Mum? *Dating?* You've got to be kidding! She's far too old to meet someone else.'

Henny felt easy tears coming and, giving Freddie a brave smile, she shook her head. 'Milly's quite right, I'm afraid, Freddie. Who's going to look at an old lady like me?' She looked down at the ground. 'Do excuse me, I must go and find Will. He said something about Sophie coming back and poor Tristan must be in an awful state.'

Freddie looked agonised and shot Milly a horrified look.

Milly bit her lip as her mother stumbled away. Why had she done that? It was as if she couldn't help herself. She realised her mother was the punchbag she needed when things weren't going her way. And she was such an easy target.

Milly put her glass on the tray of a passing waiter, feeling appalled. Her mother deserved to meet someone else after everything that had happened and she had no right to mock her when she looked so lovely today. And what must Freddie think of her? She had sounded like a monster, a spoilt brat.

'I think I owe my mother an apology,' she said to Freddie who immediately gave her a dazzling smile of approval. If only apologising wasn't so cringe-making, Milly sighed regretfully.

Chapter Seventeen

Towards the end of the evening when most of the guests had left, Tessa began to realise she might be spectacularly drunk. She and Tristan had ploughed into the champagne as if it was going out of fashion before Sophie had arrived, and after Tristan disappeared to have it out with her, Tessa vaguely remembered turning down a bowl of delectable-looking Eton Mess for yet another glass of champagne and then perhaps another . . .

Ditching her empty champagne glass and grabbing a bottle of water from the bucket of melting ice cubes by the marquee, she headed for the regal oak tree at the front of the manor house. Diving under it and kicking off her back-breaking heels, she downed the water thirstily to try and counter some of the alcohol. Leaning against the tree trunk for support, she surveyed the grounds of the manor rather drunkenly, taking in the twinkling white fairy lights that had been strung between the trees and the flickering tea lights that had been placed on every surface. Tucked inside some Moroccan tea glasses Gil had found, the candles sent out jewel-like beams that danced across the lawn like feisty dragonflies.

Tessa smiled, wishing her eyes wouldn't keep crossing. In the warm, fuzzy glow of champagne, with the sun sinking down on the horizon, it felt like a beautifully romantic scene. If only everything wasn't so gloriously screwed up, she thought with a deep sigh.

'Are you all right?'

Tessa jumped. It was Nathan, his tanned biceps flexing as he put a hand out to her.

'I'm fine, thanks,' she mumbled incoherently. 'Just need some . . . some air.'

He nodded, not quite convinced she was fully compos mentis but understanding that she needed to be on her own.

Tessa returned to her thoughts as Nathan ducked out of sight. Sophie was the girl from Tristan's portraits, the one he seemed so deeply in love with still, and if the realisation that she hadn't spotted the resemblance wasn't enough to make her feel like a complete idiot, the fact that Sophie hadn't been truthful with her was. Tessa had happily confided in Sophie about anything that had come to mind – her feelings about the Forbes-Henry family mostly, her mistrust of Will, her feelings about Tristan, for heaven's sake! And the whole time, Sophie had been hiding her true identity, keeping quiet about her past with Tristan. It made Tessa's skin prickle all over. And what about the veritable time bomb Sophie was sitting on in the shape of five-year-old Ruby?

Wincing as she ran her tongue around her parched mouth, Tessa held her hair away from the nape of her neck to cool down. No wonder Ruby had reminded her of someone so vividly the other day – she was the spitting image of Tristan! Had Sophie told Tristan about Ruby? Tessa wondered. She couldn't believe Tristan was the kind of man to turn his back on his own child; he adored children, by all accounts, so why on earth would Sophie have kept such an enormous secret from him? It was a mystery. Tessa felt betrayed, even though she and Sophie had been friends for only a short while. She had thought they trusted each other but that was obviously not the case.

She felt her BlackBerry jerk to life in her handbag and felt her spirits slump even further as she checked it. Jilly was hounding her again, certain there must be something to report back from the party. What could she tell her? That Clemmie had looked as ravishing as ever and had charmed every member of the village with ease? That Rufus had played the part of the Hollywood bad boy perfectly, strutting around in his tight jeans and occasionally throwing a hot look in the direction of a middle-aged aristocrat?

The pressure of behaving like some hardened hack while the Forbes-Henry family wove their magic around her on a daily basis was becoming too much, Tessa decided, suddenly feeling as if she needed a lie-down. And what made it even more difficult was that Clemmie seemed genuinely lovely and while Rufus wasn't the most likeable person Tessa had ever met and certainly not perhaps the most trustworthy, he didn't seem to be putting a foot wrong.

Tessa's head drooped. She was horribly drunk. She felt like a fraud, an impostor. She had befriended everyone with the best of intentions but now she felt she was compromising everyone, using them for all she was worth. Jilly had sold the documentary to Will as a dazzling advert for their new hotel when the reality was that she, Tessa, was being forced, like a ghastly puppet, to turn the programme into a sordid, celebrity exposé.

'Er . . . everything all right?' Looking awkward, Will appeared next to her, his towering height and broad shoulders immediately making her feel at a disadvantage. He had abandoned his suit jacket and his white shirt was slightly crumpled and the cuffs were turned back to the elbows. This, and the fact that his tawny-gold hair was ruffled, made him seem almost human but Tessa wasn't going to be sucked in.

Stuffing her BlackBerry into her handbag guiltily and wishing she still had her heels on, she answered Will's question by confidently shaking her head from side to side. She pulled a face and held her temples; waggling her head around at the moment was a huge mistake. God, this was the last thing she needed, Will giving a bloody lecture, she thought, eyeing him cagily.

Placing his hand on the tree trunk beside her head, Will gave her a ghost of a smile. 'A bit tipsy, are we?'

'Certainly not!' Indignation seemed the best course of action but seeing Will raise his eyebrows at her disbelievingly, she held her hands up in defeat. She could barely stand up straight, so it didn't take a genius to work out she had downed one too many. 'Well, maybe a little,' she admitted reluctantly.

His blue eyes twinkled at her unexpectedly and she found his openly friendly manner quite unnerving.

'I've had a few myself, actually,' he confessed, rubbing his eyes. He wasn't quite sure what he was doing, talking to Tessa like this, but he didn't feel like fighting today. 'It's been a long day, but a successful one, don't you think?'

'I suppose . . .'

'Obviously the incident with my parents was . . . unfortunate but everything else seemed to go well. Christ, you don't think they'll use that in the documentary, do you?'

'Doubt it.' Tessa let out a delicate burp. 'Nothing to do with the hotel, is it?' Why was Will suddenly being so nice? Had he finally realised she wasn't the devil? Or perhaps this was his way of catching her off guard before he went in for the kill, she thought, narrowing her eyes at him suspiciously.

'You're not going to start, you know, lecturing me, are you?'

'No.' He leant his back against the tree so their shoulders were touching and glanced at her sideways. 'What do you think I'm going to lecture you about?'

'Oh, I don't know . . .' Rolling her eyes with bad grace, she held her fingers in front of her eyes and counted on them. 'Talking to Henny, asking about Rufus, making friends with Tristan . . .' She paused, casting her eyes to the ground. Her voice caught in her throat, the pressure of her job overwhelming her for a minute. In her drunken state, she felt sure she was too weak to deal with one of Will's searing diatribes. 'I just . . . just don't think I could take it right now.'

Will studied her, watching her rub her bare arms with trembling fingers, her shoulders cowing slightly. Was she upset about Tristan and Sophie? he thought with a frown. Tristan claimed Tessa was nothing more than a friend and Will believed him but did Tessa's feelings run deeper than that? Will found himself feeling rather sorry for her and he was surprised he even cared.

'You're upset about Tristan.' It was a statement rather than a question.

'Tristan?' Tessa put her head back against the tree trunk and wondered why Will had picked up on that point in particular. 'Yes . . . no . . . it's just everything. The whole . . . sorry . . . mess.'

Feeling a stab in his heart he didn't understand, Will fought the urge to gather Tessa up in his arms and kiss her problems away. He was shocked at himself. Why on earth would he want to do such a thing? It was the sight of her woeful green eyes and her wide, sensual mouth drooping dejectedly, that was all, he told himself. She looked so . . . vulnerable. And so beautiful, he was astonished to find himself thinking.

'I feel sick,' Tessa said abruptly, going pale.

Seeing she was about to collapse, Will scooped her up in his arms. Completely thrown off guard, Tessa had no choice but to cling to him, curling her hands round his wide neck for dear life. Woozily, she linked her fingers under the ends of his tawny gold hair and fervently hoped her knickers weren't on show to all and sundry. She was so taken aback by Will's gallantry she didn't even feel sick any more.

'I'm taking you back to your cottage,' he said firmly, making sure he had a good grip on her before heading out from under the tree.

She wanted to protest that she was too heavy for him to carry all the way to her cottage but she couldn't help enjoying the security his massive arms afforded her. In fact, if it wasn't Will and she didn't dislike him so much, Tessa might have thought the whole thing was terribly romantic. Will seemed rather like Mr Darcy for a moment, with his masculine stride and unreadable face; all he needed was his white shirt to be soaking wet and see-through and some tight breeches around those big thighs . . .

There were hardly any guests left and, nodding politely at the few stalwarts who remained, Will headed for Tessa's cottage, bearing her as if she weighed nothing. Austin, worried that his beloved master was disappearing, followed them all the way to Tessa's cottage, lolloping alongside them, his tongue hanging out of the side of his mouth because of the heat.

Tessa wanted the ground to swallow her up at the thought that Will believed she was too drunk to stagger to her cottage unaided; he had a bad enough opinion of her as it was without him thinking she was some sort of lush. She kept catching maddening wafts of his spicy aftershave as he strode towards her cottage and she berated herself for being such a girl.

Carefully depositing her on the comfy sofa in the sitting room at the front, Will ran up the stairs two at a time and reappeared with pillows, a duvet and some blankets. Austin, thinking it was all a fantastic game, ran up and down the stairs a few times for good measure before remembering how old he was and flopping down on the rug in the sitting room as if he'd run a marathon.

'Really, you don't have to do this . . .' Tessa said, feeling foolish as Will tucked a pillow behind her head and wrapped a duvet around her. 'I'm drunk but I'm not an invalid.'

'I never said you were.' He put the kettle on and handed her a glass of water. 'You just need some strong coffee.'

As Austin turned round on the duvet next to her several times before flopping down in the crook of her legs, Tessa watched Will deftly making two mugs of coffee. He looked exhausted, the weight of his self-imposed responsibilities evident from the bags under his eyes and his slightly dishevelled appearance. As soon as he had made the coffee, she was going to insist that he left, she decided.

It was kind of him to bring her back to her cottage but there was no need for him to stay and pretend to like her because the atmosphere would be uneasy and neither of them would know what to say. Tessa wished the room would stop whizzing round her as if she was on a ride at Alton Towers and she lay back against the pillow as she fought another bout of nausea.

'I'll have this coffee and then you should try to get some sleep,' he said before she could say anything. Handing her a mug, he flung himself into the armchair next to her, throwing his huge thighs over the wooden arm. His head was almost touching hers but for some reason it didn't intimidate her.

'Make the room stop spinning,' she begged him with her eyes shut, forgetting she wanted him to leave. 'Talk . . . about anything. I don't even think I care if you have a go at me.'

Will flinched at the jibe but knew he richly deserved it. Perhaps he had given Tessa a hard time since she had been here but surely he couldn't be blamed for trying to protect his family? He remembered Tristan saying he had Tessa all wrong and that she wasn't nearly as hard-nosed as she appeared. He hadn't believed him at the time but seeing her looking so pale and weak as her hangover started to kick in early, Will wondered if there might be a glimmer of truth to Tristan's heated protests. Then he remembered the page of notes he had seen and pulled himself together. Still, now was hardly the time to discuss that particular issue.

'I'm not going to have a go at you,' he told her mildly. 'I'd like to think we're capable of having a conversation that doesn't involve sniping at each other.'

Tessa said nothing but watching her bite her lip tentatively, Will realised she was just as wary of him as he was of her. He rubbed his chin reflectively, scratching the five o'clock shadow that was already appearing. 'Right. Well, maybe a civilised chat *is* out of the question. He glanced around for something to read to her and grabbed the nearest book from the shelf. 'How about some poetry?'

She gave him an imperceptible nod so he settled back in his chair.

> 'Away with your fictions of flimsy romance,
> Those tissues of falsehood which folly has wove!
> Give me the mild beam of the soul-breathing glance,
> Or the rapture which—'

' "Dwells on the first kiss of love", ' Tessa finished sleepily. She noticed that his blue eyes darkened when he was concentrating. 'God, I love that poem.'

'You like Byron?'

'You sound surprised.' She sounded defensive and she knew it.

'I guess I am but . . .'

'I did read English Lit. at uni, you know.'

'It's not that, it's just, well, I don't know many women who like Byron, that's all.'

Actually, he only knew one and that was his fiancée. *His fiancée.* Will sat up in his chair and put his coffee mug down with a bang. He hadn't given Claudette a moment's thought for the past few hours. He had been disappointed that she couldn't make it to the party but, after that, he had been focused on making the party a success, and then he had been preoccupied with making sure Tessa was all right. Was it out of sight, out of mind with Claudette? Will was confused. It hadn't been that way for him previously. She had been on his mind constantly and he had been driven to distraction by the fact that she was still in France when he had to be in England to sort out this hotel idea, but somehow . . . Will gazed at Tessa's brown shoulders emerging from the absurdly sexy pink dress. Somehow, Claudette seemed a million miles away, further away than Paris and like a cardboard cut-out, flat and unreal. He couldn't for the life of him think why.

'I don't know many men who like Byron,' Tessa offered, interrupting his thoughts. She fixed her moss-green eyes on him, a flicker of humour in them. 'My last boyfriend thought reading poetry was something old ladies did. In fact, he once described Byron as a tosser.'

'A tosser? Interesting view.' He watched her rub Austin's ears and felt deeply and ridiculously envious of Austin.

'Isn't it?' Tessa felt rather sober all of a sudden and her eyes clouded over. 'But he also thought having two girlfriends was absolutely acceptable behaviour so I don't think we need to worry about his opinion too much.'

Will watched her long chestnut hair fall over her face and felt a rush of protectiveness which jolted him to the core. What the hell was happening to him? He didn't even like Tessa, and he certainly didn't care about her previous boyfriends! Even if this one did sound like a complete bastard. He gulped down some coffee, thinking he must have drunk more champagne than he had thought.

'Another poem I think,' he said quickly, feeling the need to steer the conversation away from Tessa's personal life. It wouldn't do to start feeling sympathy for her, he told himself forcibly. She was the enemy, he must remember that. If only she didn't look so irresistible with those smoky black smudges under her eyes and the bee-stung lips protruding sorrowfully, he thought, randomly remembering the carefree way she had run down the lawn in her underwear. He wasn't sure Byron was the right poet to be quoting if he was trying to keep his mind away from how delectable Tessa looked.

Will mentally shook himself and forced his mind to focus on the task in hand. Choosing 'Remind me not, Remind me not' because it was one of his favourites, he read the lines in a low voice. The room became darker as the evening drew in and although he felt tempted to light a candle, he didn't want to interrupt the moment. He stumbled over the words of the poem occasionally because it moved him so much, especially when he got to the part that said:

> 'And still we near and nearer prest,
> and still our glowing lips would meet,
> As if in kisses to expire.'

He wasn't sure Tessa noticed his voice cracking because her eyelids were closed. '"Which tells that we shall be no more",' he ended quietly. He was shocked when he saw a tear slowly trickling down her face.

'Shit.' He leapt out of the armchair and bent over her. 'I shouldn't have chosen that one. Did it remind you of that bastard of an ex-boyfriend or something?'

She shook her head. 'It's just so . . . so romantic,' she said, giving him a watery smile. She looked agonised and brushed frantically at her face. 'Ignore me. I'm such a wet when it comes to his beautiful words.'

Will found himself staring down at her quivering lips, longing surging through his body. Tessa really was an enigma. She was ballsy and opinionated but there was a vulnerable quality in her, Tristan was right about that. Will still didn't trust her but it transpired that that had nothing to do with how attracted to her he was. He detected a faint waft of Penhaligon's Bluebell and caught his breath. Seemingly, perfume was one of the only things he and Claudette disagreed on; she insisted on wearing some heavy, strong-smelling French perfume that was about as subtle as a slap round the face because she claimed that English perfumes smelt old-fashioned.

Reaching out and brushing a lock of hair away from Tessa's

tear-streaked face, Will fought to rationalise his thoughts. It was lust, good, old-fashioned lust that had been the undoing of many a man. The sight of Tessa tearing down the lawn in her lime-green underwear all those weeks ago had sent his head into an erotic spin, but so what? That didn't mean he had *feelings* for her; it meant that she was gorgeous and uninhibited. Discovering her intellectual side made her all the more dangerous in Will's eyes but when it came down to it, Tessa was everything he disliked in a woman. Whereas Claudette . . .

Without moving away from Tessa, Will thought hard about his fiancée. She was beautiful. Elegant and sophisticated and, yes, intellectual in her own way. She enjoyed everything he did which was something he had never experienced before in a relationship. And she loved family. Claudette knew how much family meant to him and she felt the same way, she told him so all the time. Almost absent-mindedly, Will wiped a smudge of make-up from Tessa's cheek with the edge of his thumb. What was wrong with him? He had an amazing fiancée whom he loved and planned to marry but Tessa . . . She stared back at him, her eyes widening as his hand cupped her neck.

Will glanced at her wide, sensual mouth and felt lust kick him in the groin, hard. He wanted to resist her, more than anything, but he didn't know if he could.

Tessa had no idea what Will was thinking. The air was charged with electricity and she didn't have a clue why. She was drunk, she knew that. But noticing how sexy the crinkles were at the corners of his eyes, Tessa couldn't help feeling reckless. Was he going to kiss her? Surely not! This was Will, not Tristan . . . He was engaged to be married . . . he was trustworthy, loyal . . . everyone said so. He was also predictable, wasn't he? The last person to do something wild and romantic like kissing some girl he barely knew and absolutely detested.

Feeling completely out of control for the first time in his life, Will drew Tessa's mouth close to his. Feeling her wide, soft lips parting against his, he kissed her thoroughly. It was a slow, searching kiss at first but within seconds it had spiralled into something else, something exhilarating and heady. He sank his big hands deep into her hair, pulling her towards him.

Tessa felt a shudder of lust ripple down her body as she snaked an arm round his neck and gave herself up to the kiss. It didn't make sense, but she didn't want it to stop. She sat up, her skin tingling with anticipation as Will tucked an arm round her waist until he was almost on top of her. She leant back, her mouth still on his, intoxicated by the feel of his heavy frame on her.

More turned on than he had ever been in his life, Will was struggling to control himself. He longed to kiss her until she couldn't bear it any more and he wanted nothing more than to tear the low-cut dress from her quivering body. He kissed her again, delirious with lust as her tongue mingled hotly with his. As he felt her slip a hand inside the gap in his shirt buttons and touch his bare skin with intent, Will thought he might explode.

Drawing back to look at her, he stared into her eyes which had turned so dark with desire they were almost bottle-green. Her cheeks and chest were flushed with pink and her hair was messed up around her face. He ran a thumb over her swollen lips, feeling her jerk against him, sure that if he made a serious move, she would reciprocate.

What am I doing? Will halted and sucked his breath in. He grabbed the hand that was inside his shirt and, panting, he pulled back from her. The movement broke the spell and they both stared at each other, appalled.

I can't stand her, Will told himself numbly.

I can't stand him, Tessa told herself dizzily.

He sat back on his heels and rubbed his face. He had a fiancée, for fuck's sake. What the hell was he thinking? Looking at Tessa in utter shock, he saw the same thing mirrored on her face.

'We're drunk,' she mumbled, not sure what to say. She lay back and pulled the duvet up around her chin so that her body was completely hidden from him. Anything to hide the shuddering desire that kept sending delicious tingles all the way down to her toes.

'Drunk,' he echoed, grabbing hold of the word gratefully. 'We're very, very drunk . . . you're right.'

'Too much champagne,' Tessa agreed heartily, wondering why her body was still shaking all over. She had been kissed before, many times, so why was she behaving like some sort of inexperienced teenager? 'You should go,' she said, then added hurriedly, 'I mean, you *can* go. You know, if you want.'

'I'll stay until you've fallen asleep,' Will said. He sat back in his armchair, tilting his body away from hers. 'That's what a gentleman would do.' A gentleman? What a joke. A gentleman wouldn't have thrown himself at a drunken woman he claimed not to be able to be in the same room with, he reminded himself, guilt kicking in with a vengeance.

Reeling from what had happened, Tessa wished he would leave. Knowing he would stay until he thought she was all right, she reluctantly put her head on the pillow and made a show of trying to drop off to sleep.

Watching her dark lashes sweeping down on to her cheeks, Will was flabbergasted at what had just happened. He was fairly certain he didn't need to worry about Tristan's feelings, especially now that Sophie was back, but what about Claudette? He felt remorse wash over him. She didn't deserve to be treated like this, not after everything he had promised her.

Will put his head in his hands. He was a good person, he was loyal and straight down the line – he just didn't do things like this! As he reproached himself, he glanced down at the tilt of Tessa's proud nose. There was something about Tessa that had got under his skin. In that stupid, crazy moment, he hadn't been able to resist her. He had been out of control, unable to stop himself, and it had never happened to him before.

Christ, Claudette was due to arrive any minute – what on earth was he going to say to her? But it was just a kiss, wasn't it? It didn't mean anything, it was just lust, and he was ashamed of himself for being so weak.

And what about Tessa? He stared at her thoughtfully. Had she kissed him to try to forget Tristan? He had no idea. Up until a few minutes ago, he had been sure she hated him with a passion.

Not sure if Tessa was asleep or not, Will leant back in his chair and tucked his arms behind his head. Staring up at the beamed ceiling of the cottage, he realised he wasn't going to get a wink of sleep that night. He decided to use the time wisely and figure out what the hell he was going to do when Claudette arrived.

Hours later, Tessa woke up groggily and let out a monster yawn. She was still on her sitting-room sofa with Austin curled up in the crook of her knees.

Will had gone. She had no idea when he had left, and the only sign that he had been there was a rug that was neatly folded up on the armchair and a slight dent in the fabric where his head had been. Squinting at the cheerful stream of sunlight beaming through the windows of her cottage, Tessa reached for her sunglasses. About to make herself a cup of bionic strength coffee, Tessa noticed a mug and a coffee pot on the table. Putting the back of her hand gingerly against the side of the coffee pot, she was puzzled to find it scorchingly hot. Had Will stayed all night? Pouring herself a mug of strong coffee, she picked up a scribbled note he had left, politely asking her to join them all for breakfast if she wanted to.

Ever the gentleman, she thought, throwing off the duvet and groaning at the sight of her crumpled pink dress. Or perhaps not, she thought, remembering their kiss with sudden clarity. She felt her cheeks redden with embarrassment and she tucked her legs up under her chin. How had she let that happen? She had been drunk and she had been carried away in the moment with all the Byron; that was the only explanation.

She touched her lips in wonder, remembering the kiss. It had been nothing like kissing Tristan – that had been fun and clumsy and completely meaningless but this, this had felt like something else.

'It was a moment of madness,' she said out loud, making Austin jump. 'Nothing more.' She tickled his ears. 'And I'm sure it won't ever happen again, will it, you lovely old boy?'

Realising it was nearly ten o'clock and that she was due to meet JB at the B&B in two hours, she rushed upstairs to have a shower. She got ready in record time, choosing to wear a cream denim skirt that finished a few inches above the knee and a high-necked black T-shirt that made the skirt look less slutty. Why was she taking so much trouble with her appearance? It was only the Forbes-Henrys. Tessa added a slick of pink lipgloss.

Did she even want to see Will this morning? she wondered as she tied her hair up into a ponytail. No, surely it would be horrifically embarrassing and they wouldn't even know what to say to each other. She was intrigued to know if last night had just been a one-off but she wasn't sure why. Will was still odious and over-bearing, but that kiss – wow, it had been mind-blowing.

Maybe he wouldn't be at the breakfast table, maybe he would be busy elsewhere with hotel stuff. She hoped so. Asking herself if that was really the truth, Tessa headed outside. Austin loped after her, his interest in breakfast rather more straightforward. Something had changed between herself and Will, Tessa couldn't deny it. They might claim to hate each other but they had some serious sexual chemistry going on – maybe something even deeper than that.

The marquee hadn't been taken down and there was a pile of discarded brochures by the entrance of it that looked as if Milly and India had given up on their marketing responsibilities early. The lawn was pockmarked by the plethora of high heels that had sashayed across it and Nathan, already stripped to the waist in the glaring sunshine and looking put out about all the mess, was doing his best to repair it.

'Hi!' she called out to him. 'The gardens looked fantastic yesterday, everyone said so.'

'Not any more. By the way, I put your shoes inside the house.' He gave her a knowing wink. 'You looked as if you were having fun when the lord of the manor carried you off in his arms!'

Tessa turned scarlet and hurried past him. She hoped the rest of the family hadn't seen Will carrying her; they might imagine all sorts of shenanigans had gone on, which was only half true. She was beginning to think she had made a mistake deciding to join the family for breakfast and she was just about to turn back when she heard Henny calling her name in a strangely high-pitched voice.

'Hi there,' Tessa called back gamely. The family were seated on the veranda around an oval table which was covered with baskets of bread and pastries as well as a tray of Henny's home-made jams and some tea and coffee. There was also a dish piled with crispy bacon and some scrambled eggs that were rapidly overcooking in the heat.

'How lovely to see you!' Henny trilled, looking strained. Her curls from the day before looked squashed and she was wearing one of her shapeless overalls again. 'Will said you might be joining us . . . and it's lovely to see you, really lovely!' She poured Tessa a cup of coffee and, forgetting that she took it black, slopped nearly half a pint of milk into it.

Tessa gingerly took a seat, wondering why Henny's behaviour was verging on the hysterical. The family were unusually quiet but tension crackled in the air.

'We've been inundated with hotel bookings already, even though we don't officially open until January,' Henny was saying breathily as she heaped too much ginger marmalade on to a muffin. 'And several people have expressed an interest in the wedding packages we're offering, no doubt because of Rufus and Clemmie. Isn't that wonderful news, Tessa?'

Tessa nodded mutely, throwing the cup of disgustingly milky coffee on to the grass when Henny wasn't looking and helping herself to a fresh cup. She glanced round the table, trying to work out why the air was frostier than a December morning.

Tristan, looking scruffy in yesterday's crumpled white shirt and a pair of torn green combat-style shorts, was sitting with his bare feet propped up on a nearby chair. He had one of Will's brochures balanced on one of his hairy thighs and his mouth was set in a grim line as he scribbled on it mindlessly. Judging by the set of his jaw and his rigidly bent fingers, he was obviously seething over Sophie's reappearance. Tessa didn't blame him; she was feeling rather antagonistic towards Sophie herself and she didn't have half his baggage to deal with. Tristan gave her the briefest of smiles but immediately cast his eyes down to his sketch again, and angrily slashed his pen across the paper.

Tessa slid her eyes round to Caro, surprised to see her at the breakfast table after what had happened with JB. Oddly, far from looking remorseful, Caro appeared defiant. No, scrap that, Tessa thought disbelievingly; Caro looked, well, indestructible. Wearing a short, red kimono that clashed with her Titian hair and revealed acres of pale thigh, she was nibbling unenthusiastically at a piece of dry toast without a care in the world.

'Croissant?' she said to Tessa, offering the basket of fattening pastries up distastefully. Tessa was starving but somehow taking a croissant from Caro felt like siding with the enemy. Caro hadn't exactly been friendly towards her since she'd arrived, unlike Jack who had gone out of his way to make her feel welcome. Tessa knew which side of the carefully drawn battle lines she was on and as far as she was concerned, Caro was on her own. She shook her head.

Caro shrugged. 'No? I'm the same, can't eat a thing in the mornings. And this toast is like cardboard.' She tossed it to one side in a way that suggested Henny had failed yet again.

'Most people have butter on it,' Henny snapped, fed up with Caro's sniping.

'It's obvious you do,' Caro returned, giving Henny's generous hips a pointed stare. Not having to look at Henny to know she was probably on the verge of tears, Caro turned to Jack with a smug smile. 'It went terribly well yesterday, don't you think? *Very* successful all round, one might say.'

Jack appeared not to hear. Tessa was distressed to see him looking so dejected. It didn't suit his usual air of masculine vitality and strength. The suitcase-sized bags under his bloodshot eyes revealed he had had little sleep and he looked the picture of unhappiness. Clearly nursing the mother of all hangovers, Jack was sipping iced water, his hand shaking so uncontrollably, he could barely get the glass to his lips. His blond hair was uncombed and, like Tristan, he appeared to have thrown on the nearest thing he could lay his hands on; the grubby dress shirt he had worn to a charity dinner three nights ago looking incongruous with a pair of faded blue swimming shorts covered with dolphins.

'Jack?' Caro fixed her cold blue eyes on him. She was like a cat toying with a mouse, spitefully detached and fascinated to see what would happen when she dug her claws in again. 'Did you think the party was a success?'

If Jack had heard her, he didn't react. He carried on taking tiny sips of water, shovelling down what looked like prescription-strength painkillers. Presumably they were for his throbbing head, but it was patently obvious that what Jack really needed was something to ease the pain in his heart. He slipped a pair of sunglasses on, hiding his bruised eyes from

Caro. They afforded him a modicum of privacy but he still looked like a broken man.

Tessa half wished he would throw one of his caustic remarks Caro's way so they could strike up their usual acerbic banter. But today it was obvious something had fundamentally changed and Jack's muted appearance and demeanour touched Tessa more than she could say.

What with Caro oozing poison on an uncharacteristically silent Jack, Tristan stripped of his cheerfully sunny disposition and Henny about to have a nervous breakdown, Tessa realised she had been invited to the breakfast from hell. She was relieved when Milly arrived.

'Hi, everyone. Urgghh, how can any of you contemplate eggs and bacon on a morning like this?'

'Milly, darling!' Henny's voice was getting shriller by the second. 'Would you like some tea?'

'No thanks.' Milly shuddered at the glacial atmosphere around the table and decided to ignore it. She caught Tessa's eye with feeling and picked through the pastries on the table, selecting a mini pain-au-chocolat. She was dressed in a matching vest and shorts set that she had obviously slept in and her platinum-blond hair was held up with a pencil.

'I've just finished reading *Othello*,' she told Tessa with her mouth full. 'It's fan-bloody-tastic! All that pent-up sexual tension and intense jealousy. Jesus, who could live like that?' Not seeming to realise she was describing Jack and Caro to a T, she carried on blithely. 'And that Iago, what an utter, utter bastard! Causing mischief, getting revenge and making everyone around him do terrible things . . .' She stopped as it finally dawned on her that she might now be describing JB and the farce that was Jack and Caro's relationship, and stuffed the rest of the pain-au-chocolat in her mouth.

Tessa wondered if it would be rude to make her excuses and leave. Seconds later, she sincerely wished she had.

'Hello, *darling*!' Henny jumped out of her seat and charged round to the other side of the table. 'Have the French finished their strike already? What a shame you couldn't make it to the party yesterday!'

Tessa lowered her coffee cup with trembling fingers, feeling as if she was moving in slow motion. Standing next to a sheepish-looking Will was Claudette. Larger than life, instantly recognisable from Tristan's painting and twice as beautiful. Handsome rather than pretty, her androgyny was complemented by her stylish white Capri pants and tailored navy shirt. Red lipstick finished off her chic look.

'Claudette arrived ten minutes ago,' Will explained to the table at large. Tessa couldn't bring herself to look at him. She didn't know why but the truth of the matter was that she was absolutely gutted to see Claudette. Last night she had been the furthest thing from Tessa's mind – Will's too, judging by his behaviour. Tessa felt dreadful. What kind of woman was she? She had berated Adam for stringing her along when he had someone else but she was just as bad, kissing someone who had a fiancée he was crazy about.

In a daze, Tessa watched Claudette move round the table kissing everyone on both cheeks and wafting exotic perfume everywhere.

'*Chérie!*' Claudette embraced Milly, her dark bobbed head a stark contrast to Milly's white-blond one. 'It is so lovely to see you again.' Her barely-there English accent was adorable, her golden-brown freckles even more so.

'This is Tessa,' Milly said, keen to introduce her new friend to Claudette. 'She's staying with us at the moment and filming a documentary here.'

'*Enchantée*,' Claudette said charmingly, reaching across the table to shake Tessa's hand. 'I 'ave seen you on TV, *non*?'

'No . . . er . . . maybe . . .'

'*Oui!* Breakfast telly you call it in England,' she said,

wrapping her arms round Will's waist and smiling confidently up at him. 'I love all the celebrity news, don't I, *chéri*? I cannot wait to meet Clemmie Winters. She is very popular in my country and such a good actress.'

Tessa saw Will looking awkward for a split second as Claudette snuggled up to him but he covered it up admirably and smiled down at her. Tessa wished she could rush back to her cottage and change; the short skirt and T-shirt made her feel invisible next to Claudette's soignée outfit that looked as if it had been copied straight from the glossy pages of *Vogue*.

Henny clasped her hands together. 'So you've finally managed to tear yourself away from all that marvellous charity work.'

'Yes and I was so angry about missing your wonderful party!' Claudette looked adorably furious. 'I stayed in the airport and demanded to be on the very first flight out, so 'ere I am!' She clung to Will possessively. 'I'm staying for a few weeks, maybe a month – maybe longer if I can manage it.'

'How fantastic!' Henny said.

Fantastic, Tessa echoed in her head. Clutching the arms of the garden chair with white knuckles, she looked longingly at her cottage on the other side of the lake. Couldn't she just slip away and dash back to it so she could curl up under her duvet and die?

Henny was beaming. 'Darling, what would you like to eat? You must be starving.'

'Not for food.' Claudette giggled as she kissed Will's neck and whispered something in his ear.

Will went scarlet and mumbled something about showing Claudette the new hotel rooms.

As soon as they had disappeared inside, Tessa leapt up from the table as if she'd been shot.

'Darling, more coffee?' Henny was puzzled. 'You haven't even had any food.'

'Not hungry,' she said briefly before stalking away with her head down. Feeling tears stinging at her eyelids she was startled to find Milly catching up with her.

'Isn't Claudette lovely?'

'Er . . . yes, charming.'

'I'm so glad she's here, she's like my big sister and she's always there when I need advice. Well, when she's not shagging Will, obviously.' Milly linked arms with Tessa. 'You're like my big sister too. I'm very lucky to have both of you.'

Praying tears wouldn't spill out on to her cheeks at the thought of Will and Claudette tangled up in the bed sheets together, Tessa shook her head. 'I'm not as nice as you think I am.' I snogged your favourite cousin last night, she added silently, the one with the perfect fiancée. If Milly knew what she was really like, she wouldn't want to spend time with her, Tessa was sure of that.

'Nonsense!' Milly brushed her comment away airily. She proceeded to go into minute detail about Freddie at the party yesterday, full of excitement at the thought that he might have feelings for her but not believing for one minute he did. She sounded childish and, unlike her friend India, obviously and sweetly innocent.

'Honestly, Tess, I know it sounds stupid, but I thought my heart was going to break when he took his arm away from me!'

Feeling glum as she listened to Milly happily dissecting her moments with Freddie, Tessa forced herself to get some perspective. She and Will had kissed, that was all. So why was she feeling so bloody dejected?

Chapter Eighteen

'Is it really necessary for me to have another outfit to change into in the evening?' Clemmie swallowed down one of the maximum-strength headache pills her doctor in LA prescribed her on demand. She had been on the phone to her agent for the past hour discussing details for the wedding and, sick and tired of the whole thing, Clemmie was beginning to think cancelling might be the best idea all round.

'Fine,' she conceded wearily. 'Order the vintage Valentino gown . . . the purple strapless one. And do whatever you like about the cake . . . seven tiers . . . ten tiers . . . I couldn't care less. No, I couldn't be less interested in sponge flavours. Choose spiced honey, pear and walnut or citrus-almond . . . whatever you damn well please.' She listened again, feeling her forehead pucker. Wondering if she needed a top-up of Botox, she couldn't quite believe what she was hearing. 'Jennifer, I specifically told Tessa Meadmore, the journalist, that the very notion of us capturing dragonflies in Christmas decorations was ridiculous in the extreme! Don't you dare think of such stupid ideas. What are you trying to do, get the entire contingent of animal lovers on my case in one go? This is a wedding, Jennifer, not a circus. Remember that, *please*.' She slammed the phone down hard.

Had everyone gone mad? Her wedding, supposedly the happiest day of her life, was rapidly turning into a farce, an arena for outlandish ideas and unlimited extravagance. In a rage, Clemmie deleted the email her stylist had sent her. It had dozens of photographs of wedding-dress designs attached to it and she had barely devoted more than a few seconds to choosing one of them.

It was now September, mere months until the wedding, but Clemmie couldn't seem to get her head around the idea. She and Rufus barely seemed to have time to discuss any of the details and filming at the manor house occupied most of their days. Rufus was becoming increasingly unpredictable and his presence was never guaranteed, which was a constant source of embarrassment to Clemmie, who was frequently left red-faced and scrabbling for excuses.

She sighed and stared out of the window, the stunning Cotswold countryside failing to cheer her up for once. Even the weather seemed to be conspiring against her, the watery, September sun all too often giving way to smattering rain that depressed her and made her long for predictable Californian sunshine.

Clemmie abandoned her emails and instead went to the safe she had had fitted in the study. She removed her personal photograph collection from under all the Tiffany bags and Asprey boxes containing her jewellery. Flicking through the photographs made her feel despondent. When Tessa had asked her all those weeks ago if she had any childhood photographs, she had lied without skipping a beat. Of course she had photographs of herself as a child, who didn't? The only difference was, hers travelled with her wherever she went and were locked away securely in hotel safes or private vaults, depending on her location.

Clemmie wasn't even sure why she kept them. They were dangerous and they made her sad. Was it ego? Guilt? A reminder of where she had come from and who she had been? She couldn't fathom it but she knew it was madness to even hang on to the incriminating photos. Clemmie hadn't meant to lie to Tessa, but what else could she do? She pulled out a picture of herself aged sixteen and sucked in her breath. She was unrecognisable – literally – as the awkward blonde girl who was smiling shyly at the photographer, the crooked teeth contributing to her plainness.

Who would recognise her as the same girl? Who would believe the dowdy, overweight teenager in the ill-fitting gingham dress had grown up to be a famous movie star, a svelte brunette with perfect teeth, chiselled cheekbones and a figure to die for? No one. And they were right. She wasn't the same girl.

Clemmie felt tears trickling down her cheeks. If she had surrendered these photographs to Tessa, questions would be asked. Not necessarily by Tessa but by someone – someone who would immediately spot that something wasn't quite right. They would demand to know how it was possible that someone could change so dramatically from the person they once were. Not just a different nose, suspiciously pert breasts or fuller lips – they were synonymous with any self-respecting Hollywood actress. No, this was evidence that Clemmie was now a completely different person, one who bore no physical resemblance whatsoever to her former self.

And once that question had been asked, others would follow. Who had she been? What had happened to her? Why had she changed herself? And, finally, they might think to ask: what had she done that was so terrible, so shameful, that she had been forced to remove every last trace of herself?

Clemmie allowed the tears to fall. Was she ever going to be free? She had brought this on herself, she knew that. After all, she had put herself in this position – she had searched out the limelight, even though she knew it would mean living a life of fear. She had put herself in the public eye willingly and, as such, she had offered herself up for scrutiny. At best she could expect praise and adulation; at worst, criticism and judgement. She had allowed her love of acting and her desire to follow her dream to put her in the very situation she found herself in now.

Hearing Rufus's approaching footsteps, Clemmie shoved the photographs back in her safe and slammed the door shut. She twisted the handle and rearranged the numbers just as he reached her and, not having the time to wipe her tears away, Rufus immediately spotted that she'd been crying.

'What's wrong?' He just about stopped himself sighing with boredom; Clemmie's tears were as commonplace around here as chocolate-box cottages.

Clemmie looked him in the eye with difficulty. 'Nothing, hon, I'm just feeling a bit . . . emotional.'

He helped her to her feet with a frown. 'It's probably just pre-wedding nerves. It's September now, the wedding's only a few months away – even I'm getting a bit jittery, ha ha!' In truth, Rufus was more than jittery but he sensed it wouldn't be prudent to raise the issue just yet.

'It's not the wedding. I'm fine about the wedding . . .'

At least, Clemmie would be if Rufus hadn't been so distant over the past few weeks. Why was he feeling jittery about the wedding? Was he having second thoughts? That would be terrible . . . unbearable. She slid her arms round him, feeling a familiar sense of insecurity settle on her shoulders as he stiffened slightly. She laid her head on his shoulder, listening to the steady thump of his heart through the thin fabric of his Guns N' Roses T-shirt. How she envied him his calm.

Nothing seemed to faze Rufus and aside from his recent odd behaviour, he was an open book. Everyone knew who he was and where he came from. He had no need to hide his past and he had no need to lie about his motives. Or so she had thought.

Clemmie wished she could stop worrying about why Rufus was being secretive with her. The day she had broken down in front of Henny and Tessa, Henny had ever so gently homed in on the anxiety she was feeling about Rufus's disappearances. Was he having an affair? Did he still love her?

Sensing he needed to make some sort of effort to be

affectionate, Rufus loosely put his arms round her. 'Is it the documentary? Is that why you've been crying? If it's that, just remember how much they're paying us for it. It's major!'

'We don't need the money,' Clemmie snapped impatiently.

'Yes, but it can't hurt, can it? And it's already bringing us so much publicity! My agent phoned this morning with another film offer – can you believe that?' Rufus's eyes lit up and he looked almost crazed. 'Will Smith has already signed up for it and I'd be playing his sidekick – his *sidekick*, Clem! That's the third film offer this week! They want to start filming in January so I have to get back to my agent by tomorrow to let them know what I think.'

'So you'll be flying back to Hollywood straight after the wedding?' Her voice was flat.

'I guess so.' Rufus sounded vague and he let his arms fall to his side. 'Is that a problem?'

Clemmie walked over to the window and stared out across the stunning Cotswold countryside. 'I thought we moved here to have a normal life, Rufus. I thought you were ready to settle down, for us to have a family.'

'Of course I am.' Now Rufus sounded impatient. 'But it would be madness to turn this film down, surely you can see that?'

'And what about the other two films? Will you do those as well?'

'I haven't decided yet!' He gripped her shoulder and flipped her round to face him. 'I don't remember handing my career over to you, Clemmie. I don't remember once saying to you that moving here would mean I was never going to work again.' His lip curled. 'It's all right for you, isn't it? You've got your bloody Oscar, everyone thinks you're a superstar! But I'm just starting out and I want to work. Forgive me for not realising that just because you've reached this heady level of fame, you can turn your back on acting forever.'

Clemmie's eyes clouded over with hurt. 'I worked hard for that "bloody Oscar", as you call it,' she began heatedly.

'Yes, yes, we all know what a terrible trauma it was for you to play a rape victim,' Rufus intoned, sounding bored. He rolled his eyes offensively. 'I was there for your acceptance speech, remember? You don't need to trot it out every time someone mentions awards. There aren't any cameras rolling today.'

She recoiled in shock. He had always said that he admired her performance in that film, he had always told her she deserved the success it brought her. This was a side of him she had never witnessed before.

'How can you say that? I love acting but I've had some shitty jobs in the past, like most actors. I came from nothing and clawed my way up. Making that film made everyone sit up and take notice of me. People actually took me seriously for the first time in my fucking career.'

Rufus flinched at the swear word; Clemmie rarely cursed. 'Good for you! Good for you, Clemmie. Welcome to my world – except that no one has taken me seriously yet! Everyone thinks I'm a talentless playboy who couldn't act his way out of a paper bag. I have to sit by and watch Orlando and all the rest of them get critical acclaim while I'm overlooked every time.' Childishly, he kicked the foot of the bed with his boot. 'Even Daniel bloody Craig's shit-hot these days, all for doing a few Bond films.'

Clemmie wasn't sure laughing would be the right thing to do in the circumstances but it was what she felt like doing. Was that what Rufus wanted, to be the next Bond? Or was he simply so envious of anyone who had achieved the level of success he thought he deserved, he couldn't find it in himself to congratulate them?

For once, she was lost for words. Rufus was such a child; he was so resentful that the world hadn't brought him the fame, celebrity and riches he felt he should be handed on a plate.

Remembering what she had been through to get where she was, Clemmie felt a flash of anger surge through her. Who the hell did Rufus think he was? What gave him the right to expect to not have to work hard for what other people had to fight tooth and nail for?

Staring at the man she was due to marry in a few months, Clemmie felt reality smack her round the face. The so-called 'normal' life she craved here in England with Rufus didn't exist, it was nothing but a pipe dream. Despite his attempts to convince her otherwise, Rufus still wanted to be famous. He wanted Hollywood to sit up and notice him and he still wanted to see himself splashed across celebrity magazines on a weekly basis – all the things that she herself no longer wanted.

Clemmie stared at Rufus, feeling her world crashing down around her. She knew she had no right to stop Rufus from pursuing his dream, but what about *her* dreams? Rufus's claims that he wanted children were lies, she could see that now. Lies he had offered to placate her and hide his career ambitions.

'I don't actually *want* to play James Bond, if that's what you were thinking,' Rufus chimed in sulkily. 'I was just making a point.'

'I know.' She sounded resigned.

'I'm going to do those films, Clemmie, and you can't stop me.'

'I know.'

And she did. All she needed to do now was to get her head around the idea that Rufus had tricked her into believing their move to England had been about settling down and not about promoting his career.

He loved her – or at least he had started out that way, of that Clemmie was sure. But how much of Rufus's decision to marry her had been about generating publicity for himself? How much of it had been about creating a union that was a glossy, clichéd publicist's wet dream? Rufus had simply gone along with her plans to settle down with children when his real intentions were to head straight back to a film set.

Clemmie felt as if she was about to faint. He was lucky she loved him so much. Distraught, a fresh set of tears threatened to make an appearance and she dashed them away with her hand.

Rufus had no idea what Clemmie was thinking. Frankly he was fed up with her being so over-emotional. Worse than that, Clemmie had looked for one moment as if she was mocking him. And being laughed at seriously pissed him off. It had been bad enough when Milly Forbes-Henry had cut him dead at the manor house party – he hated being made to feel like a prat; it reminded him of being at auditions when someone uttered the insincere yet immortal line: 'We'll be in touch.'

Rufus indulged himself with thoughts of India. She was becoming annoyingly clingy and he suspected she had high hopes of him dumping Clemmie and waltzing off into the sunset with her. Some chance! She had gleefully informed him that she was using a girl called Alicia as a smokescreen to put Milly off the scent or some such immature nonsense; Rufus barely listened when India got going. He simply used her to block out reality – something she was very good at. The last time he had met up with her, she had lazily sucked coke off his cock while expertly massaging his balls – and, in his final, lucid moment before his mind shot off into erotic euphoria, Rufus had asked himself what the hell he was doing even thinking of marrying Clemmie. She was good for his career, marrying her couldn't fail to give him some much-needed clout in Hollywood; in fact, it already had – look at the job offers he had just received! If he was honest, staying in LA would have been his preference but Clemmie had been hell-bent on coming here. Essentially, she was fantastic for his career and, as such, he had gone along with her plans to have a traditional English wedding and hole up in the Cotswolds for a while. But he drew the line at long-term domesticity and cooing over babies.

Rufus felt something tug at his heartstrings when he caught the panic-stricken look in Clemmie's wide, hazel eyes. Did he still love her? He must do if her misery made him feel this bad and he hated feeling guilty or responsible for anything.

But she had no right to make him give up his career. If she thought he was going to turn his back on the chance to be an A-lister himself and have an Oscar of his own to show off in the downstairs bathroom, she was very much mistaken.

He took out his phone irritably and speed-dialled India. With his phone clamped to his ear, Rufus stalked off, leaving Clemmie wallowing in self-pity. Some women were happy with a bloody necklace from Tiffany's, he told himself impatiently. They didn't need their ego stroking every two minutes – they were excited to be in his company. India certainly was.

It was only hours later that Clemmie realised it was the first time Rufus hadn't used sex to make things right between them.

Clutching her photographs and sliding to the floor in a heap, she realised she hadn't been as scared as this since she came out of prison.

Henny put the finishing touches to the cake she was decorating before boxing it up and labelling it with David's university address. She was missing him like crazy; he had only been gone a few weeks and had already been home once but he always made her feel better about Milly. Things with Milly had reached a stand-off and it was very unpleasant. Since the summer party, they had chatted about nothing but there was an underlying tension between them.

Henny sighed. Milly was a difficult child and even though it was hard sometimes, she loved her to pieces. She just wished things between them weren't so strained.

'You've been baking again.' Will came in and dropped a kiss on Henny's forehead. 'It makes the entire house smell divine.'

'This is for David but I did bake some chocolate scones for supper.' She smiled up at him and pushed his tawny hair out of his eyes. 'You must be so pleased Claudette's finally here.'

Will nodded but his eyes seemed dull. 'I must get my hair cut. Claudette hates it this long, says I look like a typical public school boy.'

'You can't help that, darling. But still, it's lovely for you to have her here. You were missing her so much.'

'I know. We've had tons of hotel bookings, I can't believe how well the party went, can you?'

Henny stared at him. Why was he changing the subject?

Will cleared his throat. 'I was thinking, would you like to go on a course about wedding planning? I thought it might boost your confidence and now that Tristan's passed on his commission money, we've got some extra funds in the pot. *Shit.*'

Henny swung round, her blue eyes fearful. 'Is money an issue, Will? Why didn't you say?'

'It's fine, really,' Will said soothingly. He must be tired; he would never have let that slip to Henny otherwise. He couldn't help feeling relieved the bookings were flooding in; he was just praying for more of the same. 'We had a cash flow problem for a few weeks but it's all flowing nicely again now. So, I'll book the course up, shall I? I think it's time you thought about yourself for a change.'

Henny smiled. Will was so sweet, so caring. How Caro had ever produced such incredible sons was beyond her.

'That's the other thing,' he said, as if he had read her mind. 'Stick up for yourself more, all right? Put Mother in her place when she picks on you.'

'I couldn't possibly—'

'Yes you could. You've been through a tough time and you're bringing two children up single-handedly. You've got a

312

backbone, Aunt Henny; you just need to start using it.' Giving her plump shoulders a squeeze, he left her gaping at him. That needed saying, he told himself. She was lovely but she was being walked all over and it was horrible to watch. His mother could fend for herself but Will was buggered if he was going to let her trample all over Henny on a daily basis.

Going in search of Claudette, Will's mind was going haywire as he worried about the stack of bills he still hadn't paid. He had been telling the truth about Tristan passing on his commission money but they weren't out of the woods by any means. Gil's taste was alarmingly expensive but having listened to the coos of delight from the guests when they saw his designs, Will knew he had to let Gil run riot and worry about the cost later. He had also hired a temporary general manager to come and run the place when they were ready to open because he wasn't sure Jack or Henny would be prepared. Will needed someone to monitor the income and the expenses, supervise and train the staff, provide reports, that kind of thing. Something he knew all about but he planned to head off as soon as the hotel was up and running. He had a life to go back to in France – although that seemed very far away at the moment.

Poking his head into the library before heading upstairs, Will wondered where Claudette had got to. He skim-read through a proposal Gil had put together to develop another wing to house a swimming pool and a spa as 'every boutique hotel hoping for first-class status boasted one of these or both'. Will stuffed the proposal into his pocket. Luxurious lighting and sumptuous home furnishings were one thing but he couldn't see how he was going to have the resources to pull off a sauna and beauty salon any time soon.

Thank God the weddings were so lucrative, Will thought. Rufus and Clemmie's wedding was turning out to be astonishingly expensive, but none of it had been paid for yet. Will was loath to prompt his old friend for the cash but he knew the conversation was going to have to take place soon. Gil had also booked Christmas Eve for his wedding to Sophie, a much smaller affair than Clemmie's, naturally, but as ever Gil was demanding the best and seemed more than happy to pay for it. Whether either wedding would go ahead was another matter, of course, Will thought with a frown. Rufus and Clemmie's relationship seemed about as stable as a homemade bomb, and as for Gil and Sophie, Will just wished he and Henny had guessed that Gil's Sophie was in fact *Tristan's* Sophie when they had taken the booking.

'Claudette!' he called, catching sight of Jack and Caro sunbathing outside at opposite ends of the lake. Their stand-off had reached epic proportions, with Jack working hard at staying away from both the booze and his wife, and Caro sneering at Jack whenever she could before slinking off to see JB in her sluttiest clothes.

Will's heart contracted briefly when he saw Tessa exercising outside her cottage wearing tight leggings and a tiny cropped top which showed off her brown abs. He had kept his distance from Tessa as much as possible since Claudette had arrived, partly out of respect because he thought he must be the last person Tessa wanted to see after what had happened, and partly (not that he had reached a stage where he could admit it out loud to himself) because he still didn't trust himself around her.

What was going on with him? If it was just a simple case of lust, it was a bad one, he thought grimly, averting his eyes as Tessa bent over, her tight backside taunting him. But it couldn't be anything more than that; he loved Claudette, right?

'Excuse me!' Milly charged past Will at high speed, her platinum plait flying out behind her. 'Late for a class!' She glanced out of the window and gave Will a cheeky grin. 'Stop perving at Tessa, you. You're engaged and Claudette told me yesterday she wants to get married this year!'

Will flushed at Milly's comment and couldn't find the words

to defend himself before she'd shot down the stairs and out of the front door. He felt his stomach flip over. Claudette wanted to be married within the year? It was the first he'd heard of it. She *had* made plenty of veiled references to their wedding since she'd arrived but Will hadn't really taken her seriously. When he had first met her, she hadn't exactly seemed like the marrying kind. They had bumped into each other at a party, literally bumped right into each other, and she had made it patently obvious she fancied him. Will wasn't prone to taking women he'd just met home for a night-long session of sex, but much to his surprise, that was exactly what had happened that night. Claudette had seduced him, telling him with wide eyes she thought she might have fallen in love with him then and there.

Will pushed the memory to one side and peeked into 'Cassiopeia', one of his favourite rooms. It had an enormous sleigh bed and a ceiling studded with stars. In a fit of minimalist chic, Will had originally thought of assigning a simple number to each room but had decided the rooms deserved better than that. Inspired by stays at Raymond Blanc's spectacular establishment, Le Manoir aux Quat' Saisons, he asked his family for lists of their favourite words and the result was a rather random but beautiful collection of room names. Each had their own significance and Gil had worked aspects of the room name into each room somehow, using books, vases, lamps or the colour scheme to tie everything in.

'Ophelia', 'Cocoa' and 'Provence' were Milly's choices, based on her new-found fascination with Shakespeare and a lasting love affair with both chocolate and France (although Will had put his foot down over her pleaded suggestion of 'Gucci'). 'Blake' (as in William), 'Rococo' and 'Alizarin' were courtesy of Tristan, and his parents, Henny and David had provided some of the others.

Will had, perhaps rashly, in view of his appalling behaviour with Tessa, allocated 'Claudette' to a pretty navy and white room at the back of the manor, which had pale floorboards, a vast bed with striped cushions and feminine touches in every corner.

Walking in, he was surprised to find Claudette speaking softly into her mobile phone. Seeing Will, she abruptly ended her call and slipped her mobile into the pocket of her wide, masculine trousers.

'*Chéri*,' she said huskily, winding her arms round his neck and leaning into him suggestively.

'Who was that?'

'A friend.' She shrugged carelessly. '*Je t'aime*,' she said, kissing him with obvious passion.

Will kissed her back guiltily, unable to push the image of Tessa with her make-up smudged sexily under her eyes from out of his head. Why did this keep happening to him every time he was with Claudette?

Feeling Claudette slipping her hand into the back of his shorts suggestively, Will desperately tried to figure out what to do. He was in trouble but he didn't have a clue how to get himself out of it.

Tristan did his best to ignore the inane tittering of his client but it was grating on him him like nails on a blackboard. He was painting a vast nude of Hannah Penry-Jones the third, Freddie's vacuous new stepmother, and he was having terrible trouble concentrating. The portrait was a Christmas present for Mr Penry-Jones from his much younger wife who had paid well over the odds to have Tristan complete it before Christmas. Which was never going to happen the way he was carrying on.

Bloody *bloody* Sophie, Tristan thought, between gritted teeth. He had avoided her for the first few weeks since the party, too furious to even contemplate seeing her again. Unfortunately, as the days passed, the temptation to see her became too overwhelming and he had found himself sitting in his car, a good distance away from the house she and Gil were renting but with a prime view of the windows at the front. He caught heart-wrenching glimpses of her as she passed through different rooms and, more annoyingly, plenty of Gil as he changed his clothes hundreds of times before heading out to Appleton Manor. Every time the front door had opened, Tristan had hastily driven off in the other direction.

Pathetic, he fumed at himself as he glanced up at Hannah again.

'I hope I'm not too difficult to paint,' she simpered, turning so her left breast pointed more directly at him. She wriggled slightly on his gilt sofa. 'I haven't done this before so I'm relying on you to give me some . . . guidance.'

His hand faltered. Tristan was used to being propositioned by his clients and had always seen their seduction of him as a perk of the job. He had lost count of the times he had been painting the wife or girlfriend of a wealthy contact, only to find them leaping up and sashaying into his arms or melting in front of his very eyes, undulating across his sofa.

Tristan sighed. If he hadn't been able to fall in love with Tessa, Hannah Penry-Jones, with her big cow eyes and thrusting bosoms, wasn't going to cut it. He looked up again, just in time to see her parting her legs and offering him a glimpse of her wetly pink labia.

'Right, that's enough for today,' Tristan said quickly, putting his paintbrush down. Bundling her out of his studio as quickly as he could manage and ignoring her comment that her bush was 'more camel than coffee', Tristan headed out to the faithful old yellow MG he had bought with his first pay cheque. He had no idea how he was going to keep Hannah at arm's length until Christmas when he would receive the last of his money but he was going to have to think of something. Putting his foot down, Tristan knew he had to have it out with Sophie because he simply couldn't concentrate.

Screeching to a halt outside her house with a thumping heart, Tristan was taken aback when Sophie tore out of the house and ran towards him at full pelt. Her face was flushed and her caramel-coloured hair flew out behind her as she dashed to his car window.

'What the hell are you doing here?' she cried, throwing a nervous look over her shoulder.

He got out, the sight of her making him feel weak again. She even managed to look gorgeous in jeans and a vest top. 'Well, I'm not here to get advice on cushion covers from your fiancé.'

'Very funny. You . . . you should have phoned or something.'

Tristan stared at her. 'I don't have your number, Soph. I'm sure you meant to give it to me the other day but you must have forgotten when you rushed off in the other direction as if I had the plague.'

Sophie pushed her hair back and looked vexed. 'Right. Yes. I see what you mean. Look, I can only stay out for a few minutes.' In answer to his quizzical look, she made up a lie on the spot. 'I'm expecting visitors and I need to tidy up.' It was the best she could come up with on the spur of the moment. She could hardly tell him Ruby was happily playing indoors.

'I see.' Tristan felt exasperated. Why was it so difficult to talk to her? 'So I can have a few minutes, can I?' He turned searing blue eyes towards her. 'Is that all I'm worth after five bloody years of nothing?'

Sophie reeled at his harsh tone. Why was he acting as if she needed to explain her absence? She wasn't the one who'd been unfaithful!

'I don't owe you a single thing,' she fired back. 'You didn't care about me or our relationship enough not to ruin it five years ago, so don't start acting like I should give you a second chance!'

'Ruin our relationship?' he repeated incredulously. 'What on earth did I do to "ruin our relationship", Sophie? Tell me, please. Did I love you too much? Did I smother you? I only wanted the best for you, for us. Surely you know that?' He gripped her arm, hating how smooth her skin felt beneath his fingertips. 'Do tell me, Sophie. Tell me what you think I did that was so fucking terrible that you had to run off without saying one word to me.'

Sophie gaped at him. Even after all this time, he still couldn't bring himself to be honest and confess.

'I looked after you, didn't I?' Dropping his angry expression for a second, Tristan looked as vulnerable as a puppy. 'You were all alone in the world and I thought we were going to be together for the rest of our lives . . . we still could be . . . if you wanted that . . .'

'I'm not one of your bloody lost souls any more, Tristan!' Sophie wrenched herself away from him. She had spent the past few weeks yearning to see him but knowing she had to stay away. He was bad for her, he had proved that and she had no urge to reopen old wounds.

And there was also Ruby to consider. How she was going to keep her a secret as time went on was anyone's guess; she could only hope Gil hurried up and completed Appleton Manor so they could move on to the next job he had lined up in Upper Slaughter. She would have preferred Scotland or somewhere equally far away but even putting a few miles between them would help her relax.

But could she really cope with never seeing him again now that they were face to face? Seeing him was difficult but not seeing him crucified her. Once or twice, she thought she had seen glimpses of his sunshine-yellow car in the distance but she told herself she had to be mistaken. She couldn't even phone Tessa for support because they still weren't speaking and Sophie knew she was the one who had to make the first move to try to salvage their friendship. She resolved to start texting Tessa relentlessly, even if she didn't respond.

'I'm well aware you're not one of my lost souls,' Tristan pointed out tersely, her silence provoking more bad feeling. 'Nor would I want you to be. You've grown up and so have I. It's just that seeing you again has brought it all back. Don't you remember what we had?' He knew he was putting himself in the firing line but he didn't care any more. His heart in his mouth, his voice came out hoarsely. 'Are you really going to marry Gil? After what we had together, can you really marry someone else?'

Sophie hung her head in despair. No matter what Tristan had done to her, his words made her want to fling herself in his arms and kiss him until all the pain had gone away. Nothing made sense. She just wanted to be with him. As he stood in front of her, looking tense and unhappy, she felt as if she could almost forgive him the stupid fling with Anna. If he touched her, she knew she'd be lost forever.

She had to be strong and she had to think about Gil and everything they had together. But somehow, their close friendship didn't seem to count for much, not when she was presented with everything she had ever wanted. How unfair of her to think such a thing, how cruel. But it was true. Almost ready to do something stupid, Sophie looked up and saw Ruby's eyes looking back at her from Tristan's face. She backed away from him, aghast.

What was she thinking? This was the man who had ruined her life; this wasn't a man who could be a good father!

Sophie bit down hard on her lip. She had no idea how she was going to go ahead with her wedding to Gil in light of her feelings for Tristan but running off with her cheating ex-lover was the worst possible thing she could do to Ruby. And Ruby was the most important person in all of this and she had to put her above everything else.

'I can't let Gil down,' she said tightly. 'And you're years too late, Tristan! I'm marrying someone else and you have to accept that.' She twisted away from him and ran back into the house. 'You have to stay away from me,' she called over her shoulder, tears coursing down her cheeks.

Feeling destroyed, Tristan drove back to Appleton Manor at breakneck speed. In his studio, he shoved the painting of Hannah Penry-Jones roughly to one side and propped up a fresh canvas. Staring at it blindly, he started mixing colours with jerky hands. He grabbed his paintbrushes and began, and once he had started, he knew he couldn't stop until he reached the end. It was something he had known he would end up doing as soon as he clapped eyes on Sophie again but he had resisted, telling himself it was too painful, knowing that to give in would mean he would be lost forever.

As the sky drew darker outside, Tristan painted his beloved muse furiously, great, sad tears splashing down on to his hands.

Chapter Nineteen

Swaddled under a duvet and alone in her freezing cold cottage, Tessa was listlessly perusing the filming schedule for the week. It was the end of September but it felt more like November.

The ancient heating system in her cottage had given up the ghost in the early hours of the morning and a bitter wind was whistling under the door and through gaps in the tiny windows. She had managed to light a fire but the wind kept snuffing it out so she had resigned herself to wearing extra layers until someone came to fix the heating.

She peered outside unenthusiastically. The sky was dark and malevolent and rain was hammering down on the grass. The lake had flooded its muddy banks and poor Nathan was beside himself to see his beautifully tended lawns swamped with puddles as, wrapped in a waterproof jacket and hood, he desperately tried to stem the damage. There wasn't much point; they still looked remarkably like Wimbledon's Centre Court on a bad day.

Tessa realised she was due at the manor house that afternoon. Preparing herself for the severe chill, she threw off the duvet. Shrieking and blowing on her fingers, she dashed upstairs and pulled on a huge, paint-encrusted jumper Tristan had lent her to keep warm and some Ugg boots. Why on earth hadn't she bought herself some wellies, she thought, clutching at her hair?

Pulling her lank hair up into a ponytail, Tessa thanked God she had a make-up artist and hair stylist to make her look passable. Not just for filming but because the last thing she wanted was to appear badly groomed next to Claudette who looked like a walking L'Oréal advert with her glossy dark hair and eyelash-perfect fringe. Tessa half expected her to purr, 'Because I am worth it, *non*?' in her seductive French drawl whenever she sashayed past with a confident flick of her bob.

Tessa pushed down the thought that she was feeling so gloomy about Claudette because of the stupid kiss at the summer party. Thinking about the kiss made her think about Will and she couldn't think about Will. Stomping outside and wrapping her arms around her to keep warm, Tessa shivered at the sight of the trees around the manor. They had been stripped of all but a few of their leaves so they resembled stark figures from a horror film and only the russet Virginia creeper covering the honey-coloured stone walls of the house remained stoically in place.

As she reached the manor's front door, Tessa bumped into Henny who was back from her wedding-planner's course. Wearing a yellow twinset with a smart new pair of wellies, she looked anything but frumpy. Her sandy hair was held up in clips and she was even wearing some pale pink lipstick.

'Wow, you look glamorous! Where are you off to?'

'I . . . I'm off to . . . well, I'm meeting . . .' Henny stammered, her voice petering out as she avoided Tessa's eyes.

She was *blushing*, Tessa thought in amusement. At least all her advice on the day of the summer party hadn't gone unnoticed – with a touch of make-up, a serious amount of hair product and a few new clothes, Henny looked positively radiant! Was it possible she was meeting a man? Tessa hoped so; Henny deserved to have some fun.

'Darling, your feet!' Henny pointed at Tessa's sodden Ugg boots. 'You must borrow some wellies, we have tons in the kitchen. Help yourself, you'll catch your death otherwise.' She squinted up at the sky. 'Isn't it dreadful out here? I do worry about poor David at university shivering away in his tiny room and not eating properly. Do you think he's going to be all right?'

Tessa privately thought David was more likely to be drinking himself stupid in the student union bar or snuggled up in bed with his new girlfriend but seeing Henny's anxious face, she immediately put a comforting arm around her shoulders.

'I'm sure David is absolutely fine. You've sent him three food hampers so he's probably eating fantastically well, in addition to making tons of friends because they'll all want to try your orange and white chocolate muffins.' She was gratified to see Henny's face brightening. 'And I think they have pretty good heating in student digs these days – it's probably warmer there than in my cottage.'

Henny clapped a hand over her mouth. 'Oh my goodness, I completely forgot to phone someone to come and look at it for you!' She glanced at her watch. 'I'm horribly late otherwise I'd do it for you now but if you give Will a shout, I'm sure he'll do it straight away.' She put her umbrella up and ran towards her car. 'And don't forget those wellies!' she shouted over her shoulder.

Her shoulders slumping, Tessa went inside. Her heating was going to have to wait; she'd rather die of hypothermia than talk to Will at the moment. Aside from the fact that he seemed to have been avoiding her ever since the party, Claudette was surgically attached to him, looking irritatingly beautiful and mistily in love. Tessa had no idea what Will was thinking because he had been polite but distant. They weren't so much at each other's throats these days as avoiding each other at all costs.

'There you are! We were beginning to think you'd both deserted us!' Joe the cameraman handed her a mug of coffee. The film crew were huddled round the vast kitchen table with steaming mugs, munching on a plate of chocolate brownies Henny had left them and staring out at the vista gloomily.

Tessa took the coffee gratefully, frowning slightly. 'What do you mean you thought we'd both deserted you?'

Jo pulled a face. 'JB hasn't turned up – again.'

Tessa tightened her grip on her mug. Since the party, JB seemed to be disappearing with increasing regularity, missing film slots and failing to turn up for meetings to review the rushes. She could only imagine he was holding his own kind of meetings with Caro, the kind that took place in hotel rooms.

So much for JB's 'life motto' or whatever he called it, Tessa thought to herself crossly as she burnt her tongue on the hot coffee. What had he said to her all those months ago? 'Get them to trust you but whatever you do, don't get attached.' He had obviously forgotten his own mantra because he was acting very much like a man besotted, loved up to distraction and incapable of functioning professionally.

'We'll just have to cope without him,' Tessa told Joe. Inwardly she was fuming. How could he do this to her again? She had enough to cope with as it was. 'We've done it before and we can do it again, Joe. You'll just have to bear with me while I get to grips with both jobs.'

He nodded approvingly and lowered his voice. 'Between you and me, even though he had some great ideas and knows what he's doing, the crew work much better without him. He's so bloody moody all the time! And such a critical bastard too.'

They set to work quickly, all keen to get filming over and done with for the day. Tessa dialled JB's mobile a few times in a half-hearted attempt to track him down but, wherever he was, he wasn't answering so she concentrated on work, running through her links efficiently and suggesting an angle that they hadn't tried before. It turned out to be successful and Tessa couldn't help feeling a rush of pride. Jilly might have written her off and her heart might not be in it, but at least she was proving that she could pull it out of the bag if she really needed to.

Tessa had been instructed by Jilly to emphasise the 'quintessential English charm' and the 'romantic, period features' the American market went so nuts over, clearly assuming Tessa was incapable of figuring this out for herself. They had already shot the library, the grand dining room and the orangery Clemmie was considering for the ceremony, with Tessa waxing lyrical about the 'enviable charm of the antique mirrors and floorboards'. Gil was hovering in the background like an overexcited three-year-old, keen to get his design slot started.

Tessa stood aside to let Gil begin his segment, knowing this was the moment he had been waiting for all his life. Watching him wring his hands and for the umpteenth time mess up the carefully coiffed hair Louise the stylist had created, Tessa wondered if he might be so nervous he would fluff his lines completely. She watched him sympathetically, knowing how terrified she had been the first time she had presented something on film. Seconds later, her mouth fell open in surprise.

'Hello, viewers, what a treat I have lined up for you!' Gil said confidently and with just the right degree of charm. 'An inside view of a gorgeous country pile with fabulous features and breathtaking views.' He winked at the camera. 'One that will be host to the wedding of the year – which should be mine but unfortunately I've been overshadowed by some serious celebrity heavyweights!'

Gil was an absolute natural in front of the camera. A little camp maybe but he completed his introductory speech in three takes and if the guffaws of the hard-to-impress film crew were anything to go by, the public were going to be utterly entranced by the finished article. Even Nathan had rolled up to watch Gil's film segment and he stood behind the cameraman wearing a skin-tight red jumper that made his upper arms look like hunks of meat. Incongruously, his skin was tanned a deep mahogany as if he'd spent the last few weeks in Hawaii rather than the depths of the rainy Cotswolds but Tessa guessed St Tropez fake tan might be behind his healthy glow. Nathan and Gil seemed to have formed a strong friendship and on warmer days would often be seen sitting on the manor house veranda, chatting about plans for the house or the garden. Nathan seemed to have become a stout fan of Gil's and he kept giving Gil encouraging nods every two seconds and calling out helpful comments.

Perhaps Jilly wasn't mentally unhinged after all, Tessa thought in amazement. Gil was made for television; he was pure gold, confident, engaging and humorous, and she berated herself for not having given him credit before. He must be the only person in Appleton who hadn't heard about the situation with Sophie and Tristan, Tessa thought, glancing down to see yet another text message from Sophie on her mobile. Thank God Gil had the documentary and the other rooms to occupy him for now.

She smiled as Gil came over.

'You were great,' she told him warmly.

'Thank you, but that wasn't why I wanted to talk to you.'

She was startled. 'Oh?'

'It's Sophie.'

Tessa looked away.

'Look, I don't know what's happened between you two but she seems really glum about the fact you won't speak to her.' Gil's expression was earnest, caring. 'I'm worried about her, Tessa. You were such good friends for a while and I really think you helped her settle into Appleton.'

'It's personal,' Tessa bit back, feeling guilty. She hated to think of Sophie being upset and, deep down, she knew she was desperate to make things up with her.

Gil put his hands on his hips, looking unconsciously effeminate. 'It's just that . . . I think she could really do with someone to talk to right now. I mean, I have Nathan which is lovely but Sophie, well, I think she could do with a friend too.'

She's not the only one, Tessa thought as she watched Gil walk back to the make-up area and hold his face up for a touch-up. Reading the pleading text from Sophie again, begging her to come over for wine and apologies later on, Tessa thought for a second before swiftly sending one back. It was time to bury the hatchet and have a proper talk; perhaps she and Sophie both needed a shoulder to cry on, she thought, catching sight of Will striding towards her with intent.

'If you don't need me any more, I'll be off,' she called to Joe who waved his free hand and glued his eye to the camera again. She dashed off in the other direction and headed for the front door, perturbed to find that Will, his big thighs covering twice the distance her legs could, had caught up with her.

'We need to talk,' he said, grabbing her hand.

'Do we?' She shook his hand off, trembling under his touch. 'I honestly don't think we have much to say to each other, do you?' Gazing into his intense blue eyes, Tessa felt herself melting. She forced herself to think about Claudette's perfect mouth on Will's and it hardened her resolve in seconds. 'Although Henny did ask me to mention my heating to you so I suppose we could always have a chat about that.'

'God, why do you always have to be so bloody . . .' Will slammed his hand on the door frame in frustration. He couldn't help a grin spreading across his face. 'You're infuriating, do you know that?'

She felt a smile twitching at her mouth and fought hard to suppress it. When Will grinned like that, he was irresistible. It was lucky he didn't do it around her more often, she thought, surprised at herself. She realised he might be much harder to resist if he did. All of a sudden, all she could think about was his hands in her hair and his mouth on hers and she looked away, flustered.

Will turned her chin towards him with his hand. 'I'll get someone to look at your heating but that wasn't why I wanted to talk to you. Tess, that night of the summer party, we . . . we . . .'

'Had too much champagne?' she offered helpfully, looking away again and feeling her heart sink to her boots. Will felt guilty, that was all, and he wanted to apologise and make amends. However boorish and rude he might be with her, under normal circumstances Will was the consummate gentleman. And that night he had done something totally out of character and it was probably eating away at him inside. Tessa glanced outside at the melancholy downpour of rain, thinking how well it mirrored how her heart was feeling. She was shocked when Will bundled her into an alcove.

'I don't know if we had too much champagne or not,' he started, 'but that kiss . . . we shouldn't have . . .'

'I know. I'm sorry. It was probably my fault . . . I threw myself at you . . . or something like that.' Her voice was flat and dull.

Will let out an impatient noise. 'Why are you being so difficult? I don't know whether to slap you or . . . or to fucking kiss you again.'

She stared at him, her heart pounding. She willed him to do the latter, shocked at herself. He leant closer and she felt her stomach fizzle with anticipation.

'What I meant was, it shouldn't have happened but it did and I've been asking myself why that is and the only explanation I can think of is that I—'

'*Chéri*, where are you?'

They both jumped guiltily at the sound of Claudette's voice and sprang apart. Will gave Tessa a loaded look before heading out of the alcove first.

'I was looking for you, darleeng,' Claudette pouted. She was wearing one of his Oxford-blue shirts, knotted loosely at the waist, teamed with a pair of trendy wide-legged trousers. Somehow, the masculine look heightened her femininity rather than hid it. She gave Tessa a slightly hostile look as she emerged from the alcove but it was so fleeting, Tessa wasn't sure if she'd imagined it.

'Er . . . Henny must have been mistaken,' she improvised hastily.

'What?' Will ran a hand through his dark gold hair and bit his lip.

'Thinking the extra welly boots were in here. They must be in the kitchen or something.' She gestured vaguely in the other direction. 'Do excuse me.' Tessa hurried away, panic-stricken as Claudette followed her.

'Wait for me!' she called out, smiling widely. She waved to Will who looked almost as disconcerted as Tessa. 'I need some of these . . . boots too. Tessa can 'elp me find some.'

Tessa bent over the pile of colourful welly boots that were stacked higgledy-piggledy by the back door of the kitchen, certain her cheeks must be stained with colour. What in God's name had Will been about to say about their kiss? What had he said? 'I've been asking myself why it happened and the only explanation I can think of is . . .' Is what? Tessa paused with a red welly boot in her hand.

'I theenk we need to talk,' Claudette pronounced, unaware she was echoing Will's words from before.

Tessa straightened and found Claudette regarding her with the kind of look a famished polar bear might give a big fat seal: determined, focused and absolutely sure it would emerge victorious. 'Er . . . do we?' Tessa put the red welly boot down cautiously and moved round to the other side of the table, convinced that putting some distance between them might be for the best.

'I theenk so.' Claudette folded her arms, her red lips pursed, and her glossy bob framing her angular face. 'I 'ave seen the way you look at Will.'

'What?' Tessa scraped her hair out of her eyes and frantically started picking brownie crumbs off the table.

Claudette's brown eyes darkened. 'Please do not insult my intelligence. You 'ave feelings for Will, yes?'

'Only murderous ones,' Tessa muttered sulkily, wondering how the hell she could escape. She threw a hopeful look over her shoulder and wondered if the back door was unlocked.

'I 'ave been watching you,' Claudette interjected, 'and I theenk you need to find your own boyfriend.' The looming clouds outside threw a dark shadow across her face, turning her smattering of freckles into chestnut smudges. 'Will is *mine*, do you understand?'

Tessa gulped.

Claudette leant over the table, her red mouth like an angry slash across her face. 'Stay away from Will. We are going to be married so you are wasting your time. Do you understand?'

Tessa flinched, feeling sick as a waft of Claudette's over-powering perfume reached her nostrils.

Claudette laughed bitchily. 'Will does not even like you, he told me so himself! What did he say about you? He said you are shallow, that you are hard,' she pronounced the 'h' with a sneer, 'and that you care nothing for family because all you care about is your job and making money.'

Tessa recoiled. Only Will could have said those words. She blinked several times, feeling tears prick her eyelids. Will really didn't know her at all! She was right; he hadn't changed his mind about her since the summer party. Their chat, their passionate kiss – it had all been meaningless. She was devastated but lifted her chin bravely.

'You have nothing to worry about as far as Will is concerned,' she told Claudette stiffly, her heart feeling like a bruised peach. 'I have no feelings towards him whatsoever – at least, none you need to be concerned about.'

Claudette's eyes watched her suspiciously until, satisfied Tessa was telling the truth, she allowed herself a smile.

'Claudette, have you got a jumper I can borrow?' Milly breathlessly rushed into the kitchen wearing a short tartan skirt with black opaque tights and a black bra that barely contained her boobs. 'Bloody Aunt Caro seems to have realised that I keep filching her cashmere so she's locked them all in a cupboard. I

331

haven't got a thing to wear and I'm due to meet India in a minute.'

Reverting back to her usual charming self in the wink of an eye, Claudette flung her arms round Milly's shoulders. 'Of course! I brought some lovely cashmere jumpers over with me. You shall choose one for yourself and keep it.'

'Really?' Milly shot Tessa a beaming smile, overjoyed at being spoilt by Claudette.

'Really! *Chérie*, you are like my little sister! You know I will do anything for you.' Claudette deliberately turned away from Tessa and led Milly from the room. 'I might even let you wear that ruby ring you love so much . . .'

Shakily, Tessa sat down at the table and stared after them. At least she knew how Will really felt about her now. She bit her lip to stop it from trembling. God, she had to get a grip! She stood up and picked up a pair of navy welly boots that were far too big for her, pulling them on mindlessly. The only problem was, even though Will still couldn't stand her and was patently in love with Claudette, Tessa had just realised that she was no longer confused about him. In fact, she knew exactly how she felt about him.

Pulling open the back door, she stepped out into the torrential downpour as tears dashed down her cheeks and mingled with the rain. She wiped them away hurriedly. She and Will had no future together, that was clear, so all she had to do was stay away from him, focus on her job and figure out how the hell to get over him.

Milly burnt her mouth on her hot chocolate and checked her mobile phone again. She was meeting India at the tea shop in the village and India was over half an hour late already. Outside, dark clouds raced across the silvery-grey sky, casting murky shadows over the village and making four o'clock seem like midnight. Where the bloody hell was India? Milly thought, feeling impatient.

She pushed away the poetry book she was failing to concentrate on and pulled at the sleeves of the charcoal cashmere jumper Claudette had given her. It was softer than any of Aunt Caro's and it had little buttons down the sleeves that made it look really expensive. She was very lucky to have people like Claudette and Tessa in her life, Milly decided, feeling very grown-up. Especially when India kept letting her down all the time, she thought darkly.

Putting her hot chocolate down, she was stunned to see David pushing open the door of the tea shop. Wearing a black overcoat that looked suspiciously like one of Freddie's and a pair of grey jeans, he looked shamefaced when he caught sight of her and he glanced back at the door as if he had half a mind to head back the way he had come.

'David!' Milly called him over, flapping her hand at him. Reluctantly, he came over to her table. 'Sit down then, you big idiot.' She pushed a chair in his direction and he slumped into it, tucking his coat around him defensively. He gave a furtive look around like a spy, narrowing his eyes at gossipy old Mrs North and some of her cronies who were tucked in a corner with one measly pot of tea between them. But Milk and Honey, Appleton's busiest tea shop, was practically empty; the horrendous weather had driven most people back home to their log fires.

'What are you doing home? I thought you weren't back until next week.' Milly frowned as David devoured a scone she had just slathered with blueberry jam and clotted cream. She noticed he now had one ear pierced and a small silver cross was dangling from it.

'I'm not – officially, at any rate,' he said, with his mouth full. 'That's why you can't say anything to Mum about me being here.' He wiped the back of his hand across his mouth. 'I'm meeting Alicia,' he added. 'But I don't want Mum to know I've come back for the weekend because I won't have time to see her so you have to keep your mouth shut about this, do you understand?'

Milly whistled. 'Oh my God! David is being rebellious for once in his life! I thought I was the black sheep of the family.' She pointed to his earring, her eyes dancing with mischief. 'Mum's going to go nuts about that, but hang on, are you sure you've got the right ear? Doesn't having that one pierced mean you're gay?'

'Oh, shut up!' David swatted her hand away and rolled his eyes. 'You can be so immature sometimes. If you must know, I had it done because Alicia likes it, all right?' He sat back, looking pleased with himself. 'I'm taking her out to dinner tonight. That fancy Italian place in the next village. I'm going to blow my rent money on lobster and champagne and whatever else she wants.'

Milly drank her hot chocolate speculatively. 'So you're trying to sleep with her then? There's no way a tight-arse like you would splash out like that if you didn't have an ulterior motive.'

David flushed, proving Milly had hit the nail on the head. 'Alicia is a virgin,' he confided suddenly, mostly because Milly was there. More to the point, he didn't dare discuss such a thing with an old pro like Freddie. 'Which I don't have a problem with obviously but she's so hot, it's getting difficult—'

'Too much information!' Milly squealed, pretending to put her hands over her ears. 'Anyway, I wouldn't worry about Mum, she's hardly around at the moment. She's been on this course and seems to have come back a new woman. She's even wearing make-up!'

'Perhaps she's seeing someone,' David said, checking his mobile phone. 'I wonder where Alicia's got to. She's late.'

'So is India. I thought they might be together, I'm sure they're best bloody friends or something now.'

'Really?' David shrugged. 'Alicia never mentions her. So do you think Mum is seeing someone then?'

Milly scooped some cream up with her finger. 'Haven't a clue. We're not really talking at the moment.'

'I'm not surprised.' David looked self-righteous. 'Freddie told me what you said to Mum at the summer party and I think you should jolly well apologise to her. You have no right to make her feel like that!' He warmed to his theme. 'Mum thinks the world of you and you just keep attacking her and blaming her for everything like a spoilt brat.'

Milly felt the beginnings of tears in her eyes and she swallowed hard, hoping to keep them at bay. David had such a way of twisting the knife until she felt terrible about things.

'There's Alicia now.' David leapt up and checked his spots in the mirror over the counter. He glanced back at Milly whose shoulders were heaving slightly. 'I didn't mean to upset you, sis,' he said kindly. 'But seriously, you've got to stop taking things out on her all the time. She's a fantastic mum and we should be looking after her, not telling her she can't be happy. Look, I'll see you soon, all right? And not a word to Mum!'

Milly gave Alicia a feeble wave and wiped the sleeve of her new jumper across her eyes. David was absolutely right; she was horrible to her mother and it was about time she grew up and stopped thinking she could get away with it. The hurt in her mother's eyes had been tangible and for the first time in her life, Milly realised she had a cruel streak a mile wide. Her eyes fell on to her poetry book, the page open at 'When You are Old' by Yeats. Unexpectedly, she was so moved by it, she felt tears running down her face. Unlike the people in the poem, her mother was never going to grow old with her father now, and she, Milly, had even laughed scornfully at the very idea that her mother might meet someone else to share things with.

Poor Mummy, Milly thought desperately. *She* was the one who had been left behind; she was the one who had to carry on living, in spite of her grief and in spite of being left penniless. Milly balled her hands into fists, thoroughly ashamed of herself.

She had blamed her mother for everything – from coming back home to Appleton which must have dented her pride immeasurably, to missing her school friends, who in truth Milly had soon forgotten about when she had joined her new school.

Seeing a shadow fall across the page, she was gobsmacked to find Freddie standing over her. He was wearing a beautiful cashmere overcoat with tight black jeans and the heavy rain had turned his jet-black hair into a slick, dark helmet. His slanting cheekbones and dazzling eyes made him look like a demigod rock star.

Milly frantically raked her fingers through her blond hair and rubbed mascara splatters from her eyes.

'Are you all right, angel?'

The look of concern in his dark blue eyes almost sent Milly sobbing into her tissue again. There was something about his terribly posh voice and the tenderness in his eyes that made her want to collapse into his arms. But that would never do. She reminded herself that Freddie simply saw her as the little sister he'd never had and that he was stepping in for David in his absence. He had been terribly sweet since David had left – checking up on her, smuggling free spliffs into her pockets and sending her funny text messages – but the likelihood of him seeing her as potential girlfriend material was pretty remote. Freddie was far too glamorous for someone like her, he deserved to be with a Scandinavian princess, or a supermodel, at the very least.

He took his overcoat off and hung it carefully over a chair to dry. 'Mind if I join you?'

'Feel free. Doesn't look like India's going to turn up.'

Freddie took a seat and put his feet up on the chair next to her. He picked up a book from the pile on the table, his fingers brushing against hers. As she revelled in his touch, he flicked through the pages, scanning the words with raised eyebrows. 'So you like this Shakespeare guy, then?'

'Well, I adore his words . . . these sonnets are incredible.' In truth, Milly had no idea Shakespeare had been such a talented, romantic guy, although discovering a picture of him in the back of one of Will's books, she had been thoroughly disappointed to find him sporting a dubious goatee and looking like a poofter in a frilly collar.

Freddie smiled and handed the book back. 'You're such an intellectual,' he teased. 'Christ, that isn't on the syllabus, is it? Not that I'm at school these days.' He ordered a large pot of hot chocolate and another plate of scones from a waitress who was practically drooling at the sight of him.

Milly gave her an acidic stare and the waitress narrowed her eyes in response, put out at being warned off by such a young girl, even if she was wearing one of the most expensive cashmere jumpers the waitress had ever seen.

'My father is livid with me actually,' Freddie continued, oblivious of the goings-on. 'He thinks I'm a waste of space, a loser. He says I'm going to end up in the gutter.' His expression became muted. 'He's threatened me with all sorts of nonsense if I don't get my A levels this time.'

'Such as?'

'Disowning me, cutting me out of the will, kicking me out of the family home, to name but a few.'

Milly was horrified. 'He wouldn't!'

'He would,' Freddie told her with feeling, surprised when the waitress slammed the pot of hot chocolate down on the table with barely concealed venom. 'Steady on! Christ, what's the matter with *her*? Anyway, my father's a very strict man when it comes down to it, Mills; ruthless, in fact. He seems tolerant but if you push him over the edge, he's capable of cutting you off without compunction. Why do you think he's had so many wives? As soon as they piss him off, they're packed up and out of the door before the ink's dry on the divorce papers.' He sipped his hot chocolate. 'Speaking of which, my stepmother

Hannah had better stop feeling my backside every time I walk in the room, otherwise she's history.'

'Does your father know about your . . . you know, extra-curricular activities?'

Freddie gave her a lopsided grin. 'You mean the drug dealing? Of course he does, who doesn't? But it's only dope, nothing serious.' He stirred his hot chocolate with downcast eyes, his absurdly long eyelashes almost grazing his cheekbones. 'He wants me to stop what I'm doing immediately and knuckle down. Or he says he's going to shunt me off to London to live with a horrid uncle who'll probably cane me to within an inch of my life.' His expression was mocking. 'Or knowing his preferences, he'll be content with buggering me senseless.'

Milly was terrified. She couldn't bear it if Freddie moved away to London. She had to help him – her life wouldn't be worth living if he left.

She turned pleading eyes towards his. 'Can't you just give it up? Your business, I mean?'

He lazily thumbed through her poetry book again but he seemed distracted. 'I'm so independent though.' He looked up, his blue eyes earnest. 'I hate people thinking I'm going to spend the rest of my life living off my father, you see, but the trouble is, I haven't a clue what I want to do with myself. There'd have to be a very good reason for me to give up the business that keeps me in cashmere overcoats, put it that way.' Freddie laughed, breaking the tension. 'I'm a sucker for the good life and I haven't been able to think of a good enough reason to give it up so far. If a beautiful woman asked me to, I might consider it but as it's my father who asked me, and he's a man who's never been known for his looks, then no can do.'

Milly thought hard. If Freddie was unwilling to give up his drug dealing, she was going to have to think of something else. Maybe . . . maybe if Freddie passed all his A levels without giving his business up, his father would forgive him anyway?

The thing was, getting Freddie to turn up for lessons would be a miracle, let alone him attending the actual exams and acing them with any conviction.

'There's nothing else for it, you're going to have to pass your A levels,' she said firmly.

Freddie looked sceptical. 'Simple as that? I haven't even been back to school this month.'

She ignored him. 'It would be that simple if you let me help you. School work comes easily to me, Freddie. It's only a few weeks into term; enrol on Monday, go to some lessons to collect the work and we'll meet every day after school to make sure you pass with flying colours. I'll coach you. I won't do the work for you but I can definitely make sure you pass.' She had a momentary loss of confidence. She hadn't even passed her A levels herself yet but they couldn't be *that* difficult. 'At least, I think I can.'

'Would you do all that for me?' Freddie turned his crushed blueberry eyes to meet hers and she nearly fainted.

'O-of course. I mean, if you want me to.'

He stared at her. 'I might just take you up on that, Milly Vanilli.'

'Great!' She leant forward with sparkling eyes, buoyed up by her plan. She was going to spend tons of time with Freddie, what could be better than that? 'Then your father won't send you away to be buggered.'

He shuddered. 'Fingers crossed. Is that my phone or yours?'

'Mine.' Milly's face fell as she opened a text message. 'I don't believe it. India's cancelled. She's not going to come and meet me because she's got to go and buy something for her project with Alicia.' Before she could stop herself, tears flooded down her cheeks. 'I-I don't even know what I've done wrong!' she wailed. 'India hates me and I don't know why. What's so special about bloody Alicia anyway? David spends every spare second with her and India can't seem to get enough of her either. I can't bear it.'

'Hush.' Freddie pulled her close and kissed the top of her head. Her hair smelt clean and fresh like daisies and it took all his willpower not to tip her head up and kiss her full, trembling mouth.

He let go of her as if she had burnt him, astonished at himself.

What was he thinking? Milly was only sixteen, although that wasn't really the problem. What sort of friend would he be to David if he swooped in and seduced Milly the second he had been entrusted to look after her?

She looked adorable, her cute, doll-like nose was all pink and her mouth, which was swollen from crying, looked strangely kissable. He looked at her again, suddenly noticing she had lost all her puppy fat. Her body was curvaceous but slender. She was wearing her blond hair loose today and it hung freely around her shoulders like an angel's.

A sixteen-year-old angel he thought of as his own little sister, Freddie reminded himself ruefully as he moved further away from her. Feeling like a bastard, he forced himself to give the stroppy waitress a searingly appreciative look to take his mind off Milly. The waitress responded as he had expected, with a seductive smile and knowing eyes, but Freddie knew his heart wasn't in it and he regretted it the instant she scrawled her phone number on the chalkboard behind the counter. Freddie turned back to Milly, overwhelmed by his feelings and incapable of figuring out what they meant.

Milly's face fell when she saw the waitress smugly gesturing to her mobile phone number on the board but she forced herself to think about how much time she was going to get to spend with Freddie.

'Let's go back to mine. I can lend you tons of books!'

Caught up with her enthusiasm, Freddie completely forgot

to look back at the waitress and he found himself excited about studying for the first time in his life. He just wasn't sure if Byron or Shakespeare were responsible for his new-found passion.

'God, that must have been embarrassing when Claudette told you to back off like that.' Sophie topped up Tessa's wine glass. 'She sounds like a bit of a nutter.'

'She's just a bit possessive.' Tessa sighed. 'And who can blame her? She's been away for months and when she turns up, I'm hanging round like a bad smell. And she doesn't even know about the stupid kiss.'

'Was it a stupid kiss?' Sophie watched her.

Tessa felt herself colouring under Sophie's scrutiny and she hid her face behind a cushion. 'Oh God, I don't know! I don't understand how it even happened but all I can say is, at the time, it felt real. You know, meaningful. But in the cold light of day, who knows? He's avoiding me at all costs and according to Claudette he still thinks I'm this hard-nosed bitch who couldn't give a shit about family and friends – which couldn't be further from the truth.'

'Although he only thinks that because that's what you've shown him,' Sophie pointed out reasonably. 'If he got to know you properly, I know he'd think the world of you, the way everyone else does. Including me.'

Tessa nudged her. 'You've grovelled enough already, Soph, you don't need to be nice to me for the entire evening!'

'I'm not! I mean, I am but only because I'm telling the truth.' Sophie's eyes were full of remorse. 'I really am sorry about everything, Tessa. I'm so grateful you've forgiven me for being such a bitch to you.'

'Shut up and open another bottle of wine. And let's stop talking about me and Will because there *is* no me and Will. I'd far rather talk about you and Tristan again.'

Tessa had called Sophie as soon as filming had finished and

after arranging for Gil to take Ruby out for a pizza with Nathan, Sophie had invited Tessa round. Aside from an awkward five minutes when Sophie opened the door, they had both ended up hugging and crying on one another's shoulders within minutes. Sophie had apologised profusely for warning Tessa away from Tristan and had convinced her that her actions were at least partly to do with protecting her friend. Over the course of three hours and two bottles of heady Merlot, Sophie had also admitted to being hideously jealous that Tristan had seemed so attracted to Tessa. She told her all about their relationship and her reason for leaving, breaking down when she told Tessa about Tristan kissing an ex-girlfriend and the terrible night she had left Appleton.

'I'm sure you're mistaken about Tristan and this girl,' Tessa said as Sophie tipped a bag of tortilla chips into a bowl. 'I mean, Tristan can be an idiot at times because he has his head up his arse when he's having a creative moment but I can't believe he'd treat you like that. He's too genuine.' She felt a hundred times better than when she'd arrived; somehow talking everything through about Will and Claudette with Sophie had put things in perspective. Tessa still had no idea what to do with her feelings but having a laugh with Sophie about it all seemed to make the whole thing more manageable.

'I know what I saw.' Sophie's mouth was set. 'Tristan was kissing Anna . . . oh God, it was horrible, Tessa.'

'Not everything is how it seems, trust me, I should know. When you work in the entertainment industry, you get to understand that so-called facts can be fabricated and real life truths can be twisted. You think you've seen something but—' She stopped short. 'Hang on, did you say she was called Anna?'

Sophie nodded gloomily. 'She was an ex-girlfriend of Tristan's but he never talked about her. He kept a portrait of her, though, so he must have been harbouring feelings, even though he was with me. It makes me sick to even think about it.' She slammed her wine glass down so hard she almost snapped the stem. 'On all those nights I was away on my art course he must have been sleeping with her behind my back the whole time.'

Tessa shook her head slowly. 'But he told me about her, about this Anna. She was a total nutter – he couldn't stand her. She stalked him for months after he dumped her and even threatened to do something terrible to Austin like that loony woman in *Fatal Attraction* – you know, boil him in a pot or stuff onions up his bum or something.'

'What?' Sophie looked disbelieving. She shook her head. 'He was only saying that so you didn't think badly of him, Tessa!'

'Why would he do that? He didn't even know I'd met you when he told me this and he barely knew me at the time so it would be strange of him to lie about something so random.' She leant forward earnestly. 'Seriously, Soph, the whole family know about that girl Anna. Milly used to do impressions of her, Tristan said. She even nicknamed her The Psycho.'

Sophie's rose-pink complexion turned ashen as the blood drained from her face. She twisted her hands desperately, unable to comprehend what Tessa was saying. Tessa had to be mistaken, she simply *had* to be. Because if she wasn't, it would mean she had run away from the only man she had ever loved over something that might not even be his fault. It didn't bear thinking about.

'But I saw . . . they kissed . . . he didn't even push her away . . .'

Tessa could see Sophie was struggling to get the words out. She didn't want to make her feel worse but if what she suspected was true, that Tristan and Sophie still had feelings for each other, didn't she owe it to both of them to try to figure out what might have happened?

'Look, what if . . . what if Anna threw herself at Tristan? What if she knew you were out of the way – she was pretty good at the whole stalking thing, after all – and she turned up unannounced and . . . I don't know, fed him some sort of sob story?'

Sophie closed her eyes as her stomach shifted. She felt Tessa take her hands.

'What if she pounced on him and he was so taken aback, he didn't move straight away?' Tessa nodded, seeing the scene in her mind. 'You might have walked in right at that moment and what you saw looked awful and incriminating, but maybe seconds later you would have seen him pushing her away. There's no way he would have done that to you, least of all with her.'

'Oh my God.' Sophie's voice was barely a whisper. She opened her eyes and they reflected her agony. 'Do you think I might have made a mistake?'

'You were shocked, you thought you saw something terrible.' Tessa did her best to be the voice of reason, even though she could see Sophie was finding the whole thing devastating. 'Let's face it, before you met him, Tristan didn't have the best reputation, did he? Milly told me he slept around like a total man-whore before he fell in love with you. It's perfectly reasonable that you might think he could do something like this, even if you did trust him. You saw something and your imagination ran riot.'

Sophie burst into tears. 'But I just ran away! I was so crushed and torn apart I didn't even give myself a chance to think about it. If you're right, Tessa . . . can you imagine how Tristan felt when I disappeared like that?'

'Sophie, calm down!' Tessa resisted the urge to shake her and instead poured some more wine into her glass and thrust it into her trembling hands. 'He was still in love with you when you disappeared, he did tons of paintings of you. I know his work and there are portraits of you in his cottage that are definitely his more recent work. You know, using the earthy colours he's into now, more focus on the face – I can't believe I didn't spot the resemblance before, but you have changed a bit since then.' She rushed to cover herself. 'You're still ravishing, of course, but your hair's different and your face has changed slightly . . .'

'Old age, childbirth . . .' Sophie sniffed wryly.

'Stop it, you're stunning.' Tessa struggled to her feet. 'Look, I have to go, Soph, I've got an early-morning meeting with Clemmie.'

'How are you going to get home? The rain hasn't stopped all day.'

'I'll be fine walking,' Tessa said gamely. She supposed she could phone someone for a lift – taxi cabs were hard to come by in such a rural area – but she didn't want to disturb anyone. She glanced at Sophie. She didn't want to risk upsetting her now that they were friends again but it seemed like the right time to voice her concerns.

'Look, if I'm overstepping the mark, please tell me but there's something I've been meaning to say to you. It's about Ruby.'

'Ruby?' Sophie didn't meet her eyes.

'Yes, *Ruby*,' Tessa emphasised pointedly, 'I know you're upset about finding out about this thing with Anna and I really feel for you. But you can sort that out with him, you can explain what happened and what you thought you saw. Tristan would forgive you, I honestly believe that. He's still in love with you.' She grinned. 'He must be if you're the reason he didn't fall in love with me.'

She ducked as a cushion sailed past her head and her expression became sober. 'But something you might not be able to explain away so easily is Ruby. You have to tell Tristan about Ruby, Sophie. As soon as possible.'

Sophie froze.

Tessa nodded fervently. 'He'd hate to hear about something as important as that from someone else. Or,' she said as she shoved her feet into the ridiculously large welly boots, 'there's always a chance Ruby and Tristan might come face to face and guess.

Because you might tell yourself they're not the spit of each other but you're fooling yourself, Soph.' She paused by the door. 'They're like a mirror image of one another. And if I've seen it, it won't be long before someone else does. You've done a bloody good job of it up until now but you can't hide her forever.'

As the door closed behind Tessa, Sophie put her head in her hands and howled.

Tessa almost fell over several times as she headed back to the manor. Had she done the right thing by telling Sophie to talk to Tristan about Ruby? She hoped so. Knowing Tristan as she did, she was fairly certain he could forgive Sophie for getting the wrong idea about the awful night she had walked in on him kissing Anna – it must have looked pretty damning, after all – but hiding his daughter from him for five years? Tessa feared Tristan might see it as too cruel a crime to forgive Sophie for.

She squinted as someone emerged from the shadows and played a torch directly into her eyes.

'Tess, is that you?' It was Tristan, wearing a bright yellow waterproof coat with a beanie hat pulled down over his curls. He held up a dog lead. 'I'm walking Austin. What on earth are you doing out on such a horrible night?'

She shrugged sheepishly, shivering in the cold night air. 'Actually, I was talking to Sophie.'

'I see.' He turned away.

She grabbed his arm, keen to explain herself. She didn't want to lose his friendship; they got on so well. 'I know you must think I'm fraternising with the enemy, Tristan, but Sophie and I were good friends before the summer party. She's been phoning me . . . I thought it about time I gave her a chance to explain herself.' She blew on her frozen fingers and watched his shoulders relax slightly.

'And did she?' He glanced at her moodily, noticing she was wearing a flimsy coat. 'Christ, what are you wearing, woman?

346

Do you actually own any practical clothes?' Tristan tore off his waterproof jacket and flung it round her shoulders before ducking under a tree with her out of the rain. 'Don't worry about me, I'm wearing three jumpers. Well, go on. What happened? Have you kissed and made up?'

'Something like that.' Tessa stuffed her hands into the pockets of his waterproof jacket, torn between her loyalty towards him and her loyalty towards Sophie. They had both been good friends to her and she was certain they were both too stubborn to back down and be honest with each other about their feelings. Would they ever talk about that night if she didn't open her mouth? Tessa faltered. She had spent the past few months trying not to get involved with the family, telling herself that interfering in things that had nothing to do with her could only end in tears.

Seeing the distressed look on Tristan's face at the mere mention of Sophie's name and convinced he was still in love with her, Tessa threw caution to the wind.

'Sophie thinks you cheated on her.'

'What?' He looked shocked at her outburst. 'What makes you say that?'

'She told me.' Tessa sighed. 'Do you remember the night before Sophie left?'

'With absolute clarity,' he replied drily.

'Good. So you remember your ex-girlfriend Anna turning up and trying to kiss you?'

He almost dropped his torch. 'How do you know about that?'

'Sophie just told me about it. And she knows because she came back early from London. She turned up at your cottage and saw you kissing Anna. Or Anna kissing you.'

'Jesus!' Tristan tore his beanie hat off and ran a hand through his damp blond curls. 'Oh my God! Can you imagine how that must have looked? Wait . . . didn't she hang on to see what happened? Didn't she see me pushing her away?'

Tessa shook her head. 'She was so upset, she just ran.'

'But . . . she couldn't possibly believe I would do something like that to her! I wouldn't . . . I couldn't . . . I loved her more than anything . . .'

'You did have a terrible reputation in those days,' Tessa reminded him gently. 'You weren't exactly known for your faithfulness.'

Tristan looked shell-shocked.

'I think what made it worse was that you didn't ever speak to Sophie about Anna. She didn't know Anna was unhinged. By the sounds of it, she was even paranoid you still had feelings for Anna because you kept that portrait and because you refused to talk about her.'

'Keeping the portrait . . . that was just ego – about my work,' Tristan ranted, almost slipping over in his agitation. 'Sophie knew what I was like in those days when I completed a portrait I thought was especially good. I couldn't even bear to let a gallery have it. It didn't mean I had feelings for the girl – I couldn't stand the sight of her!'

Tessa didn't know how to console him. 'Sophie didn't know that, Tris. You have to try to see it from her point of view. An ex-girlfriend you'd refused to talk about, a portrait you kept hold of, possibly for sentimental reasons. And a bad reputation that you'd grown out of by the time you met Sophie but she was young, maybe she was insecure about how you felt about her.'

'Fuck.' Realisation about how the scene with Anna must have looked to Sophie dawned on Tristan. 'My God, she must have hated me,' he said in a flat voice, 'and she must have thought that everything I ever told her was a lie. I didn't talk to her about Anna because I didn't want to taint our relationship. I was always terrified Anna would come back and try to get revenge; it felt better to just block her out and pretend she didn't exist.'

'Talk to Sophie,' Tessa urged as rain dripped off the hood of Tristan's waterproof jacket. Without it, he was getting soaked to

348

the skin and rain was dripping off his eyelashes. She linked her arm through his as Austin galloped up to them, his coat saturated. 'But can you do it another time? We're in danger of drowning out here.'

'But . . . I have to go to her . . . to explain . . .'

'You can't!' Urgently, Tessa held on to his arm. Gil was due back with Ruby at any minute. 'Sophie's upset . . . really upset. You have to give her time to digest everything and calm down a bit. She honestly wouldn't let you in if you did go over there now.' At least that was the truth.

'All right. Fine, I'll see her another time. God, Tess, I can't tell you how grateful I am that you've told me about this. You're such a good friend.' He hugged her.

'I wish Will thought so,' she mumbled into his jumper, feeling miserable again. She felt Tristan pull away and she froze. Had she said that out loud?

'You like Will,' he said in wonder. 'My God, when did that happen?'

Tessa poked a branch with the toe of her welly boot. 'The summer party . . . we had a . . . a moment. But you can't say anything! It was a mistake. Will loves Claudette and she warned me off today so it's nothing, do you understand?'

Tristan held his hands up. 'All right, keep your hair on. I won't say anything. But I think you and Will make a much better couple than him and Claudette – all right, Tess, I'll shut up!' He caught sight of her footwear and, in spite of his distress, burst out laughing. 'But only if you tell me why you're wearing Dad's size twelve welly boots.'

Chapter Twenty

'What do you think of this one? Grotesque, isn't it? I look like a hippo, honey, so don't even try and say otherwise.'

Tessa put her head on one side and tried to think of something constructive to say. It was early October and the weather was getting worse by the day. If that wasn't bad enough, Jilly was hassling her like a foxhound tormenting its prey. Believing she had chosen the lesser of two evils, Tessa had switched off her BlackBerry and agreed to help Clemmie choose a wedding dress. They were shut away in one of the penthouses at Appleton Manor, surrounded by dresses in every conceivable shade of white and an array of designer shoes. In the absence of Clemmie's stylist, she had enlisted Tessa to advise her before a wedding rehearsal with Rufus and the camera crew. JB had made a shock appearance and was prowling around downstairs like a snarling panther, making the camera crew hate him even more with his acerbic put-downs and generally causing havoc with his uniquely bossy form of direction.

Not that being shut away with Clemmie for the past few hours had been much fun either, Tessa thought dejectedly. Apart from getting to try on the latest Jimmy Choos, Louboutins and YSL heels and play around with the latest lust-have handbags, it had been an exasperating trial of endurance. Clemmie was down in the dumps and every designer dress was dismissed as 'ugly' and flung to the floor with disgust.

'Why don't you try the Vera Wang on again? I'd kill to wear this on my wedding day.' Tessa held up the simple, elegant dress that was made of silk and cut so beautifully, it was actually breathtaking. She held it against herself enticingly, but as Clemmie lifted her shoulders in a non-committal way, Tessa bit back a rude retort. She had spent most of her time frantically shaking the dresses out and coaxing them back into the plastic covers so they could go back to the designer unmarked, and she was at the end of her tether. Some of the wedding dresses were astonishingly beautiful and all of them had a price tag of five figures – apart from one, which tipped over into six.

'Or what about this exquisite Lawrence Steele?' The dress was reminiscent of Jennifer Aniston's at her wedding to Brad Pitt – dreamily romantic and as classy as anything.

Clemmie ignored the dress. 'Has Rufus called?'

Tessa checked Clemmie's phone again. 'Nope. Are you sure you don't want to try this one on again? You looked absolutely beautiful in it.'

Clemmie shook her head and downed another glass of champagne. 'I look fat.'

Tessa let out a frustrated sound but tried to hide her irritation. Clemmie was incredibly slender with an impossibly nipped-in waist, but every dress she tried on had been deemed unflattering because it 'drew attention to her big, Texan behind'. Having downed almost a bottle of champagne on an empty stomach, Clemmie was reeling across the floor like a drunken teenager. Which was marginally better than the sober Clemmie who had been alternating between black moments of anger to wailing misery without warning.

'He's having an affair, isn't he?' Clemmie cried, looking demented as she hurled another dress to the floor. She started pacing the penthouse in her corseted underwear, looking like some tragic nineteen thirties movie star. 'He's never at home any more, Tessa! I can't talk to him, he's shutting me out completely. I have no idea if he wants to go ahead with the wedding because

I can't even remember when we last had dinner together! He doesn't call when he says he will, he doesn't turn up when he's supposed to – it's as if he's leading a double life. I thought he loved me, really loved me, but he doesn't! I want children so desperately but we don't even have sex any more, so that won't be happening, will it?'

Tessa was astounded and she scrabbled for the right words to reassure Clemmie that this was just an unfortunate blip. She had had no idea things were that bad between Rufus and Clemmie – if they weren't even speaking, what hope did they have of getting married in a couple of months' time?

Whatever Rufus was up to, he was playing a dangerous game and hurting Clemmie immensely in the process and Tessa wished she could give him a stern talking to. For someone so career-focused, Rufus didn't seem to have thought about the consequences of cheating on someone as famous and as popular as Clemmie, if indeed that was what he was doing. Clemmie was a sweetheart in her own country, a veritable national treasure, and unless he had some unseen trick up his sleeve, Tessa couldn't see how Rufus could get away with shitting on American royalty.

Clemmie had given in to hysteria by this point, embracing it as if it was an old friend. 'That's my phone . . . that's my phone! What does it say?'

Tessa read the text message with a sinking heart. 'It's from Rufus. He says he . . . can't make it and has to cancel. He . . . er . . . doesn't say why.'

'No, no, *no.*'

Clemmie fell to the floor and curled up in a foetal position. She started rocking from side to side, tearing at her hair and weeping like a baby. Tessa rushed over and wrapped her in a dressing gown.

Helping her into an armchair, Tessa gently brushed Clemmie's hair out of her eyes. With tears streaming down her face, Clemmie clung to her tightly, as if she was the last dinghy on the *Titanic*.

'I have n-no one,' she stammered into Tessa's shoulder. 'There's no one left from my old life. I'm all alone . . . without Rufus, I have no one. My parents are dead . . . my fans will forget me if I don't make any more films . . . what will I do . . . where will I go?'

It was heartbreaking. Stroking her hair and hushing her sobs, Tessa felt immensely sorry for Clemmie. She had an enviable life on the surface of it, with all the money she had and the Oscar on her mantelpiece, but she seemed so lonely and in need of love.

'We all adore you, Clemmie. You're not alone, you're amongst friends. I know we haven't known each other that long but I really do care about you and the Forbes-Henrys adore you, especially Jack. He's absolutely smitten. You've won everyone over, I promise you.'

Clemmie lifted her hazel eyes drunkenly, trying to focus on Tessa's face. 'None of you would love me if you knew . . . none of you would want to be my friend if you knew what I'd done.'

Tessa felt a shiver down her back. 'What have you done? Nothing can be that bad.'

'Oh yes it can, honey.' Clemmie's head fell forward on to her chest as the drink took hold. 'So bad, so very, very bad. Bad Bobby-Sue . . . terrible things . . . Bobby-Sue Winterbottom . . . it all seems so long ago now.' She let out a hiccup before passing out cold.

Bobby-Sue? Tessa stared at Clemmie's inert body, slumped in the armchair. Who was Bobby-Sue Winterbottom? Seconds passed and Clemmie began to gently snore; only the ache in her knees galvanised Tessa into action as she realised how long she'd been sitting there. Calling down to Henny who rushed upstairs looking concerned, Tessa explained that Clemmie was over-wrought and emotionally drained and in need of looking after;

would Henny mind because she had something incredibly important to do?

Vaguely, Tessa noticed Henny was wearing a new jumper in a soft duck-egg blue shade which brought out the blue of her eyes and complemented her rosy cheeks. She left Henny fussing over Clemmie like an anxious mother hen and dashed to Will's office. Thankfully, he was nowhere to be seen and Tessa opened the internet on his computer with a thumping heart.

After checking several American websites, she finally found what she was looking for. A tragic incident had taken place many years ago in Texas. A pedestrian had been killed by an out-of-control vehicle. The pedestrian had been a happily married mother of three, aged twenty-four, and the driver of the car was reported as a teenage girl named Bobby-Sue Winterbottom. Tessa's mouth was dry from all the adrenalin. Depicted not so much as mentally unstable but as a tragic victim of circumstance – albeit one who must pay for the grave mistake she had made – Bobby-Sue had looked ashamed throughout the trial and had been, as it was reported, 'visibly distressed by the pain she had caused the dead woman's family'. The 'extenuating circumstances' surrounding the crash (although these were not stated in the article) and her overwhelming remorse were taken into account, and Bobby-Sue had been sentenced to one year in prison for manslaughter. Grainy photographs showed an awkward-looking young girl with big teeth and frizzy hair, her anguished eyes speaking volumes about how cut up she was by the proceedings. Despite her dramatically different appearance, there was something about the haunted look in her eyes that was instantly familiar.

'Jesus, Clemmie,' Tessa said out loud. No wonder she had reinvented herself. She must have been devastated by the damage she had done. Tessa wondered what the 'extenuating circumstances' were that had been taken into account at Clemmie's trial. They had to be serious for the sentence to be so short but Tessa couldn't find anything else about the story on the internet.

Why on earth had Clemmie wanted to become an actress after what she had been through? That was what Tessa couldn't understand. Acting was the one career that would force her into the public eye, a career that would make her live her life in constant fear of being discovered. And just how much surgery had Clemmie had? More to the point, how had she afforded it? Some of the changes were relatively simple: her frizzy blond hair dyed to a dark, glossy brunette and her crooked teeth straightened and whitened. But it wasn't just hair and teeth that had been changed; in comparison to the early photographs of her, every aspect of Clemmie's face appeared to be different. Her nose, her chin, the arch of her eyebrows, everything had been changed. Even the shape of her eyes was different, almond-shaped instead of round.

Tessa felt a new-found respect for Clemmie, sensing a level of determination in her she hadn't given her credit for. Beneath that sensual, Southern drawl and the impeccable manners was a relentless sense of purpose and a willingness to do whatever it took to shake off her old self and create a whole new person. Tessa wondered how many times Clemmie had beaten herself up for killing an innocent woman. It was a terrible secret to have to live with, but it had been an accident, a dreadful accident.

'Are you all right, darling?' Henny stuck her head through the door. 'You look like you've seen a ghost.'

'I'm fine, thanks . . . I just had a bit of a shock, that's all.' Tessa swiftly shut down the page and deleted it from the history on Will's computer. She wondered fleetingly if Rufus knew about Clemmie's past but decided he couldn't. Knowing Rufus, he'd drop Clemmie like the proverbial hot potato if he thought she could taint his career with a secret of this magnitude. 'Is Clemmie all right?'

'As right as rain,' Henny reassured her cheerfully, stopping in front of a mirror to check her hair was pinned up still. 'I managed to get some water down her when she woke up but she seemed rather distressed about something. Seemed to think she might have told you something she shouldn't have and that you might be off phoning the *Sun*, the silly thing! I told her she was being paranoid and that whatever she told you, you weren't the type of person to do something so vicious.' She smiled at Tessa openly, but her brilliant blue eyes had a glimmer of shrewdness in them. 'I was right to say that, wasn't I?'

Tessa bit her lip so hard she almost tasted blood. She knew exactly why Clemmie was so scared. This sort of information was like gold dust. Jilly's jet-black heart would be aflame with euphoria if Tessa told her about Clemmie's stint in prison. It was the scoop Jilly – and indeed Tessa – had been waiting for all her life. It would send her career into the stratosphere and would mean never having to worry about money or job opportunities again.

Tessa fingered her BlackBerry, knowing she had to make the right decision over this. It wasn't just Clemmie's career that was on the line here, it was her own. She knew no other journalist would dream of keeping such scandalous information to themselves. Most of them would probably even bypass their bosses and sell the story to the highest bidder but . . .

Tessa hesitated, knowing she would hate herself for exposing Clemmie. Did Clemmie deserve to be held up for inspection, just because she had made a mistake? The public didn't own her life, but Tessa knew if she revealed what she had just discovered, Clemmie would be in prison all over again. And any hope of returning to her career would be impossible.

'*Of course* you were right to tell Clemmie I'm not that sort of person,' Tessa said decisively. She knew what she had to do. 'Clemmie did tell me something . . . something that would make me a household name and Clemmie – well, let's just say,

Clemmie would probably be a public hate figure if I said anything. Or very misunderstood, to say the least.' She linked arms with Henny, instantly relaxing. 'But I just can't do that to her . . . not to Clemmie. She's a friend and I respect her way too much.'

Henny patted her arm comfortably. 'You're a lovely girl, Tessa. I knew you wouldn't do something like that.'

Tessa stopped her. 'I thought about it, though. Doesn't that make me a bad person anyway?'

Henny looked thoughtful as she led her downstairs. 'Darling, you wouldn't be human if you hadn't thought about doing that. Most journalists wouldn't have even thought twice about it and would have been on the phone to all and sundry by now.'

'Which just means I've lost my killer instinct,' Tessa realised, feeling low again. Jilly and JB had been right all along about her.

'No, darling.' Henny sat her down and made her a mug of strong, aromatic coffee. 'It just means you're too nice to be a journalist and that you're in the wrong job, that's all. Tristan said you were disillusioned with it all and this just proves it, doesn't it?' She gave Tessa a kindly smile and gently pushed a notepad and pen across the table. 'If I were you, I'd stop beating myself up about it and think about writing that book you've been talking about.'

Tessa sipped her coffee pensively. She wasn't sure of anything any more, her head was full to the brim with thoughts of her career, of Will and of the Forbes-Henry family. She felt as if her head might explode.

Maybe thinking about the novel she wanted to write wasn't a bad idea after all, Tessa thought. Escaping to a pretend world might be far more preferable than dealing with her real one. Pushing away scary thoughts of Jilly, Tessa pulled the pad and pen towards her and started to scribble.

Sophie stared at her reflection. The wedding dress was stunning, a masterpiece of understated class and vintage cool. As with

357

everything Gil applied himself to, his taste shone through and she couldn't fault him for having an eye for perfection. The same could be said for the other dresses he had hand-picked, all of which were lined up on a rail above her head. She had tried all of them on twice but she was no nearer to reaching a decision. Choosing a dress made the wedding to Gil real and that wasn't something she could easily come to terms with right now.

Sophie pleated the oyster silk duchesse satin between her fingers apprehensively, fighting the urge to be sick. She didn't want to cause a scene in front of Ruby who was trying on bridesmaid's dresses in rich shades of damson and raspberry; she had to be strong and pretend she was enjoying herself.

Shouldn't this be an exciting occasion? Shouldn't this be a day to remember – the day she twirled around in a gorgeous dress squealing, 'This is the *one*', delirious with happiness that she would be wearing it as she married the man of her dreams? Except . . . that wasn't the situation she was in. Sophie wasn't marrying the man of her dreams. Yes, she was marrying her best friend, someone she cared for deeply but not someone she loved to distraction. Gil was a dear, sweet man but he didn't make her heart sing. Only one man was capable of doing that and she had well and truly burnt her bridges with him.

And what about Gil, how did he feel about her? Did he love her, really love her the way Tristan did? Sophie didn't think so. She hoped he hadn't ever guessed that she didn't love him that way either but sometimes she thought she could see it in his eyes when he stared into the distance. Did she even make Gil happy? There were times when he seemed so introverted, so distant from her.

'That looks divine on you,' gushed the shop assistant, smoothing the fabric around Sophie's waist. She was a middle-aged spinster with bouffant hair and an affected manner, and she was containing her eagerness at making such a huge sale with great difficulty. The dresses on the rail were the most expensive in the shop and she was practically salivating at the thought of ringing one of them through the till. 'It's a perfect fit. Would madam like to take it?'

'I-I'm not sure. I don't know if it's me, to be honest.'

Sophie stared at her pale reflection, wondering if she'd lost weight. She had always been slender but she had never been a perfect size anything so she could only guess she had dropped a few pounds over the last month. And no wonder, Tessa's bombshell about Anna had left her reeling. For days she had convinced herself it wasn't possible and that what she had seen had been real, but the more she thought about it, the more she thought about Tristan, the more it dawned on her that she had made an appalling mistake. When she had left five years ago, she had still found it hard to believe Tristan would cheat on her. But the girl she had seen him with had been so confident and the evidence had been so damning.

However, now she knew that the girl had been stalking Tristan and was mentally unbalanced, the scene that had replayed itself in her mind constantly since that fateful day suddenly took on a whole new meaning.

With a thumping heart, Sophie allowed the shop assistant to sulkily unzip the dress so she could step out of it. Tristan hadn't betrayed her, he had been the innocent pawn in one of Anna's twisted games and he had suffered purely because of timing and circumstance. If Sophie hadn't come back early to tell him about the baby, she wouldn't have walked in on Anna kissing him against his will. She would have been none the wiser and she would have told him about the baby the next day, or whenever. She still didn't know for sure how Tristan would have reacted to the news but she was pretty sure he would have been thrilled because he adored children, and he adored her. Or he used to anyway.

A minuscule part of her felt elated at the realisation that

Tristan wasn't the bad guy she had thought he was but she felt overwhelmed by a sense of loss at wasting the past five years. She stepped into another one of the gorgeous dresses Gil had chosen, this time a nineteen thirties-style halter-neck creation in honey-coloured silk, and swallowed down a sob. She hated herself for not giving Tristan the benefit of the doubt and knowing that he was blameless in the entire scenario had the unfortunate effect of making her fall in love with him all over again – if she had ever stopped loving him in the past five years, and she knew she hadn't. She longed to dash to his side but it was so complicated . . .

'Madam seems to look ravishing in everything,' the shop assistant commented honestly but rather sourly. 'This one brings out the tones of your hair and really makes your brown eyes stand out.' The assistant suppressed a sigh. It was a Friday night and she had expected to get a sale over and done with quickly, especially since the dresses had been hand-picked by the groom and all the bride had to do was choose one of them. But several hours had passed and, frustratingly, she was no closer to chivvying this particular bride along.

'Mummy, you look *pretty*,' Ruby exclaimed as she flung herself against the bottom of Sophie's dress.

'So do you.' Sophie knelt down, her knees in a pool of expensive silk. And she did. Wearing an A-line cream dress with a wide sash the colour of deepest rubies, her daughter looked adorable. Realising she had procrastinated enough and that, in view of how things were with Tristan, the wedding to Gil was inevitable, Sophie decided to let her five-year-old daughter have the final say.

'So, do you think this is the best dress?'

Ruby nodded. Truthfully, she just wanted to get home and play with her Barbies but she did like the feel of the slithery material. She tugged at the dress as Sophie advised the shop assistant of the good news.

'Mummy, will I ever get to meet my real daddy?'

'What?' Sophie blinked at her, horrified. The shop assistant hid a smug smile as she discreetly hooked the dress back on the hanger.

Ruby repeated her question. 'My real daddy. I want to meet him.'

Sophie felt jolted. 'Where did that come from?'

Ruby shrugged.

Ignoring the penetrating stare of the shop assistant, Sophie gaped at her daughter. What on earth was she supposed to say to her?

Having taken out his anguish on several canvases in his studio, Tristan decided he needed some fresh air. Realising he hadn't spoken to Will for ages and intrigued to know what was going on with the Claudette/Tessa situation, he decided to invite him out for a game of squash. Dragging himself away from the pile of accounts on his desk, Will drove them into the nearest town and then got changed at the gym.

'God, I'm out of practice,' Will panted as he missed yet another shot.

Tristan wiped his head on a towel. 'Me too. Christ, when did we get so old and creaky?' Wearing a yellow polo shirt and some red shorts, he cut a stylish figure on the court. Not that his attire was helping his game any, he thought as he tripped over his own feet for the third time.

'Speak for yourself, little brother!'

Will whacked the ball hard and couldn't help laughing as Tristan ended up on his backside. Will was more soberly dressed in a blue T-shirt and rugby shorts but his hairy thighs and broad shoulders were gaining him any number of admirers on the other side of the glass.

Back on his feet, Tristan sent a ball ricocheting around the court, sending Will flying. He was immediately contrite. 'Sorry!

I'm finding my mojo again, watch out!' He whooped as he got to a difficult ball. He gave Will a sly, sideways glance. 'So, what's happening with you and Tessa then?'

'Me and Tessa?' Caught off guard, Will fluffed an easy shot and fell over. Sprawled out on the court, he avoided Tristan's stare. He got to his feet and busied himself with brushing himself down briskly. 'There's nothing happening with me and Tessa. Why do you ask?' Seeing the knowing look in Tristan's eyes, he realised he knew about the kiss. 'Shit, she told you about the kiss.'

'Only by accident,' Tristan said quickly.

Will smashed the ball against the wall, feeling exposed. 'I suppose she still hates me.'

'I don't think hate is the word I'd use, no,' Tristan wheezed, wondering if it was possible to develop asthma at the age of thirty. Leaning over, he tried to catch his breath.

Will's mouth settled into a grim line. It was like that, was it? He felt stupid for even daring to hope Tessa might have been disturbed by thoughts of him the way his mind had been preoccupied with unsettling thoughts of her. It had affected his ability to work, to focus on the hotel plans and, on some days, just to function as a normal human being. He felt incredibly foolish. He had obviously misread the situation entirely. 'Look, it was just one of those things . . . it happened and it shouldn't have done . . .' He stopped, realising how lame it all sounded. 'Tristan, genuinely, I have no idea how or why it happened. You know how I feel about her, she's not exactly my ideal woman! And what about Claudette? There's absolutely no excuse and I've been feeling like a shit about it ever since.'

Tristan shrugged. 'Don't get your knickers in a twist about it.' He was getting the impression his brother felt more for Tessa than he was letting on. 'So . . . just suppose Claudette was out of the picture?'

'How can I do that? We're engaged to be married.'

'Whatever. Just suppose. Would you feel differently towards Tessa?'

Contemplatively, Will drummed the bottom of his racket on the court. He glanced up at Tristan. 'Maybe. When it happened . . . the kiss, I mean . . . I felt something.'

'I bet you did.' Tristan guffawed naughtily.

'Shut up, Tris! You know what I mean . . . it felt different. As if it meant something. But if you're saying Tessa still hates me then I must have misread the whole thing and imagined something that wasn't there.'

Tristan looked bemused. 'I never said that. When did I say that about Tessa still hating you? I said "hate" *wasn't* the word I would use.' He rolled his eyes comically. 'God, no wonder women say men are obtuse.'

Will's eyes widened but before he could comment, Tristan was in full flow again. 'Anyway, are you sure you want to marry Claudette?'

'Why wouldn't I be?'

'I don't know, she might not be "the one".' Tristan looked coy as he prepared to serve. 'It would be a shame if there were someone better, someone really perfect, right under your nose, as it were.'

Not even attempting to go for the ball, Will stared into space. Was Tristan right? Was he unsure about marrying Claudette? Will grappled with himself. He had made a promise to Claudette, he had proposed because he loved her and wanted to spend the rest of his life with her. Nothing had changed; he had made a huge error of judgement and kissed another woman, that was all. A woman he didn't even like. So why was his head so full of Tessa? Why did he wake up in the middle of the night wishing she was the one sleeping next to him?

Will shook himself. He shouldn't be thinking like this. He deflected the conversation back to Tristan. 'Forget about me.

What's happening with you and Sophie?'

'Absolutely bugger all. Obviously we now know why Sophie left. Thank God Tessa told me, otherwise I think I'd still be in the dark.'

'So why haven't you gone to see her?'

Tristan put his hand up for a break and they both flopped down on the court. 'I keep wanting to and then I can't do it for some reason. I don't even know what to say to her. I mean, at least I know why she went but I can't believe she thought I was capable of cheating on her.'

Will was full of sympathy. 'Who would have thought Anna . . . The Psycho, would have been responsible for all this?'

'Unbelievable, isn't it?' Tristan agreed miserably. 'It's just so bloody stupid and pointless. A waste of five years, apart from anything else. And I feel as if I've lost Sophie for good, you know? I don't know for sure but it all seems so hopeless.'

Will nodded, swigging from a bottle of water.

'And I know how it must have looked from Sophie's point of view, walking in on Anna throwing herself at me like that, but it just makes me sick that Sophie could believe me capable of such a thing.' Tristan scowled and smacked his hand down on the court. 'Christ, couldn't she have given me a chance to explain myself? Actually, bugger that, Will, if she'd hung on for five more seconds, she would have seen me pushing that crazy woman away and telling her to get lost. That's all she had to do, wait five more seconds. But she didn't even give me that.'

Will let out an understanding sigh. 'I know it's hard for you to get your head round, Tris, but perhaps she was inconsolable after seeing something that looked so conclusive and she couldn't bear to watch.'

'Fuck knows. I'm still in love with her, Will, even if she *didn't* give me the benefit of the doubt. I've thought and thought about it, but I can't seem to get her out of my head. It's a bloody nuisance, but there you are.'

'You know she's still going ahead with her wedding to Gil?' Will asked, looking concerned. 'Gil paid the deposit this morning and Aunt Henny's throwing herself into the arrangements for Christmas Eve, even though she's loathing every minute of it.'

'She's still getting married? I can't believe it!' Tristan looked stricken. 'The last time I saw her . . . there was something in her eyes, Will . . . she feels something, I know it.' He clutched his blond hair impatiently, oblivious of the gaggle of women who had gathered on the other side to watch them. Tristan wanted to charge up to Gil, biff him on the nose and tell him to stay away from his woman – or something equally ridiculous. But how could he do that? Gil was about as macho as a stuffed panda and Tristan knew he'd end up looking the bad guy if he stormed in and started throwing his fists around.

'Christ, Will, this is all such a mess. What on earth is she doing with Gil, anyway?'

Will had no idea. 'If you feel like this, you have to go and see her, Tris. Unless you're planning to walk into the chapel and shout out, "It should have been me!" when the vicar asks if anyone has just cause to prevent the marriage, I suggest you pull your finger out.'

His face a picture of stubbornness, Tristan got to his feet. 'If she's still marrying Gil, there's no point. I'm not going over there like some sort of besotted moron, declaring undying love. I did that before and she's still going ahead with it!' He shook his head angrily. 'No, this time, if Sophie wants me back, she's going to have to come and get me. Because I'm done with crawling back on my hands and knees, Will. It's about time she made a bloody gesture for a change.' He waited impatiently for Will to serve. 'Come on, let's get on with the game. Now I've got my asthma under control, I'm going to thrash the living daylights out of you.'

Will grinned and served.

Chapter Twenty-One

Tessa opened the door of her cottage to find Clemmie standing under an umbrella, shifting from one foot to another apprehensively. On closer inspection, Tessa saw that she looked dreadful. Her skin was pasty, her dark hair greasy and unwashed and she was wearing a shapeless navy mac she had obviously borrowed from Henny. She was battling to keep her umbrella upright amidst the unrepentant sleet, her slender frame looking unexpectedly frail against the bitter elements.

'Honey, I'm so sorry to barge in like this,' Clemmie started, her voice trembling as she gripped her umbrella more tightly. Remorse was spilling out from every pore. 'But I just had to see you . . .'

'Clemmie, come in, don't stand out in the rain!' Tessa yanked her inside and shoved the soaking wet umbrella into a stand. It had been two weeks since Tessa had discovered Clemmie's secret and they hadn't spoken since. 'God, you're freezing.' She took Clemmie's frozen little hands in hers and rubbed them vigorously. Turning up the heating (Will had been as good as his word and had sent someone to fix it the day after their alcove chat), she bundled Clemmie into an armchair and put the kettle on.

In spite of the warmth, Clemmie couldn't stop shivering. Her eyes were wild and had dark grey shadows beneath them as if she hadn't slept for weeks.

'Terribly British to have tea, I know, but it really can help.' Tessa pressed a mug of hot, sweet tea into her hands and sat down opposite her. 'Clemmie, you have nothing to worry about, I promise you.'

Clemmie lifted troubled hazel eyes to Tessa's. 'But I told you things,' she whispered, frightened. 'I told you things you could use . . . you're a journalist . . . it's dynamite . . .'

'I know.' Tessa knew how hard it must have been for Clemmie to talk about what had happened. 'But you have my word, I will never tell another soul about you . . . I mean, about the whole Bobby-Sue thing. I have to confess that I did look the story up on the internet because I couldn't help myself. But I will never, ever tell another living soul about what I found out.'

Clemmie was so overcome with gratitude she broke down. Her shoulders shook with emotion and Tessa had to take the mug of tea from her. 'Sorry, this just brings up so many bad memories . . . it was such a terrible thing to happen . . .'

'It was an accident,' Tessa reminded her tenderly, feeling sorry for Clemmie and the terrible burden she had been carrying around with her. 'An accident. It was a desperately tragic story and I know you must feel horribly guilty about it. But it was so long ago now, no one needs to know.'

'But . . . but I killed that poor woman . . . I went to prison. I'm a Hollywood actress . . . with an Oscar.'

'I know.'

Clemmie gazed at her in disbelief. 'Honey, do you know how much someone would pay for this kind of information?'

Tessa nodded slowly. 'I can guess. And, honestly? I thought about it.'

'I don't blame you. Who wouldn't? You're only human. And it's your job.'

Tessa handed Clemmie some tissues. 'But then I thought about you and our friendship and what it would do to your career. My boss would kill me if she knew – you have no idea how ruthless she is. But I haven't called her and I won't.'

Clemmie sobbed into her hands, incapable of speaking.

When she did, her voice was muffled and Tessa could barely hear her. 'I was so upset . . . the day of the crash, you see. It's no excuse and I won't ever defend myself with this.'

'With what?' Tessa was intrigued.

'I was very much in love with someone . . . someone powerful and rich.' Clemmie shredded the tissues, her hazel eyes darkening at the memory. 'I was pregnant and so deliriously happy about it. But I . . . I had a miscarriage and lost the baby and my lover, he . . . he . . . dumped me.'

'What a bastard.' Tessa realised now that Clemmie had buried the idea of having children to pursue her career. Until she met Rufus, at any rate.

Clemmie nodded. 'He was a total bastard, a film executive – greedy, ambitious and ruthless. When I came out of prison, I went to see him . . . I-I don't even know why really. But seeing me scared him . . . he was married by then and a big name in films . . . he gave me thousands of dollars to never speak about what had happened. It was so insulting . . . so callous.' She squared her shoulders. 'But then I thought, why not use the money for my career? Why not make something positive out of this? I told him I wanted just one more favour later on – a lead part in a film. He was so petrified he agreed.'

Tessa let out a shaky breath. 'Then you had all that surgery . . . and completely rebuilt your career.'

'I rebuilt my career *and* my body.' Clemmie barked out a laugh. 'I became a new person from top to toe. I told myself I was like a phoenix, emerging from the ashes triumphantly to become a powerful woman in the world of films and money. But truly, I've never forgotten that poor woman and her family and what I did to them. I live with the guilt and shame every single day.'

'Clemmie, you have to let this go. It was an accident and you've paid your dues.'

Clemmie stared past Tessa. 'I wish I could. But it's so hard.

I've got to the stage where I don't even feel passionate about acting any more. I feel as if I've set out to achieve something and prove something to . . . myself? To the world? I don't even know any more. But now I feel so disillusioned . . . I feel as if I need to change something about my life.'

Tessa realised she and Clemmie had a lot in common. She gave her a sympathetic grin. 'That's two of us on the dole in the New Year then.'

'On the *what*?' Clemmie looked bewildered.

'Jobless,' Tessa explained.

'I guess so. But it doesn't feel so bad. In fact, I actually feel rather relieved to have made the decision.'

Tessa knew exactly how she felt. It was scary to be turning her back on something she had loved for so long but it was time for a change.

Looking peaceful for the first time since she'd arrived, Clemmie sat back and started drinking her tea. She had been working from such a young age, the thought of having months stretching out in front of her without a schedule and without an agent telling her what to do was a whole new experience. But it was an experience she believed she could easily embrace, if only she didn't have Rufus to consider. 'I'd better go. I've got a wedding to sort out. If the groom ever turns up,' she added, her voice cracking again as she shook out her umbrella and prepared to brave the elements.

Tessa gave her a hug. Feeling strangely proud of both Clemmie and herself, she closed the door and pulled out the notebook containing her ideas for her novel. If Clemmie could change careers, she could sure as hell give it a shot, Tessa thought. She curled up and started writing.

Milly stomped her way through piles of red and gold leaves as she moodily headed home from the library. India had promised to be there at midday, and three hours later and with the predictability of public transport, she was conspicuous by her absence.

Milly was beginning to tire of the situation. Each morning she would text India to arrange a meeting for them to chat, do some homework, listen to some music – the things girls normally did outside school. After some delay, India would reluctantly (it appeared), suggest a time. And, without exception, she would cancel, offering a variety of flimsy excuses that simply didn't ring true. Invariably, she blamed some environmental project she was doing with Alicia.

Milly demolished a carefully swept-up pile of leaves with a particularly vicious left foot, earning herself a stare of disapproval from old Mrs North who was trussed up like a packaged chicken in a vile plastic see-through mac and what looked like an old-fashioned shower cap.

'Sorry,' Milly muttered bad-temperedly and with a complete lack of conviction. She had raging PMT which had left her with a swollen belly, a circle of unattractive red pimples on her chin and hair that was uncooperative and lank. Thank God she wasn't supposed to be seeing Freddie today. Grumpily, she rammed her hands into the pockets of her trendy red Top Shop coat.

What with India's distant behaviour and Freddie's proximity, Milly's life felt weirdly paradoxical at the moment and the extreme swings of emotions she was experiencing were leaving her utterly exhausted. Forget PMT, she was on a non-stop emotional rollercoaster, rearing joyously upwards one minute and thundering relentlessly downwards the next. On the one hand, she was spending vast amounts of time with Freddie as she helped him with his studies but although they were getting on like a house on fire, it was clear Freddie didn't fancy her. And India was such a rubbish best friend, she had no one to talk to about it. Claudette, a veritable limpet these days, could barely be torn away from Will and every spare second Tessa had away from filming seemed to be spent engrossed in this novel she was writing.

Milly sighed dramatically. Being close to Freddie was incredibly distracting: he only had to hold her gaze with those crushed blueberry eyes or brush his dark hair aside with those long, sensitive fingers and she was truly lost – but they had such fun, she often found herself laughing unguardedly in his presence and forgetting to assume a more sophisticated persona. And to give Freddie his due, he was embracing his studies wholeheartedly, even suggesting additional study sessions from time to time, although Milly knew this was because he was determined to get his father off his back once and for all.

By contrast, India was giving her the cold shoulder so forcibly Milly feared she might develop frostbite. India was fiercely protective of her private life and her behaviour was becoming increasingly odd as the weeks passed. Teachers were rapidly losing patience with her as she scrutinised her mobile phone and abruptly disappeared from lessons, seemingly suffering from every ailment under the sun, trotting out glib excuses without a care in the world.

It was all because of *bloody* Alicia, Milly thought sourly as she began the long walk down the driveway that led to Appleton Manor. The trees had shed all their leaves now, discarding them like colourful autumnal ornaments and leaving themselves exposed and spiky. The Virginia creeper covering the manor house was still a riot of colour, although the continuous rain had left it looking rather bedraggled, as if it were clinging to the walls for dear life.

Crabbily, Milly picked at one of the pimples on her chin. It irked her that her stupid brother was so caught up in Alicia but, grudgingly, Milly admitted that her adversary was appealing, in a physical sense, at least. Alicia had stunning auburn hair and creamy-white skin dappled with golden freckles. Aside from that, she had an enviably slender figure topped off with heavy breasts and sensual green eyes.

No wonder David was coming in his pants every weekend home from uni, Milly thought bitterly. He was in love, in lust and everything in between and it appeared that Alicia felt the same way. They spent every spare minute together and when they were apart, they ran up extortionate phone bills. It was enough to make Milly vomit but she knew she was just being a jealous bitch. If Freddie gave her the slightest encouragement, she knew she'd be as loved up as David and Alicia. But as far as India was concerned, what on earth was the attraction with Alicia? Unless India was sexually confused and Alicia happened to be bisexual, Milly really couldn't understand why they would spend so much time together.

Through the trees, she caught sight of a flash of auburn hair as she turned towards the manor. She felt her hackles rise. Speak of the bloody devil! Tripping prettily through the mountains of leaves, wearing a smart bottle-green coat in the softest cashmere and black leather riding boots, was Alicia. She was strolling as if she didn't have a care in the world. Without stopping to think, Milly picked up speed until she was at Alicia's side.

'Oh, you made me jump!' Alicia turned her heavy-lidded green eyes in Milly's direction. They were friendly and open but there was a hint of trepidation in them too. 'I've been hoping to bump into you, actually.'

'Really? Well, I want to speak to you about India,' Milly spat out heatedly. Close up, Alicia's colouring was stunning; the russet and amber tones of her hair complementing the malted-milk complexion perfectly. Her green eyes seemed impossibly languid and enticing and with a flash of envious appreciation, Milly knew Tristan would kill to capture Alicia's likeness on canvas.

'India Taylor-Knight? You want to talk about India?' Alicia

nervously brushed a luxurious lock of auburn hair like a fox's brush out of her eyes. She cast her eyes down, marking the ground tensely with the toe of her riding boot. 'I wasn't expecting you to say that.'

Mystified by Alicia's behaviour, Milly was lost for words.

'I thought you might want to talk about David . . .' Alicia's delicate amber eyebrows knitted together and her body language became awkward. 'And I want you to know that the last thing I want to do is offend you . . . I want us to be friends, truly.' She blinked as Milly narrowed her eyes to hostile slits at this statement. 'Please know that my feelings are serious. I'm not playing around with your brother.'

Milly didn't know what Alicia was going on about. 'I don't care about David! I'm talking about India, about stealing my best friend away from me. You're only doing a bloody project together, you don't have to spend every waking hour with her.'

'Er . . . I don't.' Alicia looked baffled. 'We finished that project ages ago. And I can assure you that any spare time I have I spend with David.'

Milly stared at her.

Alicia flushed slightly. 'I assumed you had some sort of problem with me because of him. I don't know what's going on with you and India but, really, it has nothing to do with me.'

Milly was beginning to feel very foolish. 'I-I don't understand. That means India's been lying through her teeth to me. If she hasn't been seeing you, who has she been seeing?' She cringed inwardly. How ridiculous did she sound, asking Alicia if she was running off with her best friend? It was mortifying and she wished the ground would swallow her up.

'Hey, don't feel bad,' Alicia said softly, her green eyes brimming with sympathy. 'I know what it's like to lose your best friend and you're not being silly at all. It's hurtful, you wouldn't be human if you weren't upset about it.'

Milly suddenly understood why David was so smitten with Alicia, her physical charms notwithstanding.

Alicia gave her a wise nod. 'The same thing happened to me when I was in the fourth year. My best friend seemed to forget I existed and kept ignoring me.'

'What happened?'

'She'd found herself a boyfriend. A married man, no less. Much more exciting than hanging round with me!' Alicia laughed and put her arm round Milly's shoulders. 'I'm not saying that's what's happened with India, but it's possible and it might explain why she's treating you like this. It's what happens when people have sex.' She blushed prettily. 'So I'm told, anyway.'

Their moment of bonding was interrupted by the arrival of David, back from uni and sporting a black, long-sleeved 'Fall Out Boy' T-shirt. He was joined by Freddie who had an inane grin on his face. His dark blue eyes lit up when they fell upon Milly. She shrank back from his gaze, immediately conscious of her less-than-perfect complexion and the way her jeans were straining to contain her bloated, pre-menstrual tummy.

'What's going on?' David asked suspiciously. He didn't trust his sister, not at the moment. She'd been acting like a total weirdo and had been unforgivably unfriendly towards Alicia which he had finally put down to some kind of twisted sibling jealousy. Whether Milly was pissed off with him for being happy or with Alicia for taking up his time, David hadn't a clue but his patience had been stretched to the limits.

'I just had a go at Alicia for no real reason,' Milly confessed shamefacedly, hardly daring to meet David's eyes. She'd never seen him looking so grown-up and formidable before. 'Well, actually, it was about India but it was totally out of order and I *have* said sorry . . .'

'God, you are so fucking *immature*!' David roared, exploding into a temper. 'How dare you tear into Alicia like that?

She's been terribly upset about the way you've been treating her.'

As Milly shrank back, Freddie glared at David furiously, opening his mouth to say something.

'*David!*' Embarrassed, Alicia grabbed his hand. 'Please stop. It's all sorted out now and there's no need for any of this.' Her tone was soothing and, like a candle splashed with water, David visibly cooled down. 'It's girls' stuff so nothing for you to worry about. And I completely understand why Milly was so upset. And we're friends now, aren't we?'

Milly nodded, horrified to feel tears trickling down her cheeks. 'I'm really sorry. I-I just wanted to f-find out what was happening with India but she's lied to me and it's nothing to do with Alicia at all . . .'

'So you froze her out for nothing,' David said sarcastically but his eyes softened when Alicia squeezed his fingers.

Milly nodded and felt gratified when Freddie slung his arm round her.

'It sounds as if this has all been a big mix up,' he said firmly, 'but it's done now and it's probably cleared the air. Are we all OK again? Good. Let's go and get some coffee, Mills, and leave the lovebirds to it.'

Freddie led Milly into the manor house. There were security men prowling around the front entrance in preparation for Clemmie and Rufus's wedding and the manor house was full of representatives from the catering company, all of whom were crossly being interrogated by security as if they were terrorists. Milly and Freddie headed for the kitchen which was reassuringly warm, the air fragrant with tantalising baking smells and plates of cookies.

Freddie flicked his dark hair out of his eyes. 'Don't think too badly of David. You're his kid sister but I think he still wants your approval.'

Milly heaved a sigh. 'I wish I wasn't such a bloody bitch all the time. Alicia is absolutely lovely – beautiful too. Everyone thinks so.' She gave Freddie a sideways look, hating herself for feeling so obviously insecure but he'd have to be blind if he hadn't noticed how gorgeous Alicia was.

'Not me. Alicia's a sexy girl but it's all those freckles . . .' He shuddered then tucked a strand of blond hair behind Milly's ear. 'Don't ever tell David but redheads just don't do it for me.'

Milly beamed stupidly then felt her spirits plummet as she remembered how much Freddie fancied Tessa. Seemingly blondes didn't do it for him either; brunettes were more his bag.

Freddie helped himself to a cookie from the table. 'So, what do you think India is up to? Do you think she has a boyfriend? A married man or someone really old, perhaps? Perhaps he's a total minger and she's ashamed to tell you about him.' He frowned when his phone buzzed. 'It's one of my old clients wanting some more dope. I haven't told any of them yet but I'm kind of putting all that on the back burner for now.' His eyelashes swept down so his eyes were unreadable.

Milly was startled. 'I thought you were . . . I thought it was . . . you said you didn't want to give it up. You said . . . you would only do it if a beautiful woman wanted you to.'

'So I did.' He met her eyes for the briefest of seconds, seconds that were loaded with meaning. He put his hand on her arm as if he was about to say something then turned his head as Henny approached carrying a tray of canapés. Quickly Freddie removed his hand, leaving a searing imprint behind. 'Wow, Mrs H, you're looking stunning. Someone's making you smile.' Giving Milly a pointed wink, he left the room.

Milly couldn't even think straight. What did Freddie mean? He couldn't seriously be saying he was giving up his business, not after everything he'd said to her that day in the café. For one glorious moment, she thought he might have been hinting that it had something to do with her. But that couldn't be true.

He saw her as a friend, nothing more. God, maybe it was some other girl who had made him give it all up. That would be truly unbearable.

Glancing at her mother distractedly, Milly was shocked. She was wearing a pretty shirt with frilly cuffs teamed with jeans. *Jeans!* Milly had never seen her in jeans before and she looked ten years younger. Not only that, her normally frizzy sandy-coloured hair looked softer and it was pinned up with tendrils hanging round her face. Milly walked round her wonderingly, realising it was high time she made her apologies.

Henny didn't notice Milly's scrutiny. 'I never thought I'd say this but I'll be delighted when these bloody weddings are out of the way. I was nearly frisked by a security man just then!' She proffered a tray piled high with miniature doughnuts like a mountain of profiteroles. 'Try one of these, darling. Blissful, even if I do say so myself.'

Mindful of her diet but unable to resist, Milly took one. It was light and sugary and a burst of cinnamon custard exploded into her mouth. She knew the moment was right for her to apologise to her mother but she couldn't help shying away from it. 'They're fantastic. Are they for Clemmie's wedding?'

Henny set the tray down, her lips pursed. 'Actually, they're for Sophie and Gil's wedding. If it goes ahead,' she added darkly.

'I know, it sucks, doesn't it?' Milly agreed with feeling. 'Poor Tristan. I hope he manages to get Sophie to change her mind.'

'I quite agree. I have nothing against Gil but Tristan and Sophie – they're meant to be together, aren't they?' Henny eyed her daughter carefully. 'How are things going with you and Freddie?'

Milly's head snapped up. 'What? Who?'

Henny smiled, her rosy cheeks dimpling. 'Darling, I do know that you have feelings for him. I don't blame you either, he's such a hunk! Lovely manners and such a cheeky glint in his eye.'

'Mother!' Milly burst out laughing.

'Darling, I know you think I'm past it, but I can assure you, I have plenty of life left in me!'

It was the perfect moment to say something. Milly forced herself to speak, scared that the words would come out wrong. 'Look, about that . . . I've said some awful things to you and I'm so sorry.'

Thrown off course, Henny didn't know what to say.

Milly ploughed ahead. 'Those things I said about us moving here and about Daddy dying.' The words came out in a rush. 'I know it wasn't your fault and I know I had no right to make you feel guilty about us moving back here. I was just being selfish and immature and I didn't once stop to think about how you might be suffering. And as for saying you're too old to date someone, that was just horrible of me and I didn't mean it one bit . . .'

Milly's words petered out as Henny yanked her into a hug. 'Hush, darling, that's quite enough! I know you've had a hard time. I forgive you because I know you're a softie underneath all that attitude.'

'Thanks, Mum.' Milly rubbed her fist across her eyes. 'And you were right about me liking Freddie. But it's hopeless, he doesn't even know I exist.'

Henny cocked an eyebrow. 'I wouldn't be too sure about that, darling. I think he is very aware of your existence. And while we're on the subject, you should know that I've been seeing someone since the summer party. Barnaby Wellham-Cooper?'

Milly vaguely remembered a silver-haired man in a smart blazer.

'Well, anyway, I said no when he asked me out but he kept asking and Tessa and Will kept saying I deserved to be happy and that I should stand up for what I wanted more.' Henny went all shy. 'So I went for it! Barnaby's a widower so we have tons in common and he treats me like an absolute queen. Not unlike the way your father did, actually. He's a very sweet man, Milly. I do hope you like him because . . . because I think this might be something rather special.'

Out of nowhere, Milly felt a stab of disappointment that she seemed to be the only one who hadn't found someone special. Pushing the ungracious thought away, she immediately gave her mother a hug.

'I'm so pleased for you,' she said, meaning it with all her heart. 'You really deserve to be adored by someone. And I'm so sorry I've been such a bitch.'

Tessa was standing outside the B&B with JB who was chain-smoking his smelly French cigarettes like a man possessed. Fed up with covering for him and enduring Jilly's glowing comments about JB's directing style, Tessa had decided it was high time she confronted him about his absences. She found his attitude puzzling. He seemed to be almost lost in a world of his own but he was seriously on edge, his dark eyes darting around the car park crazily.

'You've missed filming on and off for well over a month now,' she howled at him accusingly. 'The crew are getting restless and I'm winging it like a nutter, doing two jobs at once and not getting a single bit of credit for it.'

JB's swarthy face tightened for a moment. For a second, he looked as if he might apologise then thought better of it and clammed up again.

Furious, Tessa wanted to shake him. 'You were the one who told me I shouldn't get too close, remember? But you're the one hopping into bed with a Forbes-Henry when you should be working.' She put her hands on her hips and went for the jugular. She knew how much JB hated being accused of being unprofessional but, right now, he deserved it. He was letting everyone down and it was about time someone told him the truth. 'You've got a bloody nerve telling me to keep my distance, JB! You're so loved up you can't even do your job properly.'

'Loved up? I wouldn't call it that.' JB's lip curled as he sent a spiral of blue-grey smoke into the air. He didn't react to the comment about doing his job badly. 'Caro is a passionate woman,' he added impassively. 'Rather . . . demanding.'

'I don't give a shit about Caro!' Tessa yelled, losing patience with him. 'You're not being fair to me or the crew, JB. If you don't want to do the job any more, phone Jilly up and tell her. Or get your bloody act together and turn up when you're supposed to. I'm sick of covering for you, do you understand?'

Not seeming to have heard her, JB lit another cigarette with an abrupt snap of his Zippo lighter. Obscurely, he said, 'They are a complex family, *n'est-ce pas*? But then . . . families are like that.'

'I wouldn't know.' Tessa frowned at him. It was the first time he had ever mentioned his family or, in fact, anything about his personal life.

JB regarded her. 'The brothers . . . Tristan and Will. Do they get on?'

She shrugged. 'Very well, I think. They're rather over-protective of each other, at any rate. And very loyal. I think they're good friends as much as brothers.'

'Good for them. Not all brothers are like that.'

Tessa detected bitterness in his voice. 'You have brothers?'

JB spat smoke out of his mouth in disgust and tossed his dark curls. 'One. But I cannot stand the sight of 'im.'

'Why not?'

'We used to be friends, he and I, but we 'ave not spoken for years. There is, as they say, no love lost between us.' JB gazed past her, his mouth twisted in a contemptuous sneer. 'Fabrice is dead to me now.'

'Did you row?'

'Something like that.' JB let out a mirthless laugh. 'And some things can never be forgiven. No, I will never speak to Fabrice again. *Salaud!*' he muttered furiously as he hurled his cigarette to the ground like a dagger. He glanced over his shoulder, a fleeting look of guilt in his eyes. 'I 'ave some things to do but I will finish the documentary, all right?' He looked lost in his thoughts again, seeming to have forgotten Tessa's existence. He made an ambiguous gesture with his hands. 'Just cover for me for a bit longer . . . I think that is all I will need.' He headed inside, leaving Tessa staring after him wordlessly.

Chapter Twenty-Two

Clemmie was rapidly falling apart. Traumatised after recalling her awful past to Tessa, she was also finding the wedding too much to handle. Slamming the phone down on another journalist who thought her impending wedding gave him the right to intrude on her personal life at any hour of the day, Clemmie was close to tears and even closer to the edge. Paparazzi had taken up residence outside the house, their long-distance lenses trained on every window and door. The phone rang morning, noon and night with journalists desperate to get an exclusive. Requests for interviews were shoved through the letter box, despite the high security around the house, and Clemmie lived in fear of someone managing to get in somehow.

Surrounded by wedding flowers, acceptance cards with greetings from celebrity friends like Brad Pitt and Angelina Jolie, Clemmie was beginning to feel as if she couldn't go through with the whole fiasco. Rufus had been conspicuous by his absence for the entire morning, a normal occurrence for him these days. She had no idea where he went when he headed out and suspected the truth would be far from palatable but it was getting to the stage where she was going to have to confront him, regardless of the outcome. Whenever Rufus was present, he declined to be involved in the wedding, alternating between affable disinterest and tight-lipped irritation, depending on his mood.

Clemmie sank down amongst the bouquets of deep red roses Henny had instructed the florist to send over for her to choose from. Her heart ached with pain. Didn't Rufus realise half of Hollywood was due to arrive in a matter of weeks? The Cruises and the Beckhams were due to fly in on their private jet, as were the Travoltas. Paparazzi had secured every available B&B room, each one hopeful of getting the money shot, even if it meant behaving like depraved animals. They had no idea what day the wedding had been booked for but they knew it was in December and Clemmie was mobbed wherever she went.

Rufus's parents were beside themselves with delight that the wedding was looming. They were due back from Portugal shortly to 'soak up the atmosphere', as they put it. And Clemmie's personal team – her version of family – were due the following week: her agent, her PA, her stylist, her hairdresser, her advisers, her personal bodyguard – the people she had gladly, willingly left behind when she moved to England, so desperate was she to avoid the media circus that was her life. The team had only remained in the States for so long because Clemmie had bombarded them with requests to liaise with security and track down elusive items she *had* to have for her big day. If truth be known, Clemmie was keeping them at arm's length for as long as possible because she was desperate to clear the air with Rufus. For all she knew, this wedding might not even take place . . .

Her lawyers had drawn up an aggressive pre-nup that she hadn't had the guts to discuss with Rufus, let alone get him to sign. Clemmie was worth a fortune, perhaps more so than Rufus realised. She owned properties in LA, Miami, the south of France, Tuscany and New York and she had countless investments which kept her millions ticking over healthily and made sure she – and any dependents – would want for nothing in their old age. Clemmie wasn't sure Rufus cared too much about her money; his family were peers and he received a staggering monthly allowance even he struggled to fritter away. He had so much inheritance coming to him, he could buy his own island if he fancied it. But there were more pressing issues than pre-nups at hand.

Tremulously, Clemmie crushed the velvety petals of the red Grand Prix roses between her fingers, feeling sick as she thought about the receipt she had found. She had been pretending it didn't exist but the sight of it was burnt on her consciousness.

Clemmie forced herself to confront a few questions she had been avoiding. What was Rufus playing at? Did he love her? Would he stick around if she wasn't so famous? Deep down, she already knew the answer to the last question and it was humiliating to face it head on. She tossed the roses to one side, crying out as a stray thorn tore into her finger. She watched, mesmerised, as blood dripped on to her lap, deriving an odd sense of relief from the sight. No wonder people self-harmed if this was the blissful sense of release it gave them . . .

Horrified, Clemmie pulled herself together. What was she thinking? She wasn't about to go down that path. She rummaged around in the kitchen drawer for a plaster, clueless as to where to find such a thing. Without even meaning to, she dragged the incriminating receipt out again, drawn to it like a moth to a flame. Tiffany's had always been one of her favourite stores because it reminded her of old-style glamour and romance. But now it had taken on a whole new meaning. Overwhelmed by the thought of Rufus's betrayal, Clemmie read the words again: . . . 'diamond necklace, a solitaire on a gold filigree chain'. She sucked her breath in. The necklace had been purchased back in July and Rufus hadn't presented her with any such gift. That wasn't what convinced her Rufus had bought the necklace for someone else, however; it was something else entirely.

'Christ, it's like getting into Fort Knox out there.' Rufus arrived and made her jump. He looked peeved that he was able to come and go when he pleased, proving once and for all that Clemmie was the only one the paparazzi were interested in. He had a cap pulled down over his eyes and she noticed his eyeliner was smudged underneath his dark eyes, the way it always looked after they had sex. Nausea rose to the surface.

Rufus ripped open a packet of salt and vinegar crisps and started devouring them. He glanced at Clemmie. She was wearing a cream tracksuit which looked as if it had cost an extortionate amount of money and her hair was pulled back in a ponytail, which made her beautiful cheekbones more pronounced. He noticed her tracksuit was spattered with blood and saw that her finger was encrusted with congealing red goo. 'What's the matter? Are you hurt?'

'Very.' Her voice broke and she fought to control herself.

'What's wrong?'

'Who is she?'

'Who?'

'The girl you're screwing. Who is she?' Clemmie congratulated herself on sounding so calm and collected, despite the vomit she could sense was only seconds away from making an appearance. Sometimes, being an Oscar-winning actress came in very useful, but there was only so long she could keep the act up in her private life.

'Clemmie, I have no idea what you're talking about.' Not sure where this accusation had come from, Rufus decided exasperation was the best tack and he rolled his eyes laconically for good measure. He sensed Clemmie meant business; her set jaw and hard eyes indicated how close she was to losing her temper.

She held the receipt from Tiffany's in front of his nose. 'I'll make myself clearer, Rufus, because you seem to need clarification. Who did you buy the diamond necklace for?'

'Oh *that*!' Rufus let out a laugh of genuine relief. A Tiffany necklace was something he could explain away, no sweat. 'Well, you've spoilt it now, haven't you, darling? I bought that to give you on our wedding day but it's not going to be much of a surprise now, is it?'

385

Clemmie calmly laid the receipt on the kitchen worktop, smoothing out the edges with infinite care. 'I'm going to give you one last chance,' she said in a scarily quiet voice. 'And if you lie to me again, I swear to you, Rufus, you will regret it.'

'Clemmie, really, this is intolerable.' He assumed a hurt expression and took off his cap to give her the full benefit of his puppy dog eyes. He hoped she didn't get too close; he reeked of India because he hadn't had a chance to have a shower before he left.

'Stop it!' she snapped icily. 'You had your chance.' She turned away from him unsteadily, not trusting herself to look at him again. With her back to him still, she turned her head slightly, her mouth quivering with emotion. 'The next time you intend to pass off one of your girlfriend's gifts as mine, you might want to remember that I never wear gold. Ever. I'm allergic to it, as you well know.' She took a few unsteady steps away from him and paused. 'If you continue with this affair, Rufus, we're over, do you understand?'

She headed for the bathroom, her dignified walk becoming an urgent dash as she realised she couldn't hold the vomit down any longer.

Rufus swallowed a handful of crisps and almost choked. How could he have been so stupid? The receipt Clemmie had found was for the necklace he had bought India for her birthday – a tiny diamond on a delicate gold chain. Rufus cursed himself. He had gone too far; he was sure of it. Clemmie had never threatened to end their relationship before and he was absolutely sure she meant what she said. Clemmie was easy-going in the extreme but he suspected she had a backbone of steel beneath the drawling Texan tones and the good-natured smile. She had hinted that she had been through some difficult times to get where she was and although he had never asked what she meant, Rufus believed her.

What was he going to do? India was becoming increasingly

clingy, demanding more and more of his time. She had sent him three texts since he had left her half an hour ago – stalker behaviour by anyone's standards but she was so good for his ego. Rufus had no idea how long he would stay with her. India, with her ginger hair and the fake tan she left smeared all over the bed sheets, was a reality TV star to Clemmie's Hollywood royalty.

But was India worth losing Clemmie over? No way. He loved the danger of his relationship with India but he loved his life with Clemmie more – that and the promise of more work and fame.

Rufus fingered the Tiffany receipt and leant back against the worktop. The trouble was, he had always been one to have his cake and eat it. He just needed to be more careful, that was all. He suspected India lived in hope of him dumping Clemmie before the wedding but he wasn't prepared to do that – not for India, at any rate. She wasn't a patch on Clemmie, however good she was in bed.

Still, every time Rufus remembered his wedding, the blood pounded round his body as if Formula One cars were using his veins as a racetrack. The very thought of standing up in front of Clemmie's celebrity friends – in front of his own parents for that matter, in a matter of weeks – filled Rufus with absolute terror. The kind that made his mouth feel as if it was filled with cotton wool balls and made his head throb with the intensity of a tequila shot hangover.

What did he want? Did he want to be single again and lose Clemmie altogether? He didn't think so. But India or someone like her and all the fun that came with such a relationship, it was tempting in the extreme and he wasn't sure he could give her up – not just yet.

Shredding the Tiffany receipt into tiny pieces in frustration, Rufus was buggered if he knew what to do next.

* * *

Tessa spotted her pashmina slung over the banisters in the hallway and grabbed it. She knew she'd left it in the manor somewhere. The rain had held off for the past week, thankfully, but as it was now November, there was a distinct chill in the air and she needed all the layers she could get. She looked up as Henny came charging down the stairs.

'Bloody, bloody Caro!' she stormed, looking enraged. 'Sorry, Tessa . . . I just can't believe that woman.'

'What's she done now?'

'Given me a dressing down for not washing a stain out of the white jeans she was wearing on her latest . . . *date* with JB. Honestly, she's the absolute limit! Poor Jack is drinking himself stupid over the whole affair and Caro doesn't care one little bit. What does she see in that JB chap anyway? I don't trust him . . . his eyes are too close together.'

Tessa suppressed a smile. 'I don't know about his eyes being too close together but he's certainly not reliable, that's for sure. When I spoke to him about missing filming all the time, he didn't even seem bothered about it. He just kept going on about families and some long-lost brother he doesn't speak to any more.'

'Really?' Henny's brows knitted together suspiciously. 'I wonder what that's all about.'

'God knows. I just wish he'd get his act together.'

Henny couldn't agree more. She caught sight of Gil and Nathan chatting and drinking herbal tea together on the lawn and jerked her head in their direction. 'You know I hate to gossip, Tess, but when I was in the village shop yesterday, I overheard Mrs North saying there was a rumour going round that Nathan is bisexual. What do you think?'

Tessa studied Nathan's biceps vaguely. 'It's possible, I suppose. Can't say I've ever really thought about it. Mind you, with a body like that, it's probably criminal to limit yourself to one sex, isn't it?' She giggled but Henny didn't join in. She was too busy watching Gil beaming like an idiot as Nathan talked about his plans for the prize-winning rhododendron bushes.

Leaving her to it, Tessa was about to go back to her cottage when she caught sight of Claudette on her hands and knees in the library. Loath to interrupt her, particularly in view of their previous, hostile encounter, Tessa was, nonetheless, intrigued as to what Claudette was up to.

The top drawer of the big bureau by the window was open and papers were scattered all over the floor. Claudette, dressed in a pair of dark jeans and one of her many cashmere jumpers, was rummaging through the paperwork with rapid hand movements, as if she was looking for something in particular. She discarded some yellowing papers covered in ink blotches and tucked her small hands further into the back of the drawer to tug at something that was stuck there.

Tessa was nonplussed. She remembered David saying he needed his birth certificate for university and Henny retrieving it from the bureau, telling Tessa the family kept all their private family documents in there under lock and key. Only she and Will had keys for it and they never let them out of their sight, by all accounts.

Speechlessly, Tessa watched Claudette pull free the stash of papers that had been trapped at the back of the drawer. These were newer-looking and appeared to be headed notepaper of the sort used by a hospital or a solicitor. Claudette's face lit up with excitement at the sight of them. Before she could stop herself, Tessa let out a gasp and Claudette's dark head snapped up like a rattlesnake's.

'*Bordel!*'

Tessa jumped.

'I was . . . looking for something.' Claudette casually slotted the papers back in the drawer but her hands shook as she did so. 'Will asked me to find some papers for 'im.' She locked the drawer and pocketed the tiny key with a careless shrug.

'Will asked you to look for private family papers?'

Claudette swept past her elegantly, wafting exotic cologne. 'But I am practically family, *oui*?' She made a show of flashing the tasteful diamond ring Will had given her under Tessa's nose.

'So you are.' Tessa smiled easily but she couldn't help thinking Claudette was being untruthful. Her jerky mannerisms, her shifty eyes and the way she had guiltily scooped all the papers back into the desk as soon as she had seen Tessa suggested Claudette was up to something. But why on earth would she be snooping in the Forbes-Henry family paperwork?

'I would prefer it if you kept this to yourself,' Claudette said, fixing her brown eyes on Tessa coolly. 'This is something between Will and myself so please stay out of it.'

'Of course.' Tessa watched her sashay out of the room. Something about what had happened didn't quite sit right with her. For a moment, she wondered if she should mention it to Will but decided against it. He wouldn't welcome any level of criticism about his fiancée – certainly not from her, anyway.

No, it was best left alone, Tessa decided firmly. Will's personal life was nothing whatsoever to do with her; as far as she was concerned, Claudette could rummage around in the family's personal effects to her heart's content.

As Tessa headed back to her cottage, she received a phone call from Sophie asking her to be a bridesmaid at her Christmas Eve wedding.

'Of course, thank you . . . but seriously, are you still actually going to marry Gil?' she said. Clapping a hand over her mouth, she was appalled that she'd blurted the comment out. Sophie rang off rather frostily and, catching sight of Will pacing next to the lake, his broad shoulders tense as he screamed irritably at someone down the phone, Tessa put her head down and made herself scarce.

* * *

Tristan was excruciatingly bored. He didn't have any more commissions until January and he was at a loose end. Will was busy with Claudette and the hotel renovations, Tessa couldn't be dragged away from her blessed notepad when she wasn't filming and Tristan was buggered if he was going to speak to Sophie. With no one to play with, he was driving Henny nuts wandering around the manor like a spare part and poking around in the boxes of Christmas decorations she had extracted from the loft. After breaking four hand-blown baubles and almost knocking a whole shelf of Henny's homemade pickles on the floor while he rummaged through the pantry, Henny finally lost patience with him and shooed him out.

'For God's sake, Tristan! Go and cause havoc somewhere else,' she chided him. 'You're about as much use as a chocolate teapot at the moment.'

Tristan looked hurt. 'I was only looking for some Jaffa cakes,' he said woefully.

Full of compassion, Henny put a motherly hand on his cheek. Wearing a pair of slouchy jeans flecked with paint and a big cream sweater and with his blond hair tousled and overlong, he looked like a fallen angel. He had bruised shadows under his eyes from not sleeping and there was fine golden stubble on his chin.

She brushed a curl out of his eyes. 'We all know why you're mooching round the house like this. And it has nothing to do with Jaffa cakes. You're pining for Sophie and feeling sorry for yourself. I don't mean to be hard on you, darling, but isn't it about time you made it up with her?' Her face softened as she saw Tristan's blue eyes cloud over. Catching sight of Gil and Nathan strolling through the grounds, nattering away like best buddies, she did something she rarely did and meddled like mad. 'Darling, Gil seems to be neglecting Sophie shamefully at the moment. She would probably welcome a chat with you.'

Tristan hesitated.

Henny went for it. 'Look, why not give Sophie a call? She must be as confused as you are about this situation but perhaps she thinks you don't want to see her. And what have you got to lose, Tris? Don't let history repeat itself, darling, it's not worth it.'

Her words hit home. Tristan wiped the glum expression from his face and his blue eyes started to sparkle like lit candles. 'You're right, Aunt Hen. What am I doing? I should be with Sophie, telling her how much I love her. If she loves that . . . that odd little man,' he gestured to Gil facetiously, 'there's nothing I can do about it. But if I don't try, I'll never know, will I?'

'That's the spirit.' Henny gave him a gentle but encouraging shove. 'Now, get out of my kitchen, will you, and don't you dare touch anything on the way out.'

Tristan grinned. 'I'm going, I'm going.' Dashing to the front door, he was taken aback to receive a text message from Tessa. It said: 'Don't panic but go to Cooper Ward in St Agnes Hospital. Sophie urgently needs you.'

Without stopping to think, Tristan tugged his car keys out of his pocket and charged outside to the garage. His old yellow MG hadn't been driven since late summer and the engine was freezing cold. Wasting valuable seconds turning the engine over and over, Tristan briefly wondered if he should borrow his father's Rolls-Royce Phantom. Knowing he would probably drive like a maniac in it and prang it, he persevered with his MG.

Speeding towards the hospital, his heart crashing uncontrollably in his chest, Tristan started praying. Please God, don't say I'm going to lose her, he begged. Not now . . . not now I've found her again. I couldn't bear it. Please don't let it be too late, he pleaded through gritted teeth.

Somehow making it to the hospital without incident, Tristan parked his car illegally on the double yellow lines near the car park and ran to the reception area, his eyes darting over the myriad signs until he found the one for Cooper Ward.

Speeding through the corridors like a madman, he didn't even notice the brightly coloured walls and piles of toys and teddy bears on the ward, instead whipping his head around for someone to speak to. Seconds later, he realised he didn't need to; huddled in the corner, wearing a blood-stained grey tracksuit, her face pale and streaked with tears, was Sophie, with a white-faced Tessa sitting next to her.

'Oh my God, you're all right!' Tristan threw his arms round Sophie and rained kisses on to her hair. He breathed in the smell of her, holding her tightly as he felt her sob against him, her hands clutching at him as if she couldn't bear to let go.

Tessa stood up and gave Tristan a meaningful look. 'I'll leave you to it,' she said, giving Sophie a reassuring nod. 'You have . . . things to talk about.' Quietly, she left.

Her words didn't register with Tristan who was busy murmuring into Sophie's hair, stroking her shoulders in relief. Under his sweater, he could feel a cold trickle of sweat sliding down his back. She was all right . . . Sophie was *all right*. The dreadful images racing around his head since he had received the text slowly started to dissipate. Images of Sophie hooked up to machines, being wheeled out of theatre flanked by stony-faced surgeons telling him bad news – shocking things he had hardly dared to allow himself to face, thankfully began to fade.

Finally, Sophie pulled away from Tristan. Her brown eyes were downcast and she didn't seem to be able to stop trembling.

'What happened?' Tristan asked gently, worried to see her so agitated. 'Have you been in an accident?'

She shook her head and tried to speak but she couldn't find the words. Tristan no longer cared that Sophie had thought badly of him over the situation with Anna, nor that she thought him capable of cheating on her. The thought of losing her had made his concerns for his wounded pride seem fatuous and all he cared about now was letting her know how much he still loved her. He started to tell her how he felt but she silenced him.

'I wasn't the one who had an accident today.'

'You weren't? Who then?'

Sophie gulped down her fear. 'It was Ruby. She . . . she had an accident. She was on her bike and she was hit by a car.' She closed her eyes and forced herself to speak. 'Ruby is my five-year-old daughter, Tristan.'

Tristan's mouth fell open. 'You have a daughter? Oh my God . . . why didn't you say so before . . .' His expression changed and he abruptly let go of Sophie's hands. The significance of her words began to dawn on him and the acute shock turned his face ashen. 'A *five*-year-old daughter? *Jesus*.' His eyes searched out Sophie's accusingly. 'Am I her father?' When she didn't answer, he lost his temper. 'Am I her fucking father, Sophie?'

Flinching at the terrible expression on Tristan's face, Sophie gave a slight nod. Before Tristan had a chance to react, a doctor emerged from the room.

'Ruby's going to be just fine,' he said with a bright smile.

Tristan stood up. Now he knew what people meant when they said their legs felt like jelly. He gripped the wall for support. 'Are you sure? Are you sure she's . . . Ruby's going to be all right?' He turned the unfamiliar name over in his mouth.

'And you are?' The doctor regarded him coolly.

'I'm . . . I'm her father,' Tristan said, running his hand through his unkempt hair. He couldn't even look at Sophie who was silently weeping into her hands. Was she crying out of relief that her daughter . . . *their* daughter was going to be all right? Or was it because she must know she had lost him forever? He stared at her, wondering if he had ever known her.

The doctor's tone and manner changed. 'Oh, I'm so sorry, I didn't realise. Well, you'll be delighted to know Ruby is on the mend. She's suffered minor concussion and we were concerned it might be more serious but she's going to be as right as rain.'

Tristan couldn't get his head round anything that was being said but somewhere in the recesses of his mind, he understood that Ruby, his own flesh and blood, was out of danger.

'There's nothing to worry about?'

'Not a thing.'

'Thanks. Thanks very much.' Once the doctor was out of earshot, Tristan turned furious eyes towards Sophie. 'How could you? How could you keep something like this from me? This is so fucking unfair, Sophie, I can't even find the words to tell you. Fucking hell, a *daughter*?' His mind felt hazy, as if he was drunk. 'We had a daughter and you didn't even tell me?'

Sophie was, quite literally, incapable of articulating. She was shocked to the core by Tristan's reaction. He looked gutted, grief-stricken, and the accusing look in his eyes tore her apart.

He turned away from her. 'I have to leave.'

'P-please don't.' She grasped his fingers; they felt cold.

'Please don't touch me, Sophie. I can't bear it. I can never forgive you for this. Never.' Tristan shook Sophie's hand off and stalked away from her.

Arriving seconds later with Nathan in tow, Gil rushed to Sophie's side.

'Is Ruby all right? We got here as soon as we could but some idiot had parked their MG right across the entrance to the car park.'

Unable to bear it, Sophie tore herself away from him and burst into hysterical sobs. Bemused, Nathan caught Gil's eye over the top of Sophie's head. They couldn't understand what was wrong with her. If the prognosis was good and Ruby was on the mend, what was the problem?

* * *

Tearing a ticket off his windscreen and driving like a maniac back to his cottage, Tristan strode into his studio and, without hesitation, dragged a portrait of Sophie from its hiding place. It was his favourite painting of her; it had been completed over the sensual summer they had spent together, at the height of their love affair. He had been obsessed with her, passionately in love, and, consumed by his muse, he had spent day and night capturing her image. The portrait was so evocative, he could practically inhale the scent of cut grass and the warm, sensual aroma of her skin as the sun beat down on her. His eyes traced the line of her long, graceful limbs, intoxicated, as ever, by the perfect line of her elegantly arched legs and the vulnerable, exposed throat. He had painted Sophie wrapped only in a length of daffodil-yellow silk which preserved her dignity but drew the eye to the curves beneath it.

The look in her eyes was pure Sophie, loving and honest, inside and out. But that wasn't who she was, not any more. Bubbling with incandescent rage, Tristan pulled out a penknife and in one fluid movement slashed the portrait from top to bottom. Sinking to his knees, he felt empty and consumed with regret. Indescribably sad, Tristan bowed his head in utter desolation. Part of him wanted to rush to his daughter's side and get to know her and make up for lost time – and part of him couldn't even bear to acknowledge her existence.

As for Sophie . . . he finally understood everything. Had Sophie been pregnant when she walked in on Anna making a play for him? Was that why she had come home early from London – to tell him? Probably. And her unwavering gratitude towards Gil, the man she was indebted to, was now painfully obvious – Gil must have taken pity on Sophie when she was alone and about to have another man's child. Who wouldn't feel beholden in those circumstances?

He looked outside. November was usually such a beautiful month at Appleton Manor, but today the view seemed bleak.

The trees, stripped of their leaves, looked stark and bare and the heavy rainfall was turning the lawns into mud baths. The autumnal leaves were now just piles of sodden foliage, their colours muted by the weather.

Angrily shoving the slashed portrait to one side, Tristan put his head in his hands. If only he could cry. Then at least he wouldn't have to deal with the crushing sensation in his chest which felt as if his heart was being gripped by an iron fist. He was sure he might feel a grudging respect for Sophie and what she had endured once the dust had settled. But right now?

Tristan fixed his eyes on the slashed portrait. Right now, he never wanted to see her again.

Chapter Twenty-Three

Tessa glanced at Clemmie worriedly as she pulled into Clemmie's driveway and almost knocked down a small group of demented paparazzi. They shook their fists and cameras at her before realising Clemmie was in the car and began to jostle for pole position. Tessa's Audi was swiftly followed by Joe the cameraman's van and the crew, which screeched to a halt beside them, showering the paps with driveway gravel.

'Are you sure you're up to this?'

Clemmie nodded absent-mindedly. Her dark hair was pulled into a messy bun and she wore hardly any make-up, not even her trademark red lipstick. She still looked flawlessly beautiful but there was a haunted look in her eyes and she was painfully thin. Her body had lost all its curves; her waist had disappeared almost to nothing and her hips seemed narrow and boyish. She wore a black wool dress that was undeniably stylish but it drained her of colour.

Tessa wished there was something she could do to help Clemmie. It was a cliché but she was a shadow of her former self. Filming was due to be completed at the manor house and, predictably, Rufus had advised he might be very late, saying he was in London for the day having a fitting for his wedding suit. Not a single member of the camera crew believed this, especially since Rufus seemed to have had more suit fittings than the average groom, but out of respect for Clemmie they were all going along with the subterfuge. Having discovered that most of the journalists who had been crowding round her house had now decided to decamp and follow her to Appleton Manor, Clemmie had tentatively asked if they could go back home where she felt safer. Rufus was unaware of the change of plans but no one expected him to make an appearance anyway.

Inside the house, Clemmie was twitching nervously as Susie the make-up artist did her best with bronzer and highlighter powder. As she gave Clemmie's pallid cheeks a final flick of the blusher brush before giving up, Tessa watched Clemmie feverishly checking her phone for the seventieth time that morning. The house was in a mess. The floor was littered with dummy flower arrangements, piles of acceptance cards and boxes of unopened wedding shoes, and even though it probably looked much like most expectant brides' houses did a few weeks before a wedding, there was an air of frozen desperation about the place, as if the very idea of an actual wedding taking place was surreal and unlikely.

'He bought a diamond necklace, did I tell you?' Clemmie's words came out in a jumble. 'A necklace that wasn't for me but he denied it. I asked him to stop seeing her . . . this girl, whoever she is, but I don't think he has. If he had, he'd be here, wouldn't he?' She lifted troubled hazel eyes towards Tessa.

Tessa was saved from having to respond by the shock arrival of Rufus's parents, looking tanned and full of vitality courtesy of their trip to Portugal.

'Clemmie, how wonderful to see you again!' Lady Pemberton gave Clemmie a warm hug, ending up with bronze smears all over her pristine white suit. Her wide, green eyes lit up with pleasure at the sight of her prospective daughter-in-law. 'We're so excited about the wedding, I can't tell you.'

Joe immediately switched his camera on and gestured for his sound and lighting crew to get into place. He wasn't sure if Rufus's parents were worth filming but he didn't want to miss anything that might give the documentary more colour.

'Delightful to see you,' Lord Pemberton said, going slightly red the way he always did in Clemmie's presence. He squinted as one of the studio lights nearly blinded him. 'Er . . . do forgive us for turning up unannounced like this, Clemmie, but we . . . er . . . we have a wonderful wedding present for you and we couldn't wait to present it to you both.'

'That's so kind of you,' Clemmie managed, her Texan accent, as ever, more pronounced when she was distressed. 'The thing is, Rufus isn't . . . he isn't here at the moment. And I'm not sure when he'll be back.'

'Let's phone him,' Lord Pemberton suggested swiftly, holding up a shiny mobile phone. 'I'm not very good with all this new technology but Rufus programmed all the numbers for me so I more or less just have to press and talk, heh, heh!'

Clemmie gave him a tight smile. 'I'm afraid there's no point. I've tried him several times this morning and there's been no answer . . .'

Stopping mid-flow, her mouth fell open as Rufus's distinctive phone ring could be heard upstairs. Cocking her ear at the ceiling, Clemmie's face crumpled. The film crew exchanged glances and Lord and Lady Pemberton raised their eyebrows.

'I thought you said he wasn't here,' Lady Pemberton ventured, glancing at her husband in bemusement. 'Did he leave his phone behind, perhaps?'

Knowing Rufus never went anywhere without his mobile, Clemmie didn't answer. As pale as a ghost, she slid off her chair and, followed hotly by the film crew, raced upstairs. Tessa dashed after her, dread seeping through her insides. For once, Rufus's parents forgot their impeccable manners and tore after them.

Looking like a woman possessed, Clemmie yanked open the door to the main bedroom. Tessa rushed in behind her, furious when Joe bumped into her and whacked her on the back of the head with his camera. About to tear a strip off him, she spun round as Clemmie let out an unholy howl.

Set against a backdrop of Clemmie's expensive face creams and red-carpet dresses wrapped in plastic was a horrific sight. Rufus was sprawled across the bed stark bollock naked, his coiffed dark hair streaked with sweat. His hands were tied to the corners of the four-poster bed and he was being ridden vigorously by a nubile young girl with long ginger hair that fell past the cleft of her bottom. The girl was clearly engrossed in the task in hand; she was bouncing up and down on Rufus's cock like a porn star, letting out breathy, rapturous gasps of ecstasy.

Rufus opened his eyes at the sound of Clemmie's voice, his face suddenly white with shock. He gabbled something incoherent and tried to pull his arms free but the girl didn't notice and kept up her rhythmic bouncing.

'Clemmie . . . what are you doing here? I'm . . . *oh shit . . .*'

The girl astride Rufus turned round, her breasts pointing arrogantly towards the camera.

'*Rufus Archibald Pemberton!*' Lady Pemberton turned purple.

Lord Pemberton didn't know where to look. 'Golly, Rufus . . . this is rather . . .' Words failed him and he clutched his wife's arm for support.

Clemmie clamped a hand over her mouth as if she might be sick and shook her head from side to side in disbelief. 'Rufus . . . how could you do this to me? In our own bed . . .'

Tessa looked more closely at the girl and gasped. '*India?*' She turned to Joe furiously. 'Oh my God, stop filming, you idiot!'

Joe, his face a picture of shock, lowered his camera without a word.

Clemmie took a few halting steps backwards.

'She's Milly Forbes-Henry's friend,' Tessa explained.

'Milly?' Clemmie asked in disbelief. 'Milly . . . the schoolgirl?'

Rufus writhed to push India off his lap and fought to free his hands from the bedposts. India squawked at him like a demented parrot, her ginger hair flying as she hurriedly wrapped herself in a sheet.

'What the hell do you think you're doing?' she screeched at him.

'Shut up!' Rufus yelled, finally pulling his boxer shorts up over a subsiding erection. He turned beseeching eyes towards Clemmie.

'It didn't mean a thing,' he spluttered. He cast wild eyes around the audience of people. He was mortified to see his parents but it was Clemmie he needed to explain himself to. 'I swear to you, Clemmie. It was just a fling . . . a last moment of madness before the wedding. It's nothing important . . . not compared to how I feel about you.'

'Nothing important?' India cried, an ugly stain colouring her cheeks. She stabbed a finger accusingly at Rufus. 'That's not what you've been telling me for the past five months!'

Clemmie looked utterly destroyed and started shaking uncontrollably. She held on to Tessa. 'You've been sleeping with this girl for five months? Oh my God, Rufus! You've played me like a complete fool, haven't you? What about the wedding? What about our life together in England? Do I really mean that little to you?'

Rufus was sweating profusely and his chest heaved as if it was on a hospital machine. 'It's not as bad as it looks, I promise.' He took Clemmie's hand and fell to his knees. 'It's nothing . . . she's nothing . . . you mean everything to me . . . we can still get married . . .'

Hopeless tears steamed down Clemmie's face. She wanted to believe him, she wanted to think they still had a future together but she knew it was impossible.

India let out a bloodcurdling scream. 'How can you say these things?' She grabbed her school rucksack from the side of the bed and searched through it like a maniac. 'Where is it, where is it?'

Tessa began to wonder if India was unhinged. Seconds later, she realised India had every right to be upset and that Rufus was even more of a shit than she had imagined.

'I'm pregnant!' India screamed at Rufus, her face streaked with crooked black lines of mascara. With her hair in disarray and her make-up all over the place, she looked like a damaged doll.

'W-what?' Still on his knees, Rufus gaped at India. 'You're lying . . . you can't be pregnant . . . you said you were on the pill . . .'

India finally found what she was looking for in her bag and with a quivering hand triumphantly held up a pregnancy test. 'It's positive. And you're the bloody father, all right?'

Rufus let out a sob of self-pity and put his face in his hands. Crawling on his hands and knees, semi-naked and vulnerable, he sat by the bed and looked very scared indeed.

Clemmie wobbled on her high heels. Tessa rushed forward just in time and clumsily caught her as she fainted. Seeing that Rufus was about to approach, Tessa put a hand up.

'Back off,' she snarled, speed-dialling Henny.

Doing as he was told for once, a suddenly much younger-looking Rufus sank back down, put his head in his hands and started to cry.

The next few hours went past in a daze. Tessa was disconcerted when Will arrived to collect Clemmie but she could see why Henny had chosen him to sort out the drama. Within minutes he had thrown the camera crew out of the house, calmed Lord and Lady Pemberton and managed to coax a stupefied Rufus into some clothes. Telling Rufus he would phone him later, Will had scooped Clemmie up in his arms and driven her back to Appleton Manor at such a high speed, the paparazzi hadn't been able to keep up. The camera crew were sympathetic but buzzing with the thrill of it all and unable to hide their exhilaration at having witnessed such an A-list meltdown in person. They headed back to the B&B in the village to dissect the goings-on over several bottles of wine while Tessa followed Will back to the manor. She knew she should call Jilly and tell her what had happened – a teenage pregnancy and non-existent wedding would send her into a delirious head spin – but Tessa's immediate concern was for Clemmie.

Having been briefed about the situation, Henny smoothly took over once Will had put Clemmie to bed. She was safely tucked away in 'Cocoa', a peaceful, private room at the back of the house with a vanilla-coloured bedspread and piles of comfy cushions in various chocolaty shades. Will had disappeared to keep the press at bay so Henny gave Clemmie a couple of her strongest sleeping tablets and a cup of camomile tea and left her to it.

'She's OK for now, but she's going to feel terrible in the morning when reality hits her.'

'And when the story comes out in the papers,' Tessa said matter-of-factly. She couldn't help feeling impressed at the way Will had handled everything but when she tried to say something to him, he had brushed her off awkwardly.

Henny looked vexed. 'God, Rufus is such an *idiot*! He was always selfish as a child but this is low, even for him. What the hell was he *thinking*? India's a schoolgirl . . . a *child*. I know you say he didn't know how young India was but still, he cheated on Clemmie and made a fool of her.'

'Who made a fool of Clemmie?' Munching on an apple, Milly strolled up, looking inquisitive.

Henny glanced at Tessa. 'She's going to find out sooner or later, isn't she? You can't say a word to anyone but Clemmie just walked in on Rufus in bed with India.'

Milly almost spat her apple out. 'What? You're kidding me!

India and *Rufus*? Oh my God, no wonder she's been acting like a nutter for the past few months – she's been shagging an old man! A famous one but still, Rufus is such a *dick*.'

Henny nodded grimly. 'Normally I'd tell you off for swearing but you're absolutely right, darling. The other thing is, India is pregnant with Rufus's child.'

Milly gasped. 'Pregnant? Jesus . . . poor, poor India.'

Tessa admired her ability to forgive India so quickly.

'Knowing India, she will have lied about how old she was,' Milly commented, thinking about it. 'I mean, he never saw us in our school uniforms, did he? India probably boosted his ego and did whatever Rufus wanted in bed. Men are suckers for things like that, aren't they?'

Henny eyed her nervously. 'Darling, how come you know so much about sex?'

'Oh, Mother! You have nothing to worry about, thank you very much.' Milly looked prim. 'I'm not stupid and I have no interest in sleeping with some vain old man when I finally get round to it.' Her nose in the air, she swept off in the other direction to get her head together. She was shocked about India but it explained her weird behaviour and secretiveness. She still couldn't believe India was preggers though.

As soft-hearted as ever, Milly took out her mobile and dialled India's number. India might have behaved appallingly for the past six months but seeing as she was up the duff and had most likely just been dumped by Rufus, she was probably going to need her best friend again.

The next few days were bleak for Clemmie. Every gossip rag in America and the UK were running the story – it was huge all over the globe. Clemmie's face was on every newspaper's front page and she was in more demand than she'd ever been in her career, but for all the wrong reasons.

'Rufus the Love Rat!' screamed one headline. 'Clemmie

Dumped for Schoolgirl!' another said. A well-known tabloid magazine had been phoning hourly, to see if Clemmie wanted to put her side of the story across and they promised to 'show her in a sensitive light and tell her story with compassion'. Tessa believed them; an exclusive with an A-lister like Clemmie was worth its weight in gold and an issue like this would fly off the shelves and give this magazine the kind of publicity their rivals would kill for.

Predictably spineless, Rufus had jumped on a plane as soon as Clemmie had been picked up by Will, and was shut away at an 'undisclosed location', according to his management team. He was no doubt sunning himself on a deserted beach somewhere while his people earned their money attempting to salvage what was left of his career, Clemmie thought resentfully. She hadn't been so lucky. Having found her house empty, the press had quickly cottoned on to the fact that Clemmie was being looked after by the Forbes-Henry family and had turned their attentions back to the manor house. Having already installed a sophisticated security system in the hotel, plus additional security which Clemmie had financed in preparation for the wedding, Will was still forced to step up the levels in view of the paparazzi interest. He employed a team of staff to keep the press out and rigged up lighting and alarm systems all over the building. It was money well spent so Will put any concerns about the finances to one side for the time being and did what was required to keep everyone safe.

The additional security did not, however, keep the more kamikaze members of the press at bay. They were swarming all over the grounds of the manor like SAS recruits, attempting to enter the building by any means and damaging the beautiful Virginia creeper in the process as they tried to climb through windows.

India's age was obviously a key point in the story but as India wasn't talking to anyone about her relationship with Rufus, it was hard to ascertain exactly when the relationship had started. This didn't stop the speculation, but Rufus's team were strenuously denying that the relationship began before India's sixteenth birthday and were doing their best to play down India's age as irrelevant, albeit without much success.

Tessa had problems of her own to deal with. Jilly was incandescent with rage that she hadn't been contacted personally by Tessa before the story broke in the papers; Tessa could virtually feel the steam coming out of Jilly's ears as she bellowed down the phone. And she refused to believe Tessa was unaware of cracks in Clemmie and Rufus's relationship and made her feelings known via a particularly heated phone call.

'So you're telling me you've been hanging round with the pair of them for the past six months or more and you didn't know the relationship was in crisis?' Jilly thundered, her voice dripping with sarcasm. 'Doesn't wash with me, kiddo. You must have known something and you decided not to say anything, although fuck knows why you would do that. Your career is on the fucking line as it is.'

Tessa had no idea what to say in her defence. She did her best to convince Jilly she had been in the dark but to her own ears her words sounded feeble. Tessa just knew she had to buy herself some time until she decided what to do. Hearing the phone slam down at the other end, she winced. She had no idea what she was going to do about her job, but she was on borrowed time, that much was clear. The documentary had been cancelled and the film crew had been instructed to head home. Tessa was lying low for a few days, avoiding Jilly's phone calls as much as she could. She was sticking around for Sophie's wedding and was thankful she didn't have to face her boss back in London.

A week later, Tessa popped into Clemmie's room with an armful of pink roses and was encouraged to see her sitting up in bed drinking a cup of strong, black coffee. She was surrounded by open newspapers and had obviously been shedding some tears but she seemed relatively composed in the circumstances.

'Come on in, honey.' Clemmie smiled weakly, cradling the steaming cup in her hands. 'Don't tell Henny, but I hate camomile tea. Milly brought this up for me, the angel.'

'How are you feeling?'

Clemmie's voice caught in her throat. 'Stupid. Really, really *stupid*.'

'Hey.' Tessa sat on the edge of the bed and laid the flowers down. 'Don't say that, this isn't your fault!' An article in the *Sun* caught her eye, the open page displaying a flattering photo of Rufus. The interview was entitled 'Seduced by a Teenage Temptress'. Tessa flipped the paper over so she didn't have to look at it. 'He's a bastard and he doesn't deserve you,' she added loyally.

'Thanks. You've been such a good friend to me.' Clemmie glanced down at the papers with distaste. 'Can you believe Rufus is doing interviews like this?'

'Yes. He's not the type to die quietly. Are you going to respond to any of this stuff?'

'I don't know. My agent is dealing with everything at the moment and she thinks I need to maintain a dignified silence. Being dignified has its place but I can't help wanting to fire back some insults. I mean, have you read some of this crap? "I loved Clemmie but she smothered me . . . I wasn't ready for marriage – I only went along with it to make her happy." Honestly! He proposed to *me*, not the other way round! And if he didn't want to get married, he could have just said so, he didn't need to screw a teenage bimbo in our bed!'

Tessa raised her eyebrows, glad to see Clemmie letting some of her anger out at last.

'Oh, this is well and truly over, honey! I've asked Will to cancel the wedding and I've written him a huge cheque to cover the losses. I won't have anyone losing out just because of Rufus.' Her hazel eyes filled with tears. 'I think we were both doing this for the wrong reasons, if I'm honest. Rufus . . . he just wanted the fame that went with marrying someone like me, and as for me . . . I fell for the idea of a normal life . . . a beautiful house in the countryside . . . children.' She looked away, overcome with emotion.

Tessa changed the subject diplomatically.

'Can you really see yourself turning your back on Hollywood?'

Clemmie nodded and leant back against the pillows with a sigh. 'I've had enough, Tessa. I'm tired! After everything that happened in the early days, all I could think about was being an actress and clawing my life back again. And I love acting but I can't stand being a celebrity. This,' she held up a red-top newspaper with her thumb and forefinger, 'this sums up everything I hate about being famous. And it's not worth it. The money is incredible and the adoration of the public is addictive but I don't need it any more. I just want to be normal – whatever *that* is.'

Tessa toyed with a pink rose. 'Do you think you could have had that kind of life with Rufus?'

Clemmie shook her head sadly. 'I had my head in the clouds. Rufus was with me to promote himself. Maybe he loved me a little but sadly not enough.' She buried her head in the flowers and inhaled their scent. 'And I don't even think we had that much in common apart from sex!' She smiled. 'Rufus is a child, not a man, Tessa, I realise that now. If I'm ever brave enough to start another relationship again, I need someone more mature, someone romantic who doesn't need his ego stroked every two minutes. I need a proper man, for heaven's sake. I'm just not sure I know any.'

Tessa thought she might know one but she kept quiet. The last thing Clemmie needed right now was another romance. She looked up as Will poked his head round the door.

'Do you have a minute?'

Tessa nodded, feeling her head throb. She joined him outside the door.

'Shall we walk?'

Not sure how to say no, Tessa hesitantly followed him downstairs. She glanced nervously over her shoulder but Claudette was nowhere to be seen.

'How's Clemmie?' Will asked pleasantly.

Tessa frowned. Was this really why Will had asked to speak to her – to ask how Clemmie was getting on? She gave him a brief update, feeling uptight as she walked alongside him. She caught a whiff of his aftershave and it sent her right back to the summer party when he had held her in his arms. She did her best to ignore it and to focus on what he was saying but it was hard when her stomach was coiled up like a spring.

'Henny tells me you've been sitting with Clemmie since it happened.'

'Filming has ground to a halt,' she told him wryly, feeling the need to brush the gesture off as unimportant. 'And it seemed like the least I could do after what she's been through. I guess I should head home now but Sophie's asked me to be a bridesmaid so I hope it's all right if I stick around. Or I can move to the B&B. God knows if that wedding will go ahead either. It seems to be all the rage to back out of them these days, doesn't it?'

'No need to move to the B&B. Stay as long as you like.' Will watched Tessa from under his eyelashes. He had heard about the tongue-lashing she had received from her boss for not calling in the story about Rufus and India and he was finally beginning to face up to the fact that he had seriously misjudged Tessa. Tristan, Henny, Milly even, they had all told him but he had stubbornly ignored them, certain he had the measure of her. But after their kiss, he had started to see things more clearly – he suddenly saw everything more clearly. Or did he?

Will kicked a clod of loose earth in frustration. It was just a

410

kiss, for fuck's sake! He really needed to get a grip. And what about that page of notes she'd left in his office? Could he really just forget Tessa's intentions to use his family to further her own career? The trouble was that when he was with her he felt utterly out of control for the first time in his life and he couldn't explain it or ignore it. And he had to admit, for a control freak like himself, he kind of liked it.

Tessa felt Will's fingers brush hers and almost leapt up in the air. She had to stop acting like some sort of teenager around him. It was too embarrassing for words.

'Er . . . have you spoken to Rufus?' she said.

Will nodded. 'He wouldn't tell me where he was but I managed to have a brief chat with him. I think he was freaking out about the wedding – which is no excuse for sleeping with a schoolgirl, obviously. But I think the thought of committing to someone, especially when he wasn't sure how he felt any more, got on top of him.'

Tessa chewed her lip. Was Will still talking about Rufus? Her heart soared momentarily but she forced herself back to reality. Of course he was! No, he would never look twice at her, she thought gloomily as she trudged along next to him, not while he was still in love with Claudette.

Will put a hand out as she stumbled over a tree root and didn't let go. He pulled her towards him, his heart thumping. Holding on to his hand tightly, she moved closer, her full lips parting as if she were about to say something. She held his gaze intensely and Will thought he could look into her moss-green eyes forever.

'I-I can stand up on my own if you want to let me go,' Tessa said, her words faltering.

Looking into his dazzlingly blue eyes, she could see he was nothing like the man she had formed a first impression of; he wasn't a lazy, stuck-up aristocrat, nor was he arrogant or boorish. In fact, she thought, he was lovely . . .

411

Will met her gaze. 'Do you want me to let you go?'

'No.'

She swallowed, feeling a flicker of lust spark up inside.

Staring down at Tessa's wide, sensual mouth and feeling her fingers snaking through his, Will felt himself losing control. He wanted nothing more than to push her into the pile of autumnal leaves Nathan had left by the base of the tree and ravish the hell out of her.

Tessa held her breath. She didn't know how they had ended up with their fingers entwined and their mouths mere centimetres from each other but the effort of not throwing herself into Will's arms was killing her. Their eyes widened at the sound of a branch snapping underfoot and the moment was shattered. Springing away from her, Will swung round to find Claudette standing there, looking cute in a green beret which was tilted at a jaunty angle and a matching scarf wrapped round her elegant throat.

'What are you doing out here?' Her accusing stare made Tessa turn puce and she quickly stuffed her hands into her pockets.

'I was . . . we were . . . talking about Rufus and Clemmie.'

'What a coincidence!' Claudette tucked her arm through Will's, smiling prettily at him. 'I had a lovely idea, *mon chéri*. Now that there is a free wedding slot with everything arranged, why don't we make it official?'

'Make what official?' Will felt the colour drain from his face. Tessa let out a jerky breath.

'Us, *silly*!' Claudette giggled, swatting him. 'Now that Rufus and Clemmie are no longer getting married, we could, couldn't we? There is a free space and everything is in place – we could just turn up and get, how you say, hitched?' She stretched up and gave Will a lingering kiss on the mouth, twisting round to throw a smirk in Tessa's direction.

Will gazed at Tessa dumbly. He couldn't believe that

Claudette was being insensitive enough to take advantage of Clemmie's misfortune.

Stricken, Tessa felt the full weight of Claudette's smugness. And she suddenly felt consumed with utter hopelessness. Claudette was never going to let Will go. And as for Will, what did she think he was going to do – dump perfect Claudette for *her*? He had never told her he had feelings for her, it was all in her head, wasn't it. She remembered what Claudette had said before about Will detesting her and, feeling deeply hurt all over again, she took a step backward, desperate to get away.

Ignoring Will's outstretched hand she stumbled away, kicking leaves out of her path. Hearing Claudette's excited squeals and assuming Will had agreed to her request, Tessa started to run, tears streaming down her face.

'I mean, how the hell am I supposed to comment on this in an exam?' Freddie held the poetry book aloft and quoted in crisp, cultured tones:

> 'And the sunlight clasps the earth,
> And moonbeams kiss the sea –
> What are all these kissings worth
> If thou kiss not me?'

Milly sighed. Freddie had no idea what it did to her when he quoted love poems out loud; he might not be directing the words at her as such but it still made her go all wibbly inside. It didn't help that he looked devastatingly handsome in a chunky jumper and a cream beanie hat which hid his dark hair but made the most of his blueberry-hued eyes and heartbreaking cheekbones.

Trussed up in scarves and gloves against the chilly wind, they were strolling through the village after school. The air was rich with the aroma of late November bonfires and earthy compost.

Flecks of ash and wood spiralled past their eyes and, along with the sound of tinny Christmas carols chorusing out of a CD player, delicious wafts of spiced apple punch drifted out of Milk and Honey, making Milly long for Christmas to arrive.

'Well?' Freddie nudged her and grinned. 'You're supposed to be helping me, young lady, not staring off into space.'

'Right.' Milly shoved her hands in her pockets and tried to concentrate. 'Well, I think what Shelley was trying to get at was that all aspects of the world are in pairs . . . so where he says, "The fountains mingle with the river and the rivers with the ocean," he's referring to the fact that love, like nature, mixes and mingles together.' She sucked her breath in as Freddie brushed a speck of ash from her cheek. 'And . . . and maybe there's someone Shelley loves that isn't returning his affections.'

Oh, how poetry reflected her own life, Milly thought achingly, touching her cheek where Freddie's fingers had just been. Studying love poems with him was like sweet torture; the poignant words mirrored her inner feelings to a T.

'You're so clever, Mills,' Freddie said admiringly. 'I really don't think I'd have a hope in hell of passing my A levels without you.'

'Don't be silly,' Milly said, going scarlet. She couldn't help wishing Freddie saw more in her than just brainpower but it seemed it wasn't to be. He spent so much time in her company, she wasn't sure how he would have time for anybody else – a girlfriend – but that was small consolation.

Milly was so distracted by her thoughts she didn't notice JB stalking towards her with his arms full of papers. She crashed into him accidentally, sending papers into the air and JB into an apoplectic rage.

'Gosh, I'm so sorry!' Contrite, Milly dropped to her knees to collect the papers, anxious as the wind picked some of them up and sent them cartwheeling down the road. Freddie helped her, grabbing sheets and putting them into Milly's gloved hands.

'Stupid fucking girl!' JB growled. He snatched some of the paperwork from her and shoved it into the file he was holding, his eyes blazing.

Milly looked shell-shocked. Still on her knees, she was staring at one of the sheets of paper with a furrowed brow.

'It was an accident,' Freddie interjected smoothly, helping Milly to her feet. His hands were shaking with anger. 'And I think you should apologise, quite frankly,' he told JB curtly.

'*Me?* Apologise?' JB had no intention of doing anything of the sort. 'Forget it.' He snatched the last sheets of paper from Milly's hands.

She looked puzzled and watched JB storm away from them, his dark curls flapping in the wind.

'Are you all right?' Freddie asked, putting his arm round her shoulders and trying not to enjoy the warmth of her body against his. Her platinum hair smelt like flowers and wood smoke and he forcibly reminded himself for the umpteenth time she was like his kid sister. It was just that . . . he wasn't sure that was how he saw her any more.

'That was really odd,' Milly said, enjoying the feel of Freddie's arm round her but baffled by what she had just seen.

'Odd? Rude more like. Arrogant tosser. What's he still doing here, anyway? The film crew have packed up and gone, haven't they, now that Rufus and Clemmie have split up?'

'Yes, they have. And that's the thing. JB's paperwork . . .'

'What about it?'

Milly's eyes looked glazed. 'That last sheet of paper, it was in French but it had words like "inheritance" and "wills" in it.'

'So what?' Freddie shrugged. He couldn't help thinking Milly looked adorable when she was deep in thought and crinkling her nose up. 'It's probably something to do with his family back in France or something.'

'That's just it.' Milly took out her mobile phone with trembling fingers. 'It wasn't about JB's family, Freddie, it was about *my* family. I saw the Forbes-Henry name mentioned several times – and my grandmother's name too.' She paused. 'Now, who would be best to tell . . . Will, probably, but he's all caught up with Claudette and this daft wedding idea – can you believe she wants to jump in Clemmie's grave and nab all her wedding ideas after everything that's happened? I'm beginning to think she's not that nice after all.' Milly thought for a second, tapping her gloved finger against her mouth. 'I wonder if Tessa might have some idea of what it's about. She probably knows JB better than most people. Thank God she's still here – if only because of Sophie's stupid wedding to Gil. Jesus, everything is so fucked-up at the moment!' She dialled Tessa's number rapidly.

'Why on earth would JB be looking at anything to do with your family, let alone stuff about inheritance?' Freddie wondered in confusion. 'I thought he was just here to direct the celebrity documentary?'

'That's what we all thought,' Milly said, her eyes sparkling animatedly. 'But perhaps he's here for another reason entirely. Tessa? Oh my God, have I got some gossip for you!'

Chapter Twenty-Four

Tessa glanced out of the window with a heavy heart. December had been heralded by the arrival of some heavy snow, and delicate snowflakes were spiralling downwards and settling on the window ledges of her cottage. The green lawns of the manor were covered in a pure, white carpet – so far, untouched and beautiful.

It seemed blissfully quiet, the snow wrapping her cottage in a safe, soundless cocoon and making the view outside look like the top of a Christmas cake. But Tessa was swept away by despair, desolate at having to watch Will with Claudette and furious with herself for falling in love with Will in the first place.

'What the hell am I still doing here?' she asked herself out loud. She fervently wished she'd never agreed to be Sophie's bridesmaid. Aside from the wedding to Gil seeming like a complete farce in view of Tristan and Sophie's blatantly obvious feelings for each other, it meant that she was trapped at Appleton Manor. But the fact of the matter was that Sophie needed her and Tessa could also admit to herself that she was dreading going home and facing the music about her career. Jilly was barely speaking to her and had snappily told her the best she could hope for in the New Year was a job on a documentary with a second-rate footballer and his high-maintenance soap star wife – a major bitch with a serious attitude problem. It was hardly an inspiring thought.

Tessa made some character notes for her novel but her heart

wasn't in it. Glancing at the romantic view outside, she remembered she had promised to help Henny and Clemmie with some Christmas preparations. She was sure they were just including her to be kind but she was grateful nonetheless. In spite of her recent traumas, Clemmie was bravely putting her life back together and who could resist an afternoon in Henny's motherly, nurturing company? It was like eating hot, buttered toast in front of the fire and frankly Tessa could do with some TLC.

Unenthusiastically pulling on Jack's navy wellies, Tessa only hoped Claudette wouldn't be in attendance, looking glorious in her cashmere knits and gloating in her general direction as she snuggled up to Will possessively. Tessa wasn't sure she could cope with that.

Will stared unseeingly at his computer screen. The finances were up shit creek and even with Clemmie's absurdly over-generous cheque, Appleton Manor was haemorrhaging money on a daily basis. Henny's Aga had given up the ghost a week ago and there was no question that it had to be replaced immediately. And in the process of overseeing the installation of the last of the bathrooms, Gil had discovered a major leak beneath the floorboards. Three rooms had needed extensive repairs and the cost had been astronomical.

Will sighed. The manor looked gorgeous – the hotel rooms were sensational and practically every inch of the house had been given a touch-up. Henny had strung fairy lights and Christmas decorations up and there were candles everywhere, filling the house with the scent of figs and pine needles. A vast Christmas tree had been ordered and all the decorations sat in boxes, ready to be put to good use. Everything felt perfect, in fact. So why did he feel so dissatisfied?

Truthfully, Will knew why he felt so unhappy. It was Claudette. Her suggestion that they should take Clemmie and

Rufus's available wedding slot seemed to have put everything sharply in perspective in his mind. It was inconsiderate to say the least, a crass error of judgement on her part. But it also spoke volumes about who Claudette was and it had made Will question everything about her. Was she really the sweet, selfless woman she had always purported to be? More to the point, had he ever really loved her or had he just convinced himself that she was perfect for him because the timing was right and he was ready to settle down?

Will did know one thing, however. He couldn't marry Claudette now. He didn't even think he could carry on with their relationship. Guiltily, he realised his change of heart had less to do with Claudette and her actions and much more to do with how he felt about Tessa. She had turned his ordered life upside down. At first he had thought it was sheer lust but now he knew differently.

Gazing outside at the tumbling snow, Will was jolted to see Tessa making her way across the lawn towards the house. He stood up to get a better view. She was wearing his father's massive welly boots and an old fleece of Milly's. Her dark hair was soaked, slicked back against her head like seal fur and the brisk chill in the air had turned the tip of her proud nose bright pink.

Slamming his hand against the window in frustration as she disappeared inside, Will knew what he needed to do. Making one of the biggest decisions of his life, he forgot about the family finances and the hotel and headed off to tell Claudette it was over.

JB and Caro strolled into the house, hand in hand, their clothes speckled with snowflakes, their cheeks flushed from the cold. Looking glamorous in a red, fur-edged ski jacket with the hood pulled up around her face, Caro was whispering something in JB's ear and, looking slightly distracted, he was giving her one of his wolfish grins. Canoodling openly, JB bundled her into one of the convenient alcoves in the hallway.

Will rolled his eyes in exasperation, hoping his father wasn't anywhere in the vicinity. Relations between his parents had completely broken down but he couldn't see Jack welcoming JB over the threshold anytime soon. Catching sight of Claudette walking purposefully towards the library with a key in her hand, Will called out to her.

'Claudette! I have to talk to you. It's . . . it's important.'

She spun round reluctantly, clearly intent on doing something else. 'I was just about to—'

'*Claudette?*'

JB stepped out from the alcove. He had a look of utter incredulity on his face and he walked slowly towards Claudette. '*Mon Dieu!*' he muttered to himself, clearly astonished.

Will looked from JB to Claudette in bewilderment and was astonished to see Claudette mouthing like a goldfish and waving her hands wildly. Her cheeks had turned ghostly white and she looked horror-struck to see JB. She took a hasty step backward and crashed into Jack who looked badly in need of a drink.

'Ouch! Look where you're going, darling.' Jack rubbed his sore toe, turning hostile, bloodshot eyes towards JB. His usual good manners and went out of the window at the sight of his wife's lover standing in his hallway as if he owned it. 'Fucking hell!' he howled. 'What are you doing here, you slimy little frog?'

JB didn't even seem to hear Jack. He advanced on Claudette, his dark eyebrows shooting up into his hair in wonder. Will couldn't understand why Claudette was shaking like a leaf, her pupils constricted with terror as she put her arms up in defence. Caro emerged from the alcove, watching JB with wide eyes.

'If you could just carry that for me, darling,' Henny was

saying to Tessa as they appeared, struggling under the weight of some huge flower arrangements studded with holly leaves and mistletoe. They came to an abrupt halt when they realised they'd walked into the middle of something.

Henny looked round anxiously. 'Is anything wrong?'

Tessa and Will's eyes met for a second before Will turned back to Claudette.

'You two . . . know each other?' he asked her, thinking he had never seen her looking so panic-stricken in his life. She shook her head but JB nodded.

'Yes, we know each other,' he said in a hoarse voice. 'But we 'ave not seen each other for years. I was not expecting to see Claudette 'ere, of all places.'

Henny barked out a laugh. 'But she's been here for ages, you must have seen her at the manor. Ah,' she said, realising how JB had missed Claudette. 'You've haven't been here filming for some months now.' She gave Caro a haughty look.

Caro narrowed her eyes venomously at Henny.

'Jean-Baptiste, do not say anything . . . I beg of you,' Claudette pleaded.

JB hesitated for a fraction of a second. 'Why shouldn't I? I 'ave no loyalty to you whatsoever.' He turned to face everyone else. 'We have not seen each other for years because she used to be married to my brother, Fabrice.'

Tessa frowned. 'The one you don't talk to any more?'

Blinking at Claudette, Will was visibly stunned. 'Is this true? You've been married before? Why didn't you tell me?'

In anguish, Claudette let out a strangled noise.

'Well? Speak up, Claudette, I can't hear you.' Will looked angry, two red spots appearing in his cheeks. 'Why didn't you tell me you were married before?'

She shrugged helplessly, twisting away from him. 'I did not . . . I could not . . . there was never a right time . . .'

Will looked disbelieving. 'I think there's always time to tell your fiancé you've been married before. When did you and this . . . Fabrice get divorced?'

There was silence and everyone waited with bated breath. Barely able to meet Will's piercing gaze, she stammered some words out.

'For the love of God, Claudette,' Jack snapped edgily. 'Speak up!'

'I didn't get divorced.' She bit her lip, feeling everyone's eyes on her. 'I'm still married.'

The crowd gasped in horror.

'*Sacre bleu!*' JB murmured under his breath, clutching his dark curls in agitation. 'He is more of a bastard than I gave 'im credit for.' He turned to Claudette and fired off at her in French, expletives filling the air. Henny was surprised the air didn't turn blue as Claudette shouted back at JB, her hands flying around randomly as she let rip.

Will understood most of the conversation but his head was spinning over Claudette's betrayal.

Tessa wanted to throw her arms around him. How could Claudette do that to Will? And if she was still married, why was she even with him – and why on earth was she pushing him to make a commitment to her?

'What the hell have you been doing with me, then?' Will asked in a low voice, asking the question on everyone's lips. 'You wanted to get married, for fuck's sake. When were you going to mention the small detail of another husband? Christ, you weren't going to say a thing, were you?'

Claudette stretched a hand out to him, cowering when he scorned her efforts. 'The divorce . . . Will, I just forgot, that is all.'

Will let out a derisive laugh. 'Don't be ridiculous, Claudette! Picking up one's dry-cleaning, that's the kind of thing people forget to do. Not getting a divorce is something quite, quite different.'

'So you are not here by accident,' JB stated, looking as if the penny had finally dropped.

'And neither are you,' she retorted sharply.

He coloured slightly, his swarthy cheeks turning sallow.

Caro pushed herself forward, grabbing JB's arm petulantly. 'What does she mean, JB? You're here to film the documentary. What other reason would there be for you to be in Appleton?'

JB couldn't look her in the eye. Claudette's mouth curved up triumphantly and she put her hands on her hips, jutting her chin forward aggressively.

'Yes, JB, what other reason could there possibly be for you to be in Appleton?' she crowed.

Clearly cornered, JB lost his temper. 'Whatever she tells you, she is 'ere for the money!' he burst out, wagging a finger at her.

'What money?' Will ran a hand through his hair, suddenly feeling exhausted by it all. 'If you think we've got thousands of pounds stashed away somewhere, you're wrong.'

'That's right,' Jack chortled. 'We used to have tons but I spent extortionate sums on booze and Caro frittered the rest away on knickers.' He gave her an icy look as if daring her to challenge him. She was too busy gawping at JB to even notice.

Will shook his head. 'No, Dad. I mean it. We really don't have any money.' He felt his mother's beseeching eyes burning into him but now wasn't the time to worry about protecting her feelings. 'Mum got involved in some . . . unfortunate investments and the hotel has swallowed up the rest of it. I've even sold all my properties in France.'

Jack's head whipped round to Caro. 'I bet it was that greasy toy boy you were seeing last year! It was, wasn't it? God, Caro, how could you be so *bloody* stupid?'

She started to tremble, knowing there was nothing she could say to defend herself.

Tessa gaped at Will, shocked. All this time, she had thought the family were rolling in money and instead Will had been desperately juggling cash in the background and getting rid of his investments to fund the family business. She couldn't believe he had made so many personal sacrifices, just to protect his family from going broke. Tessa felt ashamed for judging him so harshly.

'Oh, Will!' Henny looked distraught and lost her grip on the huge flower arrangement. 'Why didn't you tell us things were that bad?'

Will brushed her comment off. 'It doesn't matter, Aunt Henny, really.' He turned back to Claudette, his eyes full of contempt. 'So if you were with me for money, I'm afraid you've backed the wrong horse. *Chérie.*'

Claudette cast her eyes to the floor and said nothing.

'This was what Milly meant about those papers,' Tessa gasped suddenly. She turned to Will. 'I was going to talk to you about it . . . but I haven't . . . it's been difficult.' She took another breath as she felt her cheeks going pink. 'Anyway, Milly saw some papers JB had that mentioned wills and inheritance in relation to you.'

'To me?' Will looked taken aback.

'To the family,' she corrected herself hastily.

Will held his hands up helplessly, spinning back to JB and Claudette. 'Will someone please tell me what the fuck is going on?'

JB let out a heavy breath and nodded in resignation. 'I will explain everything.'

Sitting in the drawing room felt awkwardly civilised but no one wanted to stand around in the hallway indefinitely. Seated around the polished table and on sofas, with JB and Claudette looking uncomfortable up front, JB began.

'Your grandmother, Gabrielle,' he explained to Will. 'Years ago, she was married to a Frenchman.'

'That's right,' Henny chipped in. 'A rich property owner called Alain Latante.'

'Alain *Laurent*,' JB supplied tightly.

'But that's *your* name.' Tessa's head was spinning.

'Alain Laurent was my grandfather and he died at the end of last year.' JB went on to explain how Alain had pined for Gabrielle ever since she walked out on him, vowing to win her back somehow. He sent her hundreds of love letters, JB said, but Gabrielle never responded and when Alain found out she had remarried, he was heartbroken. He never stopped loving her and even though he knew she was lost to him forever and he subsequently married again and had children, Alain decided to make a pledge to Gabrielle in his will as a sign of his love for her.

'How terribly romantic,' Caro commented, tutting when everyone glared at her. 'What? I'm just *saying*.'

Jack leant forward, wishing he had a Bloody Mary to ease his crashing hangover. 'So what's the big deal about this will, then?' he barked at JB impatiently.

JB exchanged a glance with Claudette who was looking at him with imploring eyes. 'I am coming to that. My grandfather's will states that if Gabrielle was still alive five years before Alain died and the will was read, the money . . . or the property would come to the Forbes-Henry family.'

Henny looked bemused. 'That's odd. What's the significance of the five years?'

'I believe five years is how long Alain and Gabrielle were together. My grandfather always was a sentimental old fool.' JB shrugged.

Will couldn't look at Claudette. 'So, the money . . . or the property would come to my father and Aunt Henny?'

'No. Because my grandfather's other children – my father and his brother – both passed away some years ago, the property was always to be divided between the grandchildren.' JB turned to Will. 'You. And your brother, Tristan.'

'And if Gabrielle *was* dead when the will was read?' Caro asked, looking thrilled.

'If she was dead, the property would come to me. And my idiot of a brother, Fabrice.' JB jerked his head at Claudette. 'Which explains why she is 'ere, obviously. Fabrice sent you, didn't he? *Espèce de salaud!* Not content with ruining the family business by gambling everything away, the bastard wants this money too.'

Henny looked up with shining eyes. 'Our mother was in a coma before she died. That's why the five-year issue isn't cut and dried, isn't it?'

JB nodded. 'Well, it wasn't. Claudette, you 'ave come 'ere for nothing. I found out this morning that the Forbes-Henrys will inherit the money.'

Everyone gasped.

Claudette immediately leapt up and ran to Will's side. Her expression was contrite, her brown eyes innocently wide. '*Chérie*, you must believe me, Fabrice did send me to get the money but I fell in love with you . . . I did not mean to but I could not 'elp myself . . .'

Tessa let out a hiss of disgust before she could stop herself. She needn't have bothered; Will threw Claudette's arm off in revulsion. 'My God, Claudette! You'll stop at nothing. Now you know the money is coming to our family, you think you can worm your way back to me to get your hands on it!' His eyes darkened with dislike. 'The way we met at that party, all the things you said, none of it was a coincidence, was it? You planned the whole thing from the start – manipulating the meeting, ingratiating yourself with my family, and all along you were snooping around in the background trying to get your hands on the money.' Livid at himself, Will thumped his fist on the table. 'God, I've been such a fucking idiot!'

Finding Claudette on her hands and knees ·in the library

made perfect sense to Tessa now; she'd been looking for documents about Gabrielle's death.

JB's lip curled. 'It is not your fault,' he advised Will. 'Claudette is a consummate liar and just as bad as my brother. You must not blame yourself for being taken in.'

Henny looked deeply hurt. 'Darling, how *could* you?' she said to Claudette in an injured tone. 'Will adored you and we all welcomed you with open arms. And the whole time you were just after some money.'

Claudette rolled her shoulders rudely.

Caro had gone very quiet. Suddenly, her vision of a new life with JB had been shattered. His interest in her wasn't genuine; he had done exactly the same thing as Claudette and used her to get closer to the truth. She closed her eyes in horror, remembering all the pillow talk about the Forbes-Henry family, her insides curling in shame as she recalled the way she had blossomed under JB's touch, so grateful was she for his attention.

Opening her eyes, Caro found Jack staring at her. Her eyelids fluttered as she fought to hold back a sob. She felt old and foolish. How humiliating it all was . . . how *degrading*. Most crushing of all was the fact that Jack hadn't taken advantage of the moment to mock her, even though she richly deserved it. Instead, his sage-green eyes were flooded with pity. Letting out a cry of pain, Caro fled from the room.

Throwing a troubled look over his shoulder, JB lit a cigarette with a quivering hand, forgetting he wasn't meant to smoke in the house. About to give him a jolly good telling-off, Henny saw the look of distress in his eyes and decided to let it go.

'Just out of interest,' she said delicately, 'how much money are we talking about in this will?'

JB gave her a thin smile. 'My grandfather left behind a property, rather than a sum of money. It is a château.'

'A château?' Jack said, intrigued in spite of himself. 'Whereabouts?'

'It is in Burgundy. It is worth . . . rather a lot of money.'

They all waited.

'It is worth over five million.'

'Pounds or euros?' squeaked Henny.

Looking jaded, JB got to his feet. 'Pounds,' he said matter-of-factly. 'The château is worth five million pounds.'

He delivered the bombshell with aplomb, and with a great sense of timing, left the room.

Chapter Twenty-Five

A nerve twitching in his cheek, Will watched Claudette carelessly tossing her expensive clothes into her suitcase.

'I never want to see you again, is that understood?'

Claudette contemplated him coolly. 'Do not worry, Will, there is no reason for me to stay here with you now.'

Will stared at her, realising he had never really known Claudette. Everything about her was a lie, manufactured as a means to an end. Thank God he'd realised he didn't love her before her true motives were revealed or he'd be feeling crushed beyond recognition now rather than stupidly naive.

'I can't believe I was going to marry you,' he muttered without thinking, not even able to look at Claudette. 'Christ, Tessa's worth a *hundred* of you.'

Claudette threw the last of her belongings into her case and snapped it shut. 'Just remember that I *never* loved you, Will. And, if JB hadn't ruined everything, I would have got my hands on that money somehow. Never forget that.' Victoriously, she heaved the case off the bed and spun out of the room, throwing him one last insult over her shoulder. 'And that poet you love so much . . . Byron? I *detest* him.'

Downstairs, Claudette was delighted to encounter Tessa at the front door.

'He was going to marry me, you know. At some point.' Claudette's eyes sparkled bitchily.

Tessa couldn't help herself. 'Don't you already have a husband?'

Claudette smirked. 'That is not the point, is it? Whatever you think Will feels for you, you are wrong. He feels lust for you, maybe.' She shrugged. 'But so what? That means nothing. And he'll never love you. Do you know why?'

'Do tell,' Tessa said as offhandedly as she could, even though her heart was crashing against her ribs.

Claudette gave her a dazzling smile. 'Because you are not me,' she said simply. 'You'll always be second best.' Giving the rim of her hat a stylish flick, Claudette ducked out into the snow and leapt into a taxi.

Tessa watched her numbly, all the happiness draining out of her.

Fired up by Claudette's departure, Will was galvanised into action. He obtained copies of Alain Laurent's will immediately and faxed them over to his Uncle Perry in France. While Perry tangled with the delights of French bureaucracy, Will systematically set about removing any vestige of Claudette from his life. He shut down the French bank account he had set up to cover her travelling expenses and he switched the direct debit he had dutifully been honouring for her charity work to the charity itself, not wanting them to suffer because of Claudette's appalling behaviour.

Finally and most expensively, he instructed Gil to rename the suite he had named after Claudette. Using the last of his own money that he had set aside to pay the temporary manager's salary, Will made sure the room was stripped and redone and that the glossy hotel brochure he had painstakingly created was updated. He had no idea what he was going to do about the temporary manager but, for now, spending the money on the removal of Claudette's memory seemed like the right thing to do.

Answering his phone irritably, Will relaxed when he heard his uncle's voice at the other end.

'Legal Rescue here!' sang a merry voice. 'I have news, dear boy.'

Will leant back in his chair.

'You and Tristan have just inherited a stunning château in Burgundy. Or, to put it another way, if you decide to sell, you're five million pounds richer between you.'

Will rubbed a hand across his eyes tiredly. It was fantastic news; he knew that. If he and Tristan sold the château, the family would never have to worry about money again. And if Appleton Manor succeeded, they might just be able to hang on to both properties and start a chain. He wondered what Tristan would want to do but shrugged the thought off. Tristan was so screwed up about Sophie and the news about his daughter, he wasn't in a fit state to make a cup of tea right now, let alone make grave decisions about money.

'Hello? Did you hear what I just said, Will? You and your playboy brother have just inherited five million quid!'

'Sorry, Uncle. That's brilliant news. And thanks for getting back to me so speedily.' Will didn't want to sound ungrateful. It was just that inheriting this money seemed to have come at such a price.

'Ah, no problem at all, my boy. And the best thing about it is that the Laurents won't be contesting the will in the future.' Perry gave a hearty laugh. 'The document is as watertight as it gets. This Alain chap obviously wanted you boys to inherit the château, even after all this time. He must have loved Mother . . . I mean, Gabrielle very much to have put something so valuable aside like that for her grandchildren.' He sighed, audibly slurping a glass of wine. 'Obviously the car accident and coma made the whole thing more complex than he intended. Let me know if you'd like me to pop over to Burgundy at any time – it's only a hop, skip and a jump for me to get there.' Perry rang off, pleased to have been of use.

Now that he had dealt with the formalities, Will decided he needed to take some time out. Heading to the wine cellar, he grabbed three bottles of 2000 Lafite-Rothschild and carried them back upstairs. He had been saving them for a special occasion but what the fuck. Like his father, when Will got drunk, he preferred not to drink any old shit. Not even noticing the snow, he walked back to his cottage and found Austin shivering on the sofa. Whacking the heating up to full blast and grabbing a corkscrew, Will settled down with his faithful old dog and made a start.

He knew he should be pleased; the family's financial worries were over. And he was pleased. But he was also angry, incensed at Claudette and deeply frustrated with himself. He had almost unwittingly been the cause of losing Appleton Manor. He had allowed his stupid pride to get in the way of his judgement and he had put his family in danger. So much for protecting them!

He realised now he had been hasty proposing to Claudette. The time had been right for him to settle down; he had simply been waiting for the right girl to arrive. And Claudette had seemed so perfect, their meeting so romantic. But Will wondered how long he had been thinking deep down that something wasn't right about Claudette, that even though she represented everything he thought he wanted out of life, she didn't make his heart sing. What he had been searching for wasn't perfection, it was something much more straightforward than that. It was love. And it didn't need to be perfectly matched or perfectly packaged. It might be passionate and complicated and it might not make sense. It was just . . . right.

An image of Tessa's beautiful, open face swam in front of his eyes and Will's heart lurched painfully. She probably thought he was an absolute tosser.

How right she was, he thought miserably as he splashed more wine into a glass. He was sure the Lafite deserved a far more dignified outing than this but Will no longer cared. He needed to block Claudette out of his mind and he had to work out why he couldn't stop thinking about a girl that, by rights, he shouldn't be in love with. Chucking the wine down his throat, Will proceeded to get horribly drunk.

'India, it's me . . . please let me in.'

Milly had given up phoning India and was currently camped outside her house with her finger on the doorbell. She leapt back as the door was cautiously opened a fraction and Mrs Taylor-Knight beckoned for her to come in.

Milly was shocked at how haggard India's mother looked. A thin, fashion-conscious woman in her forties, she had fine ginger hair cut into an unflattering bob which emphasised her weak chin and insipid blue eyes. She seemed to have aged ten years in the past few weeks and her face sagged with disappointment.

'Is India all right?' Milly ventured, glancing around. No Christmas decorations adorned the walls and no bedecked tree stood in the corner. There was a stack of unopened Christmas cards on the hall table, the only sign that the festive season was approaching. The house was eerily quiet, as if a death, not a birth, was imminent and even the air seemed frosty. Milly shivered.

'Not good.' Mrs Taylor-Knight sniffed. 'She hasn't stopped crying for weeks and her father is barely speaking to her. The phone rings morning, noon and night with journalists offering ridiculous sums of money for the story.'

'Shit.' Milly hadn't realised things were that bad but having witnessed what Clemmie had been through, she knew she should have predicted this. 'That's grim. The press are like vultures, aren't they?'

Mrs Taylor-Knight looked indignant. 'My poor India has been tossed aside like . . . like an unwanted sock and she has every right to have her say and tell the world what a bastard Rufus Pemberton is.' She folded her stick-thin arms. 'If you want to make yourself useful, you should convince my daughter to go to the papers and get what's due to her!'

Milly traipsed upstairs. She found India curled up in a foetal position on her bed, sobbing into her hands, rambling under her breath. Milly rushed over and hugged her tightly. She wished India had trusted her enough to tell her what was going on – about the baby, if nothing else – but she understood that India had probably remained silent on Rufus's instructions.

'You must hate me,' India spluttered, raising red, swollen eyes.

'Don't be daft, how could I?'

Milly was horror-struck at India's appearance. Gone was the cocksure, vibrant person India had once been; she had been replaced by a dishevelled-looking girl who was wan and ill. Without her daily application of fake tan, India's skin was milky-white and almost transparent and her ginger hair hung in lank clumps, as if it hadn't been washed for weeks.

'I hate him!' India suddenly said fiercely. 'I hate him so much for what he's done to me.' Her bravado evaporated as quickly as it had arrived. 'But I love him too . . . so, so much. How could he leave me like this? How could he abandon me without even calling?'

Milly smoothed India's hair away from her face the way her mother did when she was sick. 'You haven't done anything wrong, India. Rufus is a bastard and he doesn't deserve you.'

'But I'm having his child!' India started to shriek. 'He said he loved me . . . he said he wanted to be with me . . . I'm going to have a fucking baby and Rufus doesn't even care!'

Milly averted her eyes from India's blossoming stomach. She didn't know what to say. She couldn't believe Rufus had been callous enough to desert India when she was pregnant with his baby. It was despicable, by anyone's standards.

'Maybe he'll come back to me.' India's puffy eyes lit up hopefully.

Milly's heart went out to her. Rufus had disappeared off the face of the earth. He had sold enough stories to the papers, though; Milly was sick and tired of seeing his pretty face plastered all over every newspaper and magazine she picked up. She was beginning to see why Mrs Taylor-Knight was so keen for India to sell her story too; after all, why should Rufus be the only one to profit from his mistakes?

'What about going to one of the papers?' she suggested gently. 'You're going to need some money and at least you could tell everyone the truth.' She caught sight of a photo of Rufus on India's bedside table and frowned. 'I think you should make the bastard suffer for what he's done.'

India exploded. 'You're just as bad as my fucking mother!' she hissed. 'I'm not selling my story, do you hear me? I won't do that to Rufus. What if . . .' She started crying again. 'What if he's thinking about coming back to me?'

Even though Milly thought that was never going to happen, she wasn't brave enough or cruel enough to destroy what little hope and self-esteem India had left. Not even bothering to tell India the news she had thought might cheer her up about the debacle with Claudette and JB and the five-million-pound château, Milly left her some of her mother's famous Christmas fudge and headed downstairs.

'Any luck?' Mrs Taylor-Knight said hopefully.

Milly shook her head. Pausing in the doorway, she turned back. 'Go easy on her, please,' she said earnestly, realising she might be speaking out of turn. She bit her lip. 'I think you might find India changing her mind about the papers when it finally sinks in that Rufus isn't coming back. She just can't let go of the idea that he might still want her, you see.'

Feeling immeasurably sad and badly in need of a shoulder to cry on, Milly dialled Freddie as soon as she left India's house. Even if he was only ever going to be her friend, she knew he'd never treat her the way Rufus had India.

Sophie hesitated outside Tristan's cottage. He wasn't there; she knew that because she'd watched him venturing outside to make a rare visit to the manor house. Thinking he probably needed sustenance and wouldn't be too long, Sophie ducked inside his cottage quickly, feeling like a criminal.

It felt strangely like coming home; the smells were the same and his studio looked just the way it always had; messy and cosily welcoming. Sophie breathed in the aroma like a junkie, assailed by memories of their time together. But she didn't have time to indulge in such things and she pulled herself together. She had to know if what Tessa had told her was true; that Tristan had painted her recently. She wasn't doing it to assuage her ego; she just had to know if Tristan had felt that way about her and if . . . if he still did.

Recalling the look on his face when she had told him about Ruby, Sophie winced. Hurting him that way had been the hardest thing she had ever done and his reaction, though not unexpected, had crucified her. She couldn't blame him, he had every right to be angry in the circumstances. If only she had known what had really happened with Anna that night! If only she had trusted him, she reminded herself guiltily.

Discovering several portraits stacked up against the wall, Sophie sucked her breath in. Tessa was right: Tristan had painted her over and over again. But what was this? She found a very recent portrait of herself and gasped. It had been slashed in two, her face ripped apart with a knife. Sophie turned away in agony.

Leaving a photo of Ruby propped up on his easel with 'Sorry' scrawled across the back, Sophie dashed out of Tristan's cottage with tears streaming down her face.

Maybe, just maybe, once he had calmed down, he would forgive her, Sophie thought as she let herself into her house. She felt her spirits rise slightly. She would tell him how much she loved him and, somehow, she would make Gil understand . . .

She cried out as the front door was flung open. 'God, Gil, you nearly gave me a heart attack!' Looking at his ashen face, she was gripped with fear. 'What's the matter? Is Ruby—'

'Ruby's fine,' Gil said in a flat voice. 'It's my father. He died of a heart attack this afternoon.'

'Oh no . . . Gil!' Sophie threw her arms round his neck in sympathy.

'He was preaching a sermon,' he mumbled into her neck. 'Keeled over in front of his congregation, can you imagine?' He pulled away from her. 'Probably how he'd want to go – isn't it? Centre stage, telling everyone else what to do.' He let out a mirthless laugh.

She squeezed his fingers. They felt cold and she rubbed them briskly to warm them up. He was in shock, she realised. 'Your poor mother must be devastated,' she said as he sank into an armchair. 'Do you need to help her with the funeral arrangements?'

Gil shook his head. 'She has it all in hand. Already. How strange. She's planned out the religious readings and the hymns . . . she actually sounded rather relieved that he had finally given up the ghost, as it were.'

'Relieved?'

'Mmmm. Can't say I blame her, I feel a bit that way myself.' Gil smiled crookedly. 'I thought we might be able to get out of getting married in a chapel now that Father's popped his clogs but my mother says it's all he ever wanted for me. So that's that, isn't it?'

Sophie didn't know how to console him. He looked like a little boy, lost and alone.

'I feel . . . free,' Gil commented out of the blue, almost as if he had forgotten she was there.

'Free?'

'Awful, isn't it? I should be distraught but all I can think of is that I'm finally free. Free from the bullying and the criticism, free to be who I really am – at *last*.'

Sophie was confused. She knew Gil had always yearned for his father's approval and that he always felt as if he had fallen short of expectations. But she had no idea what he meant about 'feeling free'. She felt a flash of guilt that only minutes before she had been contemplating leaving Gil and dreaming of reconciling with Tristan.

'Should we delay the wedding?' she asked, hating herself for her cowardice.

'The wedding?' Gil looked dazed as if he had forgotten their nuptials were a mere fortnight away. 'No, I don't think so, Soph. At least . . . not for the time being.'

Sophie felt her heart plummet. She listened to Gil recounting his father's bad points with increasing agitation and felt more powerless than ever. She couldn't let him down now, not when he needed her the most. Sophie put her own suffering to one side and did what any fiancée would do. She put her arms round Gil and held him.

Chapter Twenty-Six

Still reeling from Claudette's stinging parting words, Tessa found herself stumbling around Appleton, hardly knowing what to do next. It was torturous to be here still, so close to Will when she knew there was no future for them, but what else could she do when she had made a promise to Sophie?

Folding the dress Sophie had ordered for her over her arm, Tessa crunched through the heavy snow with the weight of the world on her shoulders. She couldn't help thinking Claudette was right. Will did seem to find her presence difficult. So it was unlikely the feelings she had seen in his eyes when they had kissed were anything other than lust. And, as Claudette so rightly said, what did lust count for when it came down to it? Not much. A quick shag maybe, but that was all. And that could never be enough. Not with Will.

Tessa caught sight of JB piling his luggage into the inadequate boot of his Porsche outside the B&B. She'd avoided him since the showdown at the manor but she thought JB deserved a goodbye, at the very least. Even if she was still furious with him for lying to them all.

'So you're off then,' she said curtly, pausing by his car. 'Are you going back to France?'

'Back to France but first I need to sort out some business things. Then I will head straight back over the Channel.' JB's dark eyes were unreadable. Slamming the boot lid down, he lit a cigarette and contemplated her through the blue-grey smoke. 'And you?' he asked. 'What will you do?'

'I have wedding duties on Christmas Eve.' She held up the bag containing the bridesmaid's dress. 'After that, who knows? I should go home for Christmas, I suppose, although Henny has invited me to stay.'

'So why don't you stay?' JB pushed his dark curls out of his eyes, seemingly oblivious of the snowflakes turning it damp. He gestured to the manor in the distance. It looked spectacular covered in snow with lights twinkling inside. 'I think Christmas there could be . . . very special.'

'I quite agree. I just . . . I don't know if I can handle it.'

JB nodded knowingly. 'These Forbes-Henrys, they get under your skin, *non*? You too 'ave fallen for one of them.'

Tessa was taken aback. 'So you *do* feel something for Caro, then? I thought so.'

'What does it matter?' JB slammed his hand against the boot. 'I used her and she knows it. There is nothing I can say to make 'er believe it wasn't all a lie. She will never forgive me, not now.'

'She might. She's forgiven Jack enough times. If you tell her how you feel, I'm sure she'll come running.' Tessa leant against his car thoughtfully. 'Caro's the kind of woman who loves a grand gesture. I'm sure you can think of something that would melt her heart.'

JB gave her a sideways glance. 'We are not so different, you and I. Do not look like that! I meant that we both came here to find something and we ended up falling in love instead. Idiots.' He smiled briefly.

'What did you come here to find?' She raised her eyebrows. 'Apart from the money, of course.'

'Ah, the money! Can you blame me? Five million pounds would change anyone's life.' JB stubbed his cigarette out. 'But I also wanted to know about the Forbes-Henry family. I wanted to know everything about Gabrielle, about this woman my grandfather was in love with for most of his life.'

'I can understand that.'

'And you, what did you come 'ere to find?'

Tessa bit her lip. 'I don't know. It sounds so clichéd, but . . . myself, maybe?'

JB unexpectedly turned and kissed her on both cheeks. 'You are a good person, Tessa. A good person and a good journalist. I am sorry I gave you such an 'ard time. Jilly, she wanted me to keep an eye on you.'

'I guessed that. You don't need to worry about me, though,' she added with a positivity she didn't feel. 'I'm not going back to television after this.'

'*Non?*' JB gave her a gallant wink. 'It will be their loss. And I mean that.'

'I really think you do,' she said, pleased in spite of herself. She nodded at him as he took his car keys out. 'Remember what I said about Caro.'

He shook his head regretfully. 'You are a romantic and I appreciate your advice. But it is too late, *chérie*. Caro and me, it is not meant to be. You 'ave a much better chance, you know, with Will?' As she gasped, he gave her one last, piratical smile. 'It is obvious, *chérie*. Anyone can see it. So . . .' he kissed her hand, 'this is *au revoir*. I do not think we will see each other again but you never know.'

Tessa watched him pull out of the B&B, the tyres of his Porsche skidding on the snow and sending a fountain of snowflakes into the air.

One thing you could say about JB, she thought with a wry smile as she trudged back to her cottage with a heavy heart: he had style.

Wandering into the kitchen in search of a sandwich, her head buried in *Much Ado About Nothing*, Milly was taken aback to find her mother sobbing into the orange and cranberry soufflés she was practising for Sophie and Gil's wedding. A complicated blend of puréed, sweetened cranberries, fresh orange zest and a delicious bitter orange liqueur, the soufflés would be difficult enough to pull off if Henny had been on form. As it was, they didn't stand a chance and there were three failed trays of sunken mixture on the Aga top to prove it.

'Mum, what on earth is the matter?' Milly put her arms round her mother. 'Blimey, what have you done to those? Slashed your wrists into them?'

'No, I bloody well haven't!' Henny cried. Yanking a tray of white soufflé dishes out of the Aga ten minutes too early, she smashed them down with a bang. 'I'm sorry, darling. I'm just so upset about everything. How could Claudette do that to Will? How could she lead him on like that, just for money?' Uncaringly, the soufflés on the tray collapsed and folded into the dishes as if they'd been jabbed with a knitting needle. 'Oh, look at these, they're ruined!'

'Mum, you're getting yourself into a right old state.' Milly helped her into a chair. 'Perhaps you should worry about the soufflés later.'

'But there's so much to do.' Henny dabbed her eyes with her floury apron. Her sandy hair looked frizzier than ever and her eyes, normally so vibrantly blue and bright, were puffed up and blotchy from crying.

'Don't worry about it! I know you think you're Superwoman, and most of the time you are, but honestly, I think you need to calm down a bit.'

'It's this bloody new Aga,' Henny said, giving it a savage glare. 'It's so temperamental and I'm not used to it yet. I'm trying out menus for Sophie's wedding to Gil and I can't bear it . . . poor, poor Tristan!' She burst into a fresh bout of noisy tears. Leaping up, she started mixing another batch of soufflés with a very heavy hand.

Wearing a slinky pink dressing gown and fluffy mules, Caro wandered into the kitchen in search of a splash of tonic for her enormous glass of gin.

'Bloody hell, who died in here?' she said with a lightness she didn't feel. Since the terrible day when JB had told them all about the will, Caro had been keeping herself to herself, licking her wounds in private. As usual, she sought solace in alcohol and had emerged for long enough to pour herself a gigantic top-up.

Hearing Caro's flippant tone was enough to send Henny bubbling over the edge. 'I don't know how you have the audacity to show your face in here,' she shrieked at the top of her voice, making Milly and Caro flinch in unison. 'Parading around like some cat that's got the cream. You should be ashamed of yourself!'

Milly was amazed at how thin Caro looked. Emaciated at the best of times, her scrawny upper arms and non-existent chest made her look like a skeleton. In spite of some heavy make-up, her blue eyes looked huge in her face and they were ringed with violet shadows. In fact, she looked the picture of abject misery. Still, it was hard to feel sorry for her when Uncle Jack was stumbling round the manor like a suicidal ghost, Milly thought, knowing exactly where her loyalties sat.

'Why aren't you chasing your French boyfriend back to bloody France?' Henny screamed at Caro. 'No one wants you here, not Milly, not me and least of all Jack.'

'I bloody well *live* here,' Caro retorted haughtily. She felt stupid enough about JB without Henny hammering the point home. 'Which is more than can be said for *you*, you bloody free-loader. Why don't you bugger off and buy your own house? Or are you hoping you might be in for a share of the millions if you stick around and make yourself indispensable?'

Milly sucked in her breath with horror. Aunt Caro had gone too far this time, even for her.

At this, Henny lost her temper completely and smashed her rolling pin into a plate of nearby cranberries. Crimson juice and pulp shot out over Caro, splattering her pink dressing gown. She blinked, looking down at herself in shock.

Milly thought that with a few more cranberries, Aunt Caro would look rather like Carrie in the film where pig's blood had been tipped all over her. Milly stifled a giggle.

Henny lowered her voice to a scarily calm level.

'You're an absolute *disgrace*,' she said. 'You've let the family down and you've embarrassed Jack in front of the entire village. You've been in cahoots with JB, which you might not have realised at the time but it serves you right.' She put her rolling pin down carefully. 'You think you can do whatever you like, don't you, Caro? You think you can treat me like some sort of punchbag in order to boost your own pathetic self-esteem.'

Milly gulped. She had never seen her mother like this before. Even Caro was stunned into silence. But Henny wasn't done.

'I warned you about JB,' she said, shaking her head. 'I knew he was trouble but you didn't listen. You were bowled over by his compliments and his ridiculous French charm, thinking he loved you when the whole time he was simply stringing you along like Claudette was with Will.'

Tears sprang into Caro's eyes and in spite of herself, Henny softened. 'I don't mean to hurt you, Caro. I don't mean to cut you down to size the way you have done me all these years. I just want you to know how much Jack loved you and that until you did this, he would have forgiven you for pretty much anything. It's such a waste, isn't it? I think you did fall in love with JB and, who knows, maybe he fell in love with you too. But Jack loved you to pieces and you threw that away, for what? Nothing, Caro. Absolutely nothing. You don't care about Jack and you don't care about this family. If I were you and, believe me, I really wouldn't want to be in your shoes at the moment, but *if* I were you?' Henny gave her a look that was almost kind. 'I'd go after JB before he leaves for France and beg him to take you with him. Because there's nothing left for you here, is there?'

Her body rocking as if she'd been punched, Caro looked as if she might faint. Slamming down her glass of gin, a cry tore from her throat and she legged it out of the kitchen in her fluffy mules.

There was silence for several seconds.

'Fuck,' said Milly, full of admiration. 'Fucking *hell*, Mum.'

Henny was too shocked at herself to care about Milly's language. 'Was I too cruel?' she said, putting her hands to her hot face and leaving great floury smears. 'The last thing I want to do is turn into Caro. I just wanted her to see what she's done to everyone.'

Milly shook her head. 'You weren't cruel. You were truthful and you said things Aunt Caro has needed to hear for a long time.' She got to her feet, feeling slightly unsteady. 'I'm really proud of you, Mum. Aunt Caro has been so horrible to you and you've finally stood up for yourself – at last!'

Henny wiped a hand across her flushed forehead, stunned that she had been able to be so calm. 'So that's what it feels like to have a backbone!' she said with a shaky laugh. She tipped the tray of soufflés into the bin and tried to get her adrenalin under control. Giving her daughter a mischievous grin, she wielded her rolling pin dangerously. 'Watch out, Mills, I could get to like this!'

Helping herself to an orange, Milly sincerely hoped she didn't. She was bloody scary in this mood, even if she had been impressive. Milly grabbed *Much Ado About Nothing* and decided it wouldn't do to get on the wrong side of her mother again.

Tessa paused outside Will's cottage. He hadn't been seen for days and according to Milly had last been spotted staggering towards it intent on getting paralytic.

She clutched the thermos of hot chocolate Henny had sent her over with. Why Henny thought she could cheer anyone up was beyond her; in fact, she thought she was probably the last person Will would like to see right now but she couldn't admit that to Henny so she kept her mouth shut and made a show of trudging through the snow to Will's cottage.

I can do this, she told herself. It's only Will. He's not going to bite. With a thumping heart, she pushed open the door as softly as she could. Tiptoeing into the lounge, she found Will sprawled across the sofa with Austin on his lap. Austin opened one bleary eye which immediately brightened when he saw her and he wagged his tail exuberantly. Stifling a laugh, she put a finger to her lips to silence him.

Taking her scarf off and kneeling down on the floor next to the sofa, she studied Will, feeling her heart lurch slightly. Fast asleep, his face was softer and he looked quite peaceful. The worry lines that gave his eyes character were relaxed and his mouth was curved into the ghost of a smile. Resisting the urge to brush his tawny gold hair away from his eyes and press her lips to his, Tessa left the flask on the coffee table and backed out of the room.

Will woke up as he heard the front door swing shut. He had been having the most amazingly sexy dream about Tessa charging down to the lake in her underwear. He stretched luxuriantly and rubbed Austin's head. He felt so much better about everything. Drinking himself stupid had been the best thing; it had purged his self-pity and cleared his head. He knew how he felt about Claudette, about his family and, most of all, about Tessa. He didn't know what he was going to do but at least he had admitted his feelings to himself at last.

Sniffing the air, Will wondered why the faint tang of Penhaligon's Bluebell hung in the air. He noticed a flask on the table next to a pink scarf.

'What's this, old boy?' he asked Austin, baffled, picking up the scarf. Burying his face in it, he realised it was Tessa's. She had been here, in his cottage. He must have just missed her. Disappointed, he sank back on the sofa, the scarf wound around his hands.

Jack put the bottle of whisky down with a trembling hand. With a monumental effort, he took a step backward from it, putting some distance between himself and the bottle. He felt like a man stranded on a desert island, desperate to avoid a broken raft that was in his line of vision. He knew it wouldn't do him any good to get drunk again, but he couldn't help thinking it might bring him short-term hope – and maybe, just maybe, it might prevent reality stabbing him between the eyes.

He hadn't had a drink for two weeks now but the temptation to blot out his pain with alcohol was a daily challenge and he was fighting it hard.

Where was she? he wondered despairingly. Caro had been missing for a couple of weeks now and she hadn't even left him a note to say where she was going. He had spent the first few days worried sick about her; leaving without contact was flagrantly out of character for her, but Jack soon found anger overpowering any anxiety he felt, leaving him prowling round the manor house, cursing her very existence and her ability to leave such damage in her wake. Part of him was numb with shock but the other part of him felt terrifyingly alive – alert, aware and twitching with pain as if he had been operated on without anaesthetic.

How could she leave him after everything they had been through together? What about Tristan and Will? Hadn't Caro given them a second's thought? They were her children, for heaven's sake! He didn't want her back, not this time, but didn't she respect him enough to leave a bloody note, at least? For Will and Tristan, if not for him? Jack had always known Caro wasn't the most maternal woman in the world but her cavalier attitude towards their children had left him furious.

Even so, Jack was floundering. He felt lost without her, as if his right arm had been chopped off. But the worst, most humiliating thing of all was that he *missed* Caro. He missed her so much, it was like a physical pain, one he was powerless to deal with and powerless to disguise from the world.

But did he miss *her*, the woman he was married to? Jack

allowed himself a rare moment of introspection. Caro had always been passionate and demanding and self-absorbed, hardly a paragon of virtue but exhilarating nonetheless. But was that the person she had been at the end? He didn't think so. Jack had an idea he simply missed the woman Caro had once been, outrageous and untamed but with a redeeming and undeniable charm. They had been partners in crime in the old days, one and the same, but they had both changed irrevocably and could therefore no longer exist together.

'Still finding it tough?' Henny appeared behind him with a kindly smile and a toasted bacon sandwich. Jack was rapidly turning into a bag of bones and she was desperately trying to feed him up.

'I haven't been at the whisky, Hen, so don't worry. I almost took the top off the bottle, but somehow I managed to abstain. I can't tell you how much of a challenge it was, but I did it.'

'I believe you. Are you really going to an AA meeting?'

He shuddered. 'I expect I shall hate it. It's bound to be full of trendy young people who think binge-drinking on a Friday night means they have a problem. They wouldn't have the first idea what it's like to *need* a drink like you need air.' Jack gazed longingly at the bottle of whisky again. 'But I need help, I know that. That bloody counsellor is going to think all her Christmases have come at once with a seasoned professional like me there.'

Henny smiled warmly at him. 'Good for you, Jack. You're doing so well.'

He stared past her. 'Where do you think she is, Hen? How could she leave us like this?'

Henny felt dreadful. She couldn't shake off the terrible feeling that it was completely down to her that Caro had disappeared. After their run-in, Caro had simply vanished into thin air. Henny had spent the past two weeks apologising to Jack and she did so again.

'It's not your fault, Hen. Caro has always been a law unto

herself and no one can stop her once she has an idea in her head. She does what she likes, when she likes.'

'She did love you,' Henny said desperately. 'I know she did.'

'What does it matter?' Jack said, his voice dead. 'She's gone and it's probably for the best.' He handed the uneaten sandwich back to Henny and drifted over to the window.

Jack longed for someone to come and put their arms round him and soothe away his troubles. He was aware he was feeling disgustingly sorry for himself but he couldn't help it, he just knew he needed someone. The thought was slowly registering that it wasn't Caro he was thinking of when Clemmie arrived, wafting Chanel No. 5 and the distinctive aroma of a brand-new waxed jacket.

'Jack! I was wondering if you wanted company on your way to your meeting?' Wearing bright pink welly boots, Clemmie's hazel eyes sparkled as she twirled a pink and white spotted umbrella at him. 'I can't believe I'm saying this but I actually think I might like your shitty English weather. Well, the snow, anyway. Isn't it beautiful?'

Jack smiled at the sight of her slender legs in the brightly coloured welly boots. Calm, gentle Clemmie with her delightful Texan accent and kind words – she was just what he needed to take his mind off Caro. Unaware that Henny was beaming happily as she backed out of the room with the cooling bacon sandwich, Jack gallantly offered his arm to Clemmie.

'How can I refuse when you've made such an effort to work the country housewife look?'

Clemmie glanced down at her feet with a giggle. 'Are the pink boots too much? I couldn't resist them, I'm afraid, they're just so *cute*.'

She took his arm and squeezed it with her fingers. The gesture was so unexpectedly tender, Jack felt himself jerk back to life.

'You're a sight for sore eyes, Clemmie. And I love the boots, they're very *you*.'

'Why, thank you, kind sir. Hey, I thought we could go for some lunch afterwards. You can introduce me to this steak and kidney pie thing and we could share a bottle of something non-alcoholic . . .'

They headed to the front door and Jack grabbed his coat, feeling a hundred times better. How about that? he thought with a grin. As he followed Clemmie out into the rain, any idea of drowning his sorrows with whisky went clean out of his head.

'If you really think it will do any good, I'll come along.' Tessa avoided Will's eyes and pulled on Jack's welly boots. What was Will doing here? He said he wanted her help with Tristan but things were so awkward between her and Will, she wasn't sure she was the best person for the job.

Will was confused by Tessa's reaction. 'Thanks. I'm just so worried about him and Christmas Eve is only a few days away.' He followed her out of her cottage and pulled his collar up. He couldn't understand why Tessa was being so frosty with him. Ever since Claudette had left, Tessa seemed to have gone out of her way to avoid him. He really wanted to tell her how he felt about her but she was being so offhand with him, he wasn't sure what sort of response he was going to get.

'Did you hear about Gil's father?' Tessa said, her voice muffled by the scarf he had returned to her that morning.

Will nodded. 'In view of all that, I feel terrible talking Tristan into going to see Sophie but we owe it to him, don't we? I mean, he loves Sophie more than anything and the thought of her wedding going ahead must be killing him.'

Tessa pulled her gloves on and said nothing. She wanted Tristan and Sophie to get back together as much as Will did; she just wished he hadn't roped her into helping out. Being around Will was agonising. She had the impression he wanted to say something to her but she wasn't going to give him the chance.

After all the terrible things Claudette had said, Tessa couldn't bear to hear it from his own lips.

In silence, they headed inside Tristan's cottage and kicked snow off their boots as they ducked under the low beam. Peering inside his kitchen which had a stack of dirty mugs sitting in the sink and two of Henny's delicious chicken casseroles sitting uneaten on the side, it was obvious Tristan wasn't back to normal. He was a naturally messy creature but he hadn't cleared up for weeks by the looks of things.

They found him slumped across his period sofa in his studio, watching TV with the sound off, his eyes fixed unseeingly on an *Only Fools and Horses* repeat. He was wearing paint-splattered jeans and a rugby shirt that had seen better days, and a half-empty bottle of whisky was on the floor in front of him.

He glared at them ungraciously. 'What do you want? I'm busy.'

'I can see that.' Will ignored Tristan's sulky stare and pointedly took his coat off. 'Are you enjoying that?' He nodded at the TV.

'It's a bloody riot.'

Will took a seat at Tristan's easel. 'I always find the jokes funnier when I can hear them,' he offered mildly.

Tristan scowled and said nothing, not even looking at Will.

Will began to feel concerned. He had never seen his brother like this before; it was worse than when Sophie had left him the first time. Convincing Tristan to approach Sophie before her wedding was obviously going to be harder than he had thought. He felt a tremor of unease and wondered if they should have left Tristan to stew.

Catching sight of Tessa over Will's shoulder, Tristan narrowed his eyes at her. 'What are you doing here? Oh, I see, you thought there was safety in numbers and that the two of you might be able to convince me I need to run to Sophie and tell her how much I love her, right?'

Tessa flinched. 'We just wanted to see if you were all right, actually.'

'Well, as you can see, I'm fine and dandy,' Tristan responded sarcastically. He had an inch of golden stubble on his chin and his blue eyes were flint-hard. 'Now, bugger off, both of you, and leave me to my misery.'

'No can do. Now, budge up,' Will said, squashing himself on the sofa next to him. 'Look, Tristan. You love Sophie and Sophie loves you. Just tell her how you feel and stop wasting time.'

Tristan glowered at him. 'You're a fine one to bloody talk!'

Will went red and avoided Tessa's gaze. 'Don't you think you need to make amends with Sophie?'

'Don't you think she needs to make amends with me?' Tristan yelled, sitting up suddenly. 'I have a child, Will. A five-year-old daughter I knew nothing about. How would you feel in my shoes?'

Will nodded. 'Like shit. I get it, Tris. I just think you need to understand that Sophie thought she was doing what was right at the time. I know it will be hard for you to forgive her but are you really going to stand by and watch her marry a man she doesn't even love?'

Tessa timidly leant forward, her green eyes compassionate. 'I think Sophie feels a duty to Gil,' she said. 'I think his father dying was the final nail in the coffin for her. She doesn't feel as if she can be the one to back out of it.'

Tristan's face crumpled. 'I want to go to her,' he admitted in a hoarse voice. 'I want to be a man about it and tell her how I feel. I want to be a father to my daughter ... to Ruby.' He shook his head hopelessly. 'But I don't know if I can put myself in that position again, do you understand? I . . . I think I'm done.' Tears slid down his cheeks.

Realising there was nothing else they could say to change Tristan's mind, Will and Tessa slipped away.

'I don't think that did much good, did it?' Will said dejectedly, shoving his hands into his pockets as they trudged away from Tristan's cottage. 'I don't blame him for being angry but I can't bear the thought of Tristan missing out on being with the woman he loves. Not again.'

Tessa bent her head. Will's words were so steeped in feeling, she could only imagine his view was coloured by losing Claudette. She hoped he would assume her watery eyes were due to the bitter wind whipping furiously around them.

'I really thought we could make him change his mind,' Will was saying, his voice muffled by his scarf. 'You two are such good friends, I was sure you could make him see sense.'

'Maybe we're not as close as you think,' Tessa mumbled, wondering why she suddenly felt so suicidal.

Will raised his eyebrows. 'What do you mean? I know you started off talking to Tris to get information but I thought you'd made a real connection with him . . . I thought you saw him as a friend.'

'To get information?' Tessa echoed. She stopped dead, her cheeks suffused with colour.

Will stared at her, beginning to feel exasperated. Was she seriously going to deny it? 'You know, like it said in those notes you left in my office? "How Best to Use the Forbes-Henry Family".' His mouth curled angrily as he finally confronted her about it.

Mortified, Tessa swung round to face him. 'Those weren't my notes . . . I mean, they were, but it's not what you think!'

'Oh, really?' Will grabbed hold of her. 'What am I supposed to think? That you *didn't* use my family when you obviously intended to do just that?'

Blinded by tears, Tessa struggled against him. So this was what Will really thought of her! She knew he'd seen the notes, of course, but they'd never discussed them and she'd forgotten all about how incriminating that page had been. God, how dreadful it made her seem!

With her heart beating madly in her chest, Tessa wondered if there was anything she could say to convince Will she wasn't the shallow, unscrupulous person he must think she was.

'My boss . . . she wanted me to use you all,' Tessa faltered. 'It looks bad, I know, and I admit I did it at the start. But after that, I couldn't . . . I fell in love with . . . I mean, I couldn't do it because you all started to mean so much to me.' She trembled in his arms.

Will gazed down at her. At the time, the notes had seemed so important, but what did all that matter now? He wasn't sure how she felt about him but he knew Tessa wasn't the person he'd first thought she was; in fact, Will knew damned well he wanted to do nothing more than to tell her exactly how he felt about her.

So what was stopping him? Will clenched his jaw fiercely. Deep down, he knew his outburst had nothing to do with Tessa's notes; it was simply his own frustration with the situation they were in.

What sort of man would he be, waving his fiancée off one minute and declaring undying love to Tessa the next? She would think he was on the rebound, that his feelings for her weren't genuine. After all, Will realised, Tessa had no idea he'd been about to break it off with Claudette. Will had always thought of himself as a man of integrity but right now he felt like the worst kind of bastard. About to open his mouth and say everything he'd been thinking, he was taken aback when Tessa twisted away from him.

'Oh, what's the point?' she cried, yanking her hands free. 'There's obviously nothing I can say to change your mind about me.'

Rubbing a hand clumsily across her face, she stalked away, leaving Will staring after her.

Chapter Twenty-Seven

Humming along to a catchy Christmas jingle on the radio, Clemmie removed a tray of cinnamon scones from the Aga, puzzled to find them burnt to a crisp. Prodding one of the blackened offerings with her finger, she wondered where she had gone wrong and stuck her head inside the Aga to see if it was working properly.

Jack strolled into the kitchen, in search of a strong coffee, and was shocked to find Clemmie with her head in the oven. His heart pounding in his ears, he yanked her out by her waist. 'Christ, woman, get out of there! Rufus isn't worth it!'

'*What?*' Startled, Clemmie started to laugh. 'My God, did you think I was trying to kill myself?' She put a reassuring hand on his arm. 'Honey, I *know* Rufus isn't worth it – he's just a gutless bastard.'

'Glad to hear it. Sorry about that.' Jack went scarlet. 'And just for the record, an Aga wouldn't be a terribly efficient way to commit suicide anyway. You'd probably just singe your eyebrows.'

'Right, I'll remember that. And thank you for charging to my rescue like that – what a gentleman.' She picked up her tray of scones with an innocent twinkle in her eye. 'Fancy one?'

He eyed them fearfully. 'Er . . . they look . . . very appetising but I think I'll pass, if it's all the same to you.' He liked her immensely but he drew the line at swallowing charcoal.

'Don't blame you.' She dumped them in the bin and stuck her bottom lip out in mock self-pity. 'I don't think baking is my strong point, do you?' Seeing Jack's smart suit, she gave him an admiring up and down glance. 'Hey, you scrub up well – is that what you English say?'

'We do. And thanks.' Jack thought Clemmie looked ravishing in a close-fitting navy dress and scarlet shoes, with her dark, glossy hair tied up in a loose knot. He wondered where she might be headed after Christmas but he was loath to ask her in case she said she was flying back to LA. Having spent so much time with her since she had moved in, Jack had a feeling he would sorely miss her.

'Have you heard from Caro?' she asked, her hazel eyes full of sympathy.

'Actually, yes. This arrived yesterday.' He tugged a postcard out of his pocket and handed it to Clemmie.

The front had some topless girls lying on a beach. Clemmie turned it over. 'In St Tropez with JB,' she read aloud. 'Sorry and all that. Sure you're all much better off without me. Much love, Caro.' Clemmie raised her eyebrows. 'How do you feel?'

Jack considered. 'Surprisingly good. At least I know where she is and even though she's run off with that treacherous French bastard, I'd probably rather she did that than gone with some random chap I don't even know.' He shrugged. 'It's all water under the bridge now, isn't it? Caro and I had a blast but things change.'

Clemmie knew exactly how he felt. Her relationship with Rufus seemed like a lifetime ago and now that the wedding day had passed without incident, she mostly felt an overwhelming sense of relief.

'What about you? Have you heard from Rufus?'

She shook her head. 'I'm glad. I'm not sure how I might feel if he begged me to come back. I hate him for what he did to me obviously but he seemed to be my Achilles heel. I really did love him,' she added sadly.

Jack made a show of looking at his watch. 'Er . . . we need to make a move, I think. The wedding is starting in less than an hour. Where are all the flowers?'

'Henny left them in the hallway. She's already down at the chapel, I think.' Clemmie whipped her apron off and checked the pins in her hair with her fingers. She paused. 'I can't believe it's Christmas Eve, Jack. It's so beautiful here . . . I'm so grateful you all asked me to stay.' And she was. Even though she'd have been married by now, she knew it was all for the best. And being with the Forbes-Henrys had healed her more than they could know.

Clemmie squared her shoulders and followed Jack out into the hallway. She was feeling stronger by the day. The stories about her relationship with Rufus were still in evidence but, without much comment from either side, new angles were thin on the ground. Rufus's camp seemed to have exhausted their supply of defensive comments, perhaps realising that if India chose to come forward and claim she had been underage at the start of their relationship, Rufus might find himself on a charge of statutory rape.

Being as famous and as pretty as he was, Rufus would find prison a scary place to be, Clemmie was sure, and the kind-hearted part of her hoped he escaped such an ordeal. Still, if Rufus had been harbouring fond dreams of 'doing a Hugh Grant' after the Hollywood Boulevard incident and playing the lovable cad, he was in for a shock. After allowing him an initial voice, the press had turned on him viciously, branding him a cheat and a liar, and stopping just short of accusations of child abuse.

Clemmie looked up at the gorgeous Christmas tree in the hallway, bedecked with glass baubles, beautiful white lights and handmade decorations. She was thrilled when Jack and Henny had asked her – no, *begged* her – to stay with them for Christmas and she had gladly thrown herself into all the arrangements, pleased to have things to distract her from her troubles. It was only at night she felt haunted by memories. Her heart longed for Rufus or for what Rufus had represented in her life, perhaps. Without him, she felt immeasurably lonely but Jack, equally lost without Caro, had barely left her side. He made her laugh and she was grateful for his company.

'Shall we?' he said, flinging her coat around her shoulders and proffering his arm with a grin.

'Why, I'd be delighted, kind sir,' she returned, exaggerating her Texan accent. She squeezed his hand. 'We're doing a good job propping each other up, aren't we? I can't believe what good friends we've become in such a short space of time, Jack.'

Suspecting his feelings ran a little deeper than the platonic, Jack said nothing and helped Clemmie out into the snow.

'You look beautiful,' Tessa told Sophie quietly. She adjusted the comb of fresh pink rosebuds in Sophie's hair and stood back to get a better look. The halter-neck ivory dress flattered Sophie's shapely body and brought out the caramel hues in her swept-up hair. Her brown eyes looked huge under the subtle, smoky make-up but they sparkled with agitation, not excitement.

'Thanks.' Sophie didn't even look at her reflection in the mirror. She'd seen the dress before; she knew what it looked like. And what did it matter? she thought despondently. If she were marrying Tristan, she would happily do it in jeans. Style was of the utmost importance to Gil but Sophie couldn't care less about all the special touches he had agonised over. Getting married shouldn't be about the dress or the flowers or the venue. Now that her wedding day had arrived, it all felt incredibly real but, as Sophie had known it would, it still didn't feel *right*.

'So . . . does anyone know where Tristan's gone?'

Tessa poured them some champagne and shook her head. Shortly after their visit to his cottage, she and Will had seen Tristan take off in his yellow MG. He had sent them both a text

458

to say he was fine but that he needed time to think. No one had heard from him at all that morning and, with less than an hour to go, Tessa couldn't help thinking Tristan was cutting it fine if he planned to change Sophie's mind. But then maybe he didn't plan to do anything of the sort.

'He still isn't answering his phone,' Tessa admitted.

'He's hurting so much and I don't know what to do.' Sophie wrung her hands anxiously, clearly sick with worry. 'If I could just talk to him, if I could just explain about Ruby, but I don't even know where to find him. I know I shouldn't have left it until today but I've been wracked with guilt over Gil and his father dying. I've been in such a state about it all but I wish I'd done something, *anything*, because this is unbearable.'

Tessa sighed sympathetically and discreetly checked her phone again. But there were no messages from Tristan. She glanced down at her berry-coloured dress and matching silk shoes, feeling sorry for Sophie. Weddings were usually such joyous occasions, full of pleasure and laughter and, most of all, expectation, but this one felt anything but upbeat. It was madness; Sophie was marrying Gil because she felt guilty and Tristan was too hurt to make amends with Sophie. And in a matter of hours, it would be too late and two people who shouldn't be together would be tied together in holy matrimony and Tristan would hate himself for letting Sophie go again.

'This is really happening, isn't it?' Sophie said to Tessa in a panicked voice. 'I'm really going to marry Gil.'

She took a long gulp of champagne, aware she needed some sort of boost to get her through the day. Gil had spent the day before in such a jittery state, Sophie had been sure he was going to cancel the wedding. He had attended his father's funeral alone, at his own insistence, and since then had behaved very oddly. One night she found him pacing around the sitting room, clutching at his hair and mumbling under his breath, and the next day he had spent hours staring into space with his fingers twisting manically in his lap. Another time she had caught him standing in the snow staring at Appleton Manor, an expression of utter peace on his face, and when she had tentatively taken his hand, he had glanced down at her vaguely as if he didn't even recognise her.

'Thank goodness Gil has Nathan to talk to,' Sophie said out loud. She frowned as Tessa shot her a funny look and gave a half-shrug back. She *was* pleased Gil had someone to talk to and that he and Nathan had formed such a close friendship. She was in such a mess over Tristan, she couldn't help feeling relieved that Nathan was shouldering some of the burden of looking after Gil.

Tessa watched her, her mind inadvertently slipping to thoughts of Will. Realising she was going to be standing inches from him in the chapel, she trembled for a second, accidentally spilling champagne all over Sophie's satin Jimmy Choos. Tessa gasped.

'Don't worry about it,' Sophie said, laughing in spite of herself. 'Just don't let Gil see them, he chose them . . . Christ, he chose *everything* for this wedding.' She glanced down at herself, realising Gil controlled most things. How had that happened? Why did she always let him dictate her life? She knew he didn't do it on purpose and that he always had her best interests at heart, but Sophie hadn't realised how much she had resented him for it until now. She downed the rest of her champagne and changed the subject. 'So, are you going to resign from your job?'

Tessa sighed. 'I think so. I'm just choosing the right time, you know? Jilly is so angry with me still and even though it doesn't really matter any more, I can't face a huge showdown with her at the moment. There have been enough of those going on around here to last me a lifetime.' She topped up their glasses. 'I still want to write my novel but I haven't touched my notes for the past couple of weeks. I just can't seem to concentrate. I'm too confused with everything that's happened. After Christmas, I think I just need to get away.'

Sophie sympathised. She felt like running away herself. 'How are things with Will now?'

'Awkward.' Tessa touched up her lipstick, pushing down the memory of his angry face when he had confronted her about using his family. 'Seriously, you could cut the air with a knife when we're in the same room together, Soph. He still doesn't trust me. And after everything Claudette said, I just can't bear being around him. I mean, I want to be, but I can't handle it.'

'I'm sure he has feelings for you, Tess. From what I remember about Will, he doesn't give his heart away easily, but when he does, he falls hard.'

'What, like he did with Claudette?' Tessa snapped back bitingly, as always feeling nauseous at the thought of Will and Claudette together. 'Sorry, Soph. I'm just feeling so awful at the moment.' She put her champagne flute down carefully. Any more and she'd be staggering around the chapel like an old lush. This was Sophie's day; Tessa wasn't going to spoil it by going on about Will.

'Forget it.' Sophie shrugged the comment off easily. 'But seriously, thinking about Will and Claudette's relationship, I reckon Will was ready to settle down when he met Claudette and she took full advantage of that.' She warmed to her theme. 'I think Will was taken in by her because she went all out to convince him that she was his soul mate. But if he really loved her, he wouldn't have kissed you in the first place, would he? And he certainly wouldn't have found it so difficult to be around you afterwards. Guilt's one thing but being deeply attracted to someone is something else entirely. Trust me.'

Sophie's rational assessment of Will's relationship with Claudette made Tessa's heart jerk with hope for a second. It sounded plausible and it fitted with the odd thing Tristan had said to her too but she couldn't shake off Claudette's departing words. She said as much to Sophie.

'Haven't you ever thought Claudette may have said all that stuff to scupper any chance of you and Will getting together?' Sophie asked astutely. 'I wouldn't put it past her.'

Tessa paused with her lipstick in mid-air. As much as she wanted to believe that, she didn't. And after Will's bad experience, he probably hated all women, let alone one whose morals he thought were questionable, she thought dismally.

No. Tessa tucked her lipstick away. She was better off trying to forget Will. After Christmas, she would leave Appleton, go back to her flat in Putney and do her best to put her life back together. The thought made her spirits plummet to her Jimmy Choo's.

'Bear in mind what I said about Claudette,' Sophie insisted. 'Not everything is as it seems, Tess. I should know that better than anyone.' She fiddled with a lock of her hair. 'And there's no point in both of us being up shit creek without a paddle, is there?'

They both laughed, especially when Ruby rushed in behind them and demanded, 'What's shit creek?' Wearing the same dress as Tessa with the addition of a big damson bow at the back, Ruby looked like a little angel. Carefully placing a garland of pink roses and ribbons in her golden hair, Tessa decided all Ruby needed was a little gilt harp to finish off the look.

'What's shit creek?' Ruby repeated huffily.

'Nothing,' Tessa told her with a grin. 'Forget you ever heard it.'

'OK. Will my real daddy be there?'

Tessa met Sophie's eyes above Ruby's head. Like most children, Ruby possessed an uncanny knack for asking pertinent questions at the most inappropriate times.

'I very much doubt it, darling,' Sophie said, forcing back tears. She stared at Ruby bleakly. 'I think your real daddy is the last person I'm expecting to be at the wedding.'

Henny checked her list again. Flowers, check. Ring cushion, check. Guests, vicar, best man, groom, check. The only thing missing was the bride, Henny thought, feeling guilty for hoping it would stay that way.

Gil was standing at the front with Nathan to his right in the role of best man. Despite having given himself a severe going over with St Tropez tanning spray the night before, Gil was as pale as a ghost and sweating profusely. He kept dabbing at his forehead with a pink silk handkerchief and Nathan, wearing trousers that were so tight every guest could guess his inside leg measurement, looked equally ill at ease.

Clothed in matching dove-grey tails and pink, Windsor-knotted ties, neither Gil nor Nathan were listening to the elderly vicar who, although he had never seen a groom wearing mascara before, didn't like to judge and was doing his best to keep their spirits up.

'Sit down, darling,' Henny's new boyfriend Barnaby coaxed her. Dressed in a smart navy suit with his silvery hair flattened with some gel, he was doing his best to keep Henny calm. 'Everything looks absolutely perfect.'

It did. Garlands of pale pink roses entwined with dark green ivy had been strung along the sides of the pews and were filling the chapel with a pleasing fragrance. Crystals had been tied to each knot of ribbon which gave everything a fairytale touch. The whole look reeked of Gil's tasteful eye and attention to detail.

Gil turned to nod to his mother. She was a small, unassuming woman dressed in a simple grey suit with a black ribbon in her steely-grey hair, the only outward sign of mourning she wore. She looked forlorn to be attending alone but she kept giving Gil encouraging smiles and was clearly very proud of him.

Henny turned to Barnaby. 'Jack looks much better today,' she whispered, nodding approvingly at Jack's blue and silver striped tie and dark suit. 'He had a postcard from Caro, did I tell you? She's sunning herself in St Tropez with JB, apparently.' Henny pursed her lips. 'I'm surprised Jack's bouncing back so well from it all. I can't imagine how he's doing it, what with giving up drink as well.'

Catching sight of Jack giggling with Clemmie in the pew next to them, Barnaby thought he had a fair idea of why Jack wasn't as devastated as he might have been. He patted Henny's hand comfortingly and said nothing. Today's wedding was fraught enough for her; she wasn't thinking straight. It was obvious to anyone that Jack was absolutely besotted with Clemmie. But Henny was too busy frowning at David. He was holding Alicia's hand and murmuring in her ear. Turning crimson beneath her freckles, she kept giggling and stroking his thigh. Henny sent a fervent prayer up to the Good Lord that David had heard of condoms. She was sure they hadn't been to bed together yet because she'd accidentally overheard David telling Milly to shut up when she goaded him about it recently, but by the look of things, close bodily contact was imminent.

Freddie rushed into the chapel and took a seat next to Milly. 'Where have you been?' She shoved him crossly, tugging at the short skirt of her scarlet suit. 'You're supposed to be my pretend date for this wedding and I've been sitting here getting chilblains all on my own.'

'I was outside with Will.' Freddie rubbed Milly's cold hands with his deliciously warm ones and admired her long, coltish legs in the black opaque tights she was wearing. 'He's just been over to Tristan's cottage but there's still no sign of him.'

'*Crap.*' Milly took out her mobile. 'I really thought he was going to do the romantic thing and declare undying love for Sophie before the wedding took place. I'm sending him another text telling him to stop being such a knobhead.'

Freddie laughed. 'That's bound to get him to change his mind.'

Outside the chapel, shivering in his charcoal-grey suit, Will was doing exactly the same thing and furiously texting a rude message to his brother.

Almost slipping over on the icy step, Will gritted his teeth. Where the bloody hell was Tristan?

Having missed Will by a mere thirty seconds, Tristan was sitting shivering in his freezing cold cottage. He had Ruby's photograph in his hands and he was unsteadily tracing his thumb around the outline of her heart-shaped face and her cute button nose.

How had he and Sophie created something so angelically beautiful? he wondered. He saw from Ruby's dancing eyes and effervescent smile that she would probably be a little handful and he loved the thought of that. But . . . he didn't know anything about her. What was her favourite food? Did she like to paint or draw?

Tristan was desperate to see her, to meet this little person who was part of him. It still hurt him to think about her – he had missed out on five years, after all. Would he be able to see her and make it up to her? If that was what Ruby wanted, he would do it, however far away she might be. He was grateful to Gil for stepping in and filling the gap in his absence but now that Tristan knew about Ruby, he wanted to be a good father, to be there for her the way a parent should be.

He felt clear about Ruby, he knew that now. It was his feelings for Sophie that were all over the place. He glanced at his watch. He couldn't remember what time the wedding was; having not slept for the past thirty-six hours while he agonised over what to do, his brain was a fuddled mess. Could he do it again? Could he put himself in the firing line and risk everything for her, not knowing if one day he might lose her all over again?

Tristan checked his watch once more and put his head in his hands. What the hell was he to do? He wanted Ruby – hell, he wanted Sophie, but stubbornly he wished Sophie would make the first move. Why? Because he felt she owed it to him, which was preposterous! It was his ego talking and he hated himself for being such an idiot. And if Sophie didn't make the first move and he sat back and let it happen, she would marry Gil and it would be too late. And wasn't there too much 'owing' and 'duty' going on already today?

Tristan stood in front of the torn portrait of Sophie, feeling her eyes boring into him, pleading with him to do the right thing. Everything he had ever wanted in his life could be his but he was so terrified of stepping off the cliff and ending up with his heart smashed into tiny little pieces again, he was incapable of action.

Did he love her enough to put his heart on the line and stop her wedding? Tristan stared down at Ruby's photograph again.

With chattering teeth, Sophie started to walk down the aisle. Walking hesitantly a few steps behind was Tessa, gripping Ruby's hand tightly. She felt Will's eyes on her as she reached his pew and flushed, avoiding his gaze and wishing he didn't have the ability to make her heart beat like an out of control shotgun.

Tessa hoped to God Sophie was going to be able to hold it together. Outside the chapel, Sophie had suffered a major anxiety attack, hyperventilating and shaking all over. Seconds away from calling an ambulance, Tessa had thrust Sophie's head between her legs to calm her down. It was only when Ruby had become tearfully agitated that Sophie made a monumental effort to pull herself together. Bravely, with the air of someone being sent to the gallows, she had assured Tessa she would be fine and that she just needed to get inside and get it over with.

Hardly the most romantic way to describe your wedding day, Tessa thought as she smiled down brightly at Ruby, trying to cheer her up.

Ruby might not have known it but every member of the

Forbes-Henry family was enjoying their first view of her and thinking she was the most adorable-looking child in the world. Henny burst into tears at the sight of her and had to bury her head in Barnaby's monogrammed handkerchief.

Ruby had no idea she was the centre of attention as she took her place next to Tessa; all she could think about was how beautiful and sad her mummy looked. She eyed Gil with slight disappointment. As daddies went, Gil was all right but he didn't like playing with her pink Barbie car and he really didn't get PlayStation SingStar at *all*.

Reaching Gil's side, Sophie was having difficulty breathing. Could she actually go through with this? She didn't love Gil, not the way she should. If that wasn't bad enough, her feelings for Tristan were almost bursting out of her chest and overwhelming her.

Is this really how my life was meant to be? she thought sadly as she stole a glance at Gil. She was perturbed to find him looking as grey as his tails. In fact, he looked rather old and haggard as he stood in front of the altar, the lines around his eyes and on his cheeks thrown sharply into focus by the glorious, technicolour streams of light from the stained-glass window above them.

Not acknowledging Sophie's existence, Gil kept tugging at the collar of his snowy-white shirt, and he was sweating so much his mascara was pooling in the corners of his eyes. In spite of her apprehension, Sophie couldn't help smiling fondly. Gil was so vain! Wearing mascara on his wedding day was one thing but hadn't he heard of waterproof?

Turning to check on Ruby, Sophie saw the look of abject sadness on her daughter's face. Suddenly, it hit her like a thunderbolt. She wasn't doing the right thing for her daughter by marrying Gil. Ruby was fond of Gil and vice versa but that wasn't enough – not any more.

Turning back to face the front, Sophie knew in that instant

467

that she couldn't go through with the wedding. She needed to go to Tristan and explain everything but even if Tristan never forgave her, even if he never spoke to her again, Sophie couldn't marry Gil. It wasn't fair on him. He had been an absolute rock and she loved him dearly as a friend but he wasn't the husband for her.

Just about to say she needed to speak to him on his own, Sophie jumped as Gil took her hands.

The vicar opened his mouth to begin.

'I . . . I'm sorry,' Gil interrupted him unceremoniously, holding up a manicured hand. 'I . . . I have to talk to Sophie.'

'Now?' The vicar looked bewildered.

'Now,' Gil confirmed determinedly. His eyes slid to Nathan imperceptibly before he took Sophie to one side. 'Look, I feel so awful about this but it's my father's death, Soph. It's made me think about everything . . . about my life. We've been through such a lot together, you and I . . . haven't we?'

She bowed her head, swallowing down a sob. Was Gil going to lay a guilt trip on her? Had he sensed her indecision and taken it upon himself to remind her of everything he'd done for her? She couldn't bear it if he did that.

Gil gripped her hands more tightly and there was a tenderness about the gesture that made her want to cry. 'I love you – you know that, don't you?'

She gave him a faint nod, feeling several sets of eyes on them as the Forbes-Henry family watched the goings-on. Not that she could blame them; brides and grooms didn't tend to take each other to one side for a chat as the vicar was getting into his stride.

'I need you to remember that in the next few hours, all right?' Gil took a deep breath and, his sense of the dramatic never far from mind, closed his eyes. 'I told you I felt free when my father died and I meant it. I feel free to be myself finally.' He opened his eyes; they were pleading, asking for her approval. Sweat was trickling down his forehead. Gil continued. 'No one should have to go through life feeling as if they have to be some-thing . . . *someone* they're not, should they, Soph? And no one should pretend to feel something they don't . . . even if they're doing it for all the right reasons.'

'I quite agree.' Her voice came out as a whisper but Sophie suddenly felt extraordinarily fearless. The look in Gil's eyes mirrored her own and although she didn't quite understand what he was saying to her, she sensed he didn't want to get married any more than she did.

She swallowed. 'And we . . . we're pretending to feel something we don't feel . . . aren't we?'

'Yes. Yes, we are.' Gil looked hugely grateful. His shoulders relaxed, as if a gigantic weight had been lifted off them. 'And we mustn't feel like that. Both of us have a right to be happy . . . don't you think?'

Sophie stood on tiptoe and kissed his cheek, relief flooding through her. 'Yes I do. And I want to thank you, Gil. For every-thing. I'll always love you for what you did for me and for Ruby. Please believe that. You've been such a good friend to me and I will never, ever forget that.' She held his hand, tears in her eyes. 'I do love you, Gil. Just not . . . not like that.'

'I understand. More than you think.'

He said the words with great feeling, but she was too busy thinking about Tristan to wonder what he meant. They had wasted so much time and she couldn't wait any longer. 'I have to go to Tristan.' She didn't actually realise she'd said the words out loud until Gil's eyebrows shot up in confusion.

'Tristan? Tristan Forbes-Henry?'

She cast her eyes to the floor. 'I should have been more honest with you, Gil, I know that now. I used to live here years ago and Tristan was my . . . he's . . .'

Gil stared past her and gaped at Ruby. He smacked his hand against his head. 'Tristan Forbes-Henry is Ruby's father,' he breathed, his voice low. 'Of course he is! My goodness, they're the spit of each other . . . I can't believe I missed that.' He gave Sophie a little shove. 'Go! Go to him and do whatever you have to do.'

'Really?'

'Really.' Gil twisted his hands guiltily. 'I have some business of my own to attend to.'

Thinking he meant making his peace with his mother, Sophie squeezed his hand to give him courage. Giving Tessa a broad wink, she thrust her bouquet of pink roses at her, grabbed Ruby's hand and they dashed out of the church together.

Shocked, the congregation turned back to Gil. He was down on one knee, having words with his mother who was nodding and sniffing into a lacy handkerchief. Finally, she patted his shoulder as if giving him her blessing and Gil's face flooded with relief.

'Vicar, I'm so sorry . . . do forgive me for what I'm about to do in this holy place.'

Stalking towards Nathan, Gil took his hand and looked deeply into his eyes. There was a collective intake of breath as Nathan gave Gil a loving kiss on the mouth before putting his arms round him. The vicar watched them gravely, shrugging wordlessly. Not sure how to respond, the Forbes-Henry family broke into a riotous burst of applause.

'At least he won't be devastated that Sophie's gone off with Tristan,' Milly whispered to Freddie. 'And Gil always *was* very in touch with his feminine side, wasn't he?'

'*Very*,' Freddie agreed.

Jack nudged Clemmie. 'I knew he was gay, right from the start,' he crowed smugly.

Clemmie rolled her eyes and laughed. 'Honey, we *all* knew Gil was gay, didn't we?'

Jack looked crestfallen.

Henny gave Barnaby a knowing wink. It was just as she had

suspected all along. Thank God both Gil and Sophie had come to their senses, she thought dreamily, her deep sense of romance satisfied by the events. She had been worried about Gil but at least he had Nathan.

Looking up, Tessa was caught off guard to find Will staring right at her. Claudette's words '*You'll always be second best*' raced through Tessa's mind. It hurt but it was enough to make her tear her eyes away from his and look straight ahead.

Sophie kicked off her satin shoes and shoved her feet into a pair of welly boots that had been left by the door. The snow was still coming down heavily, leaving a magical carpet of white across the grounds. Tucking her dress up as best she could, Sophie grabbed Ruby's hand.

'Where are we going, Mummy?' Ruby asked, with big eager eyes. She didn't know what was happening but it felt like an adventure.

'To find someone.'

'Who?'

Doing up the final button on Ruby's coat, Sophie grabbed her hand. 'We're going to find your real father.'

Ruby broke into an elated smile and jumped up and down on the spot.

Sophie had no idea where Tristan was but she was going to start with his cottage. As they started to run towards it, she almost let out a cry when she saw him emerging from it, his golden curls rapidly becoming damp from the snow.

Before he even saw her, he started running, heading in the direction of the chapel.

Suddenly he saw them both and, letting out a shout, he ran even faster towards them.

'Am I too late?' Tristan panted when they met in the middle.

Ruby stared at him hard and then pushed herself in between them. She looked up at Tristan. 'You're my *real* daddy, aren't you?' she cried, slipping her hand into his without hesitation.

Tristan's heart melted. Dropping to his knees, he let his eyes wander over every feature of Ruby's face. She was so much like him it was astonishing. He reached out a hand and touched her hair with his fingertips, marvelling at how soft it was.

'You're such a beautiful girl,' he whispered. 'And yes, I *am* your real daddy.' He glanced up at Sophie. 'Am I too late?' he asked again as he got to his feet.

She shook her head dumbly, marvelling as he and Ruby both gave her the same slightly crooked smile.

'I know you probably can't ever forgive me but if you'll let me, I'd like to try to show you how much I love you,' Sophie stated.

'I *can* forgive you,' he interrupted her, drawing her head to his. 'But only if you make me a promise.'

'What's that?'

'Never, ever leave me again.' His eyes were fierce but she understood. And he needn't have worried because, whatever happened, she was never going to let him go. She stood shivering in her wedding dress. It hadn't been designed for jogging in the snow at high speed; the bottom was sodden and dirty and the halter-neck was drenched with sweat.

Tristan flung his coat around her shoulders.

'Neither of us could go through with it in the end,' Sophie said with chattering teeth. 'I didn't want to hurt Gil but just as I started to tell him it was over, he took me to one side and did the same thing.'

'I want us to get married,' Tristan announced passionately. 'You're dressed for it . . . we could just go back and do it right now. Why don't we?'

'Tristan!' She swatted him and gave him a lingering kiss. 'I don't think it's the done thing to just "change grooms". And to be honest,' she gestured to the dress, 'this is Gil's idea of the perfect wedding, not mine.'

472

'All right. But let's get married straight away. We'll get one of those special licences everyone talks about and we'll do it however you want to.' Tristan smoothed her hair away from her face, still clutching hold of Ruby. 'You just say when and I'll be there.'

'I've heard better proposals,' Sophie mocked him, laughingly. 'But it's still the best idea you've ever had.'

Chapter Twenty-Eight

Christmas lunch wasn't going well, Tessa decided irritably. Every time she looked up, Will was studying her over the rim of his wine glass and each time she asked for someone to pass her something, he got there before anyone else, his fingers grazing hers and giving her little electric shocks. She swigged some wine and looked away, feeling her skin prickle with desire. The smouldering sexual tension between them was practically setting the tablecloth on fire but Tessa was doing her best to ignore it.

'Wasn't the wedding *romantic*?' Henny said for the fifth time as she dreamily looked outside at the glittering snow. 'How lovely that Sophie and Tristan both realised that they loved each other and had to be together. It's a shame they're not with us today but I totally understand why they need some time together as a family.'

'I think they're bloody idiots,' Milly commented cheerfully, helping herself to another serving of Clemmie's scrumptious candied yams. 'I mean, it was incredibly dramatic but did they really have to wait until the vicar was practically in full flow?'

'God, Mills!' Ravenous as always, David hoovered up the last golden potato that had been cooked to perfection in goose fat. 'You're such a cynic for someone so young. Can't you just be pleased they're back together at last?'

'Oh, shut up! You're just uptight because you haven't got your leg over yet.'

David scowled and wriggled uncomfortably. He hated to

474

admit it but his sister was right. Alicia's 'no sex yet' policy was driving him crazy and his balls felt like a couple of water balloons under the table.

'Milly!' Henny glared at her. 'It's Christmas, do try to behave.' Her eyes twinkled. 'And don't talk about your brother's sex life at the dinner table. It's hardly an appropriate topic of conversation.'

Milly folded her arms sulkily. She half wished her mother hadn't found her backbone. She was becoming increasingly difficult to get past when it came to teasing David.

Wearing a silky peacock-blue shirt and a black velvet kilt short enough to show the tops of her stockings, Milly couldn't stop wriggling around in her seat in anticipation. Freddie had asked to meet her later and, buoyed up after weeks spent in his company while they studied together, she was glowing with new-found confidence.

Milly had become increasingly confused at how attentive Freddie was towards her. He sent her texts and emails constantly, asked her opinion on everything and took any opportunity to put his arm round her. Head over heels in love with him, whatever he might feel for her, Milly had spent a vast amount of pocket money on a silver ID bracelet he had once said he loved when they were out shopping.

Wondering idly what it would be like to kiss Freddie under the mistletoe, Milly crossed her stockinged legs under the table and felt her stomach flip over. She pushed her plate to one side, knowing she wouldn't be able to eat another thing.

'Has everyone had enough to eat?' Henny asked. 'There's tons of meat left.'

'We'll have it tomorrow,' Jack said, holding his bloated stomach with a pained expression. 'God, I've totally stuffed myself. I haven't eaten so well in years. Good job, Henny and you, Clemmie – the food was fantastic.'

Aside from Will's disturbing proximity, Tessa had loved every minute of Christmas with the Forbes-Henrys. Henny and Clemmie had cooked up enough turkey to feed them all for the next two weeks, as well as a gargantuan ham studded with cloves and slathered in English mustard, piles of honeyed parsnips and a mountain of crisp, golden potatoes. Helping to clear away the dishes, Tessa was shocked to see Clemmie wiping her eyes frantically with the sleeve of her dress. Henny flapped everyone else away, roping Milly in to clearing up.

'Oh no, Clemmie, what's wrong?'

Clemmie gave her a watery smile. 'It's just Rufus, you know? I know I shouldn't even give him a second's thought, but I can't help worrying about him being all alone at Christmas. I was sort of hoping he'd contact me today because he knows I usually hate Christmas. But he hasn't and that just proves that he's moved on. Which is exactly what I need to do.'

'You're right about the fact that you shouldn't give him a second's thought,' Tessa retorted smartly, wondering where on earth Clemmie managed to find so much compassion. Her face softened. 'But I know what you mean, it's horrible to imagine someone being on their own at a time like this. I think you should change your mobile number, make some plans for the future . . . That's what I'm trying to do. Make plans, I mean.'

'Hasn't Christmas here been wonderful?' Clemmie sighed. They went into the library. Apple logs smouldered sweetly in the fireplace and there was a spicy aroma of mulled wine and Henny's gorgeous Diptyque fig-scented candles in the air.

'Barnaby's here,' Henny said, dashing past them, her face lighting up at the sound of the doorbell. Checking her smart new purple wool dress in a mirror quickly, she let him in, flushing when he gave her a huge kiss and a bag full of presents.

'You look divine, darling,' Jack commented to Tessa admiringly. He was wearing an emerald-green shirt that brought out the colour of his eyes which, thanks to his continued abstinence, were no longer red and bloodshot. 'Absolutely ravishing. I'm so glad you decided to stay with us. Fancy some non-alcoholic punch? Can't promise it's as good as the real thing but it's not too bad.'

She accepted a glass, glad she'd dressed up for the day, wearing a scarlet wrap-around dress, sheer black hold-ups and four-inch black velvet heels. Clemmie had gone to enormous trouble with her looks and she looked sensational in a designer black dress with diaphanous sleeves and a swirling skirt. Her normally porcelain-pale cheeks were flushed from exertion with all the cooking she had done that morning and her glossy hair was doing its best to escape its moorings. Dark tendrils fell around her heart-shaped face which was starting to lose its gauntness, and without the usual covering of heavy film make-up she looked several years younger.

Clemmie's new-found glow hadn't been lost on Jack, who couldn't seem to take his eyes off her.

'New shirt?' Tessa said, interrupting his thoughts with a wide smile.

'Clemmie bought it for me from some fancy shop in London. Seems to think I need smartening up – can't imagine why.'

'Well, dress shirts and swimming shorts have never really caught on, have they?' Tessa teased. She noticed Jack was looking much healthier. His skin had lost its deathly pallor and his eyes sparkled with vitality although he was still rather thin. With his faded blond hair and hooded eyes, he couldn't help looking like a jaded ex-drinker but at least the colour in his cheeks made him look vaguely human again. She wondered if he missed Caro and tentatively asked him as much.

'Caro?' A flicker of pain registered in Jack's eyes but it was fleeting. 'Not really. I knew Christmas was going to be diffi-cult . . . it's almost like when someone dies, you just remember all the good times, don't you?' He gripped the carafe with tense fingers. 'Christ, I'm better off without her, Tess. When it came to Christmas, there weren't any good times. Caro hated

Christmas with a passion and she was the most difficult woman in the world to buy presents for.' He glanced outside reflectively, watching the sun disappear behind the trees in a blaze of glory. 'I remember one year when Tristan bought all his Christmas presents in the airport on the way home from a trip to some art museums. The four hundred Marlboro Lights he got Caro were the only gifts she didn't want to exchange.' Seeing Clemmie curling up by the fire, Jack held up the carafe and made his way over to her. 'Non-alcoholic punch, darling?'

'Dad's right,' Will murmured in Tessa's ear.

'W-what?' She jumped. He looked dazzlingly attractive in a navy shirt and dark jeans but she wished he wasn't standing so close to her; she could hardly ignore him when his aftershave was making her nose tingle.

'You do look amazing.'

'Er . . . thanks.' Tessa didn't know what to say but she knew she couldn't take him complimenting her any longer. 'You look very nice too.' She moved away from him as politely as she could, needing to put some distance between them. If he whispered in her ear again like that, she might lose control of herself and do something stupid.

Will rubbed his chin, feeling aggravated. She was still upset with him – no doubt because of his ridiculous outburst the other day, but he couldn't help wondering why she flinched whenever he got close to her. He sat on the edge of the sofa, as far away from her as he could get. He splashed some more wine into his glass angrily.

'Are those two ever going to get it on?' David said to Milly out of the corner of his mouth.

'Who?' She opened a Gucci coin purse from Barnaby and squealed in genuine pleasure. 'Oh, thank you, Barnaby! This is really gorgeous.' She followed David's line of vision and watched Tessa and Will stealing glances at each other when they thought the other one wasn't looking. 'God, those two drive me *nuts*. They're worse than Tristan and Sophie. Honestly, I wish they'd stop pacing round each other and get on with it. If they don't do it soon, I might have to lock them in a room together and run away.' She looked at her watch. 'Do you think I can make a getaway yet? I'm supposed to be meeting Freddie.'

In spite of his own longing for Alicia, David took pity on her. 'Go. I'll cover for you.'

'Thanks, David.' Milly embarrassed him by giving him a kiss. 'You've come over all festive and fuzzy, I hardly recognise you.'

David went pink and elbowed her. 'Whatever. You owe me one, all right?'

She nodded, buzzing with anticipation, and fled from the room.

Charging down the driveway as quickly as she could, Milly could see Freddie at the end. Framed by a view of the village covered in snow and wearing his beanie hat over his dark hair, Freddie was pure rock star and she almost gasped at how beautiful he looked. He wore his cashmere overcoat over black jeans and boots and he was blowing on his gloveless fingers to warm them up.

She skidded to a halt beside him. He looked so drop-dead gorgeous Milly lost her nerve and suddenly felt timid and unsophisticated again. How could someone like Freddie possibly have feelings for her? He was cool and good-looking and rich – what on earth would he ever see in someone like her? She thrust her hands into the pockets of her coat and tucked her chin into her scarf. What had she been thinking of, believing Freddie might want to kiss her? How ridiculous of her, how *immature*.

Milly looked away. Around them, the air was still as snow steadily drifted down, coating their clothes and turning their hair crisp and then damp. In the distance, there were sounds of children sledging on the village green.

Clumsily, Milly thrust a carefully wrapped present into Freddie's hands. 'This is for you . . . you might not like it . . . I probably should have just bought you some gloves . . .'

'For me? You shouldn't have,' he joked, pulling the paper off. Opening the box, his eyes widened. 'Oh my God, you really shouldn't have. This looks expensive, Mills.' He tore off one of his leather wristbands immediately and snapped the bracelet on in its place. 'I love it . . . it's so cool.'

Milly felt foolish. They hadn't discussed buying presents and she was seriously regretting her decision to buy Freddie something so expensive. Now she looked like an idiot because he clearly hadn't bought anything for her.

'I wish I'd bought something for you,' Freddie said, proving her point. Her heart sank until he flipped his coat open and wrapped it round her. She shuffled closer cautiously, feeling warmth emanating from his body. What did that mean? And why was he so intimate with her if he just saw her as a friend? This was what Freddie did, he touched her like a boyfriend would and then backed off as if he felt guilty. What the hell was going on?

Milly narrowed her eyes at him, wondering why he looked so bashful. If she didn't fancy him so much, she would have gone mad with frustration by now.

'I mean, I *really* wish I'd just bought you something.' Freddie groaned and pulled his coat around her more tightly. His eyelashes grazing his cheekbones, he looked as if he was trying to summon up the courage to say something. 'Look, I wrote this poem for you, OK? I know you like poetry and I was going to give it to you but it was shit so I screwed it up . . .'

'You wrote me a poem?' Milly felt a surge of hope. Friends didn't write poems for each other, did they?

'I wrote you a *rubbish* poem,' he corrected ruefully.

Milly almost fainted when Freddie abruptly let his overcoat fall to the sides and cupped her face with his cold hands.

'I was trying to say something to you, you see,' he murmured, his dark blue eyes roaming all over her face before resting longingly on her mouth. 'Something about forbidden love for a girl I was supposed to be looking after for my friend, someone I saw as my own kid sister but couldn't help falling for . . .'

Milly gulped and watched snowflakes falling on to his beautiful dark lashes.

'I kept pretending it wasn't happening because I didn't think I should have these feelings.' Freddie ran a gentle thumb over her quivering mouth. 'But I couldn't help falling for her because she's so funny and so adorable . . . and she keeps wearing these tiny skirts that show off her fabulous legs . . .'

'Yes?' Milly yelped, hardly able to stand up. She was shivering in her minuscule skirt and stockings but inside, warm sparks were jumping around in her tummy like fireworks. If Freddie didn't do something soon, she was going to do something very uncool and throw herself at him.

Kiss me . . . please kiss me, she beseeched silently.

'And then I spoke to your brother and he gave me his blessing.'

Milly blinked. 'You spoke to David?'

Freddie nodded. 'And it might be because he's crazed with lust over Alicia but he told me he couldn't be happier. Which is why I feel I can finally do this . . .' Bending down, he put his lips to hers. They felt soft and chilly but his tongue was hot as it probed sensuously inside her mouth.

Milly clung on to him for all she was worth, kissing him back ardently. Her head in a spin, she realised her girlish dreams of snogging Freddie were nothing compared to the real thing. She felt a flip-flop of desire in her knickers as Freddie's hands slipped under her new jumper to stroke her back.

'I'm only warming my hands up,' he murmured with a smile before kissing her deeply again. Brushing a snowflake from the tip of her nose with his, he took a hand away reluctantly to pull a scrap of paper out of his pocket. 'This is the poem – just in case you thought I was fobbing you off about a present.'

Milly read it quickly. She stuffed it back in his pocket and leant her body against his, smiling.

He looked confused. 'Well, what do you think?'

'You were right.'

'What do you mean?'

'It *is* a bit shit.'

Freddie's face fell.

'But I love it.'

'What?'

'I absolutely *love* it,' she explained simply. 'Because *you* wrote it. And I don't need poems, anyway; this is all I've ever wanted – *you're* all I've ever wanted.'

'I told you it was terrible . . . God, I wish I'd paid attention in some of those lessons! I wanted to write something amazing so you'd be impressed and—'

'Freddie?' Milly let out an elated sigh and linked her arms round his warm neck.

'What?'

'I don't care about the poem.' She snuggled into his overcoat again and held her face up. 'Just shut up and kiss me again.'

Standing in the snow, they kissed until their legs went numb.

Back at the manor, the grand ritual of present-opening was taking place. Tessa had already opened a pair of bright red welly boots and a lovely cream mac from Milly and Henny, and Jack had bought her some Penhaligon's Bluebell bath oil and he kept giving her huge winks as she tore the paper off. Clemmie had given her some stud earrings that looked suspiciously like real diamonds, pressing them into her hands insistently and giving her a grateful smile as if to communicate her thanks for Tessa keeping her past a secret.

Seconds later, Clemmie was going into raptures over Jack's gift to her. 'Oh my goodness, Jack, you shouldn't have!' Clemmie stroked the buttery soft fawn driving gloves with shining eyes.

Henny looked at Barnaby, puzzled. What was so special about a pair of driving gloves?

'Thought I could teach you to drive,' Jack was saying gruffly. 'You know, while you're still here.' Over one of their many lunches after his AA meetings, Clemmie had haltingly told him about her past and he felt honoured that she trusted him with such information. Having made a multitude of mistakes in his own life, Jack had been completely unfazed by the truth and Clemmie couldn't believe how understanding he had been. Knowing how nervous she was of learning to drive again, he thought it might be nice to give her some lessons while she was still at the manor. Secretly, Jack hoped he might be able to persuade her to stay for a tiny bit longer because of it.

'That's so thoughtful of you,' Clemmie said, gazing at him as if seeing him for the first time.

'You're not driving the Phantom though,' he told her sternly. 'Not until you're good enough.'

'Honey, I wouldn't dream of it!' She laughed, planting a big kiss on his weathered cheek as he blushed wildly.

Tessa fingered the parcel by her thighs. She had been unsure of what to buy Will, or in fact if she should buy him anything at all, in view of the fact that they were barely speaking. But then she had found a rare first edition of poems, bound in beautiful brown suede, and she hadn't been able to resist it. It had cost a fortune but something had compelled her to do it, although now, Tessa couldn't imagine what she had been thinking. She only hoped Will would assume she had picked it up for a fiver in a charity shop.

'Er . . . I got this for you,' she said jerkily, almost throwing the present at him.

Will looked astonished but he opened it straight away.

'My God, Tessa. This is breathtaking.' He inhaled the pages of the book and ran his hand over the cover. 'I love it.'

Tessa cringed with embarrassment. 'It's nothing, really.'

'But this must have cost you a fortune,' Will said, staring at her. 'This is . . . I can't believe it.'

Suddenly aware that the entire family were watching the exchange with eyes out on stalks, Tessa felt like a fool. It was just as she'd thought. Will hadn't bought her anything and now she looked like an idiot for buying something so meaningful. She couldn't take it.

'I . . . I need some air,' she managed, rushing out of the room.

Forgetting to put on her wellies and not even bothering with her coat, Tessa fled from the house in her high heels.

In the library, Henny was crossly giving Will a shove. 'For God's sake, Will, you're as bad as your brother. Go after Tessa at once and tell her you love her, you fool!'

Jack nodded. 'Yes, what are you waiting for, son?'

Clemmie raised her eyebrows in agreement.

Will gaped at them all. 'I thought she hated me . . . I thought I didn't stand a chance.' He started to laugh. 'And how do you all know how I feel about Tessa, anyway?'

David rolled his eyes. 'Will, *everyone* knows how you feel about Tessa.'

'She thinks you don't love her,' Jack explained impatiently. 'Go. Now!'

Will leapt to his feet and, grabbing his overcoat, tore after Tessa. Outside, the air was still, the covering of snow marred only by the odd dent where a footstep had been. Charging past the snowman David and Milly had made, he spotted Tessa's red dress in the distance. She had almost reached his cottage.

Making short work of the space between them, Will spun Tessa round to face him. Her cheeks were stained with tears.

Out of breath, Will brushed her tears away, looking down into her beautiful moss-green eyes. This was it. Somehow, he had to pluck up the courage to tell her how he felt. Shit, why hadn't he rehearsed this?

'I have to tell you something,' he began urgently.

Tessa shivered. What was he doing here – hadn't he tormented her enough? She was ridiculously cold and wet; her scarlet dress was clinging to her like a sopping rag and her flimsy shoes were soaked through. She knew she must look something like a drowned rat right now.

Will pulled her closer, moulding her wet body against his. 'Look, the thing is, Tessa, I love you,' he said, forgetting anything flowery he might have been planning to say.

Tessa gaped at him, her heart crashing madly. 'W-what did you just say?'

'I said, I love you,' Will repeated, blinking as snow hit his eyelashes. He stroked her damp fringe out of her eyes. 'I love you because you're beautiful and mad and full of life. I love the way you've helped Aunt Henny get her self-esteem back and the way you've given Milly guidance with everything. But most of all . . .' He lowered his mouth to hers. 'Most of all, I just love you for who you are, for being *you* . . . gorgeous, crazy and utterly adorable.' Bending down, wrapped his warm arms round her waist and kissed her.

Forgetting all her good intentions, Tessa kissed him back as if it was the last thing she was ever going to do. Delving her hands into his hair, she wondered how she'd managed to survive without him for this long.

'Fucking hell, I've been wanting to do that for weeks,' Will said, wrapping his overcoat round her. 'Since the summer party, in fact. I felt so guilty about it, especially when Claudette arrived.'

Tessa wanted to believe him but the mention of Claudette brought everything sharply into focus again. 'But you don't

485

even *like* me. You said I didn't give a shit about family because all I care about is money.' She let her arms fall to her sides, bereft and trembling without his body warming hers.

Will looked confused. 'But that was ages ago when we had that talk in my office. I know I was wrong about you, Tess, and I'm so sorry. Everyone told me I was being stupid but I'm such a stubborn bastard, I wouldn't listen to them. And, Christ, forgive me for bringing up those stupid notes the other day. I don't care about them. I know it was because of your job.' His brow furrowed. 'But how do you know I thought you didn't care about family?'

Tessa looked away. 'Claudette told me. She told me . . . lots of things, actually.'

'What? What else did she say?' A nerve throbbed in his jaw and his eyes darkened dangerously. He was beginning to think he knew exactly why Tessa had been keeping her distance for the past few weeks.

'She said . . . you fancied me but nothing more. She said you still wanted to marry her and that I would always be second best in your eyes.'

'My God.' Will looked appalled. 'You didn't believe her, did you? Jesus, I bet she did that because I told her you were worth a hundred of her.' He cupped Tessa's face. 'Claudette is a monster. She could see how I felt about you and she couldn't bear it, even when she didn't need me any more.'

Tessa closed her eyes, leaning against him. She wanted to believe Will but something was holding her back.

Angrily, Will shook her. 'Don't you see that the very reason I love you so much is that you're *not* Claudette? You're everything she's not – kind, free-spirited, genuine. I was on my way to tell Claudette it was all over between us when JB came out with all that stuff about the will. I would never have married her, Tess, never!' Helplessly, he pulled a package out of his pocket and handed it over. 'Maybe this will show you I'm telling the truth.'

Tessa undid the wrapping with frozen, shaking fingers, gasping when she pulled out a pendant with a stunning, pear-shaped emerald in the centre.

'It reminds me of your eyes.' Will fixed it round her neck. 'Before you have a go at me for spending loads of money I don't have, it's a family heirloom. I had it reset in white-gold for you weeks ago. Maybe now you'll believe me when I say I love you. Because that emerald . . . well, it means you're part of the family.'

Tessa touched it wonderingly, absolutely knocked sideways by the gesture. Will loved her . . . he really did love her! She threw her arms round him and kissed him, laughing as he scooped her up in his arms. At the door of his cottage, he eased her down again, pushing her against the wall. Slipping the shoulder of her sopping wet red dress from her shoulder, he kissed her wet skin, his hands all over her body.

Tessa's fingers ventured inside his soaking wet shirt, his hot skin rippling beneath her touch. She felt his thumbs on her nipples and almost collapsed, desperate to tear all his clothes off and be with him.

Laughing as snow fell heavily around them, Will murmured against her neck. 'I don't know about you but I'm freezing. Shall we go inside? I can light a fire . . .'

'I have a much better idea,' she told him, dragging him indoors. 'What we really need is a long, hot bath.' She hurried upstairs to the bathroom, as he grinned and tore after her.

As steam started to mist up the mirror, Will knelt down and removed Tessa's ruined shoes. Sucking her breath in, she leant against the door as his hands travelled pointedly up her stock-inged thighs. She felt him sliding her sheer black hold-ups down her wet thighs with infinite care and gripped his shoulders as her knees buckled.

Will turned her round and kissed the backs of her knees before peeling her soaking wet dress over her head.

'Nice knickers,' he laughed, catching sight of her racy red

underwear. He stopped laughing, his eyes glazing over with lust. 'You're still too overdressed though . . .' As he hooked his fingers under the sides of her thong and drew it down her thighs, she pinged off her bra. Soon, she was naked in front of him, apart from the emerald glowing between her breasts.

Will stared at her, overwhelmed with longing and absolutely sure for the first time in his life that he was with the right woman . . . the one he wanted to be with for the rest of his life. 'Fucking hell,' he said out loud.

Stepping away from him, her body throbbing with desire, Tessa elegantly climbed into the bath and slid beneath the water. It was deliciously warm and definitely big enough for two.

Blowing bubbles into the air, she gave Will a coy glance. 'Who's overdressed now?'

Will gazed at Tessa, unable to believe they were finally going to be together.

'And that . . . is just one of the reasons I love you so much,' he grinned as he pulled his shirt over his head and stepped towards her.

One Month Later

'So, how does it feel this time?' Tessa teased Sophie as she handed her a posy of hand-tied red roses.

Sophie smiled and took Ruby's hand. 'This time, it feels . . . right.' She reached out and hugged Tessa with her free arm. 'Thank you . . . for everything.'

Tessa shook her head. 'Don't be daft. That's what friends are for.'

Sophie smiled. 'I'll call you as soon as I get home.'

'You'd better,' Tessa teased. 'Let's go . . . don't be late for this wedding too.'

They walked towards the willow tree that had always meant so much to Tristan and Sophie, the dying frost crunching underfoot. Tristan was waiting with a local representative from City Hall who was going to conduct the open-air civil ceremony for them. Thankfully, the weather seemed to be on their side and the sun was doing its best to push through the hazy clouds. Nearly all the snow had melted. Some pretty snowdrops, with bell-shaped heads and glossy green stalks, were pushing themselves into view by the willow tree, which even though it had been hit hard by the snow, still looked majestically beautiful.

Wearing a simple, empire-line chiffon dress in the palest ivory with a velvet brown cloak around her shoulders, Sophie looked sensational; she was positively glowing with love. Bursting with pride in his grey suit and red cravat, Tristan bent down and hugged a delighted Ruby, who looked adorable in a dark red silk dress with elongated petals for a skirt. Tucking Sophie's hand into his, Tristan stood beside Sophie, with Ruby next to them, and prepared to say their vows.

Tessa caught Will's eye and felt warm all over as he gave her a look loaded with lust. He looked gorgeous in the same grey suit as Tristan; the two brothers made a breathtaking pair as they stood side by side on the lawn.

Henny was clearly chuffed to pieces and took pictures every two seconds as Barnaby held her floppy, velvet hat in his lap.

'Milly,' David hissed, seeing that she'd been snogging Freddie for the past five minutes behind the tree without coming up for air. 'You've got the manners of an alley cat!'

Milly blinked and let go of Freddie finally. 'Sorry.' She gave David a conspiratorial wink. 'You've got that key, haven't you?'

He nodded. 'And you're sure Mum doesn't know I've got it?'

'She's too caught up with all the arriving guests to be worried about you and your sex life.' Milly giggled, linking her fingers through Freddie's.

'And I now pronounce you . . . husband and wife!' cried the City Hall rep.

Grabbing their boxes of rose petals, Tessa and the Forbes-Henry family jumped to their feet and cheered.

Henny nodded at the pretty new receptionist who was sitting behind a smart desk in the manor's hallway and beamed at Barnaby.

'Isn't it wonderful? We're practically booked up until Easter and the weddings are simply flooding in! One of them is for Gil and Nathan's civil partnership – the brief is not very Gil at all, it's "pink, glittery and disco". Nathan must have got him to lighten up a bit, thank goodness.'

Barnaby took her arm. 'You've all done a sterling job, Hen. You've taken to the whole thing like a duck to water. And the manor house looks incredible.'

'Doesn't it?' Henny greeted a guest warmly as she and Barnaby made their way to the kitchen. Looking vexed, she put the kettle on. 'Where on earth has Will got to? He said he had some idea about who could replace the manager we had to turn down but he and Tessa disappeared right after Sophie and Tristan's wedding.'

Barnaby guided her into a chair. 'Stop fretting, my love. I'm sure it's all in hand.'

'And where's David?' Henny said, with a frown. 'He and Milly were as thick as thieves earlier. They looked as if they might be up to mischief. I think I prefer it when they're at loggerheads, you know.'

'Calm down,' Barnaby soothed, patting her shoulder. He tilted her chin upwards. 'And do stop worrying about everyone else and give me a kiss.'

Realising she was probably worrying over nothing, Henny shyly held her face up. She didn't like to think of Barnaby as a replacement for her dear, departed Bobby, but he was a real gentleman, she thought fondly, smiling up at him.

'Oh my bloody God,' David panted, looking down at Alicia. 'That was . . .'

'*Lovely*,' she breathed, snuggling against him happily. 'I'm so glad we waited, aren't you?'

'Oh, absolutely,' David lied. He could have cheerfully done this months ago but it was so important to Alicia to hold off for a while, he hadn't had any choice but to bide his time and borrow a ton of Freddie's dirty mags to get by. He ran his fingers down Alicia's creamy thighs, marvelling at how perfect they were. So this was what all those books were going on about, he thought in awe.

'So, whose cottage is this?' Alicia asked, glancing round at all the canvases stacked up against the walls.

'Tristan's. Milly asked him for the key while he and Sophie

and little Ruby went on holiday . . . I can't believe my little sis actually did something nice for me. Still, she did owe me a favour so the cottage is ours for the next three weeks if we need it.'

Alicia smiled sleepily. 'Now, why would we need it?' she teased him, running her hand down his chest.

David gasped. 'So we can . . . come here . . . whenever we want to do . . . this,' he managed before launching himself on top of her again.

She stopped him with a look. 'Did you come prepared for us to do it more than once?'

He nodded, looking smug. 'Oh yes.' He grabbed the huge strip of condoms he'd invested in and dangled them in front of her. 'There's no bloody way I'm doing a Rufus, not after what happened with India.'

Alicia closed her eyes as David kissed her neck. 'Poor India.' She wriggled downwards to get into position. 'But lucky, lucky us . . .'

Preparing to have another mind-blowing bout of sex, David couldn't agree more.

Sitting outside a café in Rome, India felt relaxed for the first time in months. She rubbed her huge belly tenderly, wondering at how quickly she had adapted to the idea of having Rufus's baby. Her father was now speaking to her again and had taken the family on a much-needed holiday. India no longer felt ashamed of what had happened. She had fallen in love with a loser and she had believed his empty promises. But what girl didn't make a mistake now and again? India comforted herself.

Her mobile rang and she berated herself for the fleeting hope that it might be Rufus. Answering it, she found a very high-profile tabloid magazine at the other end. 'It's due in a few months,' she answered evasively. Sitting up suddenly with her mouth hanging open, she felt her parents move forward with instinctive protectiveness.

She waved her hand at them. 'You want to pay me *how* much?' she said into the phone, staggered.

After a few minutes, she snapped her phone shut and made an important decision. Maybe becoming rich and famous *was* still an option, after all, she thought with a self-satisfied smile. It was time to stop feeling sorry for herself and get revenge, India decided impishly, treating herself to another *gelato*.

Sitting in the room of one of the most exclusive hotels on the island of Barbados and wearing a pair of shorts that were far brighter than his mood, Rufus was scouring the papers moodily. Alone, lonely, abandoned by his agent and management team, he was in one of the hottest places in the world, yet he felt as if he had been left out in the cold. Or, more accurately, Rufus thought with a burst of self-pity, he felt as if he had been thrown to the lions.

He shoved the papers off the bed furiously. He couldn't even step outside his hotel room, let alone sit by the splendid freshwater swimming pool with a cocktail, because every time he attempted it, he was accosted by someone. The paparazzi shoved microphones in his face and innocently asked how Clemmie was before following up with questions about how it felt to father a child with a minor. Members of the public looked at him as if he was some kind of paedophile and quickly herded their children away. Judgemental bastards. It was *grossly* unfair, in his opinion.

Rufus got up and stared out of the window at the paradise outside. He could see the good-looking judge from a very popular talent show in the UK lounging next to his anorexic girlfriend, as well as a PR mogul who earned a seven-figure salary. What Rufus wouldn't give for five minutes with him to talk about resurrecting his pathetic career!

The British press were known to be brutal in these circumstances but Rufus hadn't expected them to turn on him so viciously. It was true what people said: the press liked to build someone up, only to bring them crashing down again at the first opportunity. Rufus was now infamous rather than famous and he feared he would never work in Hollywood again.

His parents had been absolutely horrified by his behaviour with India and his appalling treatment of Clemmie but they were doing their best to be supportive of their only son. God only knows what they had endured at his expense back home but Rufus still couldn't help feeling hard done by. He'd been a naughty boy, there was no doubt about it. But why did the likes of Hugh Grant manage to get away with behaving badly, while he was being hung out to dry?

Catching sight of a photograph of Clemmie tearfully clutching her Oscar in one of the magazines he had thrown on the floor, Rufus felt a pang of genuine regret. Why was it you only realised what you had when you'd let it go? He missed her, badly. Pulling out his mobile, he dialled Clemmie's number; she had left him enough messages, maybe it wasn't too late. He gulped as the line went dead. Clemmie must have a new number and that meant she didn't want to hear from him again. He had left it too long and clearly she had moved on.

Rufus flung himself down on the huge king-sized bed and beat the pillows with his fists. The only person he hadn't stopped hearing from since it all happened was India. He had forgotten about her the second he'd taken off in the plane although the thought of her unborn child regularly gave him chills. He felt panicked at the thought of being a father, let alone the prospect of some outrageous child support bill appearing in the future, but the one thing he felt sure of in all of this was India; she loved him far too much to drag his name through the mud.

Frowning as his mobile beeped again, Rufus let out an exclamation of impatience when he saw it was India – again.

Was she ever going to stop sending him texts declaring her undying love for him?

Opening the message, Rufus went white with shock. It seemed that the time had indeed come for India to stop declaring undying love. He slumped back on to the bed, realising he'd better phone his parents to warn them before the magazine with India's exposé went on sale. And he had assumed things couldn't get any worse, Rufus thought, feeling totally destroyed . . .

Caro leant over her balcony in St Tropez and inhaled deeply. Even the air smelt rich, she decided contentedly. The French Riviera really was her kind of place. It had glorious weather, glamour wherever one turned, fabulous beaches and, best of all, rich playboys with yachts and money to burn. Caro was in her absolute element rubbing shoulders with the rich and famous.

She let out a sigh and wished JB would hurry up so they could go down to the beach. Wearing an expensive and rather daring bronze swimsuit with cut-outs showing off acres of now golden flesh, Caro couldn't wait to strut her stuff on the beach.

The stunning coastline called the Baie de Pampelonne stretched out in front of her, full of glittering promise, millionaires lounging every two yards or so. Also known by the residents as 'Grania', which was pronounced 'Granny-ay', Caro was reminded of the unpalatable news that she was now a grandmother. Having phoned Tristan one evening in a fit of rare sentimentality, Caro had been astonished to learn of Ruby's existence.

'I'm delighted for you, darling,' she had told Tristan reluctantly, feeling terribly old. Speaking to her son had given Caro a pang and all of a sudden she missed her boys and Appleton Manor, yet most of all she missed Jack. But she had pulled herself together with admirable speed and reminded herself that they were better off without her. And that she was still young and vibrant and beautiful, fully deserving of the wonderful life ahead of her.

'Are you ready, *chérie*?' JB murmured, sliding his arms around her waist and thrusting his groin against her purposefully.

'Ready when you are, *mon ange*,' she returned, enjoying being so openly desired.

JB's dark eyes burnt into hers and he tossed his cigarette carelessly over the side of the balcony before ducking inside. As she turned to follow JB back into the apartment, Caro caught the eye of a strapping young man on the next balcony. Stretched out on a lounger wearing the tiniest briefs over a bulging groin, the well-muscled youth winked at her and smiled lasciviously.

Caro shot him a red-hot look of desire before sashaying inside feeling ten years younger. Some things never change, she smiled to herself.

Jack and Clemmie were strolling through the grounds of the manor side by side. The gardens were beginning to look stunning again as all Nathan's hard work emerged from under the blanket of snow. It would be a while before the flower beds were bright and colourful again but at least the lawns looked lush and green as the frost surrendered to the increasingly bright sunshine.

'Your driving lessons are going well,' Jack commented, giving Clemmie a sideways glance.

She gave him a grateful smile. 'Only because you're such a patient teacher. I can't believe how gentle you're being with me. Still, at least I've stopped having panic attacks every time I get into the driving seat now.'

Jack fell silent. It had been rather distressing to watch Clemmie relive what had happened all those years ago but at least she was getting her confidence back. He rubbed his chin awkwardly. There was an idea he was dying to talk to her about but he had no idea how she might react to it, especially since he didn't know if she had made any plans for the next few months.

As if she'd read his mind, Clemmie suddenly said, 'My agent has been on the phone with some film offers, did I tell you?'

Jack felt his chest tighten. 'Anything of any interest?' He didn't think he could bear it if Clemmie went back to LA. He would probably never see her again and that . . . well, that would be . . . unthinkable.

She shrugged unenthusiastically. 'One looked reasonable but I just don't think I'm cut out for that lifestyle any more, do you?' She gazed past him, drinking in the view of Appleton Manor dappled with hazy sunshine, the Virginia creeper struggling to rejuvenate itself after all the snow they'd had. 'The trouble is, I don't know what I'm cut out for now. I've changed so much and I know I can't go back to that other life.'

Jack decided to go for it. If he didn't do it now, he never would. 'Look, I've got this idea,' he started, taking her hand. 'You can say no and I'll understand, really.'

'What is it?'

Encouraged by the excited look on her face, Jack forged ahead. 'I'm going to help Henny out with the running of the hotel . . . as a kind of manager. Will needs to send me on some courses, obviously, but for the first time in my life, I really want to knuckle down and do something I can be proud of.'

'That's wonderful, Jack. I think you'll be great at the whole "front of house" thing.' Clemmie was pleased for him but she couldn't help feeling confused. 'But . . . what does that have to do with me?'

Jack hesitated then took the plunge, grabbing her hands. 'Look, I wondered if you might consider . . . staying here. I mean, here – at Appleton Manor.'

Clemmie looked incredulous. 'Stay at the manor? Doing what?'

'Whatever you want to!' Swept away by his own enthusiasm, Jack's eyes danced. 'Something in the background, of course, otherwise you wouldn't get a second's peace from the locals but maybe you could put together romantic weekend specials for couples or . . . help out with the designs for the cottages. You're incredibly bright and you have exquisite taste so I know you could turn your hand to anything.' He faltered, realising his idea might sound absurd to Clemmie. He was shocked to see tears in her eyes. 'Gosh, darling, what's wrong? Do you hate it here . . . does it remind you too much of Rufus?'

'Oh no!' Clemmie shook her head, smiling as she dabbed at her eyes. 'It's not that. I don't even think about Rufus any more. It's you asking me to stay . . . it just makes me feel so happy. Christmas here was wonderful; I've been absolutely dreading leaving Appleton Manor and Henny and everyone . . . and, well, and I've been kind of putting off the idea of leaving you, too.'

Jack's heart soared at her words. 'You might finally have a chance to live that normal life you're always talking about. You could be like Kate Winslet, burying yourself in the Cotswold countryside in those pink wellies you look so adorable in.'

Clemmie burst out laughing. 'How do you know about Kate Winslet?'

'Maybe I'm not as old as you think I am,' Jack protested in a huff.

She took his hand wryly. 'Don't worry, I'm probably not quite as *young* as you think *I* am, either.'

Heading towards the manor hand in hand with Jack, Clemmie felt contented for the first time in years.

'Will, I'm trying to watch this!'

Tessa rolled on top of Will and held his hands down. Lying naked and tangled up in Will's sheets, she had been trying to watch a preview of the documentary Jilly had couriered over to her. As far as she could see, Clemmie had been edited in a sympathetic light but Tessa had given up trying to watch the film because Will kept kissing her in rude places and she couldn't concentrate.

'You really are naughty,' she told him, dissolving into giggles as he nuzzled her neck. 'I owe it to Jilly to watch this and give her my thoughts.'

'You don't owe that woman anything,' Will retorted, emerging with his tawny hair all over the place. 'She's evil.'

Tessa shook her head. 'She's not, actually. I thought so too but she's given me her blessing to write my novel and has even sent me a contact she has in publishing. So she can't be all bad.'

'OK, we'll let her off.' Will traced a finger down Tessa's spine, loving the way she writhed against him. 'So, where do you plan to write this novel, then?'

Tessa buried her face in his shoulder. This was the part she'd been dreading. She couldn't bear the thought of going back to her old life in London and being away from Will but she didn't know what he planned to do. He had mentioned staying at the manor until a new manager could be found to run the place but recently he had gone quiet about the whole thing. She didn't want to assume it was all right for her to stay here uninvited.

He lifted her chin. 'Because if you're thinking of buggering off back to London, I should tell you that I intend to lock you in my cottage so you can't escape.'

Tessa's heart raced. 'Promise?'

'I promise. Because now that I've found you, I'm never letting you go.' Will kissed her thoroughly. When he came up for air, he looked sheepish. 'At least . . . look, I know I was talking about staying here as the manager but I've actually found someone else to do that.'

'Who?'

'My dad, believe it or not. And Clemmie if he can convince her to stay.'

Tessa's face lit up. 'Oh, I do hope she does! Clemmie loves it here, it's the life she's always wanted and she's so good for Jack.'

'Exactly. Anyway, this change of events leaves me at rather a loose end.' Will rolled Tessa over on to her back. 'I have an idea I want to run past you but you're probably going to think I'm mad . . .'

She stroked his broad shoulder as he eased one of his huge thighs between her legs. 'Try me.'

'Well, as you know, I only came back from France to sort the manor out. The hotel is doing fantastically well now so I was thinking . . . I was thinking I might head back to France to check out that château in Burgundy.'

Tessa's heart plummeted.

'With *you*,' he told her, rolling his eyes. 'Christ, Tess, when are you going to get your head around the fact that you're stuck with me?'

She broke into a goofy smile as he pulled her closer.

'You can bring your laptop and write your dirty novel and I can try to get my business back on track,' he mused contentedly. 'As you know, apart from the château, I'm very poor these days, so you'll have to survive on cheese, cheap red wine and the love of a good man.' Seeing Tessa's hand disappearing beneath the sheets, Will grinned down at her. 'Sorry, what do you think you're doing?'

'Research for my novel.' She giggled. 'Don't they say you should write about what you know?'

'I thought you said you weren't going to use me or the family for dastardly deeds any more?' he joked.

She swatted him. 'Shut up and help me with my research, Forbes-Henry.'

Tearing the bed sheet from her body, Will did just that and they didn't leave his cottage for a very long time.

Acknowledgements

Thanks to my mum and dad for introducing me to reading at an early age and for being so encouraging. Thank you for not telling me I was mad to leave my job and pursue a career in writing (even if you thought it!) and for being so excited about the book. Hopefully you can see that, apart from the family in this story being dysfunctional, my happy childhood and our strong sense of family have greatly influenced me. Also, Dad, please ignore all the sexy bits in the book!

Thank you to all at Bank of New York Mellon Bank who listened to me boring them for years about writing books, and to those who told me that leaving banking was the right thing to do! In particular, I must give special thanks to Nas, Collete and Michelle for their unwavering faith in me and utter conviction that I could be published one day. Every aspiring writer needs friends like you to encourage them to keep going.

And to Jeni, who was with me every step of the way . . . thank you for all the laughs and hugs and for helping me to believe this was something I could achieve. I owe so much to you – I hope you know what a great friend you are.

Huge thanks must go to Fiona Walker for reading some chapters a long time ago and for taking the time to provide invaluable feedback. Thank you for your continued support, in spite of juggling a busy writing schedule and two small children, and also for your generous advice and belief in me.

To Diane Banks, my fantastic agent, for seeing something in me and for taking the time to nurture and encourage it. I am immensely grateful for all the amazing advice and support and hard work that went into working with me on this book, but most of all, quite simply, thank you for 'getting me'.

To Sherise Hobbs, my lovely editor at Headline. Thank you for falling in love with all the characters so wholeheartedly and for all the hard work and great suggestions that contributed to improving the book. Thanks to everyone at Headline for making it all such fun and to the Creative team in particular, for putting so much thought into making the book look incredible.

Lastly, but most importantly, the biggest thanks must go to my husband Anthony. For everything . . . for encouraging me to leave my job and follow my dream in the first place, for being there when it was tough, for keeping me positive and upbeat, no matter what, and for never minding me scribbling notes or discussing plotlines in the middle of the night. Thanks for coming up with the title but, most of all, thanks for always, always believing I could do this. I love you. x